ADK-2985

Apt

10/10

MYSTERY   Sedley, Kate.
SED
          Whee

D0502967

DISCARD

WHEEL OF FATE

WHEEL OF FATE

Kate Sedley

severn House

This first world edition published 2010
in Great Britain and in the USA by
SEVERN HOUSE PUBLISHERS LTD of
9–15 High Street, Sutton, Surrey, England, SM1 1DF.
Trade paperback edition published
in Great Britain and the USA 2010 by
SEVERN HOUSE PUBLISHERS LTD

Copyright © 2010 by Kate Sedley.

All rights reserved.
The moral right of the author has been asserted.

British Library Cataloguing in Publication Data

Sedley, Kate.
  Wheel of Fate.
  1. Roger the Chapman (Fictitious character)–Fiction.
  2. Edward IV, King of England, 1442-1483–Death and
  burial–Fiction. 3. Great Britain–History–Wars of the
  Roses, 1455-1485–Fiction. 4. Detective and mystery
  stories.
  I. Title
  823.9'14-dc22

ISBN-13: 978-0-7278-6870-1   (cased)
ISBN-13: 978-1-84751-227-7   (trade paper)

Except where actual historical events and characters are being
described for the storyline of this novel, all situations in this
publication are fictitious and any resemblance to living persons
is purely coincidental.

All Severn House titles are printed on acid-free paper.

Severn House Publishers support The Forest Stewardship Council [FSC], the
leading international forest certification organisation. All our titles that are
printed on Greenpeace-approved FSC-certified paper carry the FSC logo.

 **Mixed Sources**
Product group from well-managed
forests and other controlled sources
www.fsc.org Cert no. SA-COC-1565
© 1996 Forest Stewardship Council
FSC

Typeset by Palimpsest Book Production Ltd.,
Grangemouth, Stirlingshire, Scotland.
Printed and bound in Great Britain by
MPG Books Ltd., Bodmin, Cornwall.

ONE

I have heard it said that when you are first apprised of some great, earth-shaking event, ever afterwards you can remember exactly where you were and what you were doing at the time. And I suppose it says something about the general bathos of my life that when I received the first intimations of the death of King Edward IV, I was coming out of the public latrine on Bristol Bridge.

I had spent the previous weeks happily peddling my goods among the villages and hamlets of north Somerset, revelling in the periods of solitude, enjoying the gossip of cottage and hall and the exchange of views with fellow travellers whom I met on the road. I had seen sunsets and sunrises, meadows knee-high in early morning mist, felt the rain on my face, the sun on my back, and watched the gradual greening of trees and hedgerows as March slid into April. And, above all, especially after the restrictions and restraints imposed on me during the previous year, I had known the bliss of being my own man again and the unfettered pleasures of perfect freedom. Now, I was on my way home, refreshed in mind and body, to Adela and the children. I imagined how their faces would light up at the sight of me, and could hear their welcoming, ecstatic cries of 'What have you brought us?'.

I had entered the city by the Redcliffe Gate early that morning, and it was as I was crossing Bristol Bridge that the call of nature became too pressing to be ignored any longer. I headed for the public latrine with an injunction to Hercules to 'Stay there!'. Of course, he followed me in (that dog has no sense of propriety), cocking his leg against the wooden structure in a gesture of male solidarity.

It was as we emerged, a few minutes later, that I was suddenly conscious of people rushing out of the shops and houses on either side of the bridge and running towards the town. And in the distance, I could just make out the clamour of the town crier's bell and the old Norman-French imperative of 'Oyez! Oyez! Oyez!' ('Hear ye! Hear ye! Hear ye!') being shouted at the City Cross, at the junction of High Street, Wine Street, Corn Street and Broad Street. I picked up Hercules and began to follow the crowds; but these had grown in such numbers as we crossed the quayside, that even with my height and girth I was unable to make good progress. My arrival at the top of High Street, dishevelled and out of breath, coincided with the crier's closing words.

'The king is dead! Long live our Sovereign Lord, King Edward the Fifth!'

For a moment, I felt winded, but not just from running. I felt stupefied, as though someone had punched me in the guts, and my heart was pounding. More than anyone else in that crowd, I had been preparing myself for this news throughout the past five months, ever since my return from France and the secret mission I had carried out for the Duke of Gloucester. I had known, far better than the anxious people around me, that the king's health was precarious, but I had secretly been hoping for some miracle that would preserve his life for at least several years to come. But God had not granted the miracle. The future was suddenly dark and insecure.

I realized that the crowds were dispersing. A not unfriendly voice in my ear said, 'Oi! Move you great dumb ox! Let an honest man get by.'

A man, a brewer to judge by his pungent smell, was shaking my arm and trying to squeeze between me and the Cross. He glanced at my dumbfounded expression and grimaced sympathetically.

'It's a bugger, eh? I must get home and tell my goody. She weren't able to leave the little 'uns when the bell started ringing. She'll be dying o' curiosity by now. What is it they say? Woe unto the land when her king is a child? Summat like that. Now if you'll excuse me, master!'

I grabbed the brewer's arm. 'Did you see where the crier went?'

He chuckled. 'Oh, aye! Heading straight for The Green Lattis, he was. Understandable after all that shouting.'

I thanked him and, ignoring Hercules's protests – he was all for going straight home now that his nose told him we were so close – I made my way to my own favourite drinking place and pushed my way in.

The main room was full to capacity, the majority of people clustered around the stocky figure of the town crier who was seated in one corner like a king upon his throne, holding court as he was begged for more information than he could possibly impart. And no one was asking the right questions, I could hear that. Most of them – mainly from women – were concerning the 'poor queen', the 'sweet princesses' and the 'dear little king'. This time, using my bodily strength to good effect, I shouldered a path through the crowd, turfed an apprentice off the stool next to master crier and dropped an indignant Hercules on the floor beside me.

There was a sudden lull in the vociferous questioning and the crier turned towards me, displaying a furious frown.

I ignored this and asked abruptly, 'Is the royal messenger still with the mayor?'

'Of course not,' was the truculent reply. 'He was off to Wells as soon as he'd given us the news.' I noted the 'us' and the slight swelling of the chest that accompanied it. 'He has the whole of Somerset, Devon and Cornwall to cover before the end of the week.'

'But he must have given you and the mayor and council –' I was careful to put them in that order, with a slight emphasis on the 'you' – 'some information. For instance, when did King Edward die?'

The crier was mollified, even pleased now by my interruption. Here was his chance to stress his importance.

'Last Wednesday. April the ninth. They'll be moving his body to Windsor sometime this week, for burial in St George's Chapel.'

'Where's the Duke of Gloucester?'

'Way up north apparently. At one of his castles in Yorkshire. So goodness knows when they'll be seeing him in London. He may even send for confirmation of the news. Seemingly he'd received a false report about his brother's death at the end of March, so he mightn't believe this one to begin with.'

'And where's the Prince of W–? I mean the king?' How strange it was to be calling that twelve-year-old child by his father's title. Edward IV had reigned over us for so long.

The crier shrugged. 'As far as anyone knows at present, still at Ludlow with his uncle, Earl Rivers, and the rest of his household. But he's bound to be setting out for the capital soon. So the messenger supposed. Well, I mean, stands to reason.'

I nodded and pushed an importunate Hercules aside as he tried to climb into my lap, just to remind me of his presence. He was extremely annoyed, and he had a nasty habit of peeing down my leg when displeased.

I turned again to my informant. The crowd around us had gone very quiet, hanging on his every word.

'Did the royal messenger happen to say what was happening in London? Is all peaceful there?'

The crier gave a gruff laugh. 'Far from it, I gather. Rumour has it that the late king, as he was dying, forced Lord Hastings and the Marquis of Dorset – that's the queen's elder son from her first marriage—'

'I know who the Marquis of Dorset is,' I said irritably.

He gave me a look, but proceeded affably enough. 'Well, the king insisted on their reconciliation. Seems there's always been bad blood between them, particularly of late, over some woman. One of the king's – the late king, that is – mistresses.' He added on a note of lugubrious satisfaction, 'If there's trouble between men, you can wager your last groat it'll be about a woman.'

I guessed that this lady was Elizabeth (although she was always known as Jane, presumably to distinguish her from the queen) Shore, Edward IV's favourite mistress, long coveted by both his friend and his elder stepson. I wondered which of them she would choose as her protector now that the king was dead. But such idle speculation was for another occasion. There were more important questions to be answered.

'Did the messenger say anything about events in London since His Highness's death?'

The crier sucked his teeth and looked portentous. 'He did let drop to the mayor and aldermen that things were pretty chaotic. The queen's brother, the Bishop of Salisbury, has been arming his retainers, as has Lord Hastings. And another of the queen's brothers, Sir Edward Woodville, has been moving some of the royal treasure from the Tower.'

'*What?* Was the messenger sure about that?'

'Appeared to be pretty positive. His Worship and members of the council were as shocked as you seem to be and questioned the man closely on the matter. But there was no shifting him. Said he knew it for a fact. What's more, Sir Edward is making preparations to put to sea. Says, apparently, it's to sweep the Channel clear of the French corsairs that have been raiding along the south coast in recent months. But if he takes the treasure with him, we–ell, it puts a different complexion on his actions, I would say.'

I drew a deep breath as the crowd, gathered around the crier and completely silent for the past few minutes, started muttering to one another. Then there was a general shifting of bodies as people moved to get back to work. Kings might come and kings might go, but there was always a crust to be earned in order to keep body and soul together. Life went on whatever momentous events were shaping the future.

Somebody said, 'Praise be we don't live in London, eh?'

There was a general murmur of assent, and someone else called out, 'It'll be all right once the Duke of Gloucester gets there, lad. He'll sort 'em out. He'll know what to do.'

The crier rose to his feet, pushing aside his empty mazer. 'You never said a truer word, friend. Thank God for Duke Richard! He won't stand for the Woodvilles' nonsense.'

There was ragged cheer and, in moments it seemed, the Green Lattis had emptied of all but the usual regulars, the elderly and the young layabouts who spent their days dicing and drinking, desperately trying to avoid anything in the nature of manual labour. I, too, gathered up my pack and cudgel, stirred a sulking Hercules with my foot and left the inn, crossing the busy thoroughfare of Corn Street and starting down Small Street towards my house.

I felt deeply disturbed by the news I had heard. I knew Sir Edward Woodville. He had been with the expedition to Scotland the previous year, and I had seen him in London as recently as last October, peacocking up the steps of Baynard's Castle as though he already owned the place. But more than that, I knew what I had been sent to France by Richard of Gloucester to discover, and I wondered if the Woodvilles knew it, too. Their spy was dead, but that wasn't to say they hadn't made a guess as to what my mission had been.

There was going to be trouble, I felt it in my bones, but exactly what kind of trouble I found it difficult to guess. Were the queen's family planning a coup against the absent Duke of Gloucester? Were they – heaven forbid! – even considering the possibility of taking his life? But somehow I couldn't see Earl Rivers, head of the family and an essentially gentle, extremely cultured man who frequently went on pilgrimage to Walsingham, Compostella, Rome or Bury St Edmunds, sanctioning such a move. But then again, was he capable of controlling its more violent and rapacious members? Particularly Edward Woodville, who had never concealed his dislike of the late king's surviving brother? Lionel, too, might be Bishop of Salisbury, but he was as power-hungry as the rest of his clan. And the queen's two first-marriage sons, the Marquis of Dorset and his brother, Sir Richard Grey, were a couple of roistering, swaggering young braggarts; at least so I judged from what little I had seen of them. Their stepfather had kept them firmly in their place, but now that he was dead, I could imagine that their self-importance would know no bounds. They were half-brothers to the new young king. They would be a part of the tight circle of Woodvilles who would surround him.

Well, it was none of my business now, thank God. I had played my part – under duress, I might add – last autumn and I would stay safely here in the West Country while the main protagonists played out whatever drama awaited them in London. Nevertheless, knowing what I did, my uneasiness remained and refused to be shaken off, although my step became brisker and my mood lightened as I approached my own front door.

This proved to be locked, but that in itself was not surprising. It simply meant that Adela was at market and the children with her; or, more probably, as I had not spotted them in the crowds around the High Cross, visiting Margaret Walker, my former mother-in-law and her cousin, in Redcliffe. It was disappointing, but had happened often enough before as there was no way my family could ever anticipate my arrival home from one of my journeys. I took my key from the pouch at my belt, leant my cudgel against the wall, hitched my pack to a safer height on my shoulder, unlocked the door and stepped inside.

But once across the threshold, I paused. The house being temporarily empty, naturally I was expecting no noise, but the silence struck me as unusually oppressive. Moreover, there was a mustiness that suggested it had been unoccupied for some time, days perhaps, or even weeks. Hercules had dashed ahead of me into the kitchen, but now re-emerged, looking puzzled. He barked on a querulous, questioning note and then tried to nip my ankle, a sure sign of agitation.

'All right, lad,' I said. 'What is it? Show me.'

He returned to the kitchen and indicated the spot where his feeding and water bowls should be, always left in the same place even if there was nothing in them, so that he could indicate hunger or thirst by pushing one or the other around the floor, then standing back until his needs were attended to. But they were no longer there. They had been washed and stacked neatly on a side bench along with Adela's other kitchen implements, knives, bowls, choppers, all similarly clean and unused. I stared around, bewildered. There was no fire on the hearth, not even a handful of dead ashes, and no pot hung from the iron tripod above it. The water barrel in the corner was empty, as I discovered when, in response to Hercules's frenzied importuning, I picked up one of his bowls and went to fill it. The bunches of dried herbs, tied to one of the ceiling beams, were still there, rustling in a slight draught from the still open front door, but the meat skewer with its half side of smoked bacon and the net of vegetables which hung beside it were missing.

I took the stairs three at a time and burst into the bedchamber I shared with Adela. Here, a stripped bed, the patchwork quilt neatly folded in the middle, told the same story. With trembling hands, I flung open the lid of the clothes chest to find it almost empty. All that remained were a few old things of mine, plus the two new outfits I had been given last year to wear to France and which Duke Richard, in defiance of Timothy Plummer's arguments that the ducal finances could not afford such extravagant gestures, had insisted that I be allowed to keep. The room which the two boys – my son, Adam, now almost five, and my stepson, eight-year-old

Nicholas – shared was equally devoid of any sign of recent tenure, as was the little attic at the top of the house, normally occupied by my daughter, Elizabeth.

Slowly, inexorably, it was borne in upon me that Adela and my children were gone. But where? And why?

The silence was appalling. Even Hercules had become conscious of it and had stopped badgering me for water, sniffing around the vacant rooms and whimpering pathetically. I shivered, suddenly feeling cold in spite of the thin April sunshine struggling through the oiled-parchment window panes, and I recognized it as the chill of neglect.

With legs that felt like lead and with my heart beating so fast that it seemed as if I must choke, I turned and went downstairs again. As I reached the bottom of the flight, there was a knock at the still half-open street door. I flung it wide.

'Adela?' I croaked.

But the small, neatly coifed, grey-gowned woman who stood there was not my wife, although I recognized her as one of our neighbours; one of those respectable Goodies who had objected so vociferously years ago when Cicely Ford had outraged all their finer feelings by leaving a common pedlar and his family her Small Street house in her will.

'Oh, it is you,' she said with a sniff. 'I thought it might be, but when I noticed the door was open I decided I'd better come over and take a look.' The brown eyes, set beneath eyebrows which were beginning to go grey, sparkled maliciously. 'If you're looking for your wife –' she gave the last word an insulting emphasis which indicated some doubt of the fact – 'she's been gone these many weeks and the children with her. At least, I don't know about the girl. I think she may be over with her grandmother, in Redcliffe. She's not your wife's child I've been told.'

'Is Mistress Chapman there, too?' I demanded, choosing to ignore the unpleasant and totally unwarranted innuendo. I hoped my wife had gone to stay with my former mother-in-law.

The woman shook her head. 'No. I don't know where she's gone. Someone said London, but I wouldn't know about that.' She gave a small, self-righteous smile. 'I mind my own business.'

You lying old besom, I thought viciously, but schooled my features to nothing more than a polite scepticism, asking, 'Do you have any idea exactly when it was that Mistress Chapman left?'

She wrinkled her brow, the furrowed lines bobbing up towards a thin fringe of greying hair, just visible beneath her coif.

'It must have been about a week after you, or maybe a little longer. I can't say for certain. As I told you, I'm not one of those who spies on her neighbours.' A prim smile twitched the corners of her mouth. 'But I can tell you it was the day after a woman called here. A young woman,' she added, 'carrying a baby.'

The almost opaque brown eyes were suddenly alive with prurient curiosity. A few blobs of spittle had appeared on her upper lip. She was agog with eagerness to winkle out the truth and pass it on – no doubt with her own embellishments – to other neighbours.

My mind was reeling as I tried desperately to think who this woman could have been and what she might have said to make Adela pack up and leave our home, taking the two boys with her. My guilty thoughts immediately turned to my recent lapse from grace with Eloise Grey, but common sense at once told me that even if Eloise had returned to England from France, there was no possible way she could have given birth to a child in the past six months.

I drew a deep, steadying breath. Whatever else I did, I must be sure to give this nosy old busybody no food for further gossip. (I had little doubt that she and her friends had already chewed the matter over daily since Adela's departure, and had been waiting with impatience for me to make my reappearance.)

'Ah!' I said with studied nonchalance. 'Yes. I think I know who that was. A . . . a kinswoman of my wife's first husband. Adela would not have been altogether surprised to see her. There has been some . . . er . . . trouble in the family of late and Adela had promised assistance if she could be of any use. Yes, yes! Of course. That would be it. Things must have come to a head during my absence. Adela will have gone to stay with them. The Juetts live some miles off, near . . . er . . . near Glastonbury.'

The woman seemed disappointed with this ingenious explanation, and she gave me a narrow look as if not entirely convinced by it.

I smiled blandly back at her and hoped that she was unable to hear the thumping of my heart as I waited in a fever of impatience for her to go.

'Oh well, if that's all . . .' she muttered sulkily.

'It is. You say you think my daughter is with Mistress Walker, in Redcliffe?' I asked as she finally and reluctantly turned away.

Hope flared again in the strangely dark eyes. 'So I was told. But why would your wife have left the girl, but not the boys? That's odd, surely?'

'Not at all. My stepson and son, being also my wife's children, are related to the Juetts. Elizabeth is not. As you and your friends have doubtless made it your business to discover during the years my family and I have lived in Small Street, she is my child by my first wife, Mistress Walker's daughter.'

'Hmmmph.' The noise was wonderfully indicative of her contempt for me and my household, implying that such domestic irregularities were only to be expected of a low-born pedlar.

'Thank you for your concern,' I said, preparing to close the door. 'But there is no need for you or any of our neighbours to worry any further.'

I think, even then, she was tempted to linger, prompted by a feeling that she had by no means discovered the whole truth, but by this time Hercules, too, had had enough of her unwelcome presence on his doorstep. He suddenly advanced several paces, baring his teeth and growling ferociously. The woman gave a little shriek, snatched at her skirts and ran up the street, letting herself in with more haste than dignity at her own front door.

This ignominious departure afforded me a momentary satisfaction, but it was short-lived. Now that Hercules and I were alone again, all my anxiety flooded back and I felt as if some unseen hand were squeezing my entrails. I glanced down at the dog, who was regarding me with a puzzled stare, then, for the second time, ran upstairs and into the bedchamber, unearthing from a corner cupboard a large canvas sack. Into this, I stuffed all my clothes from the clothes chest, my new garments being thrust unceremoniously in amongst the old, and made certain that the children's and Adela's coffers really were empty, ran downstairs again, Hercules at my heels. I was out in the street almost before I knew it, locking the door behind me.

I walked back to Redcliffe as fast as my legs would carry me, the canvas sack somewhat impeding my progress. The crowds around the High Cross and the Tolzey were as thick as usual but there was a subdued air about them. Shoppers were clustered together in little groups of three or four, deep in earnest conversation, speculating, no doubt, on what the future under a boy king was likely to hold and reflecting sadly on the past twelve years of peace and prosperity of the late king's reign, ever since the spring of 1471 when he had returned from temporary exile to wrest back his crown from the Earl of Warwick and the latter's attempt to re-enthrone King Henry VI. Several people hailed me, eager to hear my views, but I pretended not to see them and pressed on across the bridge to Margaret Walker's cottage.

My greatest fear was that she would be from home, but to my relief she answered the door after my first knock, staring at me for a moment as though uncertain who I was – her sight was not as good as it had once been – before her features settled into lines of accusation and disapproval. At the same time, in response to a bark from Hercules, my daughter, Elizabeth, pushed past her grandmother and flung herself into my arms.

'Father! Father! Tell Mother and Nicholas to come back! And Adam, too,' she added generously, 'if we have to have him. I miss them so much!' And she burst into tears.

My quondam mother-in-law pursed her lips. 'So you're home at last, are you?' she said grimly. She pushed the cottage door wider. 'Well, I suppose you'd better come in.'

TWO

I picked up Elizabeth – no mean feat for she took after me in both colouring and physique and was nothing like her dark, delicate, small-boned mother – and stepped into the cottage.

'Where's Adela?' I demanded, wasting no time on pleasantries.

But it was a question not destined to be answered immediately. For a start, Hercules's thirst would no longer be denied and he began barking on a high, shrill, begging note, pawing the ground and refusing to let up until his need was attended to. He had been very patient, but enough was enough.

'He's thirsty,' I said in reply to Margaret Walker's impatient glance, and Elizabeth, her sobs turning to giggles, wriggled to the ground, found an old bowl of her grandmother's and filled it from the water barrel. Hercules fell on it, slopping water in all directions and noisily drinking his fill.

'Where's—?' I began again, but was not allowed to finish.

'It's gone ten o'clock. It's dinner time,' Margaret announced, moving towards the fire over which hung an iron pot full of what smelled like rabbit stew. 'Bess, my sweetheart, put out the spoons and bowls. I daresay your father will be eating with us. I've never known him when he isn't hungry.' She added with some asperity, 'As for you, Roger, just make yourself useful and move that basket of wool out of the way and pull the table clear of the wall.'

'Where . . .?' I tried for the third time, keeping a grip on my temper.

But Margaret had turned her back and was busily stirring the stew, and I knew her sufficiently well to realize that repeated questioning would only lead to further delay. She would answer me in her own good time and not before, so I turned my attention to moving the basket of unbleached wool that stood beside her spinning wheel and shifting the table so that it could accommodate three instead of two.

Elizabeth, meanwhile, was running between it and the cupboard with bowls and knives and spoons, touching me every so often to reassure herself that I really had returned and stooping occasionally to pat Hercules on the head. (He, of course, having slaked his thirst, had smelled the stew and was busy ingratiating himself with the cook by rubbing himself against Margaret's legs.) Finally, I drew up two stools to the table, fetched Margaret's low-backed sewing chair from its corner and sat down to wait, containing my impatience as best I could.

Margaret brought the pot to the table and began ladling out the hot, delicious-smelling broth. I realized suddenly how hungry I was, tore a crust from the loaf and fell to with a will. My daughter filled another bowl for Hercules and for a moment or two there was no sound but the chomping of our jaws.

'You've heard the news, I suppose?' Margaret asked eventually, and I nodded, my mouth too full to speak. 'Well,' she continued, 'I daresay we shall survive and things will settle down just so long as the queen's family don't make too much trouble. But His Grace of Gloucester will no doubt keep them in check.'

'He'll have to be quick, then,' I mumbled, trying to clear my mouth. 'He's up north, in Yorkshire, and according to the Town Crier, the Woodvilles are already making their move. But for God's sake, Mother –' she still liked me to call her that even though Lillis had been dead for more than eight years – 'enough of that. Where are Adela and the boys? And why have they gone?'

Margaret laid down her spoon. 'As to where they are,' she said, 'they're in London, with the Godsloves. I've had one letter from Adela since they left, brought to me by Jack Nym, to say that they arrived quite safely – Jack took them in his cart, along with one of his loads – and that they were made very welcome.'

'London?' So my neighbour had been right. 'And who in the name of Jesus are the Godsloves? I've never heard of them.'

Margaret answered placidly, 'They're relatives of mine and Adela's on my father's side. Adela, if you recollect, was

a Woodward before she married Owen Juett. She used to
visit the Godsloves as a child, before they moved to London.
I visited them, myself, although not frequently. They lived
near Keynsham Abbey, a whole great tribe of them. It would
seem – surprisingly, I must admit – that Adela has kept up
a correspondence with them over the years, first while she
was married to Owen and also after she married you. Not a
very regular correspondence, I imagine, or you would have
known about it.'

'Did you know? And why wouldn't she mention the letters
to me?'

'I suppose because she didn't think you would be interested. There's no reason why you should be. She wasn't very
interested in the family, herself. She did give me news of
them from time to time, but it was dull stuff. When you
haven't seen people for years and years, you've nothing in
common with them, and more often than not you're reduced
to talking about the weather.'

'Then why did she go on writing to them?' I demanded,
upset to discover that my wife, who, I believed, had no secrets
from me – I had secrets from her, of course, but that was
different – had been writing to people I had never heard of.
'And why did she never show me the letters?'

Margaret sighed. 'I've told you why. They were dull, unin-
teresting and you didn't know the people concerned. I daresay
if you'd ever been present when she received a letter, she
would have told you who it was from. But you are so often
away from home that I suppose, by chance, that never
happened. As to why she's kept in touch with them, I can
only guess that she feels lonely. I'm her sole kinswoman
apart from the Godsloves, and I know Owen Juett had no
family. He was the only child of only children. Adela, I
suspect, is a woman who likes to belong. Anyway,' she added,
a steely note creeping into her voice, 'the Godsloves have
proved their worth. They have obviously taken her in and
provided her with a home while she decides what to do.'

'Do about what?' I demanded aggressively. At last we
were getting to the crux of the matter. 'Why does Adela need
a home apart from the one she shares with me? Why has
she gone?'

Margaret's lips set in a thin, straight line. 'Does the name Juliette Gerrish mean anything to you?'

My stomach gave a nasty lurch. 'J-Juliette Gerrish?' I repeated, and even to my own ears my voice came out far too high-pitched and loud.

My companion nodded. 'Yes, I can tell that it does.'

'I-I've met her,' I conceded, 'in the course of my investigation into the death of Isabella Linkinhorne for Alderman Foster. Why? What has she to do with the matter?'

'She came here some weeks back, not long after you'd gone on your travels again, looking for you. She had a child with her. She said it was yours.'

'She told me she couldn't have children,' I gasped, then could have bitten out my tongue.

'So!' Margaret uttered sourly. 'There *was* something between you. I told Adela that she was probably lying, but this Mistress Gerrish obviously knew enough about you to convince your wife.'

I was aghast. 'It was only once,' I pleaded frantically. 'And besides—'

'Besides what?' was the uncompromising reply.

'Besides,' I repeated, my mind racing frantically. Then I remembered something my neighbour had said about a woman carrying a baby. 'How old was this child?' I asked.

Margaret Walker shrugged. 'According to Adela four months or thereabouts.'

I gasped again, but this time with relief. 'Then it can't possibly be mine,' I said. 'It's two years ago that I was in Gloucester and made that bitch's acquaintance.'

I had always, until now, thought of Mistress Gerrish with a certain nostalgic affection, but no longer. She had to know – no one better – that it wasn't my baby, so what had been her purpose in coming to Bristol to find me? The answer could only be a desire to create mischief. Or, alternatively – and this explanation was a little more flattering to my ego – she had suddenly found herself, against all belief and expectation, the mother of a child and had decided that, of all her male acquaintance, I was the man she would most like to be its father. If that were so, perhaps I should feel proud that I had made such an impression on her during our brief night's pleasure, but the emotion uppermost in my breast was anger.

After a moment or two, however, my anger veered in another direction. 'What in God's name was Adela thinking of,' I burst out, 'to give credence to that harpy's tale? To believe it enough to take my sons and run away without even waiting to hear my side of the story?' I jumped up from my stool and began pacing furiously around the floor. 'And she knew . . .' I turned on Margaret, pausing only to thump the table so that the bowls and spoons rattled and jumped. 'She knew that all last year I was in the company of my lord of Albany and Duke Richard, in Scotland!'

'All the year?' Margaret queried, regarding me straitly. 'You took a mighty long time coming home from Scotland, my lad. The Scottish war was over by the end of August – at least, that was my information – and we didn't see hide nor hair of you until nearly Christmas. For all Adela knew, you might have visited Gloucester on your way back and spent the autumn with Mistress Gerrish.'

I stopped my pacing and stared at her, appalled.

'Adela couldn't have thought that, surely?'

'Why not?' Margaret looked down her nose. 'On your own admission, two years ago you did have a liaison with this woman.'

'It wasn't a liaison,' I shouted. 'One night, that was all! And it was a mistake.'

'Men always say that when they're found out,' Margaret sneered, then looked quickly at Elizabeth, who was regarding us both with a round-eyed interest tinged with uneasiness as she tried to follow a conversation that was, for the present, beyond her understanding. 'Well, that's as maybe,' she went on, 'but it might help matters if you could tell Adela where you were during autumn of last year.'

'I told you both where I was. Making my way home from Scotland. Once the army had been officially disbanded, it was every man for himself. And my usefulness had finished once Albany had been left behind at his brother's court. Scotland, I might remind you, Mother, is a very long way away.'

Margaret raised her eyebrows and chewed thoughtfully on a piece of meat which she had just prised loose from one of her teeth. 'Of course, if you won't say where you were . . . Adela and I did wonder where you got those smart new clothes that you brought back with you. Not off any market stall, that's plain. Good material, and a hat with a jewelled pin.'

'The "jewels" are glass,' I protested, but she ignored me.

'So when this Mistress Gerrish turned up, neither she nor the child exactly dressed in rags, Adela did wonder . . .' Margaret broke off, shrugging.

'If she gave them to me?' I demanded, horrified.

'Why not? Women have been known to reward their lo—' She again glanced towards my daughter. 'Men who please them,' she finished lamely.

'Dear, sweet virgin!' I exclaimed, flopping down on my stool and burying my face in my hands. 'A nice little tale you've concocted between the pair of you! I swear I've been nowhere near Gloucester for the past two years, nor so much as set eyes on Juliette Gerrish. If you must know, and I don't suppose it will matter if I tell you now, I was in France on a mission for Duke Richard. But mind you, Margaret,' I continued, lowering my hands and looking directly at her, 'I don't want that information passed on to Maria Watkins or Bess Simnel or any other of your little band of gossips.' Margaret started to protest, but I cut her short. 'And don't think I'm going to tell you what that mission was about, because I'm not. I've only told you as much as I have so that you can see I was out of harm's way.'

Out of harm's way! The words mocked me even as I uttered them. I might be able to prove my innocence as far as Mistress Gerrish was concerned, but what about Eloise Grey? I shuddered inwardly. Was she, too, going to turn up on my doorstep some time in the future, threatening me with my past misdemeanours?

My erstwhile mother-in-law heaved a sigh of relief.

'Well, it's no good telling *me* all this,' she said briskly, rising from her chair and beginning to clear the table. 'Not that I'm not relieved to hear it, but Adela's the one you want to tell. And if I were you,' she added, much to my surprise, 'just tell her what she needs to know and no more. You met Mistress Gerrish two years back while enquiring into the disappearance of Isabella Linkinhorne and that's all. The woman plainly has a vicious streak in her, trying to break up your marriage and saddle you with a baby that isn't yours, but she hasn't been back since Adela sent her away with a flea in her ear. Oh yes! She didn't for one moment let the woman know she believed a single word of her story, and I think that at the time she probably didn't. It was only afterwards, brooding on things, lonely and unhappy, that she began to think the tale might have some substance to it. In the end, she convinced herself of its truth and felt she must go away. I did try to persuade her to wait until you returned and hear what you had to say, but by that time there was no reasoning with her. She got Jack Nym to take her and the boys to London when he took up a load of withy slats and baskets, and went to the Godsloves while she thought things out. That was about three weeks ago, at the end of March. So!' She addressed me, arms akimbo. 'What do you intend doing about it?'

I accepted Margaret's account of events at their face value, but it did cross my mind to wonder how hard she had tried to dissuade Adela from leaving. She was fond of me, but had never quite trusted me. She could never bring herself to believe that it was Lillis who had seduced me and not the other way around.

'Do?' I said in answer to her question. 'I'm going to London, of course, to persuade her to come home. And I'll take your advice,' I added, 'about not telling everything. I'll go right away and speak to Jack. With luck, he might be carting another consignment of goods that way fairly soon. If not, I'll start walking and hope to come across other carters who'll give me a ride.'

'You're not going away again, Father?' Elizabeth clutched at my sleeve with an imploring hand.

I stooped and kissed her. 'Don't worry, sweetheart. I'm taking you with me. And Hercules.'

'You'll not be dragging that child all the way to London!' Margaret protested. 'That dog can go with you and welcome, but not a child of her tender years.'

My daughter bounced off her stool and flung her arms around my neck. 'Oh yes! Oh please do take me, Father!

I've never seen London, and it isn't fair that the boys should see it and me not. I don't mind walking if we have to, and I shall have Hercules.'

Hearing his name, the sagacious hound, stretched out beside the fire, gave a perfunctory thump of his tail, but was too replete with rabbit stew to do more.

'I'm taking Elizabeth,' I stated firmly and received another hug for my pains.

Margaret looked as though she would protest again, then hesitated, thinking things over, before nodding briskly.

'You may be right,' she conceded. 'Nicholas will be delighted to see her.' She did not add that the doubtless ecstatic reunion of stepbrother and -sister would be bound to disarm Adela and perhaps smooth my path to a reconciliation, but I guessed it was what she was thinking. I was thinking it myself.

'I'll pay Jack Nym a visit straight away,' I said. 'If I can find him.'

My luck was in. Jack was outside his cottage, loading his cart with bales of Bristol red cloth, a speciality of the city and sold all over the country. Without even bothering to greet him, I asked where this lot was going.

'London,' was the blessed answer, and I had to restrain myself from seizing his dirty face between my hands and kissing him. He tilted his head to look up at me. 'Why? You wanting a ride to London, then, Roger?' He gave a knowing chuckle. 'I took your wife and sons up there a few weeks back. You been a bad lad? I did hear a rumour. A woman, is it?' He regarded me enviously.

'It's all a mistake,' I said. 'A misunderstanding.'

He grinned disbelievingly. 'It wouldn't be a mistake if I got the chance, I can tell you. All right! All right! I'll take your word for it. So you're going after her, eh? Well, I don't know as I blame you. A handsome piece, that lady of yours. If it were my Goody, now, it'd be a different matter. Anyway, I'm off first light tomorrow morning. Be round here promptly at daybreak. I received an urgent message by old Hugo Doyle, who got back from London yesterday afternoon, that the mayor and aldermen want this stuff as soon as possible for the new king's coronation. Word is, apparently, that the queen – Queen Dowager I suppose I should call her now – and her family have fixed the date for May Day.'

'They can't do that!' I exclaimed, horrified. 'I doubt the Duke of Gloucester will even have reached the capital by then.'

'Why? Where is he?'

'Hundreds of miles away, in Yorkshire.'

Jack grimaced. 'Shit! So he couldn't have been there when the old king died.' He eyed me suspiciously. 'How do you know all this?' When I had explained, he grimaced again. 'Reckon there's going to be trouble, Roger?'

I shrugged. 'Could be! But how would I know?'

But I did know. Well, I knew something, that was my problem. I knew why Duke Richard had sent me to Paris in the autumn of the previous year, so, unlike most people, I also knew some of the thoughts that must be going through his mind at the present moment. Naturally, I didn't mention this to Jack, but I told him what else I had learned from the town crier.

He was as uneasy at the news as I had been.

'The Woodvilles are taking the crown treasure from the Tower? Can they do that?'

'I don't rightly know who could stop them,' I answered. 'If the young king can be conveyed from Ludlow to London before the Duke of Gloucester has a chance to get there, he'll endorse anything his mother and Woodville uncles tell him to.'

Jack chewed a grimy thumbnail. 'Didn't the late king name Gloucester as protector?'

I shook my head. 'I don't know. No one's said anything about that. But once the new king's been crowned and anointed, he won't need a protector. He can rule in his own right.'

'You mean the bloody Woodvilles can!'

'Unfortunately, yes.'

'Bugger!'

'I agree, but there's nothing the likes of us can do about it.' I clapped him on the shoulder. 'I'll see you in the morning then, at sun-up. Oh, I nearly forgot. I'm bringing my daughter and Hercules with me.'

Jack turned a dismayed face towards me. 'I don't mind Elizabeth. She's a good enough little soul, but I'm danged if I'll have that wretched dog of yours fouling my cart. He's a menace, he is.'

'I'll pay you extra,' I offered.

'How much extra?' he asked warily.

I named a generous price. Jack thought it over and finally, if reluctantly, agreed. 'But I'm holding you responsible for that hell-hound,' he snapped.

'He'll be as good as gold,' I assured him with what I trusted was a confident smile.

Jack snorted and turned back to his task. 'I'll keep you to that. And don't forget. I'm leaving first light. If you're not here, I shan't wait.'

'We'll be here,' I said.

During the short journey back to Margaret's cottage, I was accosted by at least three people, including Burl Hodge – who had been none too friendly these past four or so years, ever since Cicely Ford had left me her house – all of whom appeared to be labouring under the impression that I knew more about events at court than I was prepared to say. They all seemed offended by what they regarded as my secrecy and looked sceptical when I said they knew quite as much as I did.

'All right! If you want to be like that, Roger!' Burl grunted, and stomped off more out of charity with me than ever.

'Why does everyone think I'm in Duke Richard's confidence?' I demanded angrily as I closed the cottage door behind me with a bang.

'Well, aren't you?' Margaret countered. 'Twice in the last two years you've been hauled off up to London at his behest, once by no less a royal personage than the Earl of Lincoln. And that spy of his, that Timothy Plummer, or whatever his name is, is for ever lurking around in corners. And on top of it all, you were missing from May until nearly Christmastide this past year. How did it happen that you, a common pedlar, became so friendly with a duke, and the king's brother to boot? That's what I'd like to know.'

'There's no secret about it,' I answered, sitting down on one of the stools and taking Elizabeth on to my lap. 'Twelve years ago, on my first visit to London, and not long after I'd left Glastonbury, it just so happened that while I was trying to trace Alderman Weaver's son, I accidentally stumbled across the hiding-place where the Duke of Clarence had concealed his sister-in-law in order to prevent his brother, Gloucester, from marrying her. Duke Richard was very grateful, as you might imagine, and has made a friend of me ever since. Well, "friend" might be overstating the matter, but he's always trusted me and has—'

'Used you to do his dirty work,' Margaret interrupted, setting her spinning wheel in motion.

I was about to protest at the phrase 'dirty work', but my daughter, who had been trying to make herself heard ever since my return, clamped a small, none too clean hand across my mouth and asked, 'When are we going to London, Father?'

'We start first thing tomorrow morning, at sun-up,' I said, removing her hand. 'Carter Nym has to take a load of red cloth urgently to the mayor and corporation, ready for making up into new robes for the young king's coronation. So he's agreed we can ride along with him.'

'At a price, I'll be bound,' Margaret commented drily, but her voice was partially lost in Elizabeth's shouts of joy.

'And Hercules?' she demanded.

'And Hercules, on condition we keep him strictly under control. Jack's none too keen on dogs.'

'And who can blame him?' Margaret muttered. She added, 'You'd better check that the child has everything here she needs for the journey. Her things are in that box under the bed.'

I shook my head. 'No need to check. All the clothes chests at home were empty, bar mine, and my stuff I've brought with me.' I nodded towards the canvas sack which I had dropped in a corner, alongside my cudgel. 'I'll put Bess's in with mine, later on. As for tonight, Hercules and I can sleep on that pile of brushwood over there and be quite comfortable.'

'I daresay,' Margaret snorted. 'If you don't mind, I don't, though it's probably full of fleas. That dog of yours can add a few more.'

Hercules grunted and snuffled, a stupid grin on his face

as he pursued his canine dreams. They were obviously happy ones.

Elizabeth slipped off my lap and went to play with her doll, a one-armed wonder who rejoiced in the name of Christabelle, happy in the knowledge that within a week or perhaps less, she and Nicholas would be reunited. I could only hope that her confidence wasn't misplaced, and that Adela would not refuse to see me once I had arrived in London. I was relying on the children's delight at being together again to soften her heart long enough at least for me to explain matters, and to reassure her that I had been nowhere near Gloucester in the past twelve months. I could only trust that she would believe me. It's an unnerving fact, as I've noticed on more than one occasion, how the truth can so often sound like lies.

I got up and helped myself, unbidden, to another beaker of Margaret's excellent home-brewed ale, before returning to my stool, which I drew nearer to the fire, for the April day had turned chilly, and settling myself as comfortably as I could.

'So,' I said, 'tell me about these Godsloves to whom Adela's gone. You say they're a branch of your father's family, though I've never heard you or Adela mention them before. And yet, I do have a very, very faint recollection that Lillis might once have said their name, but in connection with what, I've no idea. In any case, even if she did, I took no notice.'

'That wasn't unusual,' Margaret cut in waspishly. 'You weren't married long enough for the poor girl to make you mind her.'

I could see that, if I wasn't careful, we were going to embark on profitless recriminations about my marriage to her daughter, and I resolutely ignored the lead she had given me, steering the conversation back to the subject under discussion. Well, the subject *I* wanted to discuss.

'Tell me about the Godsloves,' I said again. 'I can't go to London knowing nothing about them. For a start, whereabouts do they live?'

THREE

Margaret sat down again at her spinning wheel, but made no immediate move to resume work. She was quite ready to while away an hour or two in gossip. She frowned a little at my helping myself, unbidden, to her ale, but had obviously decided to overlook the impertinence in the interests of harmony.

'As to where they live in London,' she said, 'I believe Adela mentioned that it was out in the countryside somewhere, beyond the Bishop's Gate – wherever that is. But you'll likely know, I daresay. It means nothing to me. I've never been to London in my life, and don't want to. Nasty, dangerous place, or so I've heard. All those foreigners.'

Considering that the Bristol wharves and streets fairly teemed with foreign sailors most days of the week, I thought this a decidedly unfair stricture on the capital. All the same, I knew what she meant. It was not only a larger city but also far more populous than any other in the country, which meant more thieves, more pickpockets, more hustling salesmen and more tricksters per square foot than you were likely to encounter anywhere else.

Margaret continued, 'I think Adela said the house is called The Arbour, or Harbour, or some such name. From the description of it, it sounds a bit ramshackle; a big, rambling old place. But then it would have to be in order to accommodate all that tribe.'

'Tell me about the Godsloves, themselves,' I invited, finishing my drink and fetching myself another one.

So she did. But there were so many corrections, so much backtracking, such a deal of 'No, I tell a lie! That wasn't so-and-so, it was someone else,' that, for the sake of clarity, I will set down the history of the Godslove family as I eventually came to understand it, once I had sorted out the facts in my mind.

It begins with Morgan Godslove, who was a cousin of

Margaret's father, William Woodward, and who was born around the year 1400. He married twice. By his first wife – whose name Margaret could not remember – he had four children, three of whom were girls, Clemency, Sybilla and Charity, all born within six years of one another. The fourth child, a boy, Oswald, was ten years younger than the youngest daughter and his mother died in giving birth to him.

The following year, Morgan married again, this time a widow, Alicia Makepeace, whom he met while in London on business, and who already had two sons from her previous marriage, thus bringing their combined total of children to six. To this tally, Alicia and Morgan added two more in very short order, a boy, Martin, and a girl, Celia, with little more than twelve months between them. When the girl was only three, however, Alicia died leaving Morgan and his brood once more motherless. But this time, the widower decided against a third marriage and, instead, employed a housekeeper.

'Tabitha Maynard, that was her name,' Margaret proclaimed triumphantly, after some cogitation.

But five years later, during the terrible winter of 1455, both Morgan and Tabitha Maynard were drowned when the Rownham ferry capsized in the River Avon during a violent storm.

By this time, the three elder girls from Morgan's first marriage, Clemency, Sybilla and Charity, were grown up, all in their early to late twenties, all still unmarried, all still living at home, Oswald was twelve and their half-brother and -sister younger again. As the women appeared to be inclined to the single state, it seemed natural that they should decide to bring up the younger members of the family without calling upon any outside help; an arrangement that suited everybody and which still, apparently, pertained to the present day, even though Oswald was now a man of forty and the half-siblings in their thirties.

'Doesn't anyone in the family believe in marriage?' I had asked at this juncture.

Margaret had smiled. 'They were always, to my way of thinking, a very odd family. A very close-knit unit, who all put great store by being a Godslove and were slightly contemptuous of anyone who wasn't. It's difficult to explain to someone who's never experienced the ties of a large kinship. But even so, big families normally admit outsiders. They have to. But the Godsloves were different, Unhealthily so.' Margaret had pulled a face. 'I only visited them a couple of times, with Father, when they lived at Keynsham, but the atmosphere struck me as . . . as almost incestuous.'

When Oswald Godslove was fourteen, or thereabouts, he had suddenly taken it into his head that he wanted to study for the law, and although there were lawyers enough in Bristol willing to employ and train a clerk, his three sisters had decided that nothing else would do, but he must go to London, to the Inns of Court, off the Strand. And the rest of the family would, of course, go with him. Money, if not exactly short, was not plentiful, either, but they had what their father had left them and what they could make on the sale of the Keynsham house. Sacrifices would have to be made, but in such a worthy cause, no one was complaining. Somehow, they had scraped together sufficient money to enable them to buy the place in which they now lived, a decaying mansion just outside the Bishop's Gate, but big enough to accommodate them all, and there they had remained ever since, even though Oswald was now a successful lawyer and growing richer by the day. (As most lawyers, at least in my experience, do.)

When Margaret had finally finished telling me this complicated tale – or what she had managed to turn into a complicated tale, but was really quite straightforward once I had sorted the wheat from the chaff – I asked, 'But how does Adela fit into the story?'

Margaret considered this as she loaded her spindle with wool.

'I'm not perfectly sure,' she admitted at last. 'She could only have been about six years old when the Godsloves left Keynsham and went to London. But she had visited them once or twice, maybe oftener. I know for certain that she went once because she came with Father and me. But I feel sure that her mother, who was also Morgan's cousin, must have taken her on visits. Katharina – God rest her soul! – was a very nosy woman and was never happier than when she was prying into other folk's business. So I should guess that Adela might have become friends with Celia, the daughter of the second marriage, who was, it's true, maybe three or four years older than herself. But then Adela always seemed more mature than her actual age. Perhaps the two girls started writing to one another, and have continued to do so throughout their lives. Stupidly, I've never asked Adela who her correspondent is, which of the numerous Godsloves, but now I think about it seriously, Celia would seem the most likely person.' She continued spinning for a moment or two in silence, then suddenly laughed. 'I recollect my poor father going to see them once on his own. He came back absolutely appalled. I can remember him exclaiming, "Eight children! Eight of them! You can imagine the noise! All of them talking and shouting together!" I think it made him thankful that he only had the one.'

'And you've never written to them since they settled in London?'

Margaret shook her head. 'They meant nothing to me. And I must confess that I was astonished when Adela mentioned, a year or so back, that she was still in touch with them.'

'And I was completely unaware of the fact.'

'Ah, well,' Margaret muttered significantly, so I got hastily to my feet, in order to ward off yet another lecture about my shortcomings as a husband, and offered to pack Elizabeth's clothes in the sack along with mine.

'It will save you the trouble later,' I murmured ingratiatingly.

But I got no thanks, only a cynical smile that told me, more plainly than any words could have done, that she had my measure. So I took myself off to the Green Lattis, where I spent the rest of the day, or as much of it as I could bear until the sole topic of conversation – the death of the king, with its ceaseless, fruitless speculation as to what might happen next – drove me back to Redcliffe and an early bed (the pile of brushwood by Margaret's hearth) where I slept soundly until morning.

The sun was just showing its face above the city rooftops when an excited Elizabeth, a drowsy Hercules and I – full of porridge and with Margaret's parting admonitions still ringing in our ears – presented ourselves outside Jack Nym's cottage in the neighbouring street. But early as we were, Jack was up and about before us, busy tucking an extra layer of sacking over the bales of red cloth that filled the body of the cart. Elizabeth and I mounted the box beside the driver's seat, with Hercules curled up on my daughter's lap, where, for the moment, he seemed content to settle down.

'But watch out,' I warned her, 'for other dogs, sheep and, above all, his pet hatred, geese. If you don't hold on to him tightly, he'll be off the cart, chasing them and barking like a fiend.'

'Yes, and I'll be having summat to say about that,' Jack said crossly as he climbed up beside us, plainly not in the best of tempers and obviously regretting that he had agreed to let us travel with him.

He had just given his horse the office to start when he had to pull the animal up short as Goody Nym – as slatternly a woman as you could hope to find in a month of Sundays – erupted from the cottage and handed him an evil-smelling parcel wrapped in wilting, brown-edged dock leaves and tied around with a bit of twine so filthy it might just have been fished out of the central drain. (As indeed it was more than likely it had.)

'You forgot yer dinner,' she said, tossing the parcel into her husband's lap. And without acknowledging either Elizabeth or me, she bounced back indoors, shutting the door with unnecessary force behind her.

Jack handed me the parcel. I sniffed it cautiously and then recoiled. 'Hell's teeth, Jack! What's in it?'

He shook his head vigorously. 'Dunno. An' I don't want to know, either. Don't waste your time opening it. Just throw it overboard and leave it to poison some poor stray or other.' He turned his head to look me fully in the face for the first time since our arrival. 'I take it you've got money in your purse, chapman?'

'I . . . I've had quite a successful trip these past few weeks,' I admitted cagily.

'Right, then,' he said, flicking the reins. 'No need for us to stint ourselves on the journey. There's plenty o' decent inns and

taverns along the London road.' He grinned, his good humour
suddenly restored. 'We can sample 'em all.'

Fortunately for me, he was only joking. Well, half-joking.
We did indeed stay at a couple of small alehouses during
our journey in order that Elizabeth might have a good night's
rest. But, the April weather having suddenly turned warm in
the way that it does at that time of year, more often than not
we all bedded down in the cart, the bales of red cloth with
their protective covering of sacking proving a comfortable
enough mattress. Elizabeth, of course, thought this much
more fun than a conventional bed, even though our slum-
bers were frequently broken by Hercules's barking as he took
exception to the cries of the nocturnal creatures all around
us, and by his constant excursions into the surrounding
countryside to relieve himself.

'Damn dog,' Jack grumbled, but without rancour.

The fact was, as we soon discovered, that even had we
wished to pass each night in some hostelry or another, we
should have been hard put to it to find enough empty beds
to accommodate us. There were so many people on the move
that most inns seemed to be full. Not only were the roads
clogged with the customary itinerant friars, pedlars, farmers
driving livestock, or smallholders carrying vegetables, to
market in the nearest town, lawyers riding to the spring
assizes, west country pilgrims on their way to Canterbury,
but also with parties of minstrels and mummers leaving their
winter quarters for the summer round of manor house and
castle. And over and above all these, we met far more royal
messengers than usual, either heading back to London after
delivering their news, or outward bound for those distant
parts of the kingdom that might not yet have received word
of the late King Edward's death.

With so much traffic, our progress was necessarily slow,
and it was not until the following Wednesday, a week and a
day after leaving Bristol, that we finally reached the capital.

We had spent the previous Monday night at Reading Abbey,
in the common dormitory, where we had taken shelter from
a nasty storm that had sprung up unexpectedly. This
Benedictine monastery was a foundation of King Henry I
and famous for the number and variety of its holy relics:

two pieces of the True Cross, a bone of St Edmund the Martyr's arm, St James's hand, St Philip's stole, another bone belonging to St Mary Magdalene and a host of smaller items such as laces, girdles, combs, hairpins and a sandal that was dubiously attributed to St Matthew. (It sometimes seemed to me that the saints had been extremely casual with their personal belongings.)

The storm had abated somewhat by the time we had eaten our supper of soup and black bread in the lay refectory and then bedded down in the dormitory on two of the straw palliasses that were laid side by side along three of the four walls. The place was packed with other travellers as well as ourselves and Elizabeth was forced to share my mattress. She was so weary that she had nodded off over her supper, but nevertheless, she was restless, tossing and turning in her sleep and upsetting Hercules, who had curled up at my feet. In addition to this, the groaning, moaning and farting of thirty or so other souls, not to mention the smell, kept me awake for some considerable time, and when I finally did drop into an uneasy slumber, it was to dream that I was back in Margaret Walker's cottage while she tried to explain to me the ramifications of the Godslove family.

'"Eight children",' she was saying. 'That's what my father said, "Eight children! Thank the good lord I've only got one!"'

'How could there be eight children?' I was objecting. 'Four by the first wife and two by the second. That's six.'

'There were two stepbrothers,' was the answer. 'Alicia's sons. Her first husband's children. That makes eight . . .'

It was at this point that I awoke with a start, staring into the blackness of the dormitory, the words 'that makes eight' still ringing in my head.

Elizabeth was lying on her back, one arm flung across my chest. As I have already intimated, she was a robust child – and has grown into an even more well-built woman – and her arm was heavy, restricting my breathing. Hercules, too, was like a dead weight on my feet, but I felt certain that my discomfort was not what had awakened me. For a moment or two, nothing was to be heard except the cacophony created by my fellow sleepers, but then, over and above this, I was able to make out the noise of raised voices and the jingle of horses' harnesses. Someone – and someone of importance by the sound of it – had arrived at the abbey. Curious to discover who would be travelling so late at night, I gently rolled Elizabeth on to her side, eased my legs from beneath the rough woollen blanket that covered them, pulled on my boots and stood up, all as quietly as possible so as not to disturb my neighbours.

'Stay there!' I whispered to Hercules as I tiptoed towards the door at the far end of the dormitory.

Of course he came too, snuffling with delight at the prospect of a midnight excursion. There was nothing to be gained by arguing with him.

I made my way to the abbey's west gatehouse, with its adjoining chapel, where I judged most of the noise was coming from. And, indeed, I was not mistaken, the court-yard being overpoweringly full of horses and riders, the former breathing gustily through distended nostrils, their flanks heaving and sweating. Torches flared as monks ran from the abbey, calling to the grooms to rouse themselves and come at once to tend my lord bishop's cavalcade. Light flickered on the azure and silver threads of the saltire cross of St Andrew, emblazoned on saddles and cloaks, and I real-ized with a jolt of surprise that I recognized the central figure of the party as Robert Stillington, Bishop of Bath and Wells. My lord was not dressed so magnificently as usual, the splendid silks and velvets that he normally wore being replaced by the coarse black frieze of mourning. Members of his entourage, too, were all similarly attired.

The abbot appeared, looking flustered, his eyes blinking owl-like in the sudden blaze of light, the creases of sleep still wrinkling his cheeks.

'Your Grace! My lord bishop!' he exclaimed, hurrying to where Stillington was just dismounting, assisted by John Gunthorpe, his dean.

Stillington nodded, saying jovially, 'My lord Abbot, I trust you can offer me a bed for the night?' Having received the abbot's (probably mendacious) assurance that his own couch would be given up to the distinguished guest with the utmost pleasure, the bishop asked abruptly, 'What is your latest information from London? Has my lord Gloucester arrived there yet?'

'No, nor will he for some days, or so I understand.' The abbot dodged out of the path of the scurrying grooms as they led away their charges towards the stables. 'I sent one of the lay brothers to Windsor last week to discover what he could and he returned only this afternoon. But come in, my lord. You'll be in need of refreshment.'

The bishop, however, was more interested in such news as the abbot could give him.

'And what did this man of yours find out? When is Gloucester expected? And what of the . . . king?'

The abbot seemed not to notice Stillington's slight hesitation before the word 'king', but I did, as I sheltered in the lee of the church, holding an indignant Hercules firmly in my arms (the only way to prevent him from attacking the episcopal party). I edged forward a little as the two men, now arm in arm, began moving in the direction of the abbot's lodging.

The latter's voice, high-pitched and clear, carried easily on the still night air.

'My man spoke to Lord Hastings, after the late king's funeral, and my lord says that His Highness and Lord Rivers will not leave Ludlow before this coming Thursday at the earliest, and that my lord Gloucester has arranged to rendezvous with them at Northampton in a week's time so that he and the king may enter London together. Of course, whether or not matters will fall out as planned, who can tell? But it's certain that Lord Hastings is most anxious to see my lord Gloucester in London as things go from bad to worse there, with the queen's family having it all their own way . . .'

The voices gradually faded and died, the courtyard slowly emptied until nothing could be heard but the harsh cry of a nightjar in one of the neighbouring trees. I set Hercules down again and made my thoughtful way back to the dormitory, followed by a reluctant dog who thought poorly of my decision to return to bed so soon and after such tame sport. He had not even been allowed to bite a fat monk's leg.

All the same, he settled down again surprisingly quickly, curling up in his former position at the foot of the palliasse without disturbing Elizabeth, who seemed not to have stirred since I left her. I removed my boots and slithered down beside her, at the same time casting a leery eye at Jack. But he was snoring away, dead to the world, his mouth wide open and spittle dribbling on to the straw-filled pillow beneath his head. An unlovely sight, in comparison with which my daughter's deep, sweet breathing made a heart-stopping contrast. I bent over and kissed her lightly on the forehead. She murmured in her sleep, but did not wake.

I, on the other hand, lay stretched out on my back, staring into the darkness, unable to sleep, remembering . . .

Remembering that five years ago, although he had been released after a comparatively short spell, Robert Stillington had been incarcerated in the Tower at the same time that the late Duke of Clarence had been tried and condemned to death. Remembering, two years further back, how the couple, bishop and duke, had walked and talked together at Farleigh Castle in Somerset, heads inclined towards one another, voices low, for all the world like two conspirators. Remembering the well-known story that when, nineteen years ago, the late king had finally disclosed his hitherto secret marriage to Elizabeth Woodville, Cicely Neville, Dowager Duchess of York, had offered to declare her eldest son a bastard, the son of one of her Rouen bodyguard of archers, conceived while her husband was absent, fighting the French. Remembering, above all, my own secret mission to France the previous year, in an attempt to contact, on the Duke of Gloucester's behalf, another member of the Rouen garrison who might possibly be able to confirm the truth of a tale which Duchess Cicely had since refused to repeat. I had never managed to speak to Robin Gaunt, but his wife, a Frenchwoman, had told me of the odd affair of the two christenings.

She had recalled that Edward, the first surviving son and his father's heir, had been christened very quietly in a small chamber in Rouen Castle with little pomp and less cere-mony, whereas the second son, Edmund, had received a lavish christening in Rouen Cathedral, attended by French and English dignitaries with no expense spared. The Rouen Cathedral Chapter had even been persuaded to allow the ducal couple to use the font in which Rollo, the first Viking

Duke of Normandy, had himself been baptised, and which
had been kept covered ever since as a mark of respect.
Moreover, Edmund, later Earl of Rutland, had gone everywhere with his father, finally dying beside him at the bloody
battle of Wakefield. Not incontrovertible evidence that the
duchess had been speaking the truth, but . . . But what? A
straw in the wind?

Remembering . . . But at this point I must finally have
fallen asleep, for the next thing I knew was Jack shaking me
by the shoulder and urging me to 'shift my arse'.

'We've still got nigh on forty miles to go, Roger, and I
must deliver this cloth by Thursday at the latest or Their
Worships may cancel the order, and I don't fancy humping
it all the way back to Bristol at my own expense. So, come
on, my lad! Rouse Elizabeth and let's get breakfast.'

Grumbling, I did as I was bid.

And less than an hour later, we were on the road.

We made good enough time to reach London by Wednesday,
April the twenty-third, St George's Day. But there were none
of the usual mummings and play-acting to celebrate England's
national saint, only sober suits and long faces and a general
air of unease over all. We had stopped first at Westminster
to get some breakfast, having spent the previous night in a
barn, but even in that notoriously lax city, the pimps and
thieves and pickpockets, with which the place abounded,
seemed more subdued and less busy than normal, the shop-
keepers and stall-holders less inclined to harass you into
buying their goods with threats of bodily harm. This might
in part have been due to the fact that the streets were crammed
with Woodville retainers, all either going to, or coming from,
the palace where the queen – the dowager queen now – was
in residence with her children, the young Duke of York and
his sisters. But it was also due to a sombre atmosphere that
hung over everything, like a pall.

As we made our way along the Strand I noticed that there,
too, there was less noise than was customary, the street cries
more muted, people huddled together in little groups, talking
with lowered voices. But several bands of armed men passed
us, forcing the cart into the side of the road until one of the

wheels got stuck in a rut so deep that Jack and I, even with our combined strength, had to solicit the aid of a passer-by to help us free it.

The man, a butcher from the Shambles to judge by the state of his bloodstained apron, nodded towards the rapidly disappearing cavalcade.

'Arrogant young sod,' he growled, indicating the man at its head. I raised my eyebrows in enquiry and he went on, 'That's Sir Richard Grey, Queen Elizabeth's younger son from her first marriage. Busy as a cat in a tripe shop he's been ever since he came back from Windsor and the old king's funeral. Riding up and down this road, in and out o' the city, and every time he's got more and more men with him, and all o' them armed.'

'What do you think he's up to?' I asked.

The butcher grimaced. 'Your guess is as good as mine, friend. But whatever it is, it ain't anything good, you can take my word on that. And I don't reckon it bodes well for the Duke o' Gloucester, whenever he gets here.' His eyes suddenly filled with tears as he harked back to his previous words. 'Don't seem right to be referring to King Edward – God assoil him – as the old king. God! How the merchants and burgesses of this city loved him. And their wives even more!' His sorrow was momentarily quenched by a great guffaw of laughter, but he sobered quickly. 'Well, I must let you get on. I can see your friend is getting fidgety. And I don't much like the way that dog of yours is eyeing me up, either. Got a nasty gleam in his eye.'

I should have liked to talk to the man longer, but he was right; both Jack and Hercules were growing impatient. Only Elizabeth was content to sit and stare at the unaccustomed sights around her, her mouth slightly agape, her eyes round with wonder.

I climbed back on the seat beside Jack, and a few minutes later, we were rattling across the drawbridge that spanned the ditch by the Lud Gate. The guards, who were there to turn back lepers and other such undesirables, let us through without a murmur once Jack had stated his business and shown them the contents of his cart.

'Bristol red cloth for the mayor and aldermen,' he announced, not without a certain amount of pride – although his thick West Country vowels caused confusion for a moment or two.

But once any misunderstanding had been sorted out, we were waved through the gate and even accorded a sketchy salute.

'This is London,' I said to my daughter and laughed when she clutched me, suddenly frightened as she was swamped by the great wave of noise and activity that is the capital.

FOUR

Except for Paris, London is the noisiest city I know, a great, clamorous hive of activity, a babel of raucous street cries, the din of iron wheels rattling over cobbles, of constantly ringing bells from a hundred churches and the shrieking of kites and ravens as they scavenge for food in the open drains. Yet to me, on that St George's Day, even the normal crescendo of sound seemed muted as if the city were holding its breath, waiting for something to happen.

Not so to Elizabeth who clutched me tighter as another party of armed men rode by, the horses' careless hooves splashing us with mud.

'It's all right, sweetheart,' I assured her, putting an arm around her and giving her a hug.

Hercules, on the other hand, although momentarily cowed, began to fight back, giving voice to his outrage and barking at everything he saw. He took particular exception to the sole pair of mummers whom we encountered, one dressed as St George, brandishing a wooden sword and with a red cross painted on his tunic, the other wearing a patently homemade dragon's head, his paper tail trailing sadly in the dust. Both men looked dejected, obviously having met with no enthusiasm for their little play. Normally, by now, we should have met with half a dozen such couples, duelling 'to the death' on street corners, or with crowds watching a full-scale drama of the dragon-slaying on a raised platform in Cheapside. But today, London's busiest thoroughfare was in sombre mood, black hangings draped from upper-floor windows and ashes sprinkled before the doorways in memory of the dead king who had been the capital's darling for so many years.

Jack turned the cart into St Lawrence's Lane. 'My dropping point is Blossom's Inn,' he said, 'but if you're willing to wait while I unload, I'll take you as far as the Bishop's Gate.' He added roughly, to conceal his natural tenderness of heart. 'That girl o' yours looks tired to her very bones. You ought not to have brought her, Roger.'

I accepted Jack's offer meekly, guiltily observing Elizabeth's white face and the beginnings of dark circles beneath her eyes. All the same, I knew she would recover quickly once she set eyes on her beloved stepbrother.

Blossom's was the local name given to St Lawrence the Deacon's Inn because the painted depiction of the saint was surrounded by a border of flowers. The inn yard was also one of the regular places throughout London where carters and carriers unloaded their goods, which were then stored under overhanging balconies until the recipients called to collect them. A couple of stout-looking lads came running out of the inn to help Jack shift the bales of red woollen cloth, and I felt obliged to lend a hand as well.

'Any news?' I asked, as I had enquired at every stop along our route.

The fatter of the two shook his head. 'Nah! But everyone's jumpy, I can tell you that.'

'Why?' Jack wanted to know. 'What's there to be jumpy about? The old king's dead. Long live Edward the Fifth!'

The other man grimaced. 'Easy to say,' he grunted. 'But apart from being an unknown quantity, the present king's not much more'n a child. Twelve, so I've heard. And you know what that means. His uncles will all be grabbing for power and trying to order him about, poor little devil. And who's going to keep all those fancy lords in order now King Edward's gone, I should like to know. They tell me Lord Hastings and that Dorset, the queen's son, are squabbling like a couple of dogs on heat over who's going to get the late king's doxy, that Mistress Shore.'

'Oh well,' Jack soothed, 'I daresay things'll settle down once the Duke of Gloucester gets here, eh?'

'Perhaps,' the first man said, but without much enthusiasm. 'He's another unknown quantity. He's never come to Lunnon much, either. Mostly he's lived in the north. The north!' he added scathingly. 'Lot o' barbarians up there. We get a few of 'em here, unloading their goods. I can't even understand what the buggers are saying. Like a foreign language it is!' He stood back and surveyed the stack of bales. 'Well, we'd better cover these up until someone arrives to claim 'em. Pass us that sacking you had 'em wrapped in, carter. Then you'd better come in and get your money. Landlord said it'd been left.'

Ten minutes later, Jack emerged from a side door of the inn, clutching a leather purse that made a satisfactory jingling sound, climbed back on the cart and took the reins.

'What will you do now?' I asked.

'Hang around for a few days,' was the reply, 'and try to get a return freight. But if not here, I may be lucky and pick up something on the journey home. And you? How will you get back to Bristol?'

I shrugged. 'That depends entirely on Adela and whether she's speaking to me or not.'

Jack grinned nastily. 'I trust you've thought up a good explanation for her. But if you and Bess should need my services again in the next day or two, you'll find me at the Boar's Head in East Cheap.'

I nodded, hoping desperately that the whole family might be returning home with me, but I didn't say anything. To have done so would have seemed like pushing my luck.

We made our way along West Cheap, through the Poultry and Stocks Market as far as the Leadenhall, and turned up Bishop's Gate Street, a wealthy area where the houses were mostly constructed of stone or bricks, the latter made in their hundreds out beyond the city walls, near the lime house or the white chapel. I had been here before because the largest of the mansions, lying to our right, was Crosby's Place, usually rented by the Duke of Gloucester whenever he was in the capital, except for those occasions on which he stayed at his mother's London home, Baynard's Castle. And as we rumbled past in the cart, it was apparent from all the activity taking place in and around the house and gardens that His Grace was expected there soon. Men in the Gloucester livery, with the emblem of the White Boar emblazoned on their tunics, and who must have ridden on ahead of their royal master, were busily shouting orders at various menials and directing the unloading of an enormous bed and its hangings from a wagon that occupied nearly the entire width of the track.

'Fuck you!' Jack shouted at them as, with great difficulty, he managed to edge his cart past the obstruction, nearly colliding as he did so with another cart being driven in the opposite direction. 'Fuck the lot of you!'

Hercules, clearly recognizing his bounden duty, leapt from Elizabeth's lap and tried to bite the invitingly plump buttocks of one of the men manhandling the bed; in which purpose he would probably have succeeded had I not flung myself off the cart and grabbed hold of him before he could carry out his fell intent.

'That's it!' exclaimed Jack, pulling on the reins and bringing the horse to a standstill. 'That is it! You can walk from here, Roger. Anyway, the gate ain't very far now. Walk up past St Helen's Convent on yer right and it's straight ahead.'

I thanked him fulsomely for all his patience and trouble, helped my daughter down from her perch, shouldered my sack of belongings and tied the dog's rope collar firmly around his neck. Then I took my cudgel in one hand and Hercules's lead in the other, bade Elizabeth stay close in front of me and set off up the street.

Jack, possibly ashamed of his spurt of bad temper, shouted after us, 'Remember! If you want me in the next day or so, I'm at the Boar's Head in East Cheap.'

I raised my cudgel in valediction, but did not turn round. I was beginning to realize what, I suppose, women know by instinct; that where young children are concerned you need all your wits about you all of the time and eyes in the back of your head.

We reached the Bishop's Gate to find it and its neighbouring stretches of wall veiled in scaffolding, undergoing repairs. This was such an unusual sight in the capital, many of London's gates and much of her walls being ruinously neglected, that it took me a moment or two to recollect what I had once been told; that the maintenance of this particular gate was the responsibility of the Hanseatic merchants of the Steelyard. And it seemed that the Easterlings, with Teutonic thoroughness, took their responsibilities very seriously.

The gatekeeper let us through with no questions asked – indeed we must have looked a thoroughly harmless little band – and within seconds we were out in the pleasant open

countryside that surrounds the city. I freed Hercules from
the constraint of his lead, pushing the length of rope into
my sack, but my free hand was immediately claimed by
Elizabeth, frightened by the wild screams and weird noises
coming from the building to our left. This was the St Mary
of Bethlehem's Hospital, known to every Londoner as the
Bedlam, where the half-mad or totally insane – or even those
merely embarrassingly eccentric – were left by their unloving
kinfolk until they either recovered or were conveniently
forgotten by an uncaring world.

Some few hundred yards further along the track, to our
right this time, was the New Hospital of St Mary Without
the Bishop's Gate, generally called – and again because of
our slovenly English habit of never saying a whole word if
half a one would do – St Mary Spital, in its beautiful setting
of spreading green fields. In between these two buildings,
on either side of the road, was a scattering of cottages and
almshouses, a church dedicated to St Botolph, a tavern, a
small graveyard and, most convenient for my immediate and
most pressing need, a public latrine.

Both Elizabeth and I made use of this latter edifice, my
daughter having a rooted objection not only to exposing
herself in public, but to my doing so, as well. It puzzled me
where she got these ladylike notions from. It certainly wasn't
from me, so I could only assume it was from Adela.

Adela! That familiar cold hand suddenly clutched at my
entrails once again. I had been carefully putting off thinking
about my wife's reception of me. It had, of course, crossed
my mind from time to time, but I had dismissed the thought
as quickly as possible on the principal that sufficient unto
the day was the evil thereof. But now, as we rounded a bend
in the track to see a large, sprawling, half-stone, half-timbered
house set in an acre or so of badly maintained garden, I
could no longer postpone the dreaded moment of truth. This
surely had to be the Arbour as there appeared to be no other
dwelling of comparable size in the immediate vicinity.

I took a deep breath and braced my shoulders.

I had noted, almost without being aware of it, a little knot
of people standing outside the gates; but it was not until Elizabeth
let go of my hand and ran forward screaming excitedly,

'Nicholas! Nicholas!' that I realized that I knew them. My breath became suspended in my throat.

At the sound of my daughter's voice, heads turned sharply, and then, after a brief silence of pure disbelief, my stepson detached himself from the group and came tearing towards us with answering, and equally excited, shouts of 'Bess! Bess!' A moment later, the pair were hugging and kissing and dancing for sheer joy, with Hercules prancing around them, barking madly.

My gaze was fixed on the younger woman who still seemed rooted to the spot, staring at me as though she were unable to trust the evidence of her eyes. My heart began pounding uncomfortably fast. Then she, too, was running in our direction . . .

'Oh, Roger,' gasped my wife, flinging herself into my arms, her own entwined about my neck, 'how glad I am to see you!'

Whatever sort of greeting I had imagined, it certainly hadn't been this. Icy disdain, reproaches, angry questioning, I had been prepared for them all. But never in my wildest dreams had I anticipated a welcome of any warmth. And yet this one was positively ecstatic.

'Adela,' I said hurriedly, patting her back and dropping a kiss on her upturned face, 'that woman, Juliette Gerrish, was lying. I can explain what happened to me last year and how I couldn't possibly have been in Gloucester to father that child of hers. It's true I did meet her once, two years ago, but—'

Adela laid her fingers against my lips.

'Hush,' she said. 'Explanations can wait. Besides, I've had plenty of time to think and I've realized how wrong I was not to trust you.'

Oh, dear God! If she had planned for a year how to get her revenge, she could have thought of no better way than to announce her wholehearted (but misplaced) faith in me. She put an arm about my waist and urged me forward. 'Come and let me introduce you to my cousin, Clemency Godslove. Oh, Roger, such terrible things have been happening. We are in urgent need of your services.'

For the moment, her words failed to register properly: I was too relieved to have been let off the hook so easily to be aware of anything beyond my own sense of euphoria. And, in addition, Adam, who would be five years old in just over two months' time, was embracing me around the hips, impeding my progress.

'Hello, bad man,' he said. But as this was his customary, irreverent form of address – just to let me know, I suppose, that whoever else was fooled, he at least had my measure – I merely scooped him up in my arms and gave him a resounding kiss on one of his fat little cheeks.

'Ugh!' he said, but for once did not wipe it off, beaming at me instead. (It was beginning to dawn on me, greatly to my astonishment, that perhaps my family really did miss me when I was absent, although being torn apart by wild horses would never let them admit it.)

As we neared the gate, the woman who had been waiting so patiently beside it, looking slightly bemused, stepped forward a pace or two to greet us.

'Clemency,' Adela said, 'this is my husband, Roger. Isn't it wonderful? He's come to find us.'

'And to take you all home again,' I added firmly. 'You've trespassed on your cousin's time quite long enough.'

My wife turned a dismayed face towards me. 'Roger, no! I can't leave now. I told you, we need your help.'

'My help?' Now I came to think of it, I did recall Adela saying something like 'terrible things have been happening'.

My heart sank. I had been hoping to take up Jack Nym's offer and get us all back to Bristol as soon as possible. We could have been his return freight. I had sufficient money to be able to pay him.

But it was plainly not to be. Clemency Godslove was inviting us indoors and, most ominously, she and my wife were discussing where Elizabeth and I should sleep and deciding that Hercules would be happy in one of the outhouses with the family dogs.

'I'll be sleeping with Adela,' I interrupted in a voice my nearest and dearest knew well and which meant that I would brook no argument (not that that ever stopped them). 'And Hercules will sleep in our chamber. He gets upset in strange houses if he doesn't know where I am, and barks all night.'

'As you please.' Clemency Godslove shrugged and I noticed for the first time that she was dressed from head to toe in unrelieved black. She was plainly in mourning. I glanced at Adela and noted that she, too, was wearing dark colours.

I switched my attention back to my hostess as she led us towards the house, and saw an elderly woman – I learned later that she was in her fifty-sixth year – short but with an upright carriage that made her appear taller than she really was. I doubted that she had ever been beautiful in the conventional sense of the word, but with her high cheekbones, aquiline nose and determined jaw she must always have been striking. Even now, with the lines of age seaming her cheeks and forehead, she would stand out in a crowd. Her best feature was her eyes, a dark blue, set beneath heavy black brows, now turning grey.

Adela, meanwhile, was demanding details of my journey, but seemed happy enough with the bare bones of my reply. Her mind was patently elsewhere, although she gripped my arm hard and every now and then squeezed it as if to reassure herself that I really was there. Nicholas and Elizabeth had raced ahead of us, the dog at their heels, the former intent on showing his playmate all the hidden corners and secret places of the overgrown garden, while, for once, Adam walked sedately at my side, plotting future mischief. (I recognized that particular expression of his and it boded no good for anyone.)

Clemency Godslove led us indoors, into a high-ceilinged hall which was obviously used as the principal room of the house. A large dining table stood in the centre of the stone-flagged floor with a number of chairs and stools surrounding it. To the right was a huge fireplace, with a carved stone overmantel, in which a whole ox could have been roasted, but which boasted only a very small fire of logs, some of which were too green to burn properly, a fact which doubtless contributed to the general chill of the place. At the far end of the hall, a wide staircase led to the upper rooms, while on either side, a couple of heavy oaken doors opened, presumably, into other groundfloor chambers. The rest of the furnishings consisted of a pair of settles, pulled up close to the hearth, two chests made of Spanish leather, several piles of cushions, some of them rubbed and worn, a display cabinet showing items of silver and pewter, various candlesticks and, finally, a candelabra of latten tin suspended from the middle of the ceiling. My first impression was of a family stretched to its financial limit, but I was to learn later that there was no shortage of money at the Arbour. The Godsloves were just naturally parsimonious.

'Come to the fire and sit down,' Adela urged me, guiding me towards one of the settles, at the same time relieving me of my cudgel and canvas sack 'Are these yours and Elizabeth's clothes?' She turned to her cousin. 'Clemency, my dear, do you think one of the maids could see them taken up to my bedchamber? I'll sort them out later. And perhaps some ale for Roger?' She patted my shoulder comfortingly. 'It's almost dinnertime. I expect you're hungry.'

I suddenly realized that I was. Breakfast at the stall in Westminster seemed a long time ago.

Before I could reply, however, or Clemency could summon one of the maids to give her orders, a third female voice demanded querulously, 'What are you talking about? What's going on? Who's this?'

I looked towards the stairs where, halfway down, a woman in a long linen nightshift was supporting herself by clinging to one of the handrails. Her feet were bare and her once dark, but now greying hair tumbled loosely about her shoulders. Her extreme pallor suggested that she had just risen from her sick bed.

Clemency and Adela both started towards her.

'Sybilla, go back to your room at once,' the former ordered, mounting the stairs to take the other woman's arm. 'You're not fit to get up yet. You know Dr Jeavons told you that you must rest.'

'Oh Roderick fusses too much,' was the petulant answer. The newcomer shook off Clemency's restraining hand and descended the rest of the stairs.

At close quarters it was easy to see that she and Clemency were sisters; the same blue eyes, the same high cheekbones and imposing noses. But as well as being slightly younger and less wrinkled, Sybilla's features were less clearly defined. It was as though an artist had drawn a portrait of the older woman and then gently smudged the outline.

The outside door opened once more and a man came in, wearing a lawyer's robes and a flat black velvet cap devoid of any ornament. Again, it was not difficult to trace a resemblance to the two women except that the newcomer was much younger. I judged him to be in his early forties and there was, as yet, very little grey in his dark hair; but his eyes were the same blue beneath the same thick black eyebrows and he had the beak-like nose of his sisters. He was perhaps an inch or so taller with the older woman's upright bearing; and, as with Clemency, this made his height seem greater than it actually was.

'There is a girl in the garden,' he said in a high complaining tone, 'running around and shouting and encouraging Nicholas to do the same.' He turned to Adela. 'Cousin, I told you that I had no objection to your remaining here as long as the children were quiet and well-behaved. Who is this hoyden and where has she come from?'

Seeing from my expression that I was about to come to Elizabeth's defence in no uncertain terms, Adela interposed hurriedly, 'I'm sorry, cousin. It's my stepdaughter. She has just arrived and she and Nick are so pleased to see one another that I'm afraid they have let their high spirits get the better of them. I'll go and speak to them.'

'How has she arrived?' the man demanded, barring Adela's way.

'What? Oh . . . My husband brought her. Oswald, this is Roger. Roger, this is my cousin, Oswald Godslove.'

I made my bow, but not a very deep one. There was something about the lawyer to which I took an instant dislike. Something precise and old-womanish in his manner that irritated me and I felt no surprise that he was unmarried and still, in middle-age, living at home with his sisters, who no doubt petted and spoiled him. Indeed, Clemency was clucking with alarm that his homecoming had been disturbed by my noisy daughter and worrying that dinner had been delayed and was not already on the table. But her brother had finally noticed Sybilla and hastened forward to support her in his arms.

'What is she doing out of bed?' he asked angrily. 'Someone should have been sent to watch her. She is not yet fit to be up, Adela!'

His tone was sharp and he looked over his shoulder evidently to admonish my wife, but fortunately she had gone to bring in the children from the garden. This was just as well, because if these cousins of hers were treating her as an unpaid servant they would soon get the rough side of my tongue. I was in any case beginning to feel uncomfortable and had decided that no reason Adela could adduce would persuade me to remain in this house. We would go this very afternoon to find Jack at the Boar's Head in East Cheap and be back in Bristol within the week.

I said as much to Adela when she reappeared with a much chastened Nicholas and Elizabeth, who had obviously been severely taken to task for their unruly behaviour. We had the hall to ourselves, Oswald having supported Sybilla upstairs to bed and Clemency having vanished through one of the side doors, presumably to hurry along the arrival of dinner.

'No, no, Roger!' my wife exclaimed, clutching my arm. 'We can't do that. They are in such trouble and you are the very person to sort it out, to discover what is going on. I can't desert them. They have been so good to me, allowing the boys and me to stay here. As for Oswald, his bark is worse than his bite, and so long as Bess and Nick restrain their natural exuberance now that they're together again, we shall do very well. Adam has grown to be so good these last weeks, you'd hardly know him.' Here, I exchanged glances with my younger child, who smirked at me and cast down his eyes, the picture of sainthood. I wasn't fooled for a single instant. Adela went on, 'It's a pity you had to bring Hercules, though. None of them except Celia really cares for animals, so we must just try to keep him out of their way. I suppose Margaret wasn't too happy about looking after him?'

'I didn't ask her,' I said austerely. 'He's my dog and I enjoy his company.' Hercules, who was stretched out in front of the fire, opened one eye in acknowledgement of these sentiments, then closed it again. 'Besides, she'd been left with Elizabeth to care for since your precipitate flight to London. And why you felt that to be necessary,' I continued, working myself up into a pitch of righteous indignation, 'I simply can't imagine. Could you not have trusted me long enough to wait until you heard my side of the story? Yes, I was acquainted with Mistress Gerrish, but that was two years ago, so I could not possibly be the father of her child.' Adela started to speak, but I held up my hand, the patriarch, a man in command of his household. 'I know what you thought. Margaret told me. But I am now at liberty to reveal that my delay in coming home after returning from Scotland was because I was asked to undertake a special mission to Paris on behalf of Prince Richard. I was not in Gloucester, renewing my acquaintanceship with Juliette Gerrish.'

'Paris!' Adela echoed, astonished. 'You were in Paris?'

I nodded. 'I was. But mind, it's not something to be discussed with other people. I can't tell you what I was doing there, so you'll just have to take my word for it that I *was* there. Now—'

'Oh Roger, I'm so sorry for not trusting you,' my wife said, putting her arms around my neck and kissing me. 'I've no excuse except that you were away for so many months. And once the news reached us that the war in Scotland was over and Berwick retaken, I thought you'd be home much sooner than you were. And when you finally did turn up, you were so guarded about where you'd been and what you'd been doing. I was already feeling suspicious long before that woman arrived on the doorstep last month with her evil story. Whatever made her do it? When you knew her, did you anger or harm her in some way?'

'I barely knew her,' I lied, but was able to add truthfully, 'Why she did what she did, I've no idea. And had I been at home, I should have been able to refute her claim straight away. But knowing my calling, she may have gambled on my absence.' I returned Adela's embrace. 'Perhaps we shall never discover her motive. In any case, it's in the past now. Let's forget about it. We're together again and all's well. The only thing I want to do now is to take you and the children home. So let me have no more of this nonsense about staying here. I don't see why you think their problem is anything

I can solve. I don't know these people. I've only just learned of their existence. We'll leave this afternoon.'

Adela immediately became agitated, pulling herself out of my arms and saying, 'No, Roger, we can't. Two members of the family have already been killed and an attempt has been made on Sybilla's life. We can't just abandon them to their fate.'

FIVE

I stared at her for a moment, uncomprehending, before the sense of her words sank in.

'Two of them have been killed?' I repeated stupidly. 'And an attempt on Sybilla's life, as well?'

My wife nodded. 'And now they are inclined to think that Clemency's illness was more sinister than they all thought it at the time. You see—'

'Wait!' I said. 'We'd better sit down while you explain this to me.' And I drew her towards one of the settles beside the hearth. The three children had retired to sit around the table, Elizabeth and Nicholas catching up on one another's news, Adam sucking his thumb, staring into space and contemplating heaven alone knew what mischief. Hercules was still stretched out in front of the meagre fire, asleep and snoring.

'Now,' I asked, 'what is all this about?'

Before Adela could answer, however, the door in the far wall opened to admit a woman also dressed in funereal black, relieved by a white coif and apron, and with a bunch of keys dangling from her belt, which at once proclaimed her status as the housekeeper. She was a tall, handsome woman who carried herself as one with a sense of her own importance, and a pair of widely spaced grey eyes surveyed the world with a certain disdain. I judged her to be somewhere in her early forties or even perhaps a little younger.

'I thought I heard Oswald's voice,' she said, addressing Adela and ignoring my presence.

Adela nodded. 'Yes. He came in some minutes ago, but he's taken Sybilla back to her room. She got out of bed, which was very foolish of her, and almost collapsed. I thought you must know that Oswald is home. Clemency went to find you, presumably to say that dinner could be served and to tell you about the new arrivals.' My wife indicated Elizabeth and me. 'Arbella, this is Roger, my husband who has brought his daughter with him. I am trying to persuade him to remain here for a while before taking the boys and me back to Bristol. He is very clever at unravelling mysteries and I'm hoping he may be able to solve this one. Roger, this is Mistress Rokeswood, Clemency's and Sybilla's housekeeper. They tell me she has been with them for a few years now and is almost like one of the family.'

I rose politely to my feet, but apart from a brief inclination of her head, Arbella Rokeswood accorded me no other acknowledgement.

'Clemency and I must have missed each other,' she muttered angrily. 'I was out in the herb garden looking for some coriander, but there doesn't seem to be any left. As you know, an infusion of the leaves is good for stomach cramp, and one of the maids is complaining of bellyache.' She shrugged. 'Oh well! It can't be helped. But I do so hate not having dinner ready when Oswald comes in.' Her rather austere features softened. 'He works so hard and his sisters have never properly appreciated him.'

'Oh, I'm sure they do,' Adela remonstrated gently. 'They're all – I mean they're both extremely fond of him.' Her breath caught on a little sob, but she recovered her composure and went on, 'They mother him to death.'

'Smother him more like,' was the embittered reply as the housekeeper stalked from the room.

'Oh-ho! Blows the wind from that quarter?' I said, as Mistress Rokeswood disappeared through the farther door.

'Shush!' Adela whispered. 'She'll hear you.' But as the door closed, she nodded agreement. 'Yes, you're right. Poor Arbella is very much in love with Oswald, I'm afraid. Not that it will do her any good. Whatever she does for him – and she waits on him hand, foot and finger – as long as even one sister is alive she stands no chance with him whatsoever. I have never known such devoted siblings. At times, it seems positively unnatural. And I understand that when Charity was alive, it was worse. She was more maternal towards him than either Clemency or Sybilla. And that, my love, is saying something, believe me.'

I sought to put my thoughts in order.

'This Charity,' I said, cudgelling my brain to remember

what Margaret Walker had told me, 'was the third daughter of Morgan Godslove's first marriage. Am I right? But now she's dead? How did that happen?'

My wife clasped my arm. 'That's what I was trying to tell you when Arbella interrupted us. Charity died last year after eating mushrooms. One of them must have been poisonous. But the point is that she isn't the only member of the family who has died. The year before that, one of the stepbrothers was killed in a tavern brawl, and in the October after Charity's death, Martin Godslove – that's their half-brother and Celia's brother – was set upon by robbers late one night in Cheapside and stabbed to death. Moreover . . .' Adela paused a moment to take a breath and then continued, 'Moreover, not long after her stepbrother was killed, Clemency became very ill and nearly died. Indeed, she was so ill that she was given the last rites, but by some miracle she recovered. No one thought anything more about it – nothing, that is, except that she had been extremely sick and that their prayers had been answered – until first Charity and then Martin died so unnaturally. Then the rest of them began to get frightened. Three deaths and one near death in just a couple of years began to make them believe that either there was a curse on the family or that someone was deliberately killing them off one by one. And now, only a few days ago, Sybilla was badly injured from a falling block of stone as she was walking by the city wall. (You must have noticed that it's being repaired.) No one seemed to know how it happened. All the workmen swore they were nowhere near the particular stretch of scaffolding where the accident occurred. Except, of course, no one here really thinks it was an accident. And now they are in fear and trembling as to what will happen next. Oh, Roger, you will help them, won't you? They have been so very kind to me that I feel I must do something.'

I took both her hands in mine and attempted to soothe her agitation.

'Adela, my love,' I said, 'try to look at things calmly. For a start, why do your cousins believe that some unknown person is out to murder them one by one? Do they have any enemies? Have they offended somebody? Quarrelled with somebody? Injured someone?'

Adela shook her head. 'No, they say not. But Oswald is a lawyer and a good one so I'm told. He seems to be held in high esteem in the inns of court. Since I've been here, I've met several of his fellow advocates and they all speak highly of him. Clemency and Sybilla and Celia – that's the half-sister – think it more than likely that he has made an enemy of some felon who was sent to prison, or otherwise severely punished, thanks to his successful prosecution. Or maybe someone was executed and his family are set on revenge.'

I grimaced. 'That's possible, I suppose. Can Oswald recall any case in recent years where the accused made threats against him, or where Oswald himself felt the verdict to have been unsafe?'

'My dear fellow, don't let your wife embroil you in our affairs, I beg of you.' I turned my head to see the lawyer descending the staircase. Reaching the bottom, he came to join us at the fire. 'It's all nonsense, I'm sure, dreamed up by my sisters. It's a series of unfortunate coincidences, nothing more.'

He tried to speak nonchalantly, but I noticed that his voice jumped a little and that the corner of one eye had developed a tic.

I spread my hands. 'If you're satisfied . . .'

'No, he's not satisfied. Don't believe him,' said yet another voice behind me, making me start. I rose hastily to my feet to find a rather pretty woman standing with one hand on the back of the settle, smiling at me, and guessed that this must be the half-sister, Celia Godslove. There was a look of her half-siblings about her, a similarity of bearing in the upright carriage, but she was taller and younger – her middle thirties I judged – and the high cheekbones, determined jaw and aquiline nose were somehow softer and rounder, making her seem more approachable and friendly than the others.

'Hold your tongue, Cecy,' Oswald told her, but in spite of the reproof he went forward and not only kissed her affectionately but also hugged her, holding her close against him in what seemed to me to be a most unbrotherly fashion. I felt Adela's eyes upon me and we exchanged a fleeting glance.

The newcomer, freeing herself from her half-brother's embrace, again turned to me, holding out one hand. 'I don't know who you are,' she said, 'but take no notice of Oswald's protestations. He's just as worried as the rest of us, even if he likes to pretend he isn't.'

I took the proffered hand and bowed while Adela introduced me to this latest arrival. 'I want him to stay and help solve this mystery,' my wife explained.

Celia smiled and I saw that her eyes were greyish-blue, like smoke, rather than the deeper colour of her siblings'. At the moment, they were twinkling with secret amusement.

'The . . . er . . . the erring husband?' she queried, suppressing a chuckle.

'That's all been explained,' Adela interposed hurriedly. 'It was a misunderstanding on my part. Roger has come to take me and the boys home, but as I said, I think he should stay for a while if you'll let him, and try to discover what is going on.'

'I think that's an excellent idea,' Celia nodded before Oswald could register an objection. 'An extra mind brought to bear on the subject is just what we need. And it will be the viewpoint of an outsider who is unaffected by all these accidents and deaths.' She had quite lost her sunny smile and she pressed a trembling hand to her lips. 'Martin was my brother, you know,' she added.

'Yes, I do realize that,' I said quietly. 'I'm sorry.'

At that moment, Clemency came back into the hall, closely followed by the housekeeper.

'Oh, you're home,' she said, addressing her half-sister. 'Was the city very crowded?'

Celia kissed Clemency's cheek before replying. 'Not so crowded as you'd expect on St George's Day, and no plays or mummings, naturally. But a lot of armed bands patrolling the streets and one or two near clashes amongst a few of them. Someone told me that it's mainly between Lord Hasting's men and those of the Woodvilles, but I couldn't say for certain.'

'Most likely.' Oswald nodded in agreement. 'There has never been any love lost between the Lord Chamberlain and the queen's family. Matters can only get worse now that the king is no longer present to arbitrate and keep them all in order.' He sighed. 'I shall be relieved, I confess, when my Lord of Gloucester gets here.'

'No word of his imminent arrival?' I asked. 'I noticed that they were making ready at Crosby's Place when I passed this morning.'

At this point, Arbella Rokeswood intervened to remark acidly that dinner was on the parlour table and that unless we all came at once the food would be cold.

The parlour was at the back of the house, a large room overlooking a wild tangle of garden; a stretch of unkempt grass dotted with shrubs and trees and shadowed here and there by odd slopes and hollows. It was a children's paradise, and I could hear my stepson's excited whispers as he pointed out to Elizabeth the various hiding places it contained and the opportunity it presented for any number of games. Adam eyed them both thoughtfully but said nothing except to insist on sitting next to me at table, from time to time stroking any part of my anatomy that was available to him and smiling at me whenever I happened to glance his way.

'He's missed you,' Adela remarked quietly, as she took her place on his other side.

I realized she must be right, the more so because he was an independent child, not given to overt displays of affection. I felt a sudden surge of guilt. I left my family alone far too much. But I had to earn our daily bread at my chosen calling and furthermore, although in the past I had resolutely refused all offer of financial help from the Duke of Gloucester, of late I had accepted his assistance to a considerable degree, a fact which made all our lives a good deal more tolerable. Affluent, even. But the extra money was not a simple gift. There were always strings attached. And of late that had meant being away from home long periods at a time. More money in my pocket or more time spent with my wife and children, that seemed to be the choice. It was not an easy one.

The dinner was excellent, and it was with relief that I realized that whatever other economies the Godsloves practised, they did not stint on food and drink. A thick cabbage broth was followed by a pair of plump fowls served with a dressing of sage and wild garlic and stuffed with onions and hard boiled eggs, everything washed down with home-brewed ale. A dish of stewed apples and figs completed a meal with which even I could find no fault.

The talk at table was at first desultory, all the women, with the exception of Adela, anxiously concerned with Oswald's well-being. Did he approve of the new sauce for the fowls? Was that particular chair comfortable enough for him? Was he tired after his morning's work? How had such-and-such a case gone? Had it been as difficult as he feared? These questions were succeeded by extolling his achievements, both sisters and the housekeeper vying with one another in the extravagance of her praise, all of which the recipient appeared to take as no more than his due. Such adulation was obviously commonplace, and I reflected that I had never before come across so tightly knit and so self-regarding a family. I felt sorry for Arbella and for anyone else who tried to infiltrate their ranks.

After a while, however, there inevitably came a lull in the conversation, so I took advantage of the sudden silence to demand more details concerning the deaths, illnesses and accidents that seemed to be dogging their lives.

'Do you truly believe that someone is trying to kill you all?' I asked, allowing a note of scepticism to creep into my voice.

No one answered for a moment or two, the sisters and Arbella looking at Oswald as though waiting for permission to speak. But when he merely shrugged, Celia said firmly, 'Yes.'

Clemency added, 'It certainly seems a possibility. First, our elder stepbrother was killed in a tavern brawl. A common enough occurrence you might say, but when added to a sickness that almost claimed my life, to my sister Charity's death, to my half-brother Martin's death and now to Sybilla's near fatal accident, it seems too much to be mere coincidence.'

'What was your illness, Mistress Godslove?' I enquired, as two young kitchen maids appeared to clear the board of our dirty plates and to place dishes of nuts and raisins in the centre of the table along with a jug of dark, very sweet wine.

Clemency smiled. 'If you are to stay and help us,' she said, 'you may as well address us by our Christian names or there will be confusion between my two sisters and myself. As for my sickness, it was a fever with a headache so severe that I could not bear light anywhere near my eyes, vomiting and a rash. Roderick Jeavons, who has been our physician for many years now, declared at the time that it was a form of brain fever and that I would die. Indeed, they tell me –' she nodded towards her brother and half-sister – 'that I was delirious for days, and that when my mind finally cleared I was so weak, they were convinced I had not long to live. So while I was lucid, they sent for Father Berowne, our parish priest, who confessed me and administered extreme unction. But in the end, the Lord spared me and I recovered.'

'When was this?' I asked.

It was Celia who answered. 'The year before last, towards Christmas.'

I looked at Clemency. 'And at the time, did you accept the diagnosis that it was brain fever?'

She nodded. 'Oh, yes. Certainly. None of us made any connection then between our stepbrother's death and my illness. It was only last spring when Charity died after eating mushrooms, and when, the following autumn, my half-brother, Martin, was set upon by a gang of youths near Cheapside and killed, that we began to question whether my sickness really had been brain fever or some form of poisoning; when we began to wonder if someone is taking some sort of revenge against us.' She returned my gaze steadily. 'You're sceptical. I can see it in your face. You think, like Oswald – or as Oswald *says* he thinks – that these events, occurring one after the other, are nothing more than coincidence. But I would remind you that now Sybilla has almost been killed by a block of stone falling from the scaffolding around the Bishop's Gate. It bruised her right shoulder very badly. An inch or two more to the left and she would undoubtedly have been crushed to death.'

There was silence while I pondered my hostess's words. Out of the corner of one eye, I could see Adela regarding

me anxiously, afraid that I was going to refuse to help her
cousins. And it was on the tip of my tongue to do so. I had
no wish to linger in the capital. I wanted to go home and
take my family with me. I felt no interest in any of these
people and had not the slightest desire to get embroiled in
their affairs. It would be easy enough to convince myself
that these disasters had nothing to do with one another; that
they were simply isolated incidents which, although they
might appear sinister when taken all together, were really
unconnected. And indeed I had no need to convince myself.
I was almost sure that that was the case. But it was the
'almost' that bothered me.

Even so, I was just about to declare my opinion in no
uncertain terms when Celia said, 'Of course, it really started,
not with your sickness, Clem, but with Reynold being knifed
to death in that fight in the Voyager.'

'I did mention that,' her half-sister excused herself.

'Wait a minute!' I exclaimed. 'Reynold? The Voyager?'
A memory stirred. I suddenly recollected Margaret Walker
mentioning the fact that Morgan Godslove's second wife
had been the Widow Makepeace, whom he had met in
London. 'Are you telling me that your stepbrother was
Reynold Makepeace, the landlord of St Brendan the
Voyager in Bucklersbury?'

'Our elder stepbrother, yes.' Clemency frowned. 'You speak
as though you knew him.'

'We did know him,' Adela chimed in. 'Roger and I stayed
at the Voyager, oh it must be more than five years ago now.
It was before Adam was born.'

'It was five years ago,' I confirmed. 'It was at the time of
the little Duke of York's marriage to Anne Mowbray and the
trial of the Duke of Clarence. But I've stayed there since,
three years back when Margaret of Burgundy was here. And
I heard of Landlord Makepeace's death when I went looking
for him at the Voyager last October. I was never more shocked
in my life than to learn he'd been killed. He was a fine and
very kind man.'

'He was,' Clemency agreed, and both Oswald and Celia
nodded.

'A good man,' the housekeeper added.

'And now you all think that his death might not have been an accident?'

'Yes.' The three women spoke as one. Only Oswald said nothing, holding aloof from comment.

'It was the first of our misfortunes,' Clemency pointed out. 'The start of everything.'

This changed the complexion of things as far as I was concerned. I had counted Reynold Makepeace as much a friend as an acquaintance, and had been fond of him; fond enough at least for the news of his death, when it had finally come to my ears last autumn, to have saddened me beyond all expectation. If, therefore, there was a possibility that he had been murdered rather than killed accidentally, I felt I had to ferret out the truth.

'Are you saying, in all seriousness,' I asked Clemency, 'that you now believe your stepbrother's death to have been planned? That someone paid some ruffians to set on him and kill him?'

She returned my look steadily. 'It is precisely what happened to my half-brother last year, in Cheapside. It seemed like an attack by pickpockets, and indeed it was regarded as such by members of the Watch who brought his body home to us. The coroner, too, had no hesitation in accepting such a verdict.'

'You didn't, however?'

'No.' It was Oswald's turn to speak and he did so with the authority of a lawyer. 'Loath as I am to contribute to this idea of a conspiracy against our family, I have to admit that there were a couple of suspicious circumstances connected with Martin's death. Firstly, although London's streets are, regrettably, infested with bands of armed robbers at night, very few, if any, of these men set out deliberately to kill their victims. They might knock them unconscious, and in so doing fatally wound them, but death is not their intention. Martin, on the other hand, was stabbed simply and cleanly through the heart. Secondly, although he had a full purse of money on him and was wearing a silver chain as well as several valuable rings, only one of the rings and a little loose change in one of his pockets were taken. This was attributed by the coroner to the fact that Martin's attackers had been disturbed. He chose to ignore the other far more significant fact of the way in which my half-brother had been murdered. A knife through the heart can be no accidental killing.'

'In short,' I said, just so that there could be no misunderstanding, 'you think that these apparent robbers were really hired assassins?'

Oswald Godslove hesitated for a second, then, reluctantly, nodded.

'Well, thank the sweet Lord you've confessed as much at last,' breathed Clemency. 'You see, Roger, we need you,' she added, turning to me. 'Already you've persuaded my brother to declare openly that he agrees with us, which, up until now, he has refused to do.'

'Nonsense!' Oswald retorted, nettled. 'I've always said that there was something odd about Martin's death. But that doesn't mean I believe it's connected to the other mishaps that have befallen us.'

Clemency and Celia threw up their hands in disgust. 'Of course they are connected,' the former declared almost angrily. 'We have never discovered who it was who left that basket of mushrooms outside the kitchen door a year ago.'

I had temporarily forgotten the death of Charity Godslove. An unsolicited gift from an unknown person did sound suspicious, I had to admit.

'Did you all eat the mushrooms?' I asked.

'All except Oswald,' Celia answered, smiling faintly at her half-brother on the opposite side of the table.

That made sense. Picking, selling, buying and eating mushrooms was legally forbidden, although it was a law that many people ignored and whose flouting the authorities were inclined to wink at. But it was for this very reason – that the average man or woman was unable to tell the difference between a poisonous and a benign mushroom – that the ban had first been imposed. It was all too easy to make a murder look like an accident where mushrooms were concerned.

'So,' I said, 'if, as seems most probable, a highly poisonous variety of mushroom had been concealed amongst the others, any one of you, including Master Godslove, here, could have been the intended victim. In other words, there was no particular target, just whoever was unfortunate enough to eat it.'

Celia shivered suddenly. 'Yes,' she agreed with a nod. 'That's what makes us think that someone has a grudge against the whole family.'

'And also someone who is extraordinarily callous,' Clemency put in. 'Someone who doesn't care who gets harmed as long as he achieves his ends. The victim in that particular instance could just as well have been Arbella or one of the kitchen maids.'

'Why do you assume this unknown enemy is a man? It could as easily be a woman,' I pointed out. 'Poison, they say, is a woman's weapon. And a woman is as capable of hiring assassins to do her work for her as a man. In fact she would be more likely to do so.'

'And Sybilla's "accident"?' the housekeeper asked, speaking for the first time since the discussion began.

I shrugged. 'Again, money may have changed hands. One of the workmen repairing the city wall could have been bribed. I imagine you are all in and out of the Bishop's Gate fairly frequently. There would be no difficulty in recognizing any one of you, I should think.'

There was a sudden silence around the table, broken only by the subdued muttering and giggling of Elizabeth and Nicholas, totally oblivious to the rest of the world and its problems now that they were together again. Adam sat round-eyed and quiet, listening to everything that was said.

'Well, we know at least two things about this would-be murderer,' I suggested finally, when the silence became too uncomfortable to maintain any longer.

'And what are those?' Celia asked eagerly.

'That he or she has enormous patience. It's two years or more since Reynold Makepeace was killed. Nearly as long since your illness.' I nodded towards Clemency. 'Another year since your sister, Charity, died and six months since your half-brother was murdered. Also, he or she is persistent. Out of five attempts, two have failed, but that hasn't stopped further attacks nor, I imagine, will it. As far as our unknown killer is concerned, there is no urgency. Indeed, I suspect that the slow unravelling of events is a part of the enjoyment.'

'Are you saying that Sybilla and I can expect further attempts on our lives?' Clemency asked unsteadily

'I'm afraid so,' I answered. 'You are all in danger.'

SIX

There was an uncomfortable silence before Oswald gave an uncertain laugh. 'You paint a bleak picture, Master Chapman,' he said. 'I'm not sure that I believe it.'

I smiled. 'I'm not sure that I believe it, myself,' I admitted.

'Well, I believe it,' Celia declared roundly. 'I think Roger is in the right of it.' She dimpled slightly as she called me by my Christian name, but sobered again almost immediately. 'Three of our number are dead, two have nearly died. The only question in my mind is who is doing this dreadful thing, and why.'

'That's two questions,' her half-brother pointed out pedantically, and I was surprised to note that this was no jocular correction, but seriously meant. I was reminded that Oswald was a lawyer and used to standing on points of order, but I guessed that, in any case, he was a man who valued precision. He went on, 'But as you so rightly say, my dear Celia, who would instigate such a vendetta against our family, and for what reason?'

'I should think the answer is obvious,' Clemency put in. 'It's someone who has a grudge against Oswald because of one of his cases. We've said this before and I see no good reason to alter our opinion. And I should imagine that that is where anyone investigating on our behalf would start.' Here, she looked directly at me. 'Are we to understand, Roger, that you are willing to remain at the Arbour for the time being and help us with these enquiries?'

'Of course he is!' my wife interposed swiftly, at the same time kicking me smartly on the ankle.

'Let your husband answer for himself, Adela,' Clemency reproved her sternly. 'If he is at all reluctant, if his heart is not in it, then it would be far better if he took you and the children home tomorrow and left us to our fate.'

All eyes were turned in my direction including the children's, although they could have had no real idea of what was going on. But that didn't prevent their gaze being as reproachful as their mother's. As usual, my nearest and dearest were expecting the worst of me.

And I don't say they were wrong in that respect: every instinct urged me to get out of London while the going was good. But the relationship of Reynold Makepeace to the Godsloves, and the possibility that his death had not been accident, but murder, made a difference. Reynold had been a friend. If I could bring the villain who had arranged for him to be killed to book, then it was my duty to do so.

'Adela is right,' I said, smiling at Clemency. 'Of course I'll stay for a while and do what I can to help.'

I did not add that there would be a self-imposed time limit on this offer of assistance. Indeed, I doubted if that would be necessary. The constant presence of three vigorous children would eventually take its toll on a normally childless household; and whereas Nicholas had probably been on his best behaviour until now, Elizabeth's presence would inevitably alter that. Apart, they might be quiet and docile; together, they could put a cavalry charge to shame.

At my words, there were smiles from the women and even Oswald was unable to hide a satisfied twitch of the lips.

'Good,' said Clemency. 'So let's talk about something else for a while. Oswald, what's the news in the city this morning? Is there any word yet as to when the duke will arrive?'

Her brother shook his head. 'But there is a very strong rumour,' he hastened on, forestalling his womenfolk's groans of disappointment, 'that the king and Earl Rivers will leave Ludlow tomorrow and rendezvous with His Grace of Gloucester some time next week, at Northampton.'

He gave a self-satisfied smile, so I forbore to mention that this information tallied with what I had heard the Abbot of Reading tell Bishop Stillington, realizing that it would be impolitic to steal Oswald's thunder. He was a man with a very high opinion of himself, I could tell. And who could blame him, sated as he was with a lifelong diet of adulation from his sisters and also, nowadays, from his housekeeper? I did, however, contribute the fact that I had seen Sir Richard Grey riding along the Strand in the midst of a great bevy of retainers.

'Oh, him!' Oswald dismissed the queen's younger first-marriage son with a shrug of his shoulders. 'A troublemaker, that one. Indeed, all the Woodville faction are hell-bent on stirring the pot and making it boil. The lord chamberlain – or should I say the ex-lord chamberlain, for I doubt Hastings will continue in office under the new young king – is desperate for Gloucester's arrival, even though it's my impression that the two men have never liked one another above half. But their shared love and grief for Edward should draw them together. At least, that's my opinion. For what it's worth,' he added with a self-conscious laugh as he waited for the expected reassurance.

It came at once and in a chorus.

'You're always right, my dear, you know that,' proclaimed Clemency with a smile.

'I have never known your judgement to be at fault yet, Oswald,' Celia confirmed.

'Master Godslove is a very clever man,' Arbella Rokeswood said, addressing her words to me but keeping her eyes fixed on him and basking in the warmth of his approval.

I tried to look impressed, but Adela, who knew me better than her cousins, told me later that she knew exactly what I was thinking. ('You'd do as well to try and keep your features under control, Roger,' she warned me.)

The children were, by now, growing restless and Clemency, deciding that we had been sitting over our meal long enough, made to rise from the table.

'One moment,' I said as she did so. Everyone looked enquiringly in my direction. 'You've mentioned having two stepbrothers. Landlord Makepeace had a brother, then. Is he still alive? If so, can I meet him? Does he live near here?'

'Julian?' Clemency looked faintly surprised as if this was something I should know already. 'He's an apothecary and he, too, lives in Bucklersbury. His shop is not far from the Voyager on the opposite side of the road. You'll see his name over the door. There are a good many apothecaries' shops in that street.'

I nodded. 'So I've noticed. I'll pay him a visit later on.'

'Whatever for?' Oswald asked, frankly puzzled. 'I'm sure he won't be able to tell you anything. Nothing to the purpose, at any rate. A good enough man among his herbs and simples, but of limited intelligence I've always thought him.'

'His life might be in danger,' I pointed out. 'Besides, he may know something, have seen something, however small, that could help me solve this mystery. I must speak to your priest as well. Father Berowne I think you called him. But what would help me most of all, Master Godslove, would be if you could give me a list of any of the criminals you have successfully prosecuted lately who might have cause – or believe they have cause,' I hastily amended, 'to bear you a grudge.'

As he hesitated, Celia came round the table and laid a hand on Oswald's arm. 'Dearest, you must do this. Please. For all our sakes.'

There was a further pause. Then he patted her hand and gave her an indulgent smile.

'Very well,' he agreed. 'But I doubt if Master Chapman, here, will get much joy from it. My cases are all fairly conducted. Scrupulously so. Very few with whom I have dealings have cause to complain.'

His half-sister rubbed her cheek against his.

'We know that, my love. So do all your friends and acquaintances. But a felon wouldn't. I've heard you say often that very few of them ever admit, even to themselves, that they are guilty, or at least that they were not justified in doing what they did.'

'True,' the lawyer admitted. 'But in general they are a lazy, shiftless crowd who would find a sustained campaign of vengeance – if that is what this is – beyond the range of their limited powers. However, as you all seem to think it worthwhile, I'll see if I can think of anyone who might consider that he—'

'Or she,' I reminded him.

He turned a cold eye towards me. He did not take kindly to interruption. 'Very well! If you insist. Anyone who might consider that he or she has been unfairly treated at my hands. It will not,' he added austerely, 'be a long list.'

'Of course not,' I agreed suavely. 'But I think your sisters are right in supposing it could be the answer to recent events. Female intuition is never to be despised, my dear sir.'

I saw Adela's lips twitch in appreciation of this master stroke. The women were now solidly on my side.

We at last began to move, Nicholas and Elizabeth disappearing almost at once, presumably into the garden. The housekeeper made for the kitchens, to summon the maids to clear the table, while the rest of us returned to the great hall, where the fire had almost gone out. Celia gave an exclamation of impatience and put another log on the dying flames, Oswald announced his intention of returning shortly to the inns of court and Clemency suggested that I accompany Adela upstairs to inspect the bedchamber we were to share and to unpack my own and my daughter's clothes. In the middle of all this, there was a loud knock on the outer door, and before anyone could answer it, the latch was lifted and a man came in.

He was heavily built, with a neat curly brown beard that echoed the curly brown hair showing beneath his flat velvet cap. He was nearly as tall as Oswald but far more muscular, giving an illusory impression of squatness which a second and third glance dispelled. A pair of hazel eyes regarded the assembled company with indifference until they came to rest on Celia. Then they glowed.

He hurried forward, ignoring both Clemency and Oswald, and, bowing low, raised one of her hands to his lips.

'Celia, my dear! Lovely as ever and looking the picture of health, as always.'

Celia withdrew her hand, blushing slightly, but she did not return the greeting. Instead, she appeared embarrassed, casting a fleeting, half-apologetic glance at Oswald.

Her half-brother said coldly, 'Good morning, Roderick. Let me conduct you upstairs at once to see your patient. I think you'll find Sybilla slightly improved since yesterday.'

The physician returned the other man's look with barely concealed animosity and said, almost sneeringly, 'I'm sure I shall. There's nothing much wrong with her but a few bruises, which the salve I left for her should have eased. And the sleeping draught ought to have ensured her a restful night.'

'Sybilla is still very much shocked by what happened to her,' Clemency protested. 'Her nerves are in a very poor state.'

'She was always prone to hysterics,' was the cool response. 'I'll bleed her again. It will quieten her. Don't bother coming up with me, Clemency. I know my way.'

'I'll accompany you just the same,' Clemency said firmly, and followed the doctor up the stairs.

Reaching halfway, he turned, looking down into the hall with a softened expression on his rather harsh features.

'Will you stay to say goodbye to me, Celia?' His lip curled. 'Or have you some urgent business, as usual, that will necessitate your presence in some other part of the house?'

Once again, I thought that the younger woman seemed uncomfortable, but she answered composedly enough. 'I will stay and speak to you with pleasure, Roderick, if you wish it. In any case, I shall want to know your opinion of Sybilla and how she goes on. My sister's health is the important thing.'

'Naturally.' He laughed shortly. 'Such a devoted family!' He proceeded on his way, Clemency close at his heels.

'Well, I must be going along,' Oswald said. 'I'm due in court this afternoon.' He bent and kissed Celia's cheek. 'Don't let Roderick Jeavons rile you, my dear. If he weren't such a good doctor, and if he hadn't tended our family for so long, I'd be tempted to find another physician.'

'No, no! Don't do that,' Celia begged him quickly. 'He doesn't disturb me.'

Her half-brother patted her shoulder. 'I'm very glad to hear it,' he said. 'The Godsloves have never been dependent upon other people. We know how to look after our own.' He smiled fleetingly in my wife's direction at the same time glancing warningly at me. Adela had obviously been accepted as one of the family, however remote the connection, and it was implied that I should do well to remember that fact or I might find myself asked to leave.

I gave a brief inclination of my head and watched Oswald march briskly out of the door. Then I turned to Adela.

'Shall we go and unpack,' I asked, 'as Clemency suggested?'

Adela's bedchamber was a large and very chilly room at one side of the house and reached by what seemed to me to be

innumerable corridors and small flights of stairs, going both
up and down.

'You'll get used to it,' she laughed when I complained that
I should never be able to find my way around such a rambling,
topsy-turvy building. 'It's a very old house and I fancy bits
have been added on as its former occupants decided to
expand. That little room opening off this one –' she nodded
towards a door in one corner – 'is where the boys sleep.
Elizabeth can share it with them.'

I agreed abstractedly. I was not much interested in the
domestic arrangements except to notice with satisfaction that
the adjacent room had a bolt on our side of the door, which
could, and would, be employed in the interests of privacy. I
lounged on the great four-poster bed, with its faded hangings depicting the story of Queen Esther and King Ahasuerus,
and watched while my wife unpacked the linen sack I had
brought with me, shaking out the clothes with exclamations
of horror at the way they had been crammed in altogether,
without being properly folded.

'I'll never get the creases out of this,' she said, holding
up one of Elizabeth's gowns. She dived further down. 'Mmm.
I see you've brought your good new clothes with you.' She
looked suspicious. 'Was there any particular reason?'

I shook my head impatiently. 'I just took everything. Never
mind that.' I raised myself on my elbows. 'Adela, what is
there between Celia and the doctor? I'd swear there's something. She seems to me to be most uneasy in his presence.'

'Oh, there's no great secret, if that's what you're thinking,'
my wife replied, clucking disparagingly over the state of
Elizabeth's shifts. 'Clemency told me that some ten years
ago, after the death of his first wife, Roderick Jeavons wanted
to marry Celia. She must have been in her middle twenties
then and very pretty. He's a great deal older, but I imagine
he was always a handsome man. He still is.' There was a
gleam in Adela's eyes that I didn't much care for, but I let
it pass. 'Celia,' she went on, 'seems to have been equally
attracted to him and, without consulting the rest of the family,
agreed to wed him.'

'And when the others found out?'

Adela sat down on the edge of the bed. 'Well, you can

imagine! You've seen for yourself how they are. Clemency, of course, said no more than that Celia had later changed her mind having realized she had made a mistake. But I don't suppose for a single moment that that is the real story. My guess would be that she was overwhelmed by the others' tears and reproaches. Told she was breaking up the family. How would they manage without her? And so on. Maybe there were even threats – or implied threats – that she would be cast off completely; that they would never see or speak to her again.'

'But surely,' I protested, 'a woman in love wouldn't be swayed by that. A normal woman of twenty-odd must want a home of her own and children.'

'Not necessarily,' my wife answered abruptly, getting off the bed and turning the linen sack inside out to make sure that nothing had been overlooked. 'Some women might prefer their freedom.' She hurried on before I had time to digest this cryptic utterance. 'As I said just now, you must have noticed for yourself, even in this short time, how matters stand in this family. They mean everything to one another. There's something unnatural about it. If I were less charitable, I'd say that Celia, and indeed Clemency, are more than a little in love with Oswald. And from what I have gathered from Arbella, Charity was worse than either of them. Oswald's likes, dislikes, preferences were – still are for that matter – the hub on which the whole house turned. Turns.'

I lowered myself back against the pillows, my arms folded behind my head, wondering what I had let myself in for. The Arbour seemed to be a seething cauldron of suppressed emotions, largely incestuous. Arbella Rokeswood was plainly in love with Oswald, who was probably secretly in love with his half-sister, although that, I guessed, was something he would never admit, even to himself. And what of Clemency, Sybilla, and Charity who had died? There was more, surely, than sibling affection between them. I sighed. I felt I ought to insist on taking Adela and the children home at once, away from this unwholesome atmosphere. But, in spite of myself, my interest had been aroused, as well as an instinct that the Godsloves might be right in thinking that they could have an enemy bent on their extinction. Besides which, there was Reynold Makepeace to avenge.

Reynold. How had such a plain, straightforward, ordinary man fitted into this rarefied atmosphere? And why had he never mentioned to me that he had lived near Bristol, near enough for him, surely, to have known the city reasonably well? I must see and talk to his brother, the apothecary. Also, I must seek out the priest, Father Berowne, and make enquiries at the Bishop's Gate. Someone there could have seen or heard something suspicious relating to the attempt on Sybilla's life. Moreover, there were two potential avengers in the family's midst; the housekeeper, whose plan might be to remove Oswald's siblings one by one until he alone remained, bereft of all those he held dear and ready to throw himself into the comfort of Arbella's embrace. Or there was the physician with a similar scheme, hoping that once Celia was alone, and free of the influence of the rest, she would be glad to marry him. Or, yet again, Roderick Jeavons could simply be out for vengeance on the lot of them, Celia included.

Adela paused in her task of carefully placing my clothes in a cedar wood chest which stood against one wall.

'You're looking broody,' she said. But when I told her my thoughts, she was aghast. 'You can't possibly suspect Arbella or the doctor,' she protested.

'Why not? They both have sound reasons for murder.'

'Because . . . Because you just can't,' she said, woman's logic taking over from common sense. 'They're nice people.'

'And have nice people never been known to commit a crime?' I asked in exasperation. 'Some very good people have killed in their time, and no doubt will do so again.' (For some reason or other I suddenly found myself thinking of Duke Richard, but for the life of me I couldn't make out why.)

'I won't listen to such talk,' my wife said firmly, closing the chest with a bang. 'The killer, as Clemency says, is far more likely to be someone who has a grudge against Oswald. Surely that makes more sense, wouldn't you agree?'

'No,' I answered bluntly, meeting her outraged glance steadily. 'In my experience, felons, once they've been caught and sentenced, don't waste their energies on thoughts of revenge. Most have enough to do just surviving in prison.

Furthermore, a lot of them have an innate sense of justice that acknowledges the fact that they have done wrong and are being punished.'

Adela came and sat on the edge of the bed for a second time. 'And what of those who don't believe they have done wrong – or those who really are innocent – and are being unjustly treated?'

I rolled on to my side. 'I still don't think they would resort to killing off a whole family as a means of retribution,' I said. 'Oswald maybe. But not his brothers and sisters. And certainly not a stepbrother who didn't even live with him. No! My guess would be a person with a much more personal grudge against the lot of them.'

'I won't have it!' my wife exclaimed. 'I won't have you pointing the finger at Arbella or Dr Jeavons. If you must suspect someone unconnected with Oswald's work why not pick on Adrian Jollifant? Now, there's a man I do not like.'

'Who in the Virgin's name is Adrian Jollifant?' I demanded, once more heaving myself into a sitting position.

Adela waved an airy hand. 'Oh, he's a silversmith who has a shop in Cheapside. At least, I believe Clemency said it's really his father's shop, but the old man has retired and leaves his son to run the business for him.'

'And what has this silversmith to do with the Godsloves?' I asked.

'He wants to purchase the Arbour. Apparently, a long time ago, fifty years or so, it belonged to his family, and now he wants to buy it back again. He seems to think he has a right to it and that Oswald is under some sort of obligation to sell it to him. He's called twice since I've been here, and was most offensive to Clemency and Sybilla on both occasions. Oswald was from home. The second time, he swore he'd have it by hook or by crook and stumped out of the house in a fury.'

This was interesting. 'What's he like? Old? Young? Fat? Thin? Cross-eyed?'

That made Adela laugh. 'There's nothing special about him. No distinguishing features. Forty or so I should guess. Solidly built, but not fat. A round face, fair hair starting to go grey. I can't recall the colour of his eyes, but I think they were blue. Well dressed. Expensive clothes. If not downright wealthy, then I should say he has sufficient money and more for all his needs.'

'And he used threatening language towards Clemency and Sybilla?'

'Not threatening exactly. He was just rude in the same way Adam is when he can't get his own way.'

'Which reminds me,' I said, looking around, 'where is he?'

'Adam?' Adela smiled with the fond indulgence of a mother speaking of her favourite. (Not that wild horses would ever have got her to admit that she had a favourite.) 'I persuaded Nicholas and Elizabeth to let him play with them in the garden.'

'They'll be sorry,' I prophesied before returning to the subject of Adrian Jollifant. 'I must certainly see this silversmith for myself. I must ask Clemency if she knows his address in the city. If what you say is true, he might well be the person we are looking for. He would be a suspect at the very least. But,' I added, holding up a warning finger, 'that doesn't mean I've exonerated Mistress Rokeswood or Dr Jeavons. They both have equally good motives for wanting some, if not all, of the family members out of the way.'

'No,' Adela said 'I won't have it, Roger. It's preposterous.'

I ignored this. She knew perfectly well that I followed my own path; that I took advice from no one when solving one of my mysteries. And I had to own to myself that I was becoming intrigued by what I had at first thought to be little more than a couple of hysterical women reading more than they should have done into a string of natural accidents.

'Never mind,' my wife remarked. 'God will guide you.'

God! Of course! He was playing His tricks on me again. Why hadn't I realized that? He had guided Adela to London, knowing I would follow. Moreover, I decided, chewing my thumbnail, I wouldn't put it past Him to have put it into Juliette Gerrish's head to try and saddle me with her by-blow and thus start this whole chain of events. I had a good mind to pack up immediately and go to find Jack Nym at the Boar's Head in East Cheap. I toyed with the idea for a full minute before doing what I always did where God was concerned. I gave in, albeit ungraciously. Peace of mind returned.

I drew a deep breath. I was committed now, but I had no intention of rushing into anything. There were more important things in life and God would just have to be patient.

'Are you sure the children are in the garden?' I asked.

'Yes, of course,' Adela answered, surprised. 'If you open that window, you can see them. Why do you want to know?'

I twisted around to look to my left. 'And is that a bolt I can see on the main bedchamber door?'

'Yes.' She was frankly puzzled now.

I got off the bed and slid the bolt home.

'What are you doing?' Adela was either being deliberately slow on the uptake or we had been parted for far too long. I rather hoped it was the latter. I didn't care to imagine any reluctance on her part.

I got back on the bed and reached for her hands. 'I thought,' I said primly, 'that you might wish to give me a warmer welcome now that we are at last alone.' Then I grinned. 'I thought you might want to demonstrate how very pleased you are to see me.'

'If I am,' she answered severely, trying not to laugh.

I took no notice of this and pulled her into my arms.

SEVEN

Later that day, with a renewed spring in my step and a sparkle in my eye, I set out to visit Julian Makepeace at his apothecary's shop in Bucklersbury.

The fields around St Mary's Hospital stretched into the distance, softly green under the warm April sun. Here and there, they were starred with clumps of primroses, and beneath a stand of trees sweet violets raised their delicate, purple-veined heads. As I passed St Botolph's church, I reminded myself that I must also speak with Father Berowne, the parish priest who had attended Clemency when she was so ill the year before last; and I wondered uneasily if he were the black-robed figure emerging somewhat furtively from the nearby tavern, where the amount of noise issuing forth suggested that it was as badly run as the majority of inns and alehouses up and down the country. It was small wonder that they were generally regarded by the authorities as centres of vice and crime and closely watched. (In Bristol, I knew that the town constable kept a list of regular frequenters of its numerous places of refreshment, and I suspected that my name had to be somewhere near the top.)

I paused to use the public latrine and to allow Hercules, who accompanied me, to cock his leg against the wall of one of the almshouses, before proceeding to the Bishop's Gate. The cries coming from the Bedlam were as distressing as before, but I shut my ears to them and looked up at the men working above me, perched on the scaffolding over the gate. Experience having taught me that there are few things so unsatisfactory as a conversation carried on at a distance, I walked under the archway – waved through by a gatekeeper plainly disgruntled by the disturbance – to find that within the walls there were several workmen at ground level. One was busy mixing mortar while two others were loading stones into baskets which were then raised by pulleys to the men overhead.

I addressed the former, his grudging, almost sulky attitude towards his job informing me that, like the other hands,
he was English (although there had to be an overseer from
the Steelyard lurking somewhere about to ensure that there
was no slacking). My fellow countrymen were notorious for
being averse to too much hard labour.

'There was a lady injured here a day or so ago,' I said, not
beating about the bush. 'Did you happen to see the accident?'

'Piss off!' growled the mortar-mixer, a heavy-jowled indi-
vidual with hair that stood on end as though he had just
received a fright.

The tone made Hercules bark menacingly. I hushed him
and fingered the coins in my purse.

'Don't be like that,' I murmured. 'I feel sure this is thirsty
work.'

The man licked his cracked lips and cast a quick glance
over his shoulder, confirming my suspicion that one of the
Hanse merchants was somewhere in the offing. 'What do
you want to know?'

I transferred a couple of coins from my purse to my hand,
but still kept a tight grip on them.

'Were you present when the accident occurred?' I enquired.
He nodded and grunted. 'Well, what happened?' I demanded
impatiently as he seemed disinclined to add anything further.

'One o' them blocks of stone nearly squashed 'er flat. A
pity it didn't. Still,' he added, brightening, 'it 'it 'er a fair
whack. Set up a screech, she did. You'd of thought she was
being gutted at Tyburn.'

'You don't like the lady,' I said. 'Why not? Do you know
her?'

The man spat. 'One 'o them high and mighty bitches
from the old house up the road beyond the 'spital fields.
Brother's a lawyer, a race 'o men I detests.' He gave
another quick look around and held out his hand for the
money.

'Not so fast!' I whipped my hands behind my back. 'In
your opinion was it a genuine accident or did someone deliberately drop that block of stone from the scaffolding with
the intention of killing Mistress Godslove?'

He visibly jumped. ''Ere! What you implyin'? We're honest

men, we are. Anyway, why would anyone want to kill the
silly cow?'

'Money?' I suggested. 'Someone offered you and your
friends a goodish sum to do murder?'

The mortar-mixer advanced his ugly face to within an inch
of mine. The stink of his breath almost suffocated me.

'I told you just now to piss off and I meant it. You and
your money and that fart of an animal what's pretending to
be a dog.'

He kicked out at Hercules, who promptly bit him on the
ankle, then began barking like a fiend. Heads started turning
in our direction and the two men filling the baskets straightened their backs and glared menacingly in my direction. I
realized that I had handled the situation badly and had no
choice now but to retreat with as much dignity as I could
muster. I dropped the coins back in my purse, grabbed
Hercules and retreated to a safe distance where I bent to fix
his rope collar and lead around his neck, receiving his lick
of affection full across my nose.

'I made a mess of that,' I told him, wiping my face.

On reflection, however, I decided that something had been
gained from the encounter. The mortar-mixer had obviously
been rattled by my suggestion that one of his companions
had been paid to make an attempt on Sybilla's life. His reaction had not been the scornful dismissal of an innocent man.
Indeed, the more I thought about it, the more his sudden
spurt of anger seemed to indicate that there was some truth
in my accusation. Or was it simply righteous indignation?
Was I reading more into his belligerent attitude than I should?

I sighed. The beginning of any enquiry, before the various
pieces started falling into place to make a whole picture, was
always the same: self-questioning and doubts. I glanced down
at Hercules trotting happily by my side, eyes bright, tail well
up, not a care in the world. A dog's life. There might be
something to be said for it, after all.

As I came abreast of Crosby's Place, another great wagon
was blocking the road. On this occasion furniture, including a
couple of armchairs, seat and back-rest richly upholstered in
embroidered blue velvet, were being unloaded along with what
I guessed to be a tapestry, rolled and protected with sacking.

I looked around hoping to see a familiar face, then realized that the only member of the Duke of Gloucester's household whom I knew at all well was Timothy Plummer, his spymaster general. And he would surely still be travelling south in his master's train.

I turned right as far as the Stock's Market, left into Walbrook Street and right again, entering Bucklersbury from the Old Barge end. I walked along slowly, examining the names above the doors on my left. Someone – I couldn't recall who – had said that Reynold's brother's shop was on the opposite side of the street to the Voyager, but not too distant. And there, finally, it was. An apothecary's window full of the usual bottles and jars with, over the lintel, the faded legend: 'Julian Makepeace'.

I knocked on the door. Nothing happened, so I knocked again. Hercules, who was anxious to inspect some fly-blown offal in the central drain, pulled impatiently at his lead. I hauled him back and knocked a third time, and on this occasion my summons was finally answered. There was the sound of bolts being withdrawn and, a moment later, a sleepy young maid servant finally opened the door.

'Yes?' she yawned.

'I would like to speak to Apothecary Makepeace,' 'I answered.

The young woman shook her head. 'Master's away until next week. Gone to S'ampton to see a friend.'

I groaned inwardly. This, I knew, was merely the first setback. There were bound to be others, and my dream of solving the mystery quickly and easily and returning home to Bristol was doomed, as such dreams always were, to failure.

'To Southampton, eh?'

This time the girl nodded. 'That's right, sir.'

'Did he happen to mention which day he would return?'

'No, sir. Said to expect him when I saw him, that's all.'

I looked her over. Not the brightest of damsels I guessed. 'Is there anyone else in the house I could speak to?'

Again she shook her head. 'No, sir, there's only him and me. I'm Master Makepeace's housekeeper.'

I raised my eyebrows at that. Considering that the

apothecary, even if younger than Reynold, must be a man
of advanced, or advancing, years, this buxom young person
must surely be more to him than a housekeeper. And as if
in answer to my thoughts, she gave a provocative grin.

'Er – quite so,' I murmured. 'So . . . You can't give me
any idea when your master will be home? When it might be
convenient to call again?'

She tilted her head to one side, apparently giving my
question serious consideration, but after several moments'
cogitation, said flatly, 'No.'

Looked at closely, she really was a very pretty piece. My
respect for Julian Makepeace soared.

'I'll just have to keep trying until I find him returned,
then.'

She regarded me sympathetically. 'If it's a remedy you're
wanting, sir, there are plenty of other 'pothecaries in
Bucklersbury. You could try one of them.'

'No, it's a personal matter.' A sudden thought occurred to
me. 'Your master hasn't had any – er – any unexplained
accidents recently, I suppose? In the . . . the last year or so,
that is?'

The girl looked bemused. 'Not that I know of, sir.'

'His brother, Landlord Makepeace of the Voyager, was
murdered, I believe.'

Her eyes widened in surprise. 'Well, yes, sir, but that was
going on for two years ago, and he wasn't murdered exactly.
He was knifed in a common brawl.'

'And there was never any suggestion that his death might
not have been . . . well . . . not an accident?'

'Goodness no, sir! Leastways, the master never said
anything like that to me. Never said anything like it to no
one as far's I know. It was just some rowdy young bucks
making trouble, and poor Landlord Makepeace got in the
way, trying to calm them down. These fellows had their
knives out you see, sir. But if you don't believe me, you can
ask the master yourself when he comes back.'

'No, no, of course I believe you,' I said hurriedly. 'All the
same, I'll probably call again next week to have a word with
Master Apothecary.'

She gave me a sleepy smile. 'You do that, sir. But go gentle with him. The thought of his brother's death still upsets him even though it was all that long time ago now. They were close, being as they grew up together and had to keep one another company.'

I thanked her and made to move on. Hercules was getting annoyed at his enforced inactivity, and as I have mentioned somewhere before, he had the unpleasant habit of peeing down my leg if he were too frustrated. I heard the shop door shut behind me as I walked a yard or so along the street, where I found myself facing St Brendan the Voyager.

On impulse, and because I was growing thirsty, I crossed over, picking my way carefully through the refuse in the drain, and entered the inn. Then I wished I hadn't. The contrast between how it used to be during Reynold's time and how it was now was painful. Gone was the cleanliness and order, the smell of good meat roasting on the spit, the quiet hum of respectful conversation. In their place were filthy floor rushes, unchanged for days, the stink of urine and stale beer, raucous laughter and raised voices singing bawdy songs. And presiding over all was the slatternly red-haired woman and her two equally red-haired sons whom I had glimpsed last October when I had first learned of Reynold Makepeace's untimely death.

I nearly walked straight out again. But the sight of a sober-looking man in a plain brown tunic and hose, quietly supping and grimacing over his drink in a retired corner of the ale-room, encouraged me to squeeze on to the empty stool beside him.

'This place has changed,' I remarked as I settled myself with Hercules at my feet. (He was used to inns and taverns. He felt at home in them.)

My neighbour grunted. 'You never said a truer word, master. Heartbreaking, that's what it is. Did you know it in Landlord Makepeace's day?'

'I did,' I responded feelingly. 'I've stayed here a couple o' times. Even brought my wife here once.' I stared around me disparagingly. 'Couldn't do it today.'

'You surely couldn't,' he agreed vehemently. He spat. 'Pigsty, that's what it is now. I shouldn't bother calling for the pot boy. The ale ain't worth drinking.'

'I'm thirsty,' I said apologetically as I gave my order to the skinny waif in a dirty apron who had condescended to ask me what I wanted. 'I heard that Landlord Makepeace was killed while trying to break up a fight between two bravos. Is that right?'

My companion nodded gloomily. 'All too true, unfortunately. A bad business. The place has gone downhill, as you can see, since this bunch of cut-throats bought it. It's no better than any of the taverns along the waterfront.'

'I suppose,' I suggested tentatively, 'that it was an accident?' The man looked enquiringly at me. 'I mean there was never any talk that Reynold's death was – well – murder? That the young men involved had been, shall we say, paid to arrange it?'

'Never!' was the uncompromising answer. 'Not a whisper. What makes you think otherwise?'

'Just an idea.' I smiled lamely.

'You're not from around here, are you?' He regarded me curiously. 'West Country, would be my guess.' My ale arrived, the pot slapped down on the table so that some of its contents spilled across the board. He went on, 'Yes, definitely West Country. I worked in Bristol for a year or so when I was younger, and I've never forgotten that peculiar accent.'

'I was born and raised in Wells,' I replied huffily; but then relented. 'However, you're right. I've lived in Bristol for many years now. As I believe Reynold and his brother also did once, although he never thought to mention the fact to me.'

The stranger swallowed the last of his beer. 'That's because he never did live there. He and Julian were local lads, born and bred. Brought up by their grandmother who had a house in Candlewick Street. You're getting them confused with their mother, Widow Makepeace. Now if memory serves me aright, she did marry a man from Bristol – or thereabouts – and went to live there. The younger boy must've been about eleven, Reynold a year or two older. That was when they went to stay with their grandmother, I suppose. I think I once heard somebody say that Widow Makepeace had two more children by her second husband.'

Martin and Celia Godslove! I bit back the exclamation

and tried to appear no more than mildly interested. 'Are you saying that Reynold and Julian Makepeace never left London?'

'That's right. I don't think they ever did.' He suddenly tired of the subject. 'So, what do you think's going to happen?' he asked abruptly.

'Happen?' I stared at him in bewilderment, caught up in my own concerns.

'Now we have a child as king.' He spoke impatiently, as though the subject were of far more importance than the history of the Makepeace brothers. Which of course it was. He wiped his nose on the sleeve of his tunic. 'Who's going to control him and the country do you reckon? The Woodvilles or Gloucester?'

I forced myself to consider the subject. 'If I had to wager good money on it,' I said at last, 'it would be on the duke.'

My companion pursed his lips. 'I'm not so sure. The queen's precious family are a devious crowd. They've already secured the Tower and the royal treasure. They're probably plotting how to get rid of Gloucester at this very moment. Ah well!' He got to his feet. 'This won't buy the baby a new pair of breeches. I must be off back to the shop, or my beldame will give me a right scolding.'

I plucked at his sleeve. 'What makes you think that the Woodvilles are planning to murder the duke?'

He shushed me frantically. 'Keep your voice down for the love of God. And who mentioned the word "murder"?' But he added darkly, 'It just wouldn't surprise me, that's all. The whole clan are scurrying about like flies on a dunghill and arming themselves to the teeth. "Woe unto the kingdom whose king is a child,",' he quoted, grimacing. 'Ecclesiastes.'

The next moment, he was gone, leaving me to my uneasy reflections. Was Duke Richard really in danger from the queen's family? But then my thoughts reverted to what I had learned about Reynold and Julian Makepeace. They had never lived in the house at Keynsham. They had never left London. Mind you, I had only the stranger's word for it, and I would have to confirm the fact when I eventually spoke to the apothecary. But it seemed to be corroborated by the maid's remark that the two had relied on one another for companionship when they were young.

For some reason that I couldn't quite fathom, this piece of information disturbed me, so much so that I went as far as ordering myself another pot of the Voyager's disgusting ale and sat huddled over it, trying to work out why. In the end, however, I gave up, knowing from long experience that cudgelling my brains was never of any use. The answer would come to me in its own good time. I pushed aside my still almost full beaker and stood up.

'Come on! Let's get out of here,' I said to Hercules.

We emerged into Bucklersbury just in time to be spattered with filth from the central drain as another party of armed and mounted men clattered past, on this occasion wearing the livery of Lord Hastings. (My instant recognition was from having seen it so often during my enforced journey to Scotland the previous year.) So many contingents of armed men roaming the streets were enough to make the most sanguine person uneasy and wonder what in the name of all the saints was going on. I had been in London for less than twenty-four hours, and already the febrile atmosphere of the capital was beginning to make me jumpy and yearn more than ever for home. Once again, I was overwhelmed by the temptation to return to the Arbour, gather up my family and seek out Jack at the Boar's Head in Eastcheap. We could be on our way west tomorrow morning.

At that moment, the only thing preventing me from pursuing this plan of action was the knowledge that such a move would prove most unpopular with my family. Adela would be outraged that I had reneged on my offer of help to the Godsloves, while there would be howls of anguish from Elizabeth and Nicholas at having been robbed of all the exciting games they had planned in that intriguing garden. The only person who might be on my side was Adam, but he was, unfortunately, still too small for his opinion to be regarded. (That, of course, would change, but not just yet.)

Balked of my talk with Julian Makepeace, and not yet in possession of any names that Oswald might come up with as belonging to potential ill-wishers of his family, I cast around in my mind for someone else who had connections with the Godsloves, and remembered the parish priest, Father Berowne. Or Sir Berowne, so many of these underpaid and poorly regarded members of society preferring to be called by a title which added a little spurious dignity to a job that was, more often than not, only one notch above indigence.

I tugged on Hercules's lead, and we set off back the way we had come.

Bishop's Gate Street was just as busy, still blocked by wagons unloading furniture and hangings for Crosby's Place. The workmen were sweating and cursing, the sun having made an appearance in the way that an English April sun tends to do, with sudden and unseasonal warmth. You know very well that it won't last; even as you discard cap and tunic and shoulder cape, you're aware that in half an hour's time you'll be putting them all on again.

As Hercules and I edged our way past the various obstructions, I heard one of the workmen call out to another, 'There's a rumour now 'e won't be stayin' 'ere after all. Leastways, not until the duchess joins 'im from up north.'

'You mean all this bloody rush and bother t' get this fuckin' place ready on time's fer nothing?' demanded the second man. 'Where's 'e goin' then?'

'Baynard's Castle, so I was told. 'Is mother, the old duchess, is arrivin' shortly. So fat Magnus says, anyway. An' 'e keeps 'is ear pretty well t' the ground.'

I passed out of earshot. So it seemed, if fat Magnus could really be relied upon, that the Dowager Duchess of York, the little king's redoubtable grandmother, would be arriving in the capital some day soon. And Richard of Gloucester, as he had done so often in the past, would be taking up residence at his mother's house until Duchess Anne joined him from Yorkshire.

The same bunch of men were still working around the Bishop's Gate, but we pointedly ignored one another; I because I wanted no more trouble with them, they because an officer from the Steelyard – at least I presumed that was who it was – stood alongside the wall, watching them. The gatekeeper nodded to me as I passed under the arch.

By now, it was mid-afternoon, that dead time of day before all those people who have brought their goods to market begin to make their way home again, clogging up a city's every exit with their empty (if it has been a successful day) carts and baskets. It was good to be out in the open countryside once more, the smell of the grass fresh in my nostrils and the sound of birdsong in my ears. Although I was a mere hundred yards or so from the walls, everything here seemed somehow different, removed by miles from that unreasonable sensation of foreboding which hung over London like a pall.

Alongside St Botolph's Church was a two-storey cottage which, from its generally rundown appearance, I easily iden-tified as the priest's house. It was a typical daub-and-wattle building with a thatched roof somewhat in need of repair. Bits of straw floated about in the faint spring breeze like stray wisps of hair escaping from under a woman's coif, and I could hear a pig grunting away somewhere close at hand. There was also a whiff of goat in the air; while a small, badly cultivated patch of earth showed the sallow green of vegetables struggling for survival in poor soil.

I knocked on the door and waited, knuckles poised to rap again, but this proved not to be necessary. A small, extra-ordinarily thin woman – the sort my mother would have described as a 'rasher of wind' – answered my summons with surprising promptness and a look of annoyance creasing her narrow face.

'Yes?' she said, her tone sharp and unwelcoming.

'I should like to speak to Sir Berowne,' I requested, polite but firm.

The woman half-glanced over her shoulder, so I guessed that the priest was at home. 'What do you want?' she demanded.

I raised my eyebrows and stared down my nose (a not unimposing feature in my case). 'That is between me and the father.'

She hesitated, obviously aware that she was outstripping her authority, but reluctant, nonetheless, to give ground. Fortunately for my growing irritation, a man's voice sounded behind her.

'Who is it, Ellen?'

She turned her head quickly, a smile softening her stern expression. 'A stranger, Father. Leastways, I don't recall seeing him hereabouts before.'

'Now you know that all are welcome at my door, my child. Strangers in particular. Stand aside and let the poor man in.'

'He's a nasty, flea-bitten little cur with him,' Ellen objected, eyeing up Hercules with dislike. 'And you've enough of the creatures in this house without adding to their number.'

'Everything is God's creation, my dear, including fleas,' insisted the same pleasant voice, and the housekeeper – for I presumed she was that – was gently put aside as the priest himself finally appeared in the doorway.

He was not much taller than the woman and stood a good head and shoulders lower than myself, a fact he acknowledged with a comical grimace as he looked up into my face. He was certainly not a young man, and in spite of his slight build and the vaguely youthful air which clung about him, I decided he was nearer forty than thirty years of age. He had a pair of very blue eyes which held a lurking twinkle in their depths, and a wide, thin-lipped, mobile mouth, tending more to laughter than sadness. I liked him on sight, and when he stooped and patted Hercules, our friendship was assured.

'Come in, my dear sir,' he invited, holding open the door and ignoring his housekeeper's protests concerning 'that animal'. 'Ellen, my dear,' he added gently, smiling at her, 'run along now. You've done more than enough for one day and your own family need you. They'll be missing you. And I can smell the delicious stew you've left for my supper bubbling on the fire. I'm more than grateful, believe me. I always am. Let me help you on with your cloak, then you can be off.' He suited the action to his words and, with one arm about her shoulders, led her inexorably towards the door. 'God be with you, my child, and bless you.'

'I'll see you tomorrow morning, Father,' she said, accepting her dismissal with as good a grace as possible. 'And watch that dog. I know his sort. He'll steal your supper given half a chance.'

Hercules growled, recognizing an ill-wisher when he met one, and bared his teeth. The housekeeper departed while the going was good.

The priest closed the door behind her and gave me a

lopsided smile. 'A saintly woman,' he said. 'The salt of the earth, but sometimes a little trying.' He came towards me, holding out his hand. 'And now, my son, what can I do for you?'

EIGHT

The ground-floor room of the cottage was much as I had expected it to be: a beaten earth floor covered by a sprinkling of rushes, a table, several stools, a bench on which stood various cooking utensils, a corner cupboard and a couple of shelves supporting a candle in its holder, a tinder box, a pen and inkwell and some sheets of that thin cheap paper made from rags. (These latter items surprised me a little: not all parish priests are able to write and a few cannot even read, learning long passages of Holy Scripture by rote.) In one corner, a ladder rose to the second storey and a single window at the front of the house, at present unshuttered, let in a shaft of pale spring sunlight. An open fire in the centre of the room was straddled by a meat-stand from which hung a pot of the saintly Ellen's stew.

The priest invited me to sit down by pulling one of the stools from beneath the table and waving a somewhat grimy hand towards it. As though suddenly conscious of the condition of his nails, he said apologetically, 'I've been digging in the vegetable plot this morning. My housekeeper likes a few onions with the rabbit. And now, sir, in what way can I help you?'

I explained as briefly as I could the fears of the Godsloves, my involvement in their story (omitting, of course, the real reason for my coming to London) and my hope that he might be able to shed some light on the subject. But I could tell it was a lost cause by the expression of bewilderment on his face; and when he requested me to repeat the tale again, I guessed he could tell me nothing I did not already know.

When I had finished my account for the second time, he passed a hand across his brow, leaving a streak of mud behind, then ruffled the thick fringe of brown curly hair around his tonsure.

'A most extraordinary story,' he said finally, frowning. 'I agree that the deaths of Martin and Charity Godslove were terrible tragedies, and now it seems that Mistress Sybilla has also been hurt. Dear me! Yes, I can see why they might begin to think that the family is cursed. That God has turned His face from them. But that someone is deliberately setting out to do them harm! No, no! I can't and won't believe it. They are a most respected family, well liked in the neighbourhood, giving their mite to charity. Who would wish to eliminate them all? And for what reason? Even if one of them had an enemy, why would that person wish to kill the siblings as well? It doesn't make sense. And who is this Reynold Makepeace you mention? A landlord, you say, of an inn in Bucklersbury, killed two years ago in a tavern brawl? But what has he to do with the Godsloves? Forgive me! I expect I'm being very slow.'

'Not at all,' I assured him. 'It's a most complicated family. Landlord Makepeace and his brother were – are, in the case of Julian – stepbrothers to the elder sisters and Lawyer Godslove, half-brothers to the younger pair, Celia and her now dead brother, Martin. Widow Makepeace was Morgan Godslove's second wife.'

The priest gave his head a shake as though to clear it. 'Dear me! Dear me!' he exclaimed again. It seemed to be a favourite phrase. 'I had no idea. I'd heard of the affair at the Voyager. Word gets around, but it was all such a long time ago—'

'Two years,' I put in, and he nodded.

'A long while ago, as I said. These things happen, unfortunately. Young men get drunk and do stupid things. Wicked things. The times are growing more lawless – and likely to get worse now that King Edward's restraining hand has gone. The saints alone know what's to become of us all! The Woodvilles . . . ! But that's neither here nor there. So, the Godsloves reckon that this Landlord Makepeace was the first to die?' His face creased with the effort of remembrance. 'Two years . . . That must have been the same year that Mistress Clemency was taken ill.'

'It was not long after, I believe. At the time, no one made any connection between the two events, only later when the sister, Charity, died from eating mushrooms. And again, some months afterwards when the half-brother, Martin Godslove, was set upon by footpads and killed.'

'Oh, I remember that.' Father Berowne once more rubbed his forehead. 'A terrible thing to have happened. But there again, such murders occur almost nightly. It's what I was saying just now, law and order are breaking down. It's not at all like it was when I was a boy.'

It never is in my experience. If I had a silver penny for every time someone has lamented to me that things aren't what they used to be, I reckon I'd be a rich man. A very rich man.

I regarded the priest curiously. 'Where do you come from?' I asked. 'I'd swear there's some Irish in your voice. I can hear it every once in a while.'

My companion smiled, a sweet, twinkling smile that reached his eyes even quicker than his lips.

'Your hearing must be very acute,' he said. 'I can detect traces of it, myself, now and then, although I've never been there in my life. But my father came from the southern tip of Ireland, around Waterford. Do you know it?'

I shook my head. 'Like you, I've never been there, but it's the part of that country Bristol trades with the most, Waterford being the nearest Irish port of any size. The slavers, I fancy, use the smaller coves and inlets, not wishing to attract attention to their illegal cargoes.'

'Ah, yes.' He regarded me straitly, the smile no longer in evidence. 'I've heard that the people of Bristol still fuel that dreadful trade with their unwanted relatives and enemies, even though it was banned by the Church many centuries ago.'

His voice was suddenly so stern that I felt bound to reiterate the fact that I was born in Wells and was a Bristolian only by adoption. It surprised me how much I wanted the approbation of this simple, godly man. Even Hercules, who had been lying quietly at my feet, raised his head from his paws and – or so it seemed – stared at me reproachfully.

I must have sounded even more defensive than I felt, for my companion made haste to disclaim, 'No, no! Dear me! I was not implying that you, my son – no, indeed – that you are – were – have been – in any way involved. Forgive me! I . . .'

It was my turn to reassure him that he had in no sort given

offence; and as I had no wish for him to discover that I had, in the past, come to know at least one of the slavers quite well, I steered our conversation back into less troubled waters.

'That trace of Irishness in your tone comes, then, from hearing your father speak when you were a child?'

He nodded, eager and willing to follow my lead. 'Yes, that must be it, although few people detect it as quickly as you, if at all.'

'It comes from listening to the many Irish sailors around the Bristol docks,' I said and got to my feet. 'Thank you for your time, Sir Berowne. I won't trouble you any further.'

'No, no! Dear me!' He also jumped to his feet. 'You can't go without some refreshment. What am I thinking of? Sit down again, please.' He went to the corner cupboard and produced a flask and two beakers. 'Some of last year's elderflower wine. I make it myself and this was a particularly fine brew. And while we drink, tell me again if you please about your good self. You say you are a solver of mysteries and have had some successes in the past. I should like to hear about them if it wouldn't bore you too much.'

It would take a far more modest person than myself to resist such a flattering offer, so for the next hour, against a background of Hercules's wheezing snores, I recounted some of my more successful exploits while the priest and I gradually emptied the flask of its contents. Once I had to go outside and relieve my bursting bladder and twice the priest was forced to do the same; and finally we went together, arm in arm like two old comrades, to play the schoolboy game of who could piss higher against the wall. After which, there seemed nothing else to do but wish my new found friend goodbye, whistle up my dog and wend my unsteady way back to the Arbour.

What Adela's reaction to my drunken state would have been, had I been able to remain upright, I never learned, as almost immediately I was violently sick and collapsed into unconsciousness and delirium. After that, I was vaguely aware, on various occasions, of people coming and going, of anxious voices, of things being forced down my throat, of my wife's frightened face hovering above me, of the doctor's ponderous tones. But for the most part I inhabited an insane world of my own peopled by distorted images and horrors that made me sweat with terror; a place where the boiling seas were blood red and the earth gave up its ghosts and my heart thumped nearly out of my body; where my long dead mother waved a bony finger and warned me I was damned unless I renounced my profligate way of life and became a true believer. It seemed to go on for ever . . .

And then, quite suddenly, one morning, I awoke to the early sun rimming the shuttered window, to a feeling of light-headed calm and peace and the sight of Adela's drawn face beside me on the pillow. I knew at once that I had been ill. I also knew that now I was better.

It took me a minute or two longer to work out where I was and how I got to be there, but in a much shorter time than I would have thought possible, clarity and memory had returned and I could recollect everything that had led up to the moment of my return to the Arbour. The probable cause of my illness remained a mystery until I remembered the sour-tasting ale at the Voyager. And I had been foolish enough to order a second cup, some of which, at least, I had drunk. The smell of it, the rancid taste of it were once again in my throat and nostrils, and I felt my stomach heave in protest . . .

'Roger?' It was Adela's voice. She was awake, propped on one elbow and staring at me in disbelief and joy. 'You're better.'

I smiled weakly at her. 'How long have I been like this?' I asked. 'What day is it?'

'Tuesday,' she said, then burst into tears. 'We thought you were going to die.' She smothered my face in watery kisses.

'Tuesday?' I demanded incredulously. 'Are you telling me I've been ill for *six days*?'

She nodded, lying down again and pressing her head into my shoulder. 'We've all been so worried. Poor Father Berowne has called nearly every day. Apparently you had both been drinking his elderflower wine just before you returned here, and he's desperately afraid that it might have been the cause. Although he himself has suffered no ill effects, he fears he might have made it too strong for someone not accustomed to it.'

'Nonsense!' I declared. 'It was the rotten ale at the Voyager.'

And I told her what I had done and also what I had discovered the preceding Wednesday afternoon. I was amazed at how much the telling took the virtue out of me and how tired I felt afterwards. I was as weak as a kitten.

'Better now?' enquired a voice in my left ear, and there was Adam peering at me over the edge of the mattress. He climbed the small flight of steps at the side of the bed and, ignoring his mother's remonstrations, wriggled in beside me. He stroked my face. 'You're better,' he assured me firmly.

'Thank you, sweetheart.' I put an arm around him.

He eyed me, solemn as a little owl. '"Sweetheart" is for girls,' he said sternly. I apologized, but noted that he didn't seem to mind being cuddled.

A moment or two later, having been woken by the sound of our voices, Elizabeth and Nicholas bounced into the room. (Adela had obviously not thought it worthwhile to keep the intervening door locked during my indisposition.) They were delighted that I was my normal self again, and were the first of a stream of visitors who arrived at my bedside throughout the day with their congratulations on my recovery. I was desperate for sleep, but everyone wanted to talk. Clemency and Celia were anxious to share their fear that this might have been another attempt on a family member's life and refused to be altogether convinced by my argument that I could hardly be counted as a Godslove or be reassured that I was correct about the cause of my sickness. Sybilla also paid me a visit, but was less interested in my condition than in describing her own recent sufferings which, according to her, had been many and varied. Next, the housekeeper made a brief appearance to inform me that whatever I fancied to tempt my appetite would be prepared by her own fair hands (the kitchen maids being a couple of fools who could be trusted with only the most basic of recipes). And both the priest and doctor called, the former still anxious for confirmation that I held his elderflower wine in no way to blame for what had happened, the latter ostensibly to see how his patient fared, but in reality, I suspected, to catch a glimpse of Celia and snatch a clandestine word with her if at all possible. By the time Oswald returned from Westminster and the law courts in the late afternoon, I was feeling like one of my daughter's rag dolls after Hercules had given it a mauling.

At least with Oswald I was able have a rational conversation and glean whatever news there was to be had from the outside world.

'Has the duke arrived yet?' My companion shook his head. 'Is there any word of him? Or from him?'

Oswald pursed his lips. 'The rumour in the city – and it's a pretty strong one – is that His Grace will reach Northampton sometime today, where he is due to meet up with the royal party travelling across country from the Welsh border.' He stroked his chin. 'What is certain is that a few days ago, Sir Richard Grey left the capital for Wales with a train of some thousands strong to join his uncle and half-brother before they set out on their journey.'

'Why? Surely the king and Earl Rivers have enough men stationed at Ludlow to supply a sufficient retinue for the purpose of a peaceful entry into London?'

The lawyer chewed a thumbnail. 'One would have thought so. But it would seem the queen and members of the Woodville family think otherwise.'

I detected the note of unease in his voice. 'What do you believe is the reason?'

Oswald laughed and got up from the bed, where he had been sitting. 'Oh, I try not to have opinions. Well, my dear fellow, your first week with us has been unfortunate. I suppose you had no time, in the few hours before you were struck down, to discover anything of significance? No, obviously not. But I hope this unhappy episode hasn't changed your mind about helping us. Not for my sake, you understand. But it would bring a certain measure of peace of mind to my sisters. For my own part, I still remain somewhat unconvinced by this theory of a mysterious enemy waiting to strike us all down.' He smiled in his irritatingly superior way. 'And now I'll leave you to get some rest. I'm sure you need it.'

He was right, and I slept, on and off, for the remainder of the day and all of the night. But my powers of recuperation have always been remarkable, thanks in the main to my generally good health and the strength of my body. By the following evening, the last day of April, I was almost myself again and left our bedchamber to join the family for supper.

It was a splendid meal of mutton stewed in red wine vinegar flavoured with cinnamon and saffron, chopped parsley and onions, and followed by a curd tart with cream. It was all washed down with a pale amber-coloured wine whose name I refused to ask for fear of displaying my total ignorance, but whose soft, warm glow spread throughout my body and completed my recovery. When I finally laid down my spoon and drained my cup, I felt ready for anything.

I turned to Oswald, cutting across some desultory small talk between the three sisters (Sybilla was now well enough to leave her sickbed) and said abruptly, 'Before I was taken ill, Adela was telling me about a man who wishes to buy this house from you; a man who, for some reason, feels he has a right to it. Jollifant? Was that the name?'

The lawyer laughed dismissively. 'Oh, Adrian Jollifant! Yes, there is such a man. This house belonged to his father – or grandfather, I forget which – many years ago, but the family were forced to sell it. (We bought it, I think, from the man who bought it from them.) Now that the Jollifants are prospering again, Adrian wants it back and seems to think that I am under some obligation to oblige him. He is, of course, a fool with no knowledge of the law. But if, my dear Roger, you're thinking that he is behind these attacks on us – if deliberate attacks they really are – forget him. I told you, the man's a fool and has neither the wits nor the strength of purpose to sustain such a campaign.'

'Nevertheless, I should like to see and speak with him,' I said. I could not share Oswald's slightly contemptuous view of humanity, nor believe, as he so patently did, that the world was peopled entirely by idiots. 'If you know where he lives, I should be grateful if you could put me in the way of meeting him.'

'Nothing easier,' Oswald replied with a shrug. 'Adrian Jollifant has a silversmith's shop in Cheapside, close to St Paul's. If you care to accompany me tomorrow morning on my way to Chancery Lane, I'll point it out to you.' He gave a faint smile. 'I'm certain Clemency won't mind if you borrow her horse, Old Diggory. He's a quiet enough animal and won't play you any tricks.'

How Oswald had divined my uneasiness around horses I had no means of knowing, unless Adela had been revealing family secrets during my illness. But somehow I didn't think she would. I decided that my host's intuition, based on powers of observation, was greater than I had given him credit for.

'Thank you. I should be grateful if you would do that,' I answered politely.

He nodded and rose from the table. 'Now, if you will all excuse me, I have some work to do; case notes to look over. I shall see you then, Roger, at breakfast. I like to leave the house as soon as it's light.'

In the event, it was a good hour after sun-up before we passed through the Bishop's Gate. For this, the May Day crowds streaming out into the countryside to bring in branches of may and to dance barefoot through the grass were largely to blame. Strangers, even those on horseback, had to be stopped and kissed and garlanded with daisy chains before being allowed to go any further. The recent gloom following King Edward's death seemed to have vanished with the official arrival of spring. Oswald and I, he on his showy grey mare and I on Clemency's quiet Old Diggory, finally forced our way into the city against the outgoing tide of merry-makers, only to find ourselves, at the bottom of Bishop's Gate Street, caught up in another crowd making its way to Cornhill to dance round the maypole, which had been set up overnight. By the time we reached the Great Conduit, I was unsurprised to find my companion growing tetchy and ready to curse anyone who crossed his path.

I felt sorry, therefore, for the young apprentice who shot out of a goldsmith's shop in Cheapside and grabbed at Oswald's bridle. Before Oswald could snap at him, however, the boy gasped, 'Oh please, sir! I can see you're a lawyer by your robes. My master says will you come and speak to him and tell him what it all portends?'

'What it all portends, boy? What are you talking about?'

The apprentice's face fell ludicrously. 'Haven't you heard the news then, sir?' He turned to the old man who had hobbled out after him, leaning heavily on a stick. 'The lawyer hasn't heard anything, master.'

The goldsmith seemed bemused. 'Not heard anything? Why they've been crying it ever since midnight, or the early hours at the very least. As soon as possible, anyway, after the lord mayor and members of the great council received the news. They say the duke sent his messenger express, and that the poor man's horse was nearly dead under him when he finally arrived.'

'The duke?' I queried sharply.

'His Grace of Gloucester.'

'Where is His Grace?'

'Why, Northampton with the young king, so the crier said, and as I understand it, not like to leave there for maybe a day or so yet.' The old man continued to look troubled. 'What does it mean, sir, this arrest of Lord Rivers and Sir Richard Grey?'

'There was a third man mentioned, too, master,' the apprentice cut in. 'Vaughan, I think his name is.'

Oswald frowned. 'Sir Thomas Vaughan? Probably. He's a Woodville kinsman.' Suddenly, we could hear a bell ringing in the distance and the upraised voice of the crier. He turned to me. 'We'd better get on to Paul's Cross and see what we can find out. My good sir!' He addressed the goldsmith who was clutching at his arm. 'Kindly unhand me! I know no more than you do. Indeed, less.' And with a jerk on the rein, he set the mare in motion once again.

But the crowds around Paul's Cross were dense, and by the time we had pushed the horses through to a position of vantage, the crier had finished. Oswald was just looking around for someone he could question, when a man wearing the striped gown of a fellow lawyer came hurrying out of St Paul's churchyard – the cloisters were a favourite business place for the legal fraternity – and hailed him.

'Godslove! In a happy hour!'

Oswald dismounted, so I did the same, taking the opportunity to soothe Old Diggory, who was displaying distinct signs of unease. The newcomer indicated that we should follow him and led us back among the gravestones where it was quieter.

'I'm glad I caught you, Oswald,' he said. 'Are you in court today?'

'I shall be at Westminster after dinner, certainly. For the present, I'm in chambers. But never mind that. What in God's name is—'

'I just wanted to warn you,' his friend broke in, 'to expect trouble in Westminster. Delays getting through. The place is in chaos.'

'Chaos? Why?'

'My dear fellow, you can barely move. Carts and chests and crates all over the road.' He encountered Oswald's and my blank stare and went on impatiently, as though it were something we ought to know, 'The queen – queen dowager – is going into sanctuary, taking the princesses and the little Duke of York with her. Moreover, she's obviously anticipating a long stay. Workmen have had to knock down a part of the sanctuary wall to get all her household goods inside. You've never seen such stuff! Furniture, coffers full of clothes, chests of household linen, not to mention all the belongings of her attendants and the younger princesses' nurses. And I've heard on good authority that Dorset has been sent to the Tower to grab the remainder of the royal treasure. Edward Woodville's got the other half, and he's put to sea.'

'What in the name of all the saints is going on?' Oswald demanded, his sense of order and propriety outraged. The world was being stood on its head. 'And what's all this about Rivers, Grey and Vaughan being arrested at Northampton? I thought the idea was that the king's party and Gloucester should meet up there and then enter London all together.'

The other lawyer shrugged. 'That was the proposal as I heard it. But obviously something went wrong. My lord Gloucester must have suspected treason. A plot of some kind by the Woodvilles to take him prisoner? A threat to his life? Queen Elizabeth's flight into sanctuary could indicate something of the kind. Maybe she and Dorset are expecting to be arrested.'

I said nothing, merely stroking Old Diggory's nose, but all the while trying in my own mind to assess the possible danger in which Duke Richard now stood. Or, at least, thought he stood. Relations between him and the queen dowager's family had always been strained, one of the reasons he had stayed in his northern territories, visiting London as seldom

as possible. And he had made little secret of the fact that he
held their influence responsible for the late king's decision,
five years previously, to sign the Duke of Clarence's death
warrant. Somehow I doubted he would ever forgive them for
that, and they must know it. But would they seriously plot
either his downfall or his murder? Wouldn't they be too afraid
of the people's reaction if any harm came to Richard of
Gloucester? On the other hand, many of the Woodvilles had
proved themselves ruthless and grasping in the past, while
the queen dowager's rush for sanctuary could easily be interpreted as the action of a woman with guilty knowledge. But
there again, it could just as easily be interpreted as the action
of a frightened woman. We should have to wait upon events.

I touched Oswald on the shoulder. 'If you'll tell me where
this silversmith's shop is,' I said, 'I'll leave you now. I doubt
there's much more to be learned at present. We'll have to
contain our souls in patience until the king and duke arrive
from Northampton. We may learn more then, I suppose.'

Oswald nodded, looking gravely portentous. I dreaded
supper that evening. The women would be hanging on his
every word while he expounded his theories. Nevertheless,
as I rode back along Cheapside, I had to own to a sense of
foreboding. I wasn't sure why, but realized that the feeling
had begun two weeks ago, when I had first heard the news
of King Edward's death. I told myself that I had been ill;
that this was surely the cause of such womanish vapours,
but even so, I found it hard to dispel my gloomy thoughts.

The early morning sunshine had vanished and a thin wind,
sharp as a knife, was blowing between the overhanging eaves
of the houses. People were returning from the countryside,
bringing their branches and garlands of may with them, but
they seemed to have lost their earlier exuberance, slouching
wearily along, dragging their feet.

I shivered suddenly, for no apparent reason.

NINE

Oswald had pointed out a shop on the corner of Foster Lane and Cheapside where the latter divided, the left-hand fork becoming Paternoster Row and the right running into the Shambles. In spite of its closeness to the butchers' stalls and slaughterhouses, with their accompanying stench of blood and rotting entrails, the silversmith's seemed to be prosperous enough and attracting a high-class trade. It made me glad that I had followed Adela's advice and worn one of the two new suits of clothes provided by Richard of Gloucester's bounty for my journey to France the preceding autumn. Consequently, having tied the horse to a nearby post, I entered the shop confident that I looked my best in brown woollen hose, a pale green tunic adorned with silver-gilt buttons and a brown velvet hat sporting a fake jewel on its upturned brim.

'I've never seen you so smart,' my wife had said admiringly as I stood in the middle of our bedchamber earlier that morning while she had made final adjustments to the set of the tunic across my broad shoulders. But my sympathies had been with Elizabeth and Nicholas, convulsed by silent laughter, and with Adam who, upon coming into the room, had asked where his father was.

The ground floor of the three-storey building was part shop, for the display of finished goods, and part workshop, where the apprentices worked the bellows and stoked the furnace and the master craftsman, with his two assistants, fashioned the molten silver into cups and crucifixes, bracelets and necklaces, rings and buttons and all the other products of the silversmith's art. They glanced up briefly as I entered, but did not pause to acknowledge me, leaving that to the well-dressed gentleman seated just inside the door, who rose to greet me with a large, ham-like hand and an ingratiating smile.

'My dear sir! And what may I interest you in on this fine

Mayday morning? Something for your lady, perhaps? A trinket, a token of your affection? This ring, maybe, in the shape of two clasped hands?'

I had no difficulty in recognizing Adrian Jollifant from Adela's description of him; solidly built without being fat, fair hair turning grey, blue eyes in a round face and exuding an air of wealth and self-consequence that would not have been out of place in some of the highest in the land.

He grew impatient. 'Well sir, and what will it be?' Then he changed his tune. 'Of course, I understand. You are a stranger to London. You stand amazed at the quality and variety of my goods. Take your time! Take your time! I can wait.'

The man was a pompous idiot, that was plain, but one, I had no doubt, who could turn nasty if things did not go his way. I had met his sort before and always found them unpleasant characters. The trouble was that, in my usual careless fashion, I had failed to work out beforehand exactly how I should approach him. His desire to buy the Arbour was not, strictly speaking, my business, and I could hardly ask him outright if he had murderous inclinations towards the Godsloves. But if he did, I might only make matters worse for them by claiming to be acting on their behalf. I cursed myself, as I had so often done in the past, for my lack of forethought.

I decided to play the innocent. As he had already decided that I was not a Londoner – my clothes could not be quite as fashionable as I had thought them – my role would be the country bumpkin, overawed by everything about me. I let my jaw drop a little and exaggerated my West Country accent.

'I . . . I wanted to buy summat fer my wife, zir, and was told to come here as you had the best goods in Cheapside. But . . . I dunno. I don' think I could manage anything I can see here.'

Master Jollifant preened himself. 'Oh, I don't know. I'm sure if we try hard enough, we can find something within your means.' The condescending bastard! 'May I ask who recommended me?' He smirked. 'It could be almost anyone, I suppose.'

'Oh yes. Quite a number of people mentioned your name,' I said, taking my cue from him. 'That little ring you showed me, 'tis pretty now. How much would you be askin' fer it?'

He named a price, obviously expecting me to reject it out of hand, and looked disconcerted when I paid up without demur. (My family and I had lived free at the Arbour for the past sennight, and I had had a profitable few weeks before my return to Bristol, so I was well able to afford it.) While he packed the ring into a small wooden box for me, I continued to stare reverently about me, trying to appear suitably impressed.

'I can see you're a gen'leman of means, zir,' I remarked in a hushed whisper. 'You mun live in a gert big house, I reckon.'

Immediately, an expression of keen dissatisfaction distorted his features. 'As a matter of fact I don't,' he snapped. For a moment I could see him struggling against the indiscretion of confiding in a stranger, but in the end indignation and anger won. 'I ought to, but no!' He smacked the little box down on the counter in front of me and continued, 'My old family home has been filched from me by an unprincipled rogue of a lawyer.'

'Indeed?' I forced myself to appear goggle-eyed with interest. 'How did he come to steal it from you, zir?'

'We-ell!' The silversmith had the grace to look momentarily embarrassed before venom and spite took over, plunging him into a story of double-dealing and deliberate obstruction which had only the smallest relation to the truth. I could see that he was obsessed by his grievance to a dangerous degree; that long nurturing had turned it from a mild irritation into what he deemed to be a major injustice. But would he do murder, and multiple murder at that, to get his own way? The fanatical gleam in his eyes and the vicious thinning of his lips suggested that he might.

Clutching the ring in its little box, I left the shop, promising to call again. I was just about to untether Old Diggory, at the same time watching the turmoil that is Cheapside on a busy spring morning without really taking any of it in, when someone spoke my name and a hand was laid on my arm.

'Roger? Is it really you after all these years?'

I turned quickly to find myself confronting a fashionably dressed woman whose painted face was considerably more raddled than on either of the two previous occasions when our paths had crossed. For a moment I was nonplussed, then recognition dawned.

'Mistress Napier,' I said with a polite bow. 'As lovely as ever.'

She flushed. 'You always did have a cruel tongue, Roger. I'm fully aware that time has not dealt kindly with me. You, on the other hand, appear to be as handsome and certainly more prosperous than heretofore.'

'Appearances can be deceptive,' I told her. 'And how is Master Napier faring nowadays?'

She gave a short bark of mirthless laughter. 'Gregory? Oh, he's been in his grave these three years past, praise be!' The thin, carmined lips twisted into a smile. 'The house in Paternoster Row is all mine now, as is the shop. With a coronation in the offing, I'm expecting to do extremely well in the next month or two.' The sudden pealing of bells from St Paul's and half a dozen other nearby churches drowned out her voice for several moments, but as soon as she was able to make herself heard again, she said, 'It's dinnertime. Why not come and share mine? There's a stable around the corner where you can take your horse.'

I hesitated for perhaps a second or two, but then agreed. Paternoster Row was near at hand, whereas to ride back to the Arbour would take some time. She smiled, laying long-nailed fingers on my proffered arm.

I had first met Ginèvre Napier eight years earlier while investigating the mysterious disappearance of two children from their home in Totnes, in Devon, and had encountered her again three years later while enquiring into a case of apparent murder by a cousin of the late King Edward's mistress, Jane Shore. I had not much liked her then, nor did I now, but it occurred to me that she might know something about Adrian Jollifant that could be useful.

The parlour of the house in Paternoster Row was much as I remembered it. (In fact I was surprised at just how much I could remember.) The ceiling beams, once aglow

with red and gold paint, were faded now and the wall tapestries had lost their pristine freshness. But the armchairs and
the table, fashioned from the finest oak, and the corner
cupboard, with its opulent display of gold and silver, were
still the same, as was the candelabra with its many tinkling
filigree pendants. Ginèvre waved me to a chair and told one
of the servants to bring dinner as quickly as possible.

'I don't know about you, but I'm starving,' she murmured,
seating herself opposite me. Her foot brushed against one of
mine under the table. I conquered the urge to withdraw it
and returned her smile, although half-heartedly. She then
utterly discomposed me by laughing out loud and saying,
'All right, Roger, let's dispose of the pretence that you like
me and you can tell me exactly why you accepted my invitation to dinner.'

When I had stumbled through a few disclaimers at this
devastatingly forthright speech – disclaimers which she
neither believed nor wanted – I told her as briefly as possible
what I was doing in London, including the reason for my
being there in the first place, and finished by asking her what
she knew of Adrian Jollifant.

Ginèvre considered this while the maid was serving us
with the first course, a shrimp soup flavoured with garlic,
and eventually gave her measured response to the question.

'He's a man with an obsession,' she said, 'but I imagine
a smart young fellow like you has already worked that out
for himself. Would he be capable of murdering an entire
family in order to satisfy that obsession? Then my answer
to that would have to be yes, I think he probably might well
be.' She drank some soup, her expression thoughtful. 'A few
years ago,' she went on, 'when his first wife died unexpectedly, there was a good deal of whispering among the other
residents of the Cheap that she had died very opportunely,
it being well known that Adrian and a certain sprightly young
widow who lived in Muggle Street – Monkswell Street, if
you prefer its proper name – were more than nodding acquaintances. There was no proof, mind you, that these rumours
were anything more than malicious gossip, but it's true that
his mourning was of the briefest. A little more than three
months after the first Mistress Jollifant's death, the second

was queening it around the shop and decking herself out in the best wares that it had to offer.' The thin, painted lips sneered. 'I've never seen a woman so loaded down with necklaces and other ornaments. A silly creature with no taste; no idea of when enough is enough.'

I finished my soup and leant back in my chair. 'That was delicious,' I complimented her. 'You have an excellent cook. But returning to Master Jollifant, I was told that he is not the owner of the shop; that it belongs to his father who has retired.'

Ginèvre nodded, laying down her spoon and leaving at least half the soup in the bowl, too affectedly ladylike to drink it all.

'Yes,' she agreed, 'but that's another cause for talk. The old man is rarely, if ever, seen. It is presumed that he lives on the top floor of the house, but no one knows for certain. At one time, he was a popular and well-known figure around Cheapside, even after he retired.' She rang a little silver bell and the maidservant reappeared to clear the dirty dishes before bringing in the next course, braised veal in a white wine sauce. (If this had originally been intended as a meal for one, it was difficult to understand why my hostess was not as fat as a sow instead of the near emaciated figure she presented.) 'But of late, there has been no sighting of him, not even at the top floor window overlooking the street.'

I tucked into my veal with relish. 'So, what do people think has happened to the old man?' I asked.

Ginèvre shrugged. 'They don't know. There's gossip, of course, but then there always is. Some fools whisper that he's been done away with, but what would be the point of that? If Adrian wants to be master of the shop, he needs it to be known that his father is dead. There could be no point in doing things in secret.'

I agreed. 'And what do you think?'

She laughed. 'Me? Oh, I mind my own business.'

'But you must have an opinion,' I pressed her.

'I think the explanation is probably much simpler. I think the old man is ill, confined to bed. Adrian Jollifant has never encouraged his neighbours to probe into his affairs, which he keeps to himself – with one exception!'

'The fact that he believes he has a right to the Arbour?'

'Yes. This house, which you tell me now belongs to these relatives of your wife, that is his abiding grievance. Obsession is perhaps the better word, as I said. He is not rational on the subject. He speaks as though it has somehow been stolen from him instead of being the present owners' by legal purchase.'

I broke a hunk off the fine white loaf placed in the middle of the table and began mopping up my gravy. 'And this is a man,' I said thickly without waiting to empty my mouth, 'whom his neighbours believe might have killed his first wife? I agree with you about his father. To do away with him and not produce a body would be to defeat his object. Nevertheless, people seem to believe Master Jollifant capable of murder.'

Ginèvre rang the bell again. This time, when the dirty plates had been removed, wine and dishes of nuts, raisins and last autumn's little sweet apples were placed before us.

'I suppose you could say that almost anyone is capable of murder given the right circumstances,' she answered judiciously, pouring wine into two fine glass goblets. (The goldsmith's shop was certainly thriving as well as it had done in her late husband's day. But then, I had always thought her a shrewd woman with a clever head on her shoulders.) 'But if you want my own opinion, I would say yes, I think Adrian Jollifant more capable of it than most.'

'Because of this obsession of his?'

'Oh, certainly. Anyone with such an overwhelming belief that something belongs to him by rights and who feels himself robbed of those rights, is irrational enough to believe he is justified in using any means at his disposal to achieve his ends.'

I drank my wine in silence, mulling over what Ginèvre had said. It made sense. But whether it meant that the silver-smith actually had resorted to killing members of the Godslove family one by one was a different matter. Why would he bother murdering Reynold Makepeace, who had no interest in the Arbour and had never lived there? But for that one fact, I might have been inclined to believe that I had found my killer. In the circumstances, however, I could not be sure and I decided that it was time for me to pay another visit to Bucklersbury to see if Julian Makepeace had returned from his visit to Southampton.

As soon as I decently could, therefore, I thanked Ginèvre for an excellent dinner and excused myself on the grounds of having a commission to execute for Adela.

'And the present from Master Jollifant's shop?' she queried with a lift of her plucked eyebrows, nodding towards the little box which I had placed on the table beside me. 'Something to keep your wife sweet and allay her suspicions still further?' She smiled a fraction too widely, and I noticed for the first time that one of her front lower teeth was missing while another was rotten and black. 'Does she have real cause for her misgivings, Roger? During the two brief periods of our former acquaintance, I always felt that you might prove to be an unreliable husband. And, believe me, I know what I'm talking about having been married to Gregory.'

I felt the colour flood my face and silently cursed this tell-tale sign. But I bluffed it out. I was not admitting Ginèvre Napier any further into my confidence. I had been a fool to tell her as much as I had done already.

'Adela and I love one another,' I said flatly, rising to my feet, but perfectly aware, as my hostess was herself, that this was no answer to her question.

She accepted it, however, as all she was likely to get and rang the bell yet again for the maid to bring me my hat. But I wasn't to escape that easily, and when I had put the hat on, she came to stand close to me, pretending to adjust it. I could smell the wine on her breath and felt the slight pressure of her thighs against mine. But thankfully she did not attract me, and I could see by the suddenly hostile glint in her eyes that she knew it.

'Well, if I can be of any further service to you, my dear,' she said coldly, stepping back and extending her hand, 'please don't hesitate to call on me, either here or at the shop.' She was not an easy woman to discourage. 'Promise!'

I promised, gallantly kissing her proffered hand, but I gave a long sigh of relief once I stood outside in Paternoster Row and heard her door close behind me. I did not like Ginèvre Napier, but neither could I regret the meeting. I had learned some valuable information concerning one of my suspects that I probably could not have obtained any other way.

I realized that I was feeling rather dizzy: my illness had taken its toll and I was not yet as fit as I thought myself. Nevertheless, I refused to give in to such weakness. I resolutely straightened my shoulders, fetched Old Diggory, now watered and fed at my expense, made my way back along Cheapside as far as the Great Conduit and turned into Bucklersbury. Mid-morning trading was at its height, carts rattling over the cobbles, street traders bawling their wares, blue-coated apprentices trying – sometimes physically – to entice passers-by into their masters' shops, women, baskets on their arms, pausing to chat with friends and acquaintances. It was London at its busiest, and yet, this particular noonday, there was something subdued about everyone's demeanour. Conversation was earnest and there were no sudden bursts of laughter, no light-hearted banter, no cheery waving and shouting from one side of the street to the other. The news from Northampton was plainly the main topic of discussion and people's looks were grave, even bewildered, as they tried to make sense of it.

I knocked on the door of Julian Makepeace's shop, having once more tied up the horse, and it was answered by the same buxom young creature as before. This time, however, she appeared wider awake and there was a sparkle in her eyes that had not been there previously. I guessed I was in luck: the apothecary had returned.

'Oh, it's you,' she smiled. 'I wondered if you'd come back. I've told the master about you. Wait there and I'll go and tell him you're here.'

After a few moments' delay, the rustle of an apothecary's gown heralded Julian Makepeace's arrival and the man himself stood before me. I should have known him anywhere for Reynold's brother. Indeed, although I judged him a year or so younger, he was the identical stocky build, had the same bright hazel eyes and thinning brown hair and exuded a similar warmth and friendliness that reached out to embrace all the world.

'Master Chapman?' He held out his hand. 'Naomi told me you had called and that your visit had something to do with

my brother's death.' He frowned, his face clouding over. 'Or
did she misunderstand?' He smiled tenderly. 'A sweet soul,
but not the brightest of girls.'

'No,' I said. 'She understood me well enough. May I come
in and explain?'

'Yes, of course you may.' He held the door open for me
to pass inside. 'Pardon me saying so, but you don't look too
well.' He ushered me through the shop and into a private
parlour behind, indicating a chair. 'Sit there, sir, while I
prepare you a reviving draught.' And he hurried away on his
mission of mercy, returning after a short space of time with
a glass of some green liquid in his hand. 'Drink this,' he
ordered. 'It should refresh you.'

It tasted strongly of mint, a flavour I am not partial to,
but it did the trick. Within a few moments I was able to sit
up straight and hand back the glass with a smile.

'A remarkable concoction,' I said. 'What was in it? Apart,
of course, from mint?'

Julian Makepeace laughed. 'Come, Master Chapman! You
don't expect a man to give away all his trade secrets, do
you? Now, what did you want to see me about? Something
to do with my brother's death, I gather. But that was two
years ago and there was no secret about it. A taproom brawl
at the Voyager, and my poor Reynold was unfortunate enough
to be caught in the middle of it.'

'Could you – would you – be kind enough to tell me
exactly what happened? If you'll bear with me, I'll explain
my reason for asking later.'

The apothecary hesitated for a moment, then shrugged.
'Why not? There was nothing extraordinary in it. It's what I
said, a most unlucky accident.' He got up and went to the
door, calling to his housekeeper to bring a jug of ale and
two beakers before coming back and resuming his seat
again. 'During the past few years, this whole area around
Bucklersbury has, most unhappily, become far seedier than
it used to be. The tenements in the building known as the
Old Barge, at the Walbrook end of the street, have fallen into
the hands of a rougher kind of tenant as former inhabitants
have died off and the rooms been re-let. Moreover, word of
the Voyager's reputation for good food and ale spread, and

in a way Reynold's success as a landlord contributed to his downfall. Foreign sailors, dockers, began walking up from the wharves to sample what he had to offer and bringing their uncouth habits with them. There was, of course, nothing my brother could do about it. A hostelry is there for everyone's enjoyment and trade was certainly brisk. Apart from anything else, Reynold couldn't afford to turn away the custom.'

At this point, the young girl called Naomi entered with our ale and beakers on a tray. She gave me a provocative wink which she made no attempt to conceal, but Julian Makepeace only smiled indulgently and patted her rump with a loving hand, telling her she was a minx and sending her on her way. As he poured the ale, I asked, 'What happened to Landlord Makepeace's wife? I seem to remember that when I first met him, five years back, he was married.'

Julian handed me a beaker. 'You're quite right, but my sister-in-law died of the plague one summer . . . oh . . . I couldn't say exactly when. I'm only thankful she didn't live to know of my brother's miserable end. Now, where was I?'

I sipped my excellent ale. 'You were saying that the customers of the Voyager were not what they had once been.'

'Yes. There's not much more to tell. There had been a fight or two in the taproom on various occasions between some of the foreigners and the locals, but only fisticuffs, a few knocks and blows. And if you knew Reynold at all well, you'd know that he wouldn't stand for a disorderly house. He and his tapster soon broke up such brawls with a few well-placed blows of their own. But the evening he died, it was different. A couple of Genoese sailors, newcomers to the Voyager, drew knives on one another. The quarrel grew nasty, terrifying such women as were present, and Reynold decided he must stop the fight before anyone was seriously hurt. Foolishly, he sent the tapster to summon the Watch while he tried single-handedly to prevent murder being done.' Julian broke off, his lips quivering. He was forced to wait a moment or two while he got his emotion under control, then finished. 'Unfortunately, murder was done, but it was his own.'

Silence ensued. Somewhere in the house, I could hear

Naomi singing, a bright, popular street ditty of the moment, while she went about her work. I reached out and laid a hand on Julian's wrist. 'I'm sorry,' I said. The trite little phrase had never sounded so inadequate. I added, 'I liked your brother as much as any man I've ever met.'

My companion nodded. 'Everyone liked him,' he responded huskily. He remained lost in thought for a moment, then asked, 'So what else is it you want to know?'

I hesitated to cause him further distress, but my question needed an answer. 'Was there a suggestion at the time – any suggestion, however slight – that Landlord Makepeace's death might not have been an accident?'

Julian looked puzzled. 'I don't understand,' he said.

I cleared my throat. 'Was there any hint . . .? Did any of the onlookers get the impression that the two sailors might . . . well, might have been paid to kill your brother? That their quarrel was faked in any way?'

The apothecary was frankly bemused. 'Faked?' he demanded incredulously. 'No, of course it wasn't faked! Why do you ask such a stupid question? What is all this about?'

'Forgive me,' I said. 'I've upset you. Let me explain.'

'I should be glad if you would. If you can,' he answered coldly. But by the time I had finished my explanation, Julian's attitude had grown less frosty. 'What an extraordinary tale,' he said slowly. 'Naturally, I know the Godsloves. Four of them are my stepbrothers and -sisters, and two my half-siblings, but neither Reynold nor myself ever had anything much to do with them. I did inform them when Reynold died, but they meant very little to us, you see. We never lived with them. We were never part of their family. After our mother met and married Morgan Godslove – she met him while he was here in London on business – and went away to Bristol, Reynold and I went to live with our grandmother in Candlewick Street. We were informed, of course, when our half-brother and -sister were born and also of our mother's death six years after her marriage, but none of it meant very much to us. We had lost touch with her by then. Members of the family, particularly Martin and Celia, did come to visit us when they moved to London – that would be . . . oh . . . about twenty-three, twenty-four years ago – but, as I say, we were never close.

I knew that my half-brother had died, but not in such a fashion. Maybe I was told, but I was still mourning Reynold – I suppose I still am – and it didn't sink in. Last autumn, you say?' He regarded me thoughtfully. 'How odd,' he said, 'that both my brother and half-brother should have died violently within such a short time of one another.'

TEN

'Very strange,' I agreed. 'Perhaps now you can understand, why the Godslove family are worried. And added to those two deaths are the near fatal illness of the eldest sister, the death by mushroom poisoning of another and the narrow escape of the second eldest, Sybilla, from falling masonry at Bishop's Gate wall. Your half-sister, Mistress Celia, and the head of the family, Oswald Godslove, are the only two who have so far suffered no apparent attempt on their lives.'

Julian Makepeace gave a wry smile. 'And myself,' he pointed out. 'If you intend to include Reynold as a family member, then I suppose I must regard myself as one, too. Although I have to stress that neither he nor I ever considered ourselves as such. Polite acquaintances, maybe, but no more than that. Even our mother became a stranger to us after she went away. We never saw her again once she had left London, and Morgan Godslove we met only at the wedding. He was Reynold's and my stepfather, but I doubt if we thought of him in that way. I doubt if we ever thought about him at all, if the truth be told. I can't speak for my brother, of course, but I know I didn't.'

'I don't think he can have done, either,' I said, 'or, knowing that I was from Bristol, I feel he would probably have mentioned something of the circumstances to me. But he never gave the smallest indication that he had any connection whatsoever with the city.'

'There you are then.' The apothecary spread his hands and shrugged. He went on, 'I'm unable to believe that Reynold's unfortunate death has anything to do with these other accidents that have befallen my stepfamily.'

On the face of it, his argument seemed reasonable enough, but I couldn't allow myself to be convinced. To a deranged mind, nothing was simple or straightforward. But the thought occurred to me that whoever the killer was, he or she must have intimate knowledge of the Godsloves' complicated family history. There had been no obvious tie between them and the Makepeaces; nothing to tell an outsider that they were even on speaking terms. Which, to be fair, ruled out even further the possibility of Adrian Jollifant being the moving spirit behind the killings, leaving the finger of suspicion pointing at Roderick Jeavons and Arbella Rokeswood as the more likely suspects.

Julian Makepeace refilled my beaker with ale and pushed it towards me.

'Drink up,' he urged. 'You look very tired, like a man who should be home resting in his bed, rather than worrying his head over things that don't concern him.'

I gave a rather strained laugh. 'I'm afraid my wife wouldn't agree with you. She's made the Godsloves' concerns her own and therefore mine.' I added, with seeming inconsequence, 'Are you married?' (I had guessed that he wasn't.)

It was his turn to laugh, flushing slightly as he shook his head. 'Women, eh?' he said, but his quick glance towards the door told me that my surmise was probably correct. The lucky devil was bedding young Naomi.

I swallowed my ale and set the empty cup back on the tray. My companion was right: I was extremely tired and wanted nothing more than to return to the Arbour and Adela's loving embrace. But there was one other question I had to ask.

'Master Makepeace,' I said, 'has anything untoward, however slight, happened to you recently?'

He looked astonished. 'To me? No, of course not. Oh come, Master Chapman! You surely didn't take me seriously just now?'

'I'm not saying you really have anything to worry about,' I protested. 'I'm merely asking if anything has occurred lately that you couldn't explain. Anything in the nature of an accident or a near miss that could have injured you.'

He shook his head. 'Nothing,' he answered firmly, 'nor, frankly, do I expect it to. In spite of all you've told me, I still believe that Reynold's death was an accident. He simply got in the way of a knife intended for another man.'

'Were either of the Genoese seamen caught?'

'No, but there's nothing to be read into that. When they saw what had happened, they were out of the Voyager before anyone could stop them. Indeed, I doubt if anyone tried to stop them with those knives in their hands and their apparent readiness to use them. They were never found in spite of enquiries by the sheriff's men. They must have gone straight back to their ship where they laid low, protected by their fellow shipmates and the master of the vessel. I never had any expectations that they would be taken. Nor, I think, did anyone else.'

Of course not! It was the simplest explanation. And hadn't William of Ockham always taught that the simple explanation was usually the correct one? Ockham's Razor, men had called it since the thirteenth century.

I rose to my feet, steadying myself on the edge of the table as a slight dizziness threatened to overcome me.

'Are you feeling unwell?' the apothecary enquired anxiously, also getting up and putting out a steadying hand.

'It's nothing,' I said quickly. 'A momentary weakness, that's all.' I squared my shoulders. 'I'm better now. Master Makepeace, thank you for your time and patience. I'll relieve you of my company.' He followed me out into the shop, where he hovered, a worried frown creasing his brow. I forced a reassuring smile. 'There truly is nothing wrong with me. But promise me you'll take care. Watch your step, and if anything should happen that gives you the slightest cause for concern, please let me know at once. You know where the Arbour is.'

It was not a question, but he nodded and said, 'Of course,' then stood in the shop doorway until I had untied and mounted Old Diggory and ridden off up the street. 'God be with you!' he shouted after me.

I raised a hand and waved.

It seemed to have grown warmer since I entered Bucklersbury half an hour or so earlier (but May is that sort of month, when all four seasons can happen in one day). I suddenly found that I was sweating profusely, while all about me the city noises assaulted my ears and everyone I met seemed intent on doing something to annoy me. Other riders jostled my horse, beggars rattled their tins under Old Diggory's nose, making him shy nervously or come to a complete standstill, abandoned garlands of mayflowers littered the roadway and the stench from the central drains, normally something I didn't even notice, made my belly heave. I felt that at any moment, I might disgrace myself and throw up all down my smart green tunic and nice brown hose.

But by the time I reached Bishop's Gate Street, I no longer cared if I were sick or not. Old Diggory was heading home without any guidance from me, which was just as well as my senses were swimming so much that I was barely conscious of my surroundings. I was vaguely aware that the thoroughfare was still blocked, but that was all. I had just enough strength left to pull on the reins and bring the horse to a halt before I swayed in the saddle and began to fall into darkness . . .

I opened my eyes and stared up at the richly carved, red and gold ceiling above me. Light flooded in through spacious, lofty windows, one an oriel window of peculiar size and beauty. I could also see a minstrel's gallery and the floor beneath my trailing hand was marble. For a moment, I wondered if I had died and gone straight to heaven, until conscience told me that such a contingency was highly unlikely. After that common sense reasserted itself and I realized that not only was I still very much alive, but also that I knew this place. I had been here before.

I was lying on a velvet day-bed. Somewhere behind me, a door opened and closed.

'Well, well, well!' said a familiar voice, and a hand was placed on my forehead. 'Drunk again, eh, Roger? And not long gone noon.'

I sat up with such violence that the room spun around me and I was forced to lie down again in a hurry. But at least now I knew where I was – in the great hall of Crosby's Place – and I knew who was speaking, although I hadn't expected him to be in London yet awhile.

'You know damn well I'm not drunk, Timothy,' I snapped. 'Even you can't be such a fool as to believe that.'

He came closer, where I could see him, pulled up a low, velvet-covered stool and sat down beside the couch.

'There's the smell of ale on your breath,' he said, 'but I must admit I've never seen you drunk in the middle of the day.'

'Nor at any other time,' I declared. 'I can carry my ale as well as the next man. I've been ill this past week and only got up from my sick-bed yesterday. What happened? How do I come to be in Crosby's Place?'

'One of the workmen, unloading the duke's furniture, caught you as you fell out of the saddle. And by the way, that sorry piece of horseflesh you were riding has been put in the stable here for the time being. I've sent for some decent wine. It should settle your guts and make you feel better. Now, when you feel able, sit up carefully and then you can tell me what you're doing in London.'

'And you can tell me what *you're* doing in London,' I retorted. 'I thought you'd be with the duke – wherever he is.'

At that moment, a serving-man arrived with the wine and two Venetian glass goblets on a silver tray which, having dragged over a beautifully carved small table with his free hand, he placed at Timothy's elbow. By the time he departed as noiselessly as he came, I had once more pulled myself into a sitting position, but with greater caution than before. The room stayed steady. The nausea had gone.

I breathed a sigh of relief and nodded towards the goblets. 'Doing yourself proud while His Grace is still absent, eh? Which reminds me, I heard he wasn't coming here until the duchess arrives. Going to his mother's at Baynard's Castle was my information.'

A shade of annoyance crossed Timothy's face. 'Now, how by the Holy Mother do you know that? It's not supposed to be common knowledge.'

I grinned. 'Dear God, how old are you, Timothy? Don't you know by now that the man in the street always gets the news before the man in the council chamber? So it's true. But what in Jesu's name is going on? Earl Rivers arrested! Sir Richard Grey as well! And what's happened to the king? The whole city's buzzing with the news. And, as I said just now, why are you here in advance of the duke?'

He handed me a brimming goblet and filled one for himself,

sipping the golden liquid with relish, in contrast to myself, who had emptied half the glass in one go.

He winced, eyeing me up and down. 'You never did have any appreciation of good wine, Roger. So! You want to know what I'm doing here. Very well! But first tell me why you're in London, less than six months after you vowed never to return if you could possibly help it.'

Once again I repeated my story, but with variations. I wasn't stupid enough to tell Timothy Plummer, of all people, the real reason for my being in the capital. In this version, Adela and the children had come on a visit to her relations and I had arrived simply to escort them home. The rest of the tale I was open and honest about, feeling sure that Timothy would have no interest in the plight of the Godsloves. And I was right. He had too much else on his mind.

He was silent for at least a minute after I had finished, staring at me speculatively over the rim of his goblet, which he finally replaced carefully on the tray. Then he leant forward, his elbows propped on his knees.

'Well,' he said at last, 'there's no reason why I shouldn't tell you the truth. In any case, the reason behind the arrests will have to be made public sooner or later. And it may be providential that you're in London, Roger. I might have need of your services.'

'Oh no you won't!' I spluttered, showering both myself and Timothy with spittle. 'You're not playing that game again. I've had enough of that, and so I told you last autumn. I've done obliging you and the duke. Most of last year away from home! First Scotland, then France! This time you can find someone else to do your dirty work.'

'Just hold your tongue and listen, will you?' he demanded savagely, wiping his face in his sleeve. He relieved me of my goblet and placed it beside his own. 'The duke is in danger, Roger. Serious danger. The Woodvilles are out to make trouble and this city is a hotbed of intrigue. That's why I've come on ahead, to spy out the land and see if I can find out exactly what's going on. I rode with the messengers sent yesterday. We got here at midnight and I haven't been to bed since. I'm telling you this so that you won't try my temper too far. I'm dog tired and I'm worried as I've rarely been worried in my life before.'

I lay back against the pillows of the day-bed. I could see that he was rattled. 'All right,' I said. 'Tell me what went on at Northampton. I promise I won't interrupt. If I've any questions, I'll keep them to the end.'

He took a deep breath and nodded. 'Very well, then. Here's what happened. The arrangement was that the duke, en route from York, and the king's party, coming across country from Ludlow, should rendezvous at Northampton. That was clearly understood from the messages sent and received. But when we reached Northampton early on Tuesday afternoon, there was no sign of the king or his entourage. At first, the duke assumed they'd been delayed on the road, but then, to his utter astonishment, he discovered that the royal troops, with Rivers and Grey at their head, had passed through the town that morning, but had ridden straight on, heading south, towards London.

'I've never, in all the years that I've known him, seen the duke so angry. John Kendall – you know, his secretary – told me that at one point he was literally shaking with rage. But I fancy there was an element of fear in it, too. He's been jumpy ever since he got news of the late king's death. But then, midway through the afternoon, Earl Rivers appeared, attended by a small number of his immediate circle, as pleasant as you please, full of smiles and apologies. The king had thought Northampton not big enough to house both his retinue and his uncle's, so had ridden on to Stony Stratford, where he would wait until the duke caught up with him yesterday morning.'

Timothy sniffed. 'Well, the story had an odd ring to it, Northampton being not exactly short of inns and with plenty of open fields around it for the troops to camp in. And Stony Stratford is a much smaller place. But the duke chose to accept it, calmed down and invited Earl Rivers to take supper with him. However, the meal had hardly begun when the streets were suddenly filled with all the clatter and bustle of someone arriving. And someone damned important by the sound of it. I was having my meal in an alehouse a little way down the street, but I sent one of my lads' – presumably

Timothy meant one of his fellow spies – 'to find out what the commotion was all about and when he came back he said that the Duke of Buckingham had just turned up with a following several hundreds strong, and had joined Duke Richard and Earl Rivers for supper at the duke's inn.'

I knew vaguely of Henry Stafford, Duke of Buckingham. He was a descendant of yet another of the third Edward's brood of sons – if ever a king could be said to have had too many sons it was that lusty monarch – and was therefore cousin, in the second, third or even fourth degree, to every other member of the royal family. I had seen him once, five years earlier, when he had been appointed Lord High Steward at the trial of George of Clarence, but my memory of him was not vivid. If the truth were told, I couldn't recall his face at all, but I nodded as though I knew him intimately.

Timothy continued, 'Well, we thought nothing of it and went to bed. But yesterday morning I was wakened with the news that Earl Rivers had been arrested an hour or so earlier. The inn where he was sleeping had been surrounded under cover of darkness and the earl had been taken into custody as soon as it was light. Moreover, Duke Richard and his cousin were already on the road to Stony Stratford to bring the king back to Northampton – which they did several hours later, together with his half-brother, Sir Richard Grey, and another of his kinsmen, Sir Thomas Vaughan, also under arrest.'

Timothy paused to refresh himself with more wine. I broke my promise and asked impatiently, 'So what was it all about?'

My companion regarded me reproachfully and I hurriedly apologized. He went on, puffing out his skinny chest a little, 'I was called to see Duke Richard that afternoon and informed that I was to ride to London within the next hour or so with the messengers he was sending to the mayor, to explain his actions. There was a Woodville plot afoot, he said, to take him prisoner until after the king had been crowned and the dowager queen's family established in all the positions of power.'

'Sweet Jesus!' I breathed. 'But – well, how did he know?'

Timothy became his usual pompous self. 'Perhaps you don't realize, my dear fellow – indeed, I suppose there's no

reason why you should – that the Duke of Buckingham is
married to Catherine Woodville, one of Queen Elizabeth's
sisters. He was forcibly married to her many years ago by
command of the late king, and has deeply resented the fact
ever since. Unlike his cousin, he did not consider an upstart
Woodville a fit mate for a Plantagenet. My guess is, however,
that although he may have scorned her, the lady has always
done her best to woo him—'

'With the result,' I cut in, 'that she has told him all about
this plot to take Duke Richard prisoner on his way to London.
I begin to see. When my Lord of Gloucester, all unsuspecting,
and Earl Rivers got to Stony Stratford yesterday morning, the
duke would have been . . . Been what?' I frowned.

Timothy gestured excitedly. 'He would have been told
that the king had gone to rest at Grafton Regis. Grafton
Regis,' Timothy explained, 'is the Woodvilles' principal seat.
It's where King Edward first met Elizabeth Woodville and
where he secretly married her all those years ago. And, most
significantly, it's not many miles from Stony Stratford! Once
there, Duke Richard would have been taken prisoner without
any fuss and probably died of a "seizure", like Humphrey
of Gloucester in the late King Henry's reign. Meantime, Earl
Rivers and Sir Richard Grey would have been on their way
to London to stage a triumphal entry as sole protectors of
the young king. And if my Lord Buckingham hadn't ridden
all through the day on Tuesday to apprise my lord of the
Woodvilles' intentions, the chances are that their treacherous
plans would have gone smoothly. And that's why I'm here,
in order to foil any other of their little plots.'

I gave a long, low whistle. 'Dear God . . . The dowager
queen's gone into sanctuary, taking the Duke of York and
the princesses with her. Are you aware of that?'

'Of course I'm aware!' Timothy bade me sit up straight
and handed me more wine. 'And Sir Edward Woodville has
put to sea taking most of the fleet with him, not to mention
a good half of the royal treasure from the Tower.'

'And I hear that the Marquis of Dorset was despatched to
grab the other half this morning.'

I had, astonishingly, managed to tell Timothy something
that he didn't know.

'What?' he yelped, spilling half his goblet of wine down his tunic. 'Are you sure?'

I nodded smugly. 'At least, that's what I was told in the city this morning. And it would seem the natural thing for him to do.'

My companion was already on his feet, the precious glass goblet dumped back on the tray as carelessly as if it had been a wooden beaker.

'I must go at once,' he said. 'I'll leave you to find your own way out. Your horse is in the stables.'

'Yes, you said. And thank you for your assist . . .' But he was gone before I could finish the word, a small whirlwind of activity, leaving me to sit pensively on the edge of the day-bed, turning over and over in my mind what he had told me.

If all of it were true – and I saw no reason why it should not be – it was disturbing news indeed. It meant that Richard of Gloucester's life had already been in jeopardy and could well be again. In my own mind, I doubted if Earl Rivers had planned the duke's death, only his detention until the Woodvilles had seized power. (I had got to know a little of the earl during the Scottish campaign the previous year, and judged him to be less ruthless than the rest of his family.) But I had no such reservations concerning the remainder of that tribe. One of the dowager queen's brothers was already at sea in possession of half the royal treasure, having ordered the fleet to sail with him. Another, Lionel, Bishop of Salisbury, was no doubt busy stirring up sedition throughout the capital. And added to this poisonous brew was something that only I and a very few others knew about: Duke Richard's conviction that the late king had been his mother's bastard by an archer called Blaybourne and that he was already, given his brother Clarence's attainder, the rightful king.

This, however, was something the duke was unable to prove, because of Duchess Cicely's refusal either to confirm or deny the accusation she had made at the time of her eldest son's marriage. But the information I had brought back from France six months earlier, concerning the christenings of Edward and Edmund, the next brother to him in age, must have confirmed Duke Richard in this belief. And now, to discover that the Woodvilles had been seriously plotting his downfall and possible murder could only exacerbate an already dangerous situation. I shivered. The future seemed suddenly uncertain. It was like looking down a long, dark tunnel and seeing no light at the end . . .

I stood up slowly, experimentally testing my legs. But they appeared to have regained their strength, and the dizziness, thanks be to all the saints, had gone. Indeed, I felt remarkably refreshed and clear-headed. Deciding that the wine must be a contributory factor to my recovery, I helped myself to another glass before making my way to the stables to find Old Diggory. The house and magnificent gardens were still so crowded with servants and workmen that no one questioned my presence or challenged my right to be there, and I was able to collect the horse and ride out of Crosby's Place with no more than the odd inquisitive glance from a couple of busy gardeners and a half-hearted attempt by one of the grooms to discover my identity. I rode off unhindered up the street towards the Bishop's Gate, continuing to mull over all that Timothy Plummer had told me. But after a minute or so, my own concerns began to intrude upon my thoughts once more, and I stopped worrying about Duke Richard's affairs to wonder why I found the history of Reynold and Julian Makepeace so disturbing. Julian's version of his and his brother's life story had only served to confirm that given to me by the stranger in the Voyager, and I had no reason at all to doubt it. Yet something about it bothered me. But what? The more I chased the possible reason round and around in my head, the more it eluded me. With a sigh, I abandoned the quest. My brain would spew up the answer eventually. Until then I should do well to let it be.

The stonemasons were still at work on the wall and barely accorded me a glance as I passed through the gate. Even the gatekeeper nodded me through as if I were an old acquaintance, continuing his argument with the owner of a cartful of cabbages over the correct tariff necessary to bring it into the city.

'I dunno,' the countryman was grumbling, 'the bloody taxes keep going up every soddin' week as if they 'ad a soddin' life of their own. When's it goin' to end, that's what I want t' know.'

'Don't we all?' snapped the gatekeeper. 'But for now, just pay up and stop whinging. There's a queue forming behind you.'

I left them to it. There must be arguments like this going on at every gate in every city in the land. Having deliberately emptied my head of all thoughts regarding my own and Duke Richard's concerns, I began to feel extremely sleepy – Old Diggory's plodding gait rocked me gently from side to side – and there is little doubt that, for the second time that day, I would have fallen from the saddle had I not been jerked awake by a voice asking, 'Chapman, is something wrong?'

I pulled myself upright, blinking stupidly against the gentle afternoon sunlight, and looked down into the concerned, bright-eyed gaze of Father Berowne.

'Yes, yes! I'm quite well, I thank you. A little tired, perhaps.'

'You've been doing too much too soon,' he said accusingly. 'You've not long risen from your sickbed, and I saw you ride off with Master Godslove at a very early hour this morning. Come inside and have a cup of my elderflower wine. That . . . That is . . .' He broke off, looking flustered, suddenly recollecting that I had fallen ill shortly after drinking it the last time.

I grinned. 'I won't, I thank you, Father, but not for the reason you're thinking. I exonerate your elderflower wine entirely. But I've been drinking already this afternoon' – I didn't say where or whose wine – 'and I'm sleepy enough as it is. Besides, I can see you're busy.'

I indicated his earth-stained cassock and his mud-encrusted hands, one of which he was using to push back his unruly fringe of curls.

He laughed guiltily. 'Gardening is one of my great pleasures in life, I'm afraid. I do it when I should be on my knees, praying. But somehow, I find it easier to talk to God in the open air, rather than in a stuffy church. Oh dear, oh dear! Is that very wrong of me? Not,' he added, 'that I've much of a garden here. Just this little plot. But I do what I can.'

'And you do it very well, Father,' I assured him, 'very well indeed. And now I must get on. You're right. I have done more than I should today. I shall be glad of a rest.'

I jerked Old Diggory's reins and we plodded on up the track, pursued by the priest's good wishes, until, round the second bend, we came in sight of the Arbour. I expected to find it dozing in the warmth of mid-afternoon. Instead, there seemed to be a flurry of activity, with people milling around the gate and looking anxiously up and down the road. Adela was one of them, but as soon as she sighted me, she came flying towards me, just as she had done the day of my arrival. But this time, it was not good news.

'Oh, Roger!' she gasped. 'Thank God, thank God you're back at last! Celia's disappeared! We can find no trace of her anywhere!'

ELEVEN

I dismounted and, grasping her by the shoulders, gave her a little shake.

'Slowly, my love, slowly! Just tell me quietly what has happened.'

Before Adela could speak again, however, she was joined by Clemency and Sybilla, both out of breath from running and both talking at once.

'. . . hasn't been seen since breakfast . . .'

'. . . garden with the children . . .'

'. . . hide-and-seek . . .'

'. . . completely vanished . . .'

'Oh, Roger, do something,' begged my wife.

The three children and Hercules had now arrived, the former looking sulky and more than a little defiant as children often do when they think they are being blamed for something that is not their fault, while the dog, catching the general mood of panic, began to bark, short, distressing yelps that pierced the ears and made them sing. Old Diggory snorted and tossed his head.

I dealt with first things first.

'Quiet!' I yelled at Hercules, my stentorian tones for once cowing him into immediate submission. I then soothed the horse before waving a hand at Clemency and Sybilla, commanding their silence, and turned once more to my wife.

'You say Celia is missing?' She nodded, ready to burst forth again, but I said firmly, 'Wait! Wait until we are indoors and I can listen to you all properly. The horse must be stabled, too. He needs feeding and watering. Is there anyone who can see to this?'

'I can,' said a firm voice, and I realized that, in the last few seconds, the housekeeper had also joined us. In her usual competent fashion, she took the reins from me, adding, 'Go in, all of you. I've put ale and wine and some of those little cinnamon doucettes Sybilla likes so much on the table in the hall. Calm yourselves, then you can acquaint Master Chapman with such as there is to tell.' Arbella shrugged. 'For my own part, I think the three of you are making a to-do about nothing. Celia has probably just gone for a walk.'

But when all the facts had been presented to me, I wasn't so sure that I agreed with her. It seemed that after the five women – the three sisters, Adela and the housekeeper – had breakfasted, together with the children, Celia had announced her intention of playing hide-and-seek in the garden with Nicholas, Elizabeth and Adam.

'I have the headache and shall be all the better for a little air,' she had argued, brushing aside her sisters' concern and their advice to lie down upon her bed. 'For sweet heaven's sake, I'm not ill,' she had reproved them. 'A slight pain behind the eyes, that's all. Besides, I feel sure that Nick and Bess can't have discovered every nook and cranny of that garden and it's such a long time since I walked all round it. I used to love it when I was young. I was ten,' she had told Adela, 'when we first came here, and I thought it paradise.'

And so she had gone out of doors with the children, all three of whom liked her much better than her half-siblings, and, as far as Adela could tell, seemed perfectly content to accept her company. But not long after the four of them, with Hercules yapping at their heels, had disappeared into the wilderness which was the Arbour garden, the reason for Celia's sudden desire for fresh air appeared in the shape of Roderick Jeavons. He had, ostensibly, come to see Sybilla and how she was progressing, but it was immediately apparent to the other women that the real purpose of his visit was to speak to Celia. He had plainly been angry at what he saw as her contrived absence and had declared his intention of following her and forcing his presence on her. In this, he had apparently been dissuaded by Adela who, with her quiet common sense, had persuaded him that such confrontations invariably ended in quarrels.

'But it seems,' my wife said with a sigh, 'that he changed his mind. The children say he did eventually seek them out somewhere in the garden and began urging his attentions on Celia.'

'He put his arms round her and kissed her,' Elizabeth

disclosed with a little shudder of excitement, obviously unsure whether she found such rough treatment masterful or repellent. (On the whole, I fancy she rather inclined to the former.)

'And Celia slapped his face and called him a lot of names,' Nicholas added, round-eyed. 'And Physician Jeavons called her a lot of names back and said she was an . . . an in . . . in . . . in-something whore.' I guessed the missing word to be incestuous, but refrained from saying so. 'I didn't understand what he meant.'

'Yes, well never mind that,' I said hastily. 'What did the doctor do then?'

'He went away,' Elizabeth said. She looked disappointed. 'And we didn't see him any more.'

'He did say he'd get even with her,' my stepson pointed out. 'And I don't think he would have gone away then if Hercules hadn't started barking at him and trying to bite his ankles. It made Celia laugh and that made the doctor even crosser.'

The housekeeper had entered the hall in time to overhear Nicholas's last remark and she smiled sourly. 'Oh, Celia enjoys humiliating the poor man,' she said, starting to pour the wine which we had so far neglected. She pushed full beakers towards us. 'You'd think,' she went on angrily, 'that a woman of her age would be grateful for a handsome man like that to come courting her. Plump in the pocket, too. Celia will soon be thirty-six. High time she was in an establishment of her own.'

'Be quiet!' Clemency ordered her furiously. 'I don't want to hear any more of such talk. Celia's happy here with us, and that's how we want it to remain. You'd better not say those things in front of Oswald. It would be as much as your place is worth.'

Arbella Rokeswood flushed painfully and her mouth shut like a trap. If looks could have killed, Clemency would have been a dead woman. And so would Sybilla, who was nodding vehemently in agreement.

'I'm not sure I shan't tell him,' the latter told the housekeeper spitefully.

I slapped my open hand on the table making them all jump and spilling some of the wine.

'These squabbles will get us nowhere,' I reproached them. I turned again to Nicholas and Elizabeth. 'After Dr Jeavons left, what happened next?'

'We went on playing hide-and-seek,' my daughter said. 'It was Celia's turn to seek, so Adam and Nick and I ran off to hide. Nick and I went together because we'd found a little stone hut at the end of a long, twisty path – I don't know where Adam and Hercules went – and we waited and waited, but Celia never came. In the end, we thought she'd just got tired of playing and gone back indoors, so we came out and started a game of our own. Then, after a bit, we found Adam and Hercules. Adam had taken his shoes and hose off and was paddling in a stream at the end of the garden. Hercules was splashing about as well. They were both in a terrible state,' Elizabeth added virtuously, wrinkling her nose.

I gave Adam an admonitory glance, which he returned with a wide-eyed, innocent stare.

'And then?' I prompted.

'And then it was dinnertime,' Adela said. 'I went out to call the children in, but there was no sign of Celia. And when I asked where she was, Nick and Bess said she'd gone back to the house, but she hadn't. Clemency, Sybilla and I searched everywhere, but there was no sign of her. Sybilla and Clemency then went outside to search the garden – I had to clean up Adam and Hercules – but again, they could find no trace of her.'

'I tell you, you're making a fuss about nothing,' Arbella put in irritably. 'Celia's gone for a walk to clear her headache. She'll be home presently, you mark my words.'

'She didn't come home for dinner.' Sybilla began to cry. 'It's hours now since anyone's seen her. She wouldn't stay out walking all this time. Something's happened.' Her voice rose shrilly. 'Someone's killed her. Whoever it is who's trying to harm us. I think we ought to send for Oswald. He'll know what's to be done.'

Clemency put an arm around her sister's shoulders. 'Hush, my dear. Let's not jump to conclusions. As Arbella says, there may be a perfectly satisfactory explanation.' But her voice quavered and I could hear the panic behind the sensible advice.

'I'm presuming Dr Jeavons got into the garden without returning to the house,' I said. 'Am I right? Is there a separate entrance to the garden?'

Clemency nodded. 'There's a side gate that leads through from the little copse.'

'The copse?'

'A thick stand of trees that grows some way back from the main track,' Adela explained. 'It's not a part of the Arbour land. It just happens to be on the other side of the gate.'

'And has the copse been searched?'

Clemency and Sybilla looked guiltily at one another. 'We . . . we didn't think . . .'

'Stay here,' I commanded. 'I'll go and look. Just tell me how to find this gate.'

'We'll show you,' my daughter volunteered, catching hold of Nicholas's hand.

'You'd better let them, Roger,' my wife advised. 'You've only seen the garden from the windows. It's more of a labyrinth than you imagine.'

She was not exaggerating. Nothing had apparently been done to it in the quarter of a century that the Godsloves had lived there. It had simply been allowed to return to its natural state. Here and there could still be discerned the remnants of a formal layout: a rose garden, a shrubbery, a sunken herb garden, the stone hut at the end of an overgrown path which had probably once served as repository for picks and spades. But now the roses ran riot, the once exotic blooms reverting to the single, pallid dog-rose of the hedgerow, the shrubbery a mass of stunted, scrubby plants that impeded progress and tore at one's hose, but which provided wonderful cover for secret games and hide-and-seek. There was a stream, too, at the far edge of the property, forming its western boundary, the clear water rippling over pebbles and shale with little black minnows swimming in its depths. A child's paradise indeed, and yet, to my mind, there was something sinister and a little forbidding about it as perhaps there always is when the wilderness takes back its own.

Nicholas and Elizabeth seemed not to share my feelings, forging ahead of me along narrow pathways, advising me where to step in order to avoid the worst of the encroaching stems and branches and pointing out various hidey-holes which they had discovered. At last, however, we arrived at the pretty wrought-iron gate which opened into the small copse beyond. Ordering the children to stay where they were, I pushed it wide and stepped into the shadow of the trees.

Adela had been right: the copse was not large but it was dense, a stand of ancient oaks, a remnant, I guessed, of more extensive woodland that had once covered the surrounding countryside. I moved forward cautiously, my heart beating a little faster as I did so, half expecting to find a body lying on the ground. No such grizzly sight awaited me, however, but the earth beneath the trees was muddy, no sunlight penetrating the thick canopy of branches, just beginning to green with new leaf. And I noticed one place in particular where the mud had been churned up as though a horse had been tethered there.

But that, of course, was more than likely as Roderick Jeavons must have tied his mount up somewhere when he entered the garden to seek out Celia. The animal could have been standing there some while as he had first to find her before he could press his suit. And I was then able to see the imprints of his boots deeply gouged into the earth, a man in a fury at being rejected yet again, mounting his horse and riding away. But had he? Or had he re-entered the garden and vented his anger by abducting Celia – or worse, by killing her?

I pulled myself up short. If the former, she would have screamed and resisted. One of the children must have heard her and gone to see what was wrong. If the latter, where was the body? Clemency and Sybilla had, according to the women's account, thoroughly searched the garden and nothing had been found. Besides, the good doctor would surely not have risked his livelihood and reputation by anything so crude. If someone really was trying to murder the Godsloves, one by one, then he or she was demonstrating greater patience and subtlety than that. And another thought struck me. If Roderick Jeavons were the man, then he would most certainly not wish to kill Celia, who was the object of his desire. On the other hand, he might have grown tired of waiting and simply abducted her, but where would he hide her until he could force her consent to their marriage? Presumably he led a perfectly normal domestic life with a housekeeper to attend to his well-being. Or did his house have a cellar where he could keep her captive? Where he could . . . ?

I shook my head angrily and the visions of torture and rape receded. I was letting my imagination run away with me. I was getting as bad as the women and allowing their hysteria to influence my way of thinking. Arbella Rokeswood was probably right, I told myself. There was a perfectly logical explanation for Celia's disappearance, and the answer would soon be revealed.

I went back to the garden, carefully closing the little gate behind me. Elizabeth and Nicholas had vanished, fed up with waiting for my return, but I could hear their voices somewhere in the distance, laughing and chattering in callous disregard for the troubles and problems of their elders. (Which, of course, is as it should be in my view, although perhaps not many of my coevals would agree with me.) I therefore made my slow progress back to the house where Clemency and Sybilla (the latter by now in floods of hysterical tears) together with my wife and the housekeeper, were anxious for my report.

'Did you find anything?' Clemency asked, barely able to speak for fear of what my answer might be.

I shook my head, and there was a collective gasp of relief. I realized that they had all been fearing the worst: that I had stumbled upon Celia's murdered body. Sybilla's sobs abated a little.

'I found nothing in the copse,' I said, 'except a patch of churned up earth where Dr Jeavons must have tethered his horse while he went to look for Celia in the garden.' I didn't add, Away from your prying eyes and interference, although it was on the tip of my tongue to do so. But a steely glance from Adela, who had divined my intention with her usual acumen, made me think better of it. I continued, 'I think Mistress Rokeswood could well be correct in believing that Celia either simply grew bored with playing hide-and-seek or needed to calm herself after the encounter with Dr Jeavons.'

'Of course I'm correct,' the housekeeper said in a satisfied tone. 'Thank goodness someone at last has the good sense to agree with me. And now,' she added irritably, 'supper will be delayed on account of being short-handed in the kitchen.' Several enquiring looks were bent in her direction and Arbella pointed an accusing finger at Sybilla. 'She insisted that I send one of the girls all the way to Westminster, to the courts, to inform Oswald that Celia is missing.'

Clemency looked reproachfully at her sister. 'Oh, Syb! I know you're worried, dear, but there was no need to bother Oswald yet awhile. Not until we're absolutely certain that something's wrong.'

Sybilla, who had been bravely choking back a fresh bout of tears for the last few minutes, began to cry again, but quietly this time, her whole body shaking.

'But something is wrong,' she persisted. 'I can feel it in my bones.'

'Nonsense!' the housekeeper declared stoutly. 'I tell you, Celia's just gone for a walk.'

'Gone for a walk,' confirmed a small voice as Adam, looking unusually spick and span, having been thoroughly washed after his paddle in the stream, climbed into his mother's lap and solemnly surveyed the assembled company.

There was a moment's pregnant silence while we all stared at him. Then I sat down in a chair next to Adela's and, leaning forward, took both his little hands in my own.

'What do you mean, sweetheart?' I asked gently. 'Do you know that Celia went for a walk?'

He nodded. 'Went for a walk,' he repeated. 'Said she'd get her cloak.'

There was another silence, profounder than before.

'Did . . . Did she tell you that?'

Adam shook his head impatiently. 'Not me. Person she was talking to.'

'And where was this?' I kept my tone low and unhurried.

'Oh, never mind where it was,' Sybilla broke in, her voice rising to a shriek. 'Who was it she was talking to?'

Adam moved closer to his mother. My wife's arms tightened about him protectively.

'Don't know,' he said. 'Didn't see. I was hiding behind the bushes.'

'But . . . But surely you came out to see who it was?' Clemency demanded, adding her mite to the interrogation.

Adam sighed. 'We wos playing hide-n'-seek,' he explained patiently. ''F I'd come out, Cilly would've known where I was hiding.'

He glanced at me in indignation, plainly seeking guidance as to why adults asked such very stupid questions. I gave a little shrug and pulled down the corners of my mouth, which seemed to placate him.

'Was it a man or a woman Celia was talking to?' I asked, stroking the backs of his little hands with my thumbs.

His brow puckered while he considered the matter, but he eventually shook his head. 'Don't know,' he said.

'Oh, nonsense!' Clemency exclaimed. 'You must know if you heard a man's or a woman's voice, you silly boy.'

'That will do, cousin,' Adela retorted angrily, springing to the defence of her young. 'Adam is not quite five years old. He's still a baby.'

'Not a baby,' declared her ungrateful offspring. 'I's a big boy. Didn't hear the other person 'cause they were outside the gate. Just heard Cilly say, "I'll get my cloak".'

'So someone asked her to go somewhere with him . . . or maybe with her?' I gave his fingers a squeeze. 'Is that what you're saying, Adam?'

My son regarded me blankly. 'Went to get her cloak,' he repeated, taking refuge in what he was sure of. He began to look distressed again.

I leant forward and kissed his soft cheek. 'All right, sweetheart, you've been a very helpful, clever boy. Just a few more questions to make sure I understand you properly. This was by the garden gate that opens into the copse? The little wood?' He nodded vigorously. 'And what happened next?'

'Waited and waited for Cilly to come and find me.' His voice rose in outrage. 'But she never came. I waited a long, long time. Then Her'cles found me, so I stopped hiding, but Cilly wasn't there, so I went away and played with Her'cles and we paddled in the stream.'

'What do you think happened to Celia?' I pressed him.

He squirmed a bit on Adela's lap. He was tiring of this catechism and wanted to get down.

'Went to get her cloak. Went for a walk. But I thought she'd find me first,' he added, his sense of grievance coming to the fore once again. And with a final wriggle, he escaped from Adela's clutches and trundled off on his own. Wisely, she let him go.

I looked at the others. Arbella Rokeswood had forgotten all about supper and still made one of our sombre little conclave.

'So,' I said, after a moment's silence, 'it would seem that someone – a man or a woman, we don't know which – asked Celia to accompany him or her somewhere, although for what reason we again don't know. But whatever it was, she agreed. Which suggests that she recognized and trusted the person in question. She said she'd fetch her cloak. Is there any way she could have done so without anyone seeing her come back into the house?'

Arbella, Clemency and Sybilla nodded almost in unison, but it was the housekeeper who answered. 'There's a passage behind the kitchen where we keep old cloaks and pattens for when it's raining and we have to go outside. A side door opens into the passageway from the garden. The entrance to the kitchen itself is further along, so Celia could easily have come in, fetched a cloak and gone out again without anyone seeing her. In any case, the two girls and I were busy preparing dinner – that was a good meal gone to waste! – and I doubt we'd have heard anything either. There's always too much clattering and banging of pots and pans with those two clumsy creatures about, and even though the kitchen window was open, Celia could have taken half a dozen paths back to the gate without one of us spotting her. But,' she finished, 'why you've all got such long faces still, I'm sure I don't know. Surely this proves my point. Celia went out for a reason, and will be home any time soon.'

'But who did she go out *with*?' Clemency demanded, the knuckles of her tightly clasped hands showing white against her dark dress. 'Who was it came to the garden gate and asked for her company, and why?'

'Oh for sweet Jesu's sake!' Arbella exclaimed, exasperated. 'She has acquaintances among the cottagers who live around the Bishop's Gate. She's very good to some of the poorer ones. Takes them soup and bread when we can spare it from the kitchen. It was most likely one of them seeking her assistance. And apart from standing around here, wailing and wringing our hands and assuming the worst, not one of us has done more than search the garden for her.'

She had a point, and a good one. I was a little shocked to realize how I had allowed the febrile atmosphere and general sense of panic to blunt my common sense. A wider search should have been instituted for Celia's whereabouts before we all decided that she had been abducted, or worse. It suddenly dawned on me that three or four or possibly more hours had passed since Celia's absence was discovered, and no one had thought to enquire beyond the environs of the house itself. Even Adela, normally so level-headed, had succumbed to the fear that held Clemency and Sybilla in its paralysing grip.

Although still feeling a little shaky after my queer turn earlier that afternoon, I recognized that, as the only man present, it was undoubtedly my duty to bestir myself and undertake more extensive enquiries than had so far been set afoot. I stood up.

'Where are you going?' Adela asked sharply, and I recognized the underlying note of concern.

I smiled reassuringly at her. 'I'm going to ask around the Bishop's Gate, in the houses and the alehouse, if anyone's seen Celia. If she went that way, someone might remember her passing by, and might even have noted who she was with.'

'A very sensible notion,' the housekeeper approved. 'Not that I think you'll get much joy of it. There's so much traffic around the gate, what with the workmen, folk visiting the hospital or the Bedlam or the alehouse, and the cottagers in and out of the city all the time, that one woman, or a man and a woman, could easily pass unremarked. Not that I'm trying to deter you, Master Chapman. Indeed, I blame myself –' she glanced scornfully at Clemency and Sybilla as she spoke, clearly indicating that it was not merely herself she blamed – 'for failing to have done so already. But better late than never. And now I must go and see what disaster has befallen in the kitchen during my absence. With only Audrey in charge, we shall be lucky to get any supper at all.'

I recollected that the other maid had been sent to Westminster, a long journey for the poor child on foot, to find Oswald and wondered how soon we could expect to see him. I hoped not too soon; I suspected his presence would only add to the general sense of doom.

I took my cudgel to lean on, glad of its support as I trudged south again in the direction of the Bishop's Gate. Arbella Rokeswood had been right, there were plenty of people about on a warm May Day afternoon. Even though the drovers and swineherds had driven their animals to market far earlier in the day, there were still carters bringing in wagonloads of vegetables and plants from smallholdings further up the track, in the hope of making a late sale to those goodwives who had been out bringing in the may that morning.

I pressed on, my eyes constantly searching the crowds, desperately seeking for a glimpse of Celia's trim form.

'Roger! Roger Chapman!'

I turned my head quickly, trying to see who was calling my name.

'Roger!' Father Berowne was beside me, a detaining hand on my shoulder. 'Is anything wrong? Why are you wearing that worried frown? And why aren't you laid down upon your bed? You're still far from well and shouldn't be junketing about the countryside in this foolish fashion.'

'Father!' I exclaimed thankfully. 'You haven't by any chance seen Celia pass this way any time today, have you? She's been missing from the Arbour since this morning, after breakfast.'

He smiled tolerantly. 'She's a grown woman, Roger. There's probably a perfectly simple explanation for her absence. But yes, now you ask, I think I may have seen her earlier today, before dinner in fact. She was wearing that blue cloak of hers and going towards the city.'

TWELVE

I caught my breath.

'You saw her? You're sure of that?'

'I'm not absolutely certain, no. But as sure as I can be. As I said, she was walking towards the Bishop's Gate. I was just on my way to ring the bell for sext, or I would have tried to attract her attention. That's how I know it was before dinner.'

I frowned. 'I thought sext was at noon.'

'Not in the summer,' he reminded me gently. 'The office is said earlier once the warmer days arrive.'

'I'd forgotten,' I answered vaguely, my mind only half on what the priest was saying. I laid a hand on his arm and shook it. 'Can you recall if she was alone, Father, or was there someone with her?'

Sir Berowne shook his head. 'Now that I couldn't tell you. There were so many people abroad this morning. What with it being May Day and then folk crowding into the city to hear the Duke of Gloucester's proclamation at Paul's Cross as well as all the usual traffic of a normal day, the track was very crowded. Mistress Godslove might have been accompanied, it's true. There was a man close on her heels, but that could just have been coincidence. I've told you, the roadway was busy. Even busier than normal. But for sweet heaven's sake, my son, why are you so concerned? At the risk of repeating myself, Celia is a grown woman; even, some might think, a little long in the tooth. Oh, don't misunderstand me.' He threw up his hands, grimy as always from digging in his garden. 'An attractive enough woman, but long past the age when she should be wed. And she's not a prisoner. Surely, she can come and go as she pleases?'

Impatiently, I pulled him into the side of the track where we were less likely to impede the progress of others. We had already given offence to more than one person in a hurry and caused at least three carts to swerve to avoid us.

'You don't understand, Father,' I said. 'Celia went out
without leaving word for anyone as to where she was going
or who she was going to visit, and has not been seen since
early this morning. She joined the children in the garden,
just after breakfast, to play hide-and-seek . . .'

'Oh, was that all the noise I heard, then?' my companion
interrupted with an air of enlightenment. 'I had occasion to
visit one of my parishioners who lives further up the track,
a poor childless widow who has been unwell, and as I passed
the Arbour I could hear the children laughing and shouting.
Such a merry sound I thought it, and just what that old house
needs, so sombre and gloomy as it always seems. And good
for Mistress Celia, I should—'

I cut in ruthlessly on these happy reflections. 'For heaven's
sake, man, Celia hasn't returned from wherever it was she
was going and it's nearly suppertime! Her sisters are frantic
with worry after all that's occurred these past two years.
They are beginning to believe that something terrible has
happened to her. So try to remember, I beg of you, what
exactly you saw this morning.'

The blue eyes widened in sudden comprehension. 'Dear
me! Dear me! How very stupid of me not to have thought
of that. But do you know, Roger, I've never really believed
in this mysterious stranger who is trying to kill them all, one
by one. Nobody has that sort of time and patience. People's
sense of injury cools, you know. All right!' Once again he
flung up his hands, but this time in a gesture of submission.
'I accept that the Godslove family believe it, so naturally
they are worried about Celia's absence. But I'm afraid I've
told you all that I can regarding my sighting of her this
morning. There was a man behind her, it's true, near enough
to make me think that he could have been accompanying
her. Then again, he could have been a stranger walking a
little too close, in a hurry, trying to get past. Why? Do you
think there might have been someone with her?'

I explained about Adam and what he had overheard. Father
Berowne remained unimpressed.

'There you are, then! Somebody came for Celia's help. It
was urgent and all she had time to do was to grab a cloak.
She probably thought it wouldn't take long and that she

would be home again in time for dinner. But, as I know from my own experience, these cries for assistance are not always as simple and straightforward as they seem. She'll be back eventually telling you all not to be so foolish.'

But plausible as his words sounded, and much as they chimed with my own ideas on the subject, I wasn't entirely convinced. A nagging worry was beginning to eat away at my common sense.

'Can you recollect anything at all about this man?' I persisted.

The priest sighed and shook his head. 'No, nothing,' he said, 'except that he wasn't young and was smartly dressed.'

My thoughts went at once to Adrian Jollifant, but after a moment's consideration, I rejected the possibility. Coming from Cheapside, he would hardly have travelled on foot. And the same reasoning applied to the doctor. Indeed, we knew for certain that Roderick Jeavons had been on horseback, so where would he have stabled his mount? And why would he have left it behind? No, the whole idea was ridiculous. No one had been following Celia, who was about some business of her own.

I smiled wanly and clapped Sir Berowne on the shoulder. 'Just one last question, Father. Can you tell me the names of any persons hereabouts who might ask for Celia's help if they were in trouble of any sort? Mistress Rokeswood did mention that Celia occasionally took food to one or two of the families near the Gate.'

The priest seemed vaguely surprised to hear this and said austerely he was unaware that the Godslove family had ever assisted any of the poor in the vicinity. I think it was the first time I realized that, taken as a whole, he did not like them very much. Until then, I had thought him their friend – and no doubt there were some members he preferred to the others – but his tone of voice was suddenly cool and even a little hostile. He must have been aware of it himself because he became anxious to make amends.

'I'm not saying that they don't,' he added hurriedly. 'It's just that I've never heard it mentioned.'

I wanted to reassure him that I didn't care for the Godsloves myself and could hardly blame him if he didn't either. They

were not, in my estimation, a lovable family, but somehow
I was unable to say the words. I was a guest in their house
and they were, however tenuously, related to my wife. So I
thanked him for his help and said I would make enquiries
in the cottages and at the Bedlam and St Mary's Hospital
before returning to the Arbour to tell them what he had
told me.

As I turned away, I heard my name shouted yet again and
saw Oswald Godslove riding like a madman towards me. He
drew rein and fairly fell out of the saddle, his face white,
his limbs shaking. He clutched at my sleeve.

'Celia,' he croaked. 'One of the girls came to find me at
the courts. Says she's missing.' He could barely get the words
out. 'S-say it's not true!'

'I'm afraid it is,' I said, supporting him about the waist.
'She hasn't been seen since this morning, but we don't know
for certain that any harm has befallen her. Indeed,' I went
on bracingly, 'it's more than probable she'll turn up again
soon, alive and well.'

Oswald made no answer, and, with a little moan, burst
into tears.

The priest aimed an ineffectual pat at his back, missed,
then stood looking at me, faintly embarrassed. I tightened
my grip on Oswald and urged him to complete his journey.

'Your sisters will be glad to see you,' I said. 'They'll tell
you all that's happened. Meantime, I'm going to make a few
enquiries of my own, but I'll join you at the Arbour just as
soon as I've done so. Pull yourself together, man.' Oswald's
noisy sobs were beginning to attract unwelcome attention.
'Father Berowne and I are both agreed that there is probably nothing to worry about. Celia may have gone on an
errand of mercy and will return of her own accord shortly.
But, as I said, Clemency and Sybilla will explain everything
to you.'

Oswald knuckled his eyes like a child and, also like a
child, turned on me viciously, transmuting his fear into anger
and venting it on my innocent head.

'Of course you're not worried! What's Celia to you? Or
him?'

He flung out a hand, catching the priest a painful blow

on the side of his jaw. I wondered if it were as accidental as it appeared to be, and I saw the same thought flicker at the back of Father Berowne's eyes, but his expression of concern didn't alter, nor did he raise a hand to rub his face.

'You're overwrought, Master Godslove. Go home,' he said, adding his voice to mine. 'While Master Chapman, here, knocks on a door or two, allow me to walk as far as the Arbour with you. I'll lead the horse. Short as the distance is, you're in no fit state to ride.'

This kindly offer was spurned, not in words but in action. Oswald flung himself back into the saddle and galloped off up the track, at a pace which forced all oncoming traffic out of his path, with a total disregard for anyone else's convenience.

The priest sighed. 'We must make allowances for a very frightened man,' he said magnanimously, at the same time tenderly feeling his jaw. 'Now, away you go, my son, and make your enquiries. And God grant that you discover something useful as to where Mistress Celia might have gone, or even where she is, and put her poor family out of their misery.'

An hour later, footsore and weary, hoarse from asking the same question over and over again, and depressed from receiving the same negative answer each and every time, I returned to the Arbour no wiser as to Celia's whereabouts than when I set out. I did not see Father Berowne, but I heard vespers being sung as I passed St Botolph's church, a reminder that I had been lax in my attendance of late. I couldn't remember the last occasion on which I had been to confession.

As I passed the almshouses, I overtook a small, weary figure trudging up the road and recognized it as one of the Godsloves' kitchen maids; the one, presumably, who had been sent to Westminster to fetch Oswald home. I offered her my arm to which she clung gratefully.

'Couldn't your master have taken you up behind him?' I asked indignantly.

The girl looked shocked. 'Oh, no, sir! He'd never do that. He would never overburden his horses, and besides—'

'Besides what?'

'Well, he wouldn't want to be seen with the likes of me, now would he, sir? Him a smart lawyer and all.' She turned her head to look at me, taking in my brown hose and green tunic with its silver gilt buttons, and finally my hat with its fake jewel on the upturned brim. 'And you're looking very fine, sir. Are you sure you don't mind being seen with me?'

'Of course not! You're a very pretty girl.' I felt suddenly angry with Oswald and was made sharply aware of how much I disliked the man. Perhaps, after all, it was not impossible that someone, somewhere, wanted to harm him and his.

'Is there any news of Mistress Celia?' my companion asked as we left the houses behind and rounded the bend into open countryside, the Arbour, set in its rambling garden, coming into view.

'No, nothing, I'm afraid. I've been making enquiries around the Bishop's Gate in the hope that she was visiting one of the cottages there, but no one's seen her. I even asked at the hospital and the Bedlam, but to no avail. Everybody knows her by sight, of course, but very few know her to speak to. Mistress Rokeswood said she took soup and bread to the poorer families, but I don't think it was true.'

The girl shook her head. 'I've never seen her do so. Master Godslove wouldn't let her, for one thing. He'd be too frightened she'd catch something nasty off one of 'em. He's that fond of Mistress Celia, you wouldn't believe.' There was nothing in her tone to suggest she found this circumstance in any way odd, and she went on, 'I suppose it's because of that terrible secret they all share.'

I caught my breath. 'What secret?' I asked, my voice coming out as a croak.

Our feet had been dragging for the past few yards, and now we both came to a halt. The girl turned her head and regarded me with concern.

'Are you getting the rheum, sir? You really ought to be careful. You only got up out o' your sickbed yesterday. You shouldn't be running about like this.'

'No, no! I'm quite all right,' I answered hurriedly. 'What terrible secret do they all share?'

'Sir?'

'You just said that Master Godslove and his family share a terrible secret. What secret?'

She laughed, taking my arm once more as we slowly resumed our walk.

'Lord, sir, if I knew that it wouldn't be a secret, now would it?'

'Well, then—' I was beginning impatiently, but she interrupted me.

'It was just something I overheard once when nobody knew I was by. Mistress Rokeswood had sent me to fetch a bowl she needed from the big cupboard in the dining parlour, and the window was open into the garden. Master Oswald and Mistress Clemency were outside, talking about the attack on Master Martin. Him that was killed when he was set on by footpads,' she added by way of explanation.

'Yes, yes! I know about that! Go on, girl! Go on!'

She eyed me curiously, and I could see her wondering if she ought to say anything further. But she continued, 'Well, Mistress Clemency was saying she thought the attack hadn't been footpads at all. Leastways, not real ones. She thought they were people who'd been paid to murder Master Martin, and that someone was trying to kill the lot of them, one at a time. Master Oswald wouldn't have it. Said she was talking nonsense. Who'd want to do such a thing, he said. And why?'

We had stopped again, outside the Arbour garden wall, close to the gate. 'Go on,' I urged my companion as she paused for breath.

'Well, then Mistress Clemency said something about the terrible secret they all shared, but the master told her not to be so foolish. No one knew about it except themselves. He said, sort of sharpish, "You haven't told Arbella, have you?" That's Mistress Rokeswood.' I nodded and she went on, 'Mistress Clemency said she'd never breathed a word to anyone, ever, and Master Oswald said that was all right, then.' The girl's forehead puckered momentarily. 'But he did say something rather odd.'

'What?'

'He said something like, "After all, they never knew themselves, did they? So we're quite safe." And he laughed. After that he and Mistress Clemency moved away and I didn't hear any more. I took the bowl and went back to the kitchen and got a right telling-off from Mistress Rokeswood for having been so long.'

I took a deep breath. 'Have you ever told anyone else about this?' I asked. 'About what you overheard?'

The girl shook her head. 'I never give it another thought, really. Not until this minute. I didn't understand it prop'ly, so I forgot it. Should I have done?'

'No, by no means. You're sure you didn't even tell your little workmate?'

The girl snorted. 'And have her snitching on me that I'd been eavesdropping on the master and his sister? I'd have lost my place as quick as winking. Same if I'd told Mistress Rokeswood. I just forgot about it.' A sudden doubt shook her. 'You won't go telling on me, will you, sir? I didn't mean to say anything to you. It just popped out somehow, when we were talking.'

'I won't say anything,' I promised her, 'not to anyone. Not even my wife.'

But I shan't forget it, either, I thought as we entered the Arbour garden and approached the house, my companion to drag her weary limbs round to the back door and thence into the kitchen – where she would doubtless receive scant sympathy for her long, dusty walk to Westminster and back – and I to join Adela and the remaining Godsloves in the hall.

As I entered, four pairs of eyes swivelled in my direction.

'Roger!' Adela exclaimed, starting towards me. 'Have you any news of Celia?'

I sank down thankfully on to one of the settles, easing my legs out before me. 'No, nothing I'm afraid. At least, not this side of the Bishop's Gate. I didn't go further. Father Berowne is the only person who thinks he might have caught a glimpse of her sometime this morning. But even he isn't sure. He thinks there might have been someone with her, but again, he can't be certain.'

Sybilla burst into noisy sobbing, but while Adela and Clemency went to comfort her, a white-faced Oswald, who seemed to have regained a precarious control over his emotions, announced savagely, 'Your efforts were a total waste of time, my dear Roger. Any fool could have told you that. It's as plain as the nose on your face that Roderick Jeavons is the villain of this affair. I've heard how he accosted Celia in the garden and inflicted his unwelcome attentions on her.'

'But according to Elizabeth and Nicholas, he went away again,' I pointed out. 'He didn't force Celia to go with him.'

'Not then, no. But your other son overheard her talking to someone later. It's perfectly obvious to all but the meanest intelligence' – mine, I supposed – 'that he returned and persuaded her to accompany him somewhere or other.'

'But would Celia have gone with him,' I protested, 'in view of their previous quarrel?'

'God knows what blandishments and persuasive arguments he used to lure her away. Celia has far, far too kind a heart. She can be so easily led, particularly by a rogue such as Roderick Jeavons. Why, once he even persuaded her into a betrothal against her will.'

'Are you sure it was against her will?' I asked quietly. Adela sent me a warning glance, but I chose to ignore it. 'Couldn't she have been genuinely in love with the man?'

Oswald turned on me as though I had uttered the worst kind of blasphemy. He was shaking with temper and his eyes burned with fury in his parchment-coloured face.

'Celia would never have married him! Never! She would never have deserted the rest of us.' He gave a wild sob that caught in his throat, before once more making a visible effort to take himself in hand. 'In those days, of course, Charity and Martin were still alive. We were a close-knit, loving family. Celia would never seriously have considered leaving us for a stranger. But Roderick Jeavons has been trying for years to make her change her mind, all to no avail, and now he's become desperate. He's abducted her by force.'

'In broad daylight?' My tone was sceptical.

Oswald's voice rose almost to a shout. 'He's lured her away with some story or another, I tell you, and then imprisoned her.' The spittle flecked his lips. 'That's why we're going straight away, now, to visit him.'

'We?'

'You have to come with me, Roger. He's more likely to

admit the truth if he's confronted by two of us instead of one.'

'No.' It was my wife who spoke in the tone of voice she reserved for the children when she intended to brook no argument. 'Roger has been ill. He only got up yesterday. He has already over-taxed his strength with all he's done today. He looks worn out and I insist that he rests.'

Oswald and his sisters looked shocked. 'After all we've done for you, Adela,' Sybilla breathed accusingly.

The colour suffused my wife's face, but she stood her ground. 'I'm aware of that, Sybilla, and I'm very grateful, believe me. But I will not have Roger's health put at risk.'

'Roger's health!' Oswald flung back at her. 'What's that compared to the fact that Celia's life might be endangered?'

At this point, Arbella arrived to tell us that supper was ready at last, urging us to come to table before it got cold, only to find her words falling on deaf ears. Clemency informed her brusquely that no one present felt like eating, but to see that the children were fed.

'What is this nonsense?' the housekeeper demanded angrily, adding gruffly, 'Celia wouldn't want you to make yourselves ill, you know, whatever has happened to her.' She glanced towards Oswald and real concern lit her eyes. She laid a hand on his arm. 'My dear man, you look done to death. Come and get some food inside you, and if Celia still isn't home by the time you've finished, then go and alert the Watch, the sheriff's men or whoever you think fit, but—'

Oswald flung off her hand and turned on her, his features contorted with fury. He was a desperately frightened man and, as before, his fear was transformed into rage. If I hadn't begun to dislike him so much, I could have found it in my heart to be sorry for him.

'Don't call me your dear man,' he hissed, 'and don't ever lay a hand, unbidden, on me, again. You can throw supper out for the pigs for all I care. Get Old Diggory saddled. Master Chapman and I are riding to Dr Jeavon's house and demand that he tell us what he's done with Celia.'

Arbella Rokeswood's face had turned as red as his was white, and she was breathing short and fast. Her whole body was rigid with humiliation and suppressed rage. I saw her hands clench into fists, but she said nothing, swinging abruptly on her heel and going out of the hall, walking blindly as though unaware of what she was doing or where she was going.

'You shouldn't have spoken to her like that, my dear,' Clemency said unhappily. 'You've hurt her feelings. Besides,' she added tentatively, 'Adela's right. It would be foolish for you or Roger to neglect yourselves and become ill. What good would either of you be to Celia then?'

I could see that Oswald was more than tempted to brush this good advice aside; his impatience to be gone was palpable. But he was a lawyer, with a lawyer's logical mind, and he knew that what Clemency said made sense.

'Very well,' he breathed at last. 'One of you run and tell Arbella that we'll come at once, but there's to be no delay in serving the food.' As Sybilla hurried from the room, Oswald rounded on Adela. 'And keep those children quiet. I'm in no mood for their chatter.'

At that moment I was very close to rounding up my wife, my children and my dog and quitting the Arbour altogether, leaving this unpleasant family to wallow in their misery and sort matters out for themselves. Moreover, if what my little friend, the kitchen maid, had told me were true, then their troubles might well be of their own making. According to her, Clemency had referred to a 'terrible secret' which the Godsloves all shared, and which Oswald had not denied. Had she heard aright? Was there the slightest possibility that she could have mistaken what was said? I didn't think it likely. And then there was Oswald's reply. 'After all, they didn't know themselves, did they?' I longed to demand an explanation, but without betraying the girl's confidence and probably getting her dismissed, my hands – or, at least, my tongue – was tied.

Supper was eaten in almost complete silence. Adela had no need to keep the children quiet, the atmosphere alone was sufficient to dampen their usual high spirits. Hercules was not present, nor was Arbella Rokeswood. She made the excuse of having the horses to saddle, and although my wife would again have protested against my accompanying Oswald, I gave a little shake of the head. My natural curiosity, now thoroughly aroused, would not allow me to abandon the investigation at this juncture, and the excellent food and wine were sufficient to reinvigorate me. It had been a very long day, it was true, and one full, if not over-full, of incident, but I knew I could summon up from somewhere enough energy to see it through.

Oswald and I rode back into the city, passing under the Bishop's Gate arch where the workmen were still toiling away on this fine Mayday evening, an overseer from the Steelyard continuing to hover in the background, keeping a beady eye cocked for anyone who might feel like slacking.

'Where does Dr Jeavons live?' I enquired as we rode down Bishop's Gate Street and approached the outer wall of Crosby's Place, where the morning's activity had slackened somewhat so that only a solitary cart, and an empty one at that, stood outside its gates. Of Timothy Plummer there was, of course, no sign.

'Not far from Alder's Gate, in Old Dean's Lane. Near St Paul's,' my companion grunted, in between roundly cursing everyone and everything that impeded his progress. 'I knew we shouldn't have wasted time eating,' he snarled, as we were again forced to pull the horses into one side of the road in order to let a troop of men, all wearing Lord Hastings's livery, overtake us.

It seemed to me that the mood of the city was gloomier than that of the morning, when people had at least roused themselves to go out maying, and when news of the three arrests at Northampton had not really had time to sink in. Now, as we rode along Cheapside, through Paternoster Row and turned into Old Dean's Lane, faces were even more solemn, the street cries of the vendors even more muted as if, I thought, people were bracing themselves – but for what?

'Here we are!' Oswald had reined in outside a three-storey house about halfway along the lane. He threw himself out of the saddle and, without bothering to tether his horse, hammered with both fists on its nail-studded, oaken front door.

THIRTEEN

I t was answered by a tall woman, sharp-featured and thin to the point of emaciation. In spite of this, it was nevertheless possible to recognize an elusive resemblance to Roderick Jeavons – there was a similarity about the eyes – and I guessed her to be his sister. Oswald, however, noting only the bunch of keys at her waist and the gown of brown homespun beneath an apron as white and spotless as her coif, at once assumed her to be the doctor's housekeeper. He would have pushed past her into the house had she not showed a surprising strength in barring his way.

'Let me in, my good woman,' he snapped. 'I need to speak to your master.'

'My brother,' she replied firmly, 'is not here. He was called away urgently this afternoon to attend the deathbed of an uncle of ours in Barnet. If you require a physician, there is one in—'

'You're lying!' Oswald roared, causing several passers-by to turn and stare. One even fingered the dagger at his belt, as though wondering if he should come to the protection of a goodwife being harassed by a couple of ruffians.

I laid a restraining hand on my companion's arm. 'Calm down, man, calm down.' I turned to the doctor's sister. 'Mistress . . . Jeavons, is it?'

'Ireby,' she corrected with dignity. 'I am a widow, sir, and have kept house for Roderick for a year now, ever since my husband died. May I know who you and this . . . this gentleman are?'

'For God's sake, Roger,' Oswald exclaimed, 'stop wasting time!' And without further ado, he forced his way past Mistress Ireby. 'Where is she?' he demanded. 'What has your brother done with my sister?'

He began to yell the doctor's name. Hurriedly, I closed the street door and, turning to a by now very frightened woman, attempted to explain the situation. And it said much for Mistress Ireby's strength of character that she not only listened to what I had to say, but having grasped the gist of my story, exhibited a certain amount of sympathy and understanding. But she was highly indignant that her brother should be thought capable of such a dastardly act as abduction.

'I know of this Celia Godslove, of course. Roderick has, naturally, talked of her to me. I know him to be in love with her. But that he would try to coerce her . . . How can you suppose such a thing?'

To his credit, Oswald did momentarily look a little ashamed of himself, but the next minute he announced his intention of searching the premises and, without waiting for Mistress Ireby's permission, stormed off to do so. He returned a little while later, frustrated and angered by his lack of success, but still unconvinced of Dr Jeavons's innocence.

'Is there a cellar to this house?'

'No, there is not,' our unwilling hostess retorted. She had by now recovered both her poise and her courage and would no longer allow herself to be intimidated. She drew herself up to her full height and turned on Oswald. 'You fool!' she upbraided him scornfully. 'Do you think I wouldn't know if my brother had returned home with an unwilling woman? Do you think she wouldn't have set up a screech? Do you think the neighbours wouldn't have heard? You're at liberty to interrogate them if you wish. I'm sure they'll tell you that they heard nothing.'

'He might have drugged Celia,' Oswald argued. 'He's a doctor, after all, and has such things in his medicine chest. And how do I know you're not aiding and abetting him? You might be in this together.'

'And why would I want your sister here?' Mistress Ireby scoffed. 'I've no wish for my brother to get married again. At least, not since the death of my husband. I've been very comfortable here these past twelve months, caring for Roderick. I have no desire to live alone.'

I doubted if Oswald had heard much of this. He was chewing his lower lip and pursuing some thought of his own.

'You say your brother has gone to visit an uncle at Barnet. Whereabouts exactly does this man live?'

Mistress Ireby sucked in her breath. Her eyes were like flints.

'I have told you, my uncle is reported to be on his deathbed. Do you really suppose I would give you his direction so that you could blunder in with your wild accusations against Roderick and disturb his final hours? Get out of this house now, Master Godslove, before I summon my neighbours to help eject you.'

'We're going, Mistress,' I said gently, 'but before we do, would you be gracious enough to describe to us your brother's movements today. We know that he was at the Arbour this morning after breakfast and had words with Celia.'

'Words!' Oswald interjected furiously. 'He damned well forced his unwelcome attentions on her if your children are to be believed.'

I frowned him down. 'Did he return here afterwards, Mistress Ireby?'

Her thin bosom swelled and, ignoring Oswald, she addressed herself to me. 'Roderick did return for his dinner, yes. Then he went out to see one of his patients in Paternoster Row, and it was while he was gone that a man servant of our uncle's arrived to request his presence urgently at Barnet. As I told you, our uncle is thought to be dying. When Roderick returned, he paused merely to pack a few necessaries in his saddlebag and he was off. He told me to expect him when I see him. There's no telling how long Uncle Silas might linger.'

I thanked her again for her courtesy, took Oswald firmly by the arm and led him out to the patiently waiting horses. He was my host and I could hardly criticize his behaviour, but as we rode back through the city, I did venture to remark that Roderick Jeavons seemed to be innocent of whatever had befallen Celia.

'If you think that, you're a simpleton,' he answered scornfully. 'I'm not at all convinced that he knows nothing. In fact, I intend having that house watched for the next few days, and I'm entrusting the task to you, my dear Roger.'

I was so taken aback that I found myself unable to utter a single word of protest, and we completed our journey in almost total silence, passing out through the Bishop's Gate with only minutes to spare before the curfew bell tolled. (We heard the gate creak shut as we drew abreast of St Mary's

Hospital.) But I had plenty to say to Adela as we fell wearily into bed after what seemed like one of the longest days of my life. (I had hoped against hope that Celia might have returned during our absence with some perfectly reasonable explanation for her disappearance, but the long faces of the women had told their own story.)

Adela said now, snuggling into my side, 'You really aren't perfectly well yet, sweetheart, but I don't see that you can refuse. And they are all in such distress, and so frightened after the other dreadful things that have happened to them, and they have all been so kind to me during the past few weeks that it would be worse than churlish to say no.'

It was on the tip of my tongue to point out that if she had trusted me more, been less willing to believe Juliette Gerrish's pack of lies, we would be under no obligation to the Godsloves: we would never have set eyes on them nor become involved in their sorry saga. But suddenly I felt too tired, too bone-weary even to speak. I could hear the children's muffled snorts and snufflings from the neighbouring room, reassuring sounds that there was some sanity left in a world that suddenly seemed bleak and menacing, so I put my arm around Adela and went to sleep.

For the next two days, while Oswald half-heartedly pursued his calling, either in chambers, off Chancery Lane, or in the law courts at Westminster – I felt sorry for his clients who could not possibly have been commanding his full attention – I spent much of my time in and around Old Dean's Lane, watching for signs of Roderick Jeavons's return. On more than one occasion, when Mistress Ireby left the house, I had to dodge about on the opposite side of the street, hoping she would not notice me, and I lived on meat pies and small beer obtained from vendors of these commodities in Westcheap. This diet, plus the conviction that I was wasting precious hours when I could be pursuing other lines of enquiry else-where, in no way improved my temper or my digestion. On Saturday evening, therefore, I told Oswald bluntly that in future, while I was prepared to visit Old Dean's Lane once a day until I was satisfied that the doctor had finally come home, I refused to hang around the district all day, every day.

'It's folly,' I said. 'I shall be bound to know when he's returned.'

Oswald, whose features were as ravaged as his sisters' and whose eyes were like two dark bruises from lack of proper sleep, was forced, in the end, to agree with me.

'But we'll go together tomorrow,' he insisted, 'after Mass. We'll all go to St Botolph's in the morning to pray for Celia's safe return . . .'

His voice broke and he pushed aside his half-eaten supper with a trembling hand, an act which set Clemency and Sybilla off crying again, the former quietly, the latter with her customary noisy abandon. Hercules, who had somehow managed to creep unseen into the dining parlour, started to howl in sympathy. Elizabeth, Nicholas and Adam were looking frightened and Adela shepherded them away to play upstairs. She pressed Clemency's shoulder as she passed her cousin's chair, but I could see that she, too, was beginning to wish we were well out of a situation that seemed to grow more dark and menacing with every passing day. The Arbour, with its increasingly fraught and fearful atmosphere, was fast becoming no place for children.

In bed that night, we talked again of returning home, and this time Adela agreed with me. But, yet again, we decided that to do so would be both mean and cowardly. Adela would have to devote herself to keeping the children – and, of course, the dog – amused, while I did my best to unravel the mystery of who hated the Godslove family enough to try to kill them.

'Have you,' I asked, 'ever heard any one of them mention, or perhaps hint at, something in their past that could be in any way . . . disgraceful?'

Adela raised her head from my shoulder and stared up into my face, her forehead, as far as I could see in the gloom, creased in puzzlement. 'No, never. Why? Do you know of something?'

I broke my promise and told her what the little kitchen maid had said to me, having first obtained her promise to utter not a word to anyone else about it. But when I had finished, she was as bemused as I was.

'The child must have been mistaken in what she heard.

Or thought she heard. What possible secret – "terrible secret" – could any of them possibly have?'

I kissed her. 'If we knew that, my love, we might have a better idea of who it is who is trying to murder them all.'

'You don't really believe it?' Her tone was indignant. 'They have their faults like all of us, but essentially they're very good people.'

They were related to her by blood, however remotely, and she did not care to believe ill of them. Moreover, as she kept repeating, they had been kind to her.

'It's quite possible that the girl was mistaken,' I answered soothingly, but kept my true opinion to myself: that the household was a peculiar one; that the almost lover-like devotion of the siblings was unhealthy and unnatural, a potential breeding ground for evil. 'Go to sleep now and forget about it.'

I would have made love to her, but my wife is a good daughter of Holy Church, which decrees that copulation is sinful before going to Mass. So I lay staring into the darkness, stifling my urges, listening to Adela's even breathing as she sank deeper into slumber, longing for home and wondering where it would all end, and when.

The five of us with the children and Arbella – and it struck me forcibly that the Godsloves, who had originally been six in number were now only three – went to St Botolph's, before breakfast, for early Mass. (St Botolph, I'm ashamed to confess, was not a saint I was well acquainted with, although I knew that in Lincolnshire he was considered of sufficient importance to have a town named in his honour. Unhappily for the poor man, due to our lazy English predilection for shortening everything whenever possible, St Botolph's Town had rapidly become St Bo's Town, and is nowadays called simply Boston.) The other members of the congregation, standing together in the nave, eyed Oswald and his sisters curiously, having been alerted by my questioning to Celia's disappearance; but either they were not on sufficient terms of intimacy with the family, or were too indifferent, to enquire further. The only person anxious for news was Father Berowne, who, as soon as the service was over, scurried across to Oswald, laying an eager hand upon his shoulder.

'Have you heard anything?'

Oswald shook his head. 'But we are keeping a watch on Dr Jeavons's house, near Alder's Gate. We think he may know something.'

The priest's eyes widened in surprise and he was plainly agog to hear more, but Oswald hurried us all away, back to the Arbour. Thankfully, Arbella insisted that he and I stay and eat breakfast, plying us with hot porridge, oatmeal cakes and honey and pickled herrings.

'You'll make yourselves ill if you don't eat properly,' she scolded, 'and I repeat, where will that get you? You'll be of no use to Celia if you're laid up in bed.'

There was much to be said for this common sense view of things, but I regret to say that I was the only one, apart from the children, who took her advice and made a hearty meal, a fact which earned me reproachful looks from the others. But my appetite had returned, and after a week of near starvation when I was sick, I needed to build up my strength.

A Sabbath calm reigned as Oswald and I rode through the Bishop's Gate, and I could see that the work was nearly finished. There was only one small stretch of wall still under repair and that would probably need less than a week to complete. But the site of Sybilla's accident reminded me of something I had been meaning to say.

I turned to my companion. 'It occurs to me that this enemy of yours must have money.'

'Why do you say that?' Oswald spoke sharply.

'Because, if we're right, he, or she, has already bribed someone to kill your stepbrother, Reynold Makepeace, and your half-brother Martin, and someone else to attempt the murder of Sybilla. You don't persuade ruffians to do that sort of work for a pittance. If they're caught it means Tyburn and the rope's end for them. And then again, you have to know where to find these people.'

'You're right.' Oswald took a deep breath. 'And who fits that description better than Roderick Jeavons? I've never yet encountered a poor physician, and I happen to know that he inherited money from his wife. Besides which, he has a large practice. He probably meets all kinds and conditions

of people, some of whom most likely can't pay his bills.
Threatened with the debtors' prison, I've no doubt some
of them would be desperate enough to carry out his evil
work for him. Don't you see? He's been trying to scare
Celia into marrying him, but now he's grown too impatient
to wait any longer and he's abducted her.'

I was about to point out the many flaws in this convenient
theory, but at that moment we were brought to a standstill
by total confusion outside of Crosby's Place. Carts were again
blocking the road while sweating workmen carried in yet
more furniture and a number of leather, brass-bound clothes
chests.

I leant from the saddle and tapped the nearest man on the
shoulder. 'What's going on?' I asked. 'I understood, from what
I heard one of you fellows say, that Duke Richard is going to
stay at Baynard's Castle with his mother. That is, when he
finally gets here.'

The man turned a hot, red face up to mine. 'Well, he's got
here, Master Nosey,' he snapped. 'Leastways, he's getting here
today. This morning sometime. And 'e can't go to Baynard's
Castle 'cause Duchess Cicely ain't in London yet, so it's all
hands to the pump here, I'll tell you! Look, you and your
friend'll have to wait until we get these coffers in, then we'll
move one o' them carts out yer way.'

'Is the king with him?'

'O' course the king's with him! They were leaving St
Albans at the crack o' dawn, and the mayor and aldermen
have all ridden to meet 'em. Where you been? Don't you
know nothing? Look, I've got to get on. The king and his
party'll be riding in through the Cripples' Gate any time
soon.'

The speaker and his mate strained and heaved the
remaining chest on to their shoulders and vanished through
the gates of Crosby's Place. I raised my eyebrows and looked
at Oswald, but he seemed as bemused as I was and shook
his head.

'I must admit I've heard nothing,' he mumbled guiltily.
'At least, if I have, it . . . it just hasn't sunk in.'

The truth was, of course, that we had both been so absorbed
by the riddle of Celia's disappearance that the rumours and

murmurings in the city had completely passed us by. Events in the larger world had ceased to interest us. But now it seemed that, at long last, on this Sunday morning, the fourth of May – on what had originally been designated his coronation day by the Woodvilles, had their plans not miscarried – the young king was finally about to enter his capital, three and a half weeks after his father's death.

Even if we had been inclined to doubt our informant's word, we should have been convinced of his veracity long before we reached the Poultry and pushed our way on towards West Cheap. Not only was the Great Conduit running with wine instead of water, but the mass of people had become so dense that we were forced to dismount and proceed on foot, stabling the horses at a convenient inn. Fortunately, Oswald had chosen to don his lawyer's robe, which gave him instant authority amongst the crowd, while I had been bullied by Adela into wearing my second set of decent clothing, blue hose and a yellow tunic, and my despised hat, with its fake jewel and upturned brim. I therefore looked to be a citizen of some substance, a totally erroneous impression which my height and girth did nothing to dispel.

At the corner of Wood Street, where the road from the Cripples' Gate joins the Cheap, it was almost impossible to move for the press of bodies hemming us in on all sides. Nevertheless, by dint of much shoving and heaving on my part and haughty glares from my companion, Oswald and I managed to force a passage through the crowds until we were very nearly in the front row of those being held back by a line of men-at-arms. And here we had to remain, it being impossible to go any further until the royal party had entered the city and passed us by. Oswald might fume, but I was curious to see our new young king and was glad of the enforced delay.

But as I peered over the heads of those in front of me, all I could see at the present moment were four great carts, rumbling and swaying across the cobbles, piled with weapons and armour. I turned to my neighbour, a large, red-faced man, who informed me that he was a chandler by trade, for enlightenment.

'What's going on?' I shouted, trying to make myself heard

above the clang and clatter of the bells from a hundred churches.

He yelled something in reply that I didn't quite catch, but then, thankfully, some of the bell ringers took a rest from their labours and the noise diminished a little.

'They say,' the chandler repeated, dropping his voice to a more conversational level, 'that these are the weapons gathered by Earl Rivers and the rest of the Woodvilles for use against the Duke of Gloucester when they planned to take him prisoner at Stony Stratford.' He nudged me in the ribs. 'Here you are! Here are the criers now, to cry the tale.'

And indeed men in the Gloucester livery, men with stentorian voices, had caught up with the wagons and were repeating the same story to the crowds. 'See! Here are the Woodville arms, the family crest and motto on this piece of harness. And on this! It was intended to overwhelm His Grace's forces and take His Grace, himself, prisoner. And who can say but that his life, itself, may have been in danger!'

There was much more in the same vein before the wagons and the criers passed on to regale the crowds waiting in Cheapside and the vicinity of St Paul's with the same information. I heard a good deal of indignant muttering among the people around me, and cries of, 'Hang the bastards!' or 'Hanging's too good for 'em!' But I also noticed that quite a few of my neighbours, including the chandler, looked sceptical.

'You don't believe in this plot against the Duke of Gloucester?' I asked him.

He pursed his lips. 'We-ell . . . Frankly, I dunno what to think, sir. (Adela was right: decent clothes certainly fooled people.) What do we know about the man, after all? He's lived away up north for years and years.' The chandler spoke of the north, as did most southerners of my acquaintance, as though it were the dark side of the moon. 'Oh, he's been in London now and again, I grant you, but not for any length of time. Not so's you could get to know him. He was always loyal to the late king, I grant him that; not like the other one, the Duke of Clarence. Regular turncoat he was. But as I say . . .' He broke off, shrugging, then added, 'All those arms and things they just showed us, they could be left over from the Scottish campaign, last year.'

'You don't believe the Woodvilles would try to seize power?' I felt in duty bound to defend Duke Richard, even though I felt a worm of doubt wriggling around in my own entrails. I suppressed it firmly. 'Do you know that Sir Edward Woodville has put to sea, taking half the royal treasure with him? And if there was no plot against the duke, why did Queen Elizabeth rush into sanctuary as soon as she heard of her brother's and son's arrest?'

My new friend was saved from answering by the sudden pealing forth again of the bells as the ringers returned to the fray with renewed vigour, refreshed by their well-earned break. Moreover, the cheering from higher up Wood Street was growing louder and more insistent by the minute. A moment later, the first of the City fathers, resplendent in fur-trimmed scarlet, came into view, followed by three hundred of the most eminent burgesses, dressed in violet velvet. Then came the Lord Mayor and his aldermen and the hundreds of Welshmen who had accompanied the king from Ludlow, together with my lord of Gloucester's Yorkshire troops. It was probably a good half hour before the last of them had passed, and the impatience of the crowd had reached a pitch of frenzy that had become not only unpleasant, but dangerous as well as bodies pressed against one another on all sides, making it almost impossible to breathe. I was sweating profusely and, glancing at Oswald, I was afraid that he might be going to faint.

There was a sudden, blessed lull in the shouting and cheering before it started up again, but this time laced with a quieter, more reverential note. The 'oohs' and 'aahs' of the women onlookers, further up Wood Street, could be detected amongst the more vociferous greetings of the men, and we guessed that the young king had finally come into view. It must, however, have been another ten minutes or so before he reached the turning into West Cheap, but at the eventual sight of him people, even men, choked with emotion and several women burst into tears.

He rode a white palfrey and was dressed in blue velvet, that fair hair, which he inherited from both his parents, gleaming in the pale spring sunlight; 'Almost,' breathed some fanciful person behind me, carried away by the emotion of the moment, 'as if he has been blessed by heaven.' (I could see that sentimentality was going to be the order of the day.) On his right hand rode his uncle of Gloucester, and on his left – somewhat, I think, to everyone's surprise – his uncle-by-marriage, Henry Stafford, Duke of Buckingham. Both men were arrayed in unrelieved mourning black, with not a jewel nor any splash of colour in sight; and the unfortunate impression conveyed to my eyes, at least, and no doubt to some others, was that of a prisoner escorted by his gaolers.

It was an impression underscored by the expression of bewilderment and sullen defiance on the young sovereign's face. But then, I thought, a boy of twelve, abruptly robbed of the company of an uncle and Woodville kinsman whom he had known and trusted for all of his short life – a man he had grown up with – and thrust into the company of another uncle whom he barely knew, had every reason to be upset, if not frightened. Knowing my lord of Gloucester as I did, I had no doubt that he had not only treated his nephew with every kindness, but that he had had good reasons for his arrest of Earl Rivers and Sir Richard Grey. (Unlike the chandler, I was quite ready to believe that the wagonloads of arms belonged to the Woodvilles and had been intended for use against the duke and his retainers.) But the young king could hardly be expected to regard his Uncle Richard's actions in that light. I noticed, also, that one side of the boy's jaw seemed swollen and that he rubbed it from time to time, as though it hurt him. He was slow to respond to the crowd's ecstatic cheers of welcome, and only did so when prompted by one or the other of his uncles.

As the king and two dukes finally drew abreast of us, I could not help wondering what was going on in Prince Richard's mind. Was he remembering that information I had brought him back from France, the previous year; the story of the two christenings? Was he thinking that he was really the rightful king, and not this scion of the detested Woodvilles? The thought had barely crossed my mind before I was suddenly aware of him staring straight at me over the heads of the intervening crowds, and I saw his eyes flicker in surprise and recognition. It was only for the briefest moment, then he turned away to acknowledge the cheers of the people to his right. But I was certain he had seen me, and once again cursed my height.

It must have been yet another half hour before the tail of the procession finally passed us, but by that time everyone was congregating around St Paul's where a service of thanksgiving for the king's safe arrival was to be held. It would be impossible to push on to Old Dean's Lane and I said as much to Oswald.

He nodded wearily. 'Let's go home,' he said.

FOURTEEN

I t was not, however, to be that simple.

It seemed as if everyone in London, as well as his brother and his wife, had gathered in and around Cheapside to see the young king's entry into his capital. It was almost inevitable, therefore, that Oswald and I would chance upon someone whom we knew. Or, rather, that they would chance upon us, for neither of us was looking for company. Oswald was sullen and ill-tempered because his plans had been thwarted and yet another day must pass before one of us – in all probability me – could return to Old Dean's Lane to find out if Roderick Jeavons had at last come home.

For my part, I was busy assessing the scene I had just witnessed, particularly mulling over in my mind the angry and chagrined expression on the face of Lord Hastings, who had been riding several paces to the rear of the king, his handsome person lost among the crowd of other dignitaries and nobles pressing in upon their sovereign. I had little doubt that he was furious at this relegation to a minor role when he had had, quite justifiably, every expectation of occupying the place now usurped by Henry of Buckingham. After all, it was he who, since the death of his lifelong friend and master, King Edward IV, had constituted himself chief champion of the Duke of Gloucester against the Woodvilles, interpreting, both verbally and in writing and in the most favourable light, the former's action at Northampton. In his shoes, I should have expected to be rewarded with the distinction of being at least second-in-command to the man who was now the true ruler of the country. I could foresee trouble ahead, and was thankful that it was none of my business. But I didn't envy Timothy Plummer.

As Oswald and I turned eastwards along Cheapside – where the crowds had now thinned out, everyone hurrying towards St Paul's – making for the inn where we had stabled the horses, a hand smote me on the shoulder and a pleasant voice queried, 'Master Chapman?'

A glance behind me revealed the smiling face of Julian Makepeace, attired in his Sunday best and with an equally smiling and smartly dressed Naomi clinging to his arm. He went on, 'I thought I recognized your back. You've come, like us I suppose, to get a glimpse of our little king.' He glanced down teasingly at his housekeeper. 'Naomi, here, is near swooning with excitement. All her maternal instincts have been aroused by that angelic young face. Hers and nearly every other woman's in the crowd, I imagine.' He suddenly caught sight of my companion and jerked out his hand. 'Why, Oswald, my dear brother, how nice to see you again. We don't meet nearly often enough. Indeed, it's hard to recollect when we did last speak to one another. And how are my stepsisters? Nothing further untoward has befallen you all, I trust?'

Oswald, ignoring his stepbrother's hand, gave a groan and looked imploringly at me, plainly unable to cope with the thought of an explanation; so I drew Julian, together with his companion, into the side of the road, beneath the shelter of a shop's overhanging gable, and gave him the facts of Celia's disappearance as briefly as I could. He was horrified and at once offered his services if there was anything we thought he could do.

'Anything at all,' he insisted. 'Don't hesitate to call on me at any time. Business is not so brisk these days that I can't shut up shop for an hour or two.' He turned back to Oswald, looking doubtful. 'You say you suspect Roderick Jeavons of having a hand in Celia's disappearance? No, no, my dear brother. I think you're making a mistake, if you'll pardon my saying so. I know Dr Jeavons and I simply can't believe him capable of being the author of all your troubles; of paying someone to murder Reynold and our half-brother. Impossible!'

Oswald's face flushed a dark, angry red. 'If that's all you have to say, I'll bid you good-day, Julian. I appreciate your offer of help, but it won't be needed.'

The apothecary grimaced apologetically. 'I'm sorry, Oswald. I had no intention of offending you. And the offer stands. If there is any way at all in which I can be useful . . .'

'We'll let you know at once,' I said. 'And thank you.'

He nodded, smiled ruefully and walked away, Naomi still clutching his arm. I stared after him for a moment or two, unable to fathom why the sight of him suddenly made me feel so uneasy. Something he had once said to me – or was it, perhaps, something that he had not said? I was no longer certain – gnawed at the edges of my mind, but try as I might, I still could not work out what it was.

Oswald thumped me on the back. 'Let's get on,' he said. His tone was surly, and I bit back the retort that if he did not treat people with more consideration, he would find himself without support. But then I recollected what he and his family had suffered, were still suffering, and thought better of it.

'Very well,' I agreed. 'There's nothing further to be done today.'

But once again, we were not allowed to escape so easily. Yet another hand on my shoulder accosted me for a second time, but on this occasion it was a woman's voice that spoke my name.

'Roger! How pleasant! We meet once more.'

Ginèvre Napier.

Forcing a smile, I bowed over the hand she extended towards me, and then, in answer to her raised eyebrows and pointed glance in Oswald's direction, felt in duty bound to perform the introduction. He grunted something in reply to her civil words, his impatience to be gone almost palpable, but it would take more than a little discourtesy to deter Ginèvre.

'I'm surprised your sisters aren't with you, Master Godslove. And your wife, Roger. I would have expected a glimpse of our new little king – and such a pretty child, even if he does favour his mother's family too much for my taste – would have appealed to them more than to you two men, hard-hearted creatures that you are.'

I could have told her that such coquettishness was wasted on a man like my companion, impervious as he was to any female charms apart from those of his sisters. But instead I drew her aside and, yet again, repeated the story of Celia's disappearance and the real reason for our presence in Cheapside.

'We are about to return home,' I said in conclusion.

'There's small chance of pressing on to Old Dean's Lane now. The crowds around St Paul's will be thicker than flies in summer.'

She agreed, adding, 'I, myself, am simply wasting time until I can comfortably return to Paternoster Row. Although I daresay that if I spoke some kind gentleman fair, he would force a passage for me amongst the crowds.'

This was so suggestive a remark that, in another second, I would have found myself offering to be her escort, had not an unwelcome diversion occurred in the person of the silversmith, Adrian Jollifant. Until that moment, I had failed to appreciate that we were standing directly outside his shop, and his sudden appearance with his key in his hand, preparatory to letting himself in, came as an unexpected shock. (He had evidently been as far as St Paul's, but decided that enough was enough and had returned home for a little peace and quiet.)

He did not immediately recognize either Oswald or myself, pausing merely to greet Ginèvre as an old acquaintance. She, recalling our conversation of three days earlier, did make a momentary effort to distract him, but then that malicious streak in her nature surfaced and she deliberately drew his attention to Oswald's presence.

'You know Lawyer Godslove, I think.'

The silversmith spun round, his face white with anger. 'Y-you!' he spluttered. 'W-what are you doing here?' His slightly protuberant eyes lit with sudden hope. 'Or perhaps you've come to tell me that you've finally seen the justice of my claim and are willing to sell me the Arbour?'

Oswald's face was livid and all at once he looked a lot older than his forty years. 'No, I have not, you stupid old fool,' he hissed and moved forward, shouldering the other man none too gently out of his way. 'The Arbour is mine and will stay that way until there are no more Godsloves left to protect it.'

In the circumstances, it was, perhaps, an unfortunate choice of words. I know I thought so, and I saw Ginèvre raise her eyebrows and pull down the corners of her thin, painted mouth. As for Master Jollifant, he was literally jigging up and down with rage, not only furious at being addressed as a stupid old fool in the open street, but also burning with a misplaced sense of righteous indignation. He bounced forward and advanced his face to within an inch or so of Oswald's.

'Well, maybe there will come a time when there won't be any of you left,' he uttered venomously. 'Have you ever thought about that?'

For several seconds, Oswald stood as though turned to stone. Then, before I could guess what he would be about, he had seized the silversmith by the throat and forced him back against the wall of the shop.

'What do you mean by that?' he screamed. 'Where is she? What have you done with Celia?'

It took all my strength to loosen his grip. Passers-by were beginning to take an interest, grinning to see a respectable lawyer involved in a street brawl like any apprentice.

'Stop it!' I shouted, forced to raise my own voice in order to penetrate his inflamed senses. 'The man doesn't know what you're talking about, can't you see that? Besides, you can't have it both ways. If you're so convinced Roderick Jeavons has abducted Celia, then Master Jollifant is innocent. He's just a bit mad, that's all. He's just a prey to this ridiculous belief that he has some sort of claim to the Arbour.'

In my own mind, I wasn't so convinced of the silversmith's innocence, but that was because I was unconvinced of the doctor's guilt. Both were suspects as far as I was concerned, and in some ways Adrian Jollifant's was a less stable character than Roderick Jeavons's; his grudge against the Godslove family had far less reason behind it than the older man's. Indeed, it was totally unreasonable, whereas Roderick's resentment sprang from the very credible belief that Celia's rejection of his love and his suit had undoubtedly been influenced by her siblings.

My intervention had drawn attention to myself, and Master Jollifant gave a start of recognition. Rubbing his mangled throat, already beginning to show a bruise where Oswald's fingers had gripped it, he managed to croak, 'You're that country bumpkin what bought the ring off me! And not speaking the way you spoke then.' His anger almost choked him. 'If-if I'd known you were hand in glove with that . . . that

thieving rogue, I'd never have let you have it so cheap. Sorry
for you, that's what I was!'

Without warning, he pushed himself away from the shop
wall and launched himself at me, trying to punch me on the
nose. But I was too quick for him, releasing Oswald's arms
and spinning round to parry the blow with one of my own,
which caught my would-be assailant neatly under the jaw
and sent him crashing to the cobbles.

On a day when the wine, flowing freely in the Great
Conduit and others throughout the city, was the cause of
many a fight amongst the drunken London citizens, our little
spat was of minor interest to the Watch or anyone else in
authority. Nevertheless, Ginèvre suggested – not without an
ulterior motive, naturally – that Oswald and I accompany
her to Paternoster Row and take some refreshment to calm
our nerves before attempting a return to the Arbour.

'The crowds will surely have eased a little by now,' she
said. 'The service of thanksgiving for the king's safe arrival
must be well underway by this time.'

Oswald refused point-blank, making it plain that he
expected me to do the same. But I was in a mood to distance
myself from the whole tribe of Godslove and their affairs,
so I accepted with an enthusiasm that seemed to surprise
Ginèvre. I told Oswald that I would collect Old Diggory
from the inn stable when I was ready and follow him home
at a later hour. He was obviously displeased, but was too
tired and dispirited to argue. The day had been a disaster as
far as he was concerned.

I turned to the silversmith to help him to his feet, but he
had disappeared indoors while we had been talking, for which
I was thankful. I could not have hit him as hard as I had
feared. I offered Ginèvre my arm and we began walking
back along Westcheap.

The crowds had not thinned out as much as we had hoped,
many people waiting patiently in the vicinity of St Paul's
for another glimpse of their young king when he emerged
after the service. From within the great church, the sound of
the Te Deum rose in a surge of praise and thanksgiving,
answered at once by a chorus of chirping sparrows and

starlings that made their home amongst the churchyard trees. Moreover, the surrounding streets and alleyways were thronged with the grooms and horses and general retainers of the nobles inside, the different liveries and trappings making a colourful display that vied with the tapestries, rugs and floral garlands suspended from the windows of the neighbouring houses.

Ginèvre and I were at last within sight of Paternoster Row when we and others were pushed unceremoniously to one side to make room for a latecomer who, for some reason, had failed to keep up with the rest of the procession. I had a brief impression of hot, sweaty faces creased in anxious lines, a strong smell of horseflesh, the flurry of priestly vestments and the blur of white saltire crosses against an azure ground. I knew at once who the tardy prelate was.

'Robert Stillington,' I informed my companion. 'Bishop of Bath and Wells. He arrived at Reading Abbey the same night that my daughter and I were staying in the guest hall there.'

Ginèvre made no comment then; but half-an-hour later, when we had finally reached the relative peace and quiet of her house in Paternoster Row and were sipping wine and nibbling at little almond doucettes – typical women's fare which I would willingly have traded for a good, honest pot of ale and a hunk of bread and cheese – she remarked, 'Stillington! I seem to recall that His Grace suffered a spell of imprisonment around the time that Clarence was arrested and executed. Does that fact have any significance, do you think?'

I had always thought her an astute woman, who kept a finger on the pulse of public life, unlike most of her sex who found politics a bore.

'It might well have,' I agreed. 'The two men were always friendly in a conspiratorial sort of way. I saw them together once at Farleigh Castle, near Bath. I thought then that they shared some secret. But I could be wrong, and probably am. Certainly at Clarence's trial, the bishop's name was never mentioned. Which reminds me,' I went on, 'are you still friends with the Babcary family?'

Miles Babcary was – or had been – a goldsmith in Cheapside,

and five years earlier I had been instrumental in proving his daughter, Isolda Bonifant, innocent of poisoning her husband.

Ginèvre shook her head. 'Miles sold the shop two years ago and they moved away, or so I was told. But where they went, I've no idea. Nor care. They were nothing to me. Weren't they related in one degree or another to the late king's mistress, Jane Shore?' When I nodded, she gave a sneering little laugh and went on, 'Not much of a connection now that Edward's dead. They say that at the moment her favours are being shared by both Hastings and Dorset, but if young Edward's to be influenced by his Uncle Gloucester, there'll be no place for her at court.'

'No. I remember the duke didn't like her.' I bit into another doucette.

Ginèvre leant back in her chair. 'He wouldn't. He's too puritanical, my dear. Besides, he blames people like her and poor old Hastings for his brother's decline in both health and morals.' She laughed again.

I fired up in the duke's defence as I always did, even at merely implied criticism of him. 'Not that puritanical, surely. He has two acknowledged bastards.'

'Both born before his marriage to Anne Neville. For the past twelve years, he's been a model of propriety and the husbandly virtues.'

'You seem to think that something to be scoffed at.'

She gave me a leery, sidelong glance. 'I should have thought, after all you've told me, you'd agree.'

Once again, I regretted having been so frank with her regarding Juliette Gerrish, and was thankful I'd made no mention of Eloise Gray.

'I admire the duke,' I answered briefly. 'A man of integrity. I wish I were more like him.'

She gave an angry snort and changed the subject abruptly. 'Tell me about the disappearance of Lawyer Godslove's sister. Did I understand aright? Does he really suspect Roderick Jeavons of abducting her?'

I gave her a more detailed explanation of events at the Arbour during the past few days. 'Although,' I hastened to add, 'I don't share Oswald's conviction of the doctor's guilt.

But then again, he can be forgiven for his suspicions – which might, after all, prove to be right.'

Ginèvre poured herself more wine and offered to refill my cup, but I waved the jug aside. She shrugged, her disappointed expression indicating that she found me less amusing company than she had hoped.

'I wouldn't like to say that Lawyer Godslove is entirely wrong about Dr Jeavons,' she admitted at last, having mulled the matter over in silence. 'Roderick's a passionate, strong-minded, strong-willed man –' she gave a small, cat-like, reminiscent smile obviously meant to pique my curiosity – 'and any woman's a fool who tries to play fast and loose with him. I can see that he might be provoked into taking matters into his own hands. But I very much doubt that he'd continue to hold this Celia against her will. As soon as he discovered that his action had upset her, that she really was averse to his advances, he'd let her go and return her to her family. Besides,' Ginèvre added shrewdly, 'you think Roderick's in love with Mistress Godslove. Surely that doesn't sort with the terrible things you say have been happening to the other members of her family?'

'It might,' I argued, 'if he were trying to rid himself of all the obstacles to his ultimate goal of marrying Celia.'

'Then why not carry out his plan? Why ruin everything by abducting her before disposing of all her siblings? According to what you tell me, this person, whoever he or she is, has been a model of patience so far, so why suddenly abandon his deep-laid scheme? It makes no sense.'

I nodded, sighing. 'I agree with you,' I said. 'And in any case, Celia isn't in Old Dean's Lane. Oswald forced his way in and searched the house. There was no sign of her.'

'Not even in the cellar?' Ginèvre mocked. 'Or didn't the brave lawyer go down there for fear of the rats?'

'What do you mean?' I asked sharply. 'Mistress Ireby, the doctor's sister, told us that the house has no cellar.'

My companion looked startled, raising a hand, childlike, to her mouth, plainly regretting this unguarded remark. Then she shrugged fatalistically. 'I don't know why Mistress Ireby should have said that. All the houses in Old Dean's Lane have cellars.' We regarded each other significantly for a moment or two before she laughed. 'Oh, come on, Roger! You can't read anything into that! The poor woman just wanted you both out of the place. You had no right to be in there anyway, without an invitation. She didn't want Lawyer Godslove rampaging down to the cellar and disturbing whatever bottles of wine Roderick keeps there.'

'I suppose not,' I said slowly, trying to look convinced, and turned the conversation back to other things.

Ginèvre seemed more than willing to follow my lead and we chatted desultorily for a while longer about the death of the late king, about the uncertainties of a minority reign and of the unpleasantness that was obviously brewing, stirred up by the Duke of Gloucester's sudden preference for his cousin, Buckingham, instead of for Lord Hastings, who undoubtedly, in his own mind, had cast himself in the role of the duke's right-hand man. But after a while, when I realized that the dinner hour was past and that Ginèvre was not asking me to stay, I took my farewell. She made no effort to detain me, but, having accompanied me outside, she laid a hand on my arm.

'Take care, my dear,' she said. 'Don't do anything foolish.' With which somewhat cryptic utterance, she returned indoors, closing the door firmly on both me and on the crowds milling around St Paul's.

These were still thick, the service not yet being over and the women anxious for another glimpse of that seemingly angelic face with its thatch of blond hair encircled by a golden filet studded with rubies and sapphires, the latter emphasizing the intense blue of the young king's eyes. I contemplated the possibility of forcing a passage the length of Paternoster Row into Old Dean's Lane, but then abandoned the idea. If, when I got there, Mistress Ireby refused to let me in, what could I do? There were far too many people about to overcome her resistance by forcing an entry, as Oswald had previously done. And even if the lady were out, enjoying the Sunday holiday, making one of the excited press that continued to throng around the church, the same reasoning applied: I could hardly search for a way to break in with so many onlookers to observe me. So I decided that, for the present, there was nothing to be done but to return to the Arbour, where at least I would be fed. Wearily I made my way back along Cheapside to the inn where I had stabled Old Diggory.

By the time I passed through the Bishop's Gate, having been held up for a good five minutes by the increased activity outside of Crosby's Place, I was debating with myself whether or not to tell Oswald of Ginèvre Napier's revelation concerning the houses in Old Dean's Lane. If I told him, I could guess his probable reaction. He would almost certainly read something sinister into Mistress Ireby's deception and insist on returning at once to Roderick Jeavons's house. But I was too tired, too bone-weary and still feeling the effects of my recent illness to undertake the ride and brave the crowds again. I could, I supposed, let him go on his own, but in his present state of mind, he was liable to do something violent if Mistress Ireby refused him entry. And, if there was truly nothing to find, it would be disastrous for one of his profession to be taken up by the Watch and brought to court. I owed him something for his unstinting hospitality of these past two weeks and for the weeks before that during which he had housed my wife and sons. So I decided to say nothing, but to return to Old Dean's Lane the following day and see what I could discover for myself.

I looked forward to spending the rest of Sunday as quietly as circumstances would allow, helping Adela to keep the children and Hercules in check in a house that was now plunged into renewed mourning, something of which the Godsloves had had more than their fair share in recent years. But alas for such plans! As I stepped across the threshold into the hall, I was met by a distressed Adela with tears in her eyes.

I groaned inwardly as I folded her in my arms. 'Sweetheart, what's amiss?' I nearly added the word 'now' but thought better of it.

'The ring you bought for me, it's missing. The children and I have searched every inch of the bedchamber, but we can't find it anywhere.' She added, 'I don't want to say anything to the others until I'm absolutely certain that it's nowhere to be found.'

'When did you see it last?'

'Earlier this morning. It was in its little box on top of the clothes chest. The box is still there, but the ring has gone.'

'Have you worn it today?'

She shook her head. 'No, because after breakfast I was playing with the children in the garden. When we came indoors, I went to put it on, but the box was empty.'

I accompanied her upstairs to our bedchamber, where the children were still hunting for the missing ring. Judging by the state of the room, they had entered into the spirit of the thing with enthusiasm, but the search had yielded nothing.

'It's not here,' Elizabeth announced as we entered. 'We've looked everywhere.'

'Looked everywhere,' confirmed Adam, while Nicholas just nodded.

They had even stripped the bed of its coverings, tossing them on the floor, and Hercules emerged from beneath the pile, barking delightedly at my return. He obviously thought it some new game, devised expressly for his enjoyment.

I hushed him and began my own search of both our and the children's chamber, but after almost an hour, hot, thirsty and extremely dusty, I was forced to admit that they were right. The ring was nowhere to be found.

'It's no good,' I said. 'We shall have to tell Clemency and Arbella about it.'

My wife looked unhappy. 'They'll think we're accusing one of the maids.'

But when we descended to the dining parlour, where we had all been summoned for a belated dinner, no one expressed any surprise, only dismay.

'What else has been taken?' Oswald demanded, staring about him. 'I've told you women time and again about leaving the doors unlocked. You know perfectly well how many thefts there have been in this neighbourhood in the past few years.'

Clemency nodded sadly. 'It's true,' she said. 'Even the church was broken into. A valuable pyx was taken from St Botolph's, and a man living near the Bedlam, who kept all his savings in a secret hiding-place under the floor had them stolen. It was a shock to us all because no one I've ever spoken to was aware that he had a penny to his name. But someone knew and robbed him.'

'And now,' Oswald shouted furiously, 'that same someone has walked all over this house, taking what he wanted, while you precious three were no doubt gossiping in the kitchen.' He slammed his hand down hard on the table, making everyone jump.

Sybilla burst into tears.

FIFTEEN

That night, in bed, snuggled within the shelter of my arm, Adela expressed a strong desire to go home.

'This house is becoming no place for children. Nor, indeed, for dogs,' she added with a little catch of laughter in her voice, as Hercules, who had made our bed his own, snuffled and grunted and wheezed as though in the midst of an uneasy dream. She went on, 'I'm sorry for my cousins, that goes without saying, but the wheel of fortune has spun so low for them, I'm beginning to be afraid that some of their ill-luck will rub off on us.' She shivered. 'After all the other things which have happened, I don't know why losing my ring and this story of the robberies has upset me so much. But it has. The thought that someone, some stranger, has been roaming at will around this house, fingering our belongings, makes me feel that I can't possibly stay here another day.' And to my great consternation, she started to cry. She made no sound, but I could feel the shaking of her body as it pressed closer to mine.

I tightened my hold. She was right; the wheel of fortune, of fate, of life, whatever you want to call it, had spun so low for the Godslove family that the good luck sign must almost have reached its nadir. I had no wish for my wife and children (and, of course, dog) to be touched by such misfortune. Moreover, the resultant gloomy, despondent atmosphere was depressing us all: it could do no other. Since Celia's disappearance, the house was like a tomb, and Adela felt it increasingly necessary to suppress Elizabeth's and Nicholas's high spirits and to keep Hercules from barking at any stray rat or cat that ventured into the house or garden.

I kissed her gently on the forehead.

'I'll visit Blossom's Inn tomorrow,' I promised, 'and try to find a carter going to Bristol. It may take a day or two, but I'll pay the landlord to send me word as soon as he knows of one.'

Adela propped herself on one elbow. 'Oh, Roger, we can't. We can't just run away and leave Oswald and Clemency and Sybilla in such distress. You know they're counting on you to solve the mystery for them.'

I snorted. 'That's in God's hands. But no! I wasn't intending to come with you. I feel I owe it to your cousins to make a further effort to discover what lies at the root of this mystery. Would you be willing to go without me? You'll have Hercules for protection.'

The dog suddenly sat up, gave a little bark and then lay down again. I always have an uneasy feeling that, even in his sleep, he understands exactly what I'm saying. Ridiculous though it may seem, I often find myself guarding my tongue in front of him.

Adela clung to me. 'I don't want to go and leave you here.'

I was tempted to point out that no such scruples had weighed with her when she quit the Small Street house on the flimsiest evidence of my infidelity – I felt a glow of totally unmerited and unjustified self-righteousness – but decided it was foolishness to rake over dead ashes. Besides, I loved her.

'It's for the children's sake,' I urged. 'You said yourself that this is becoming no fit place for them. And it may not be for a day or two – maybe even a week or two – because we must wait for a carter going all the way home. I won't have you stranded in some strange town looking for another carter to take you the remainder of the journey. Now, will you promise me that you'll go if I can arrange it?'

After a pause, she finally nodded, her long dark hair tickling my bare chest. 'Yes, if you wish it,' she agreed. 'I'll tell Clemency in the morning. Somehow, I don't think she'll mind. Indeed, I think she might even be relieved. I'm sure Oswald and Sybilla will be. When will you go to Blossom's Inn?'

'Sometime tomorrow. I'm going into the city to keep a further watch on Roderick Jeavons's house. But first, I must ask for the name and direction of this man who was robbed of all his money and then visit Father Berowne at St Botolph's.'

Adela raised her head. 'You think these robberies have some bearing on what's been happening to Oswald and the others? But how can they?'

'I don't know,' I answered. 'I just have a feeling in my bones that they could. I've no idea why.' But I did. It was God putting it into my mind. I had no doubt by now that He was behind my coming to London. He could never keep His fingers out of my sauce dish: He was constantly stirring. It was His revenge for my having abandoned the religious life. 'Go to sleep now,' I added. 'Perhaps I can prevent the wheel of fortune turning any further for Oswald and Clemency and Sybilla before they all drop off the bottom.'

Next morning, I left Adela and the children (and, needless to say, the dog) sleeping the sleep of the just and went downstairs to break my fast with Oswald who, looking like Death at a wake, was forcing himself to eat prior to setting out for his chambers near the Strand.

'I'm glad you're up early,' he said. 'I was hoping for a word with you before I left. Today, you're to go back to Old Dean's Lane and keep an eye on the house.'

It was more a command than a request, and he had no need to specify which house was meant. I had no difficulty in giving my promise as that was already my intention; but before reassuring him on that head, I told him of my plan to return Adela and my family to Bristol, forestalling his angry protest by revealing that I would stay on. After that, he was all compliance, even going so far as to say he thought it for the best, as he believed the children were growing homesick. And Arbella, coming into the parlour at that moment with a plate of freshly baked oatcakes, agreed wholeheartedly with the scheme as soon as she was made aware of it.

'You really ought to go with them, Roger,' she said. 'You can do no good here. I think we're all cursed.'

This remark not only drew a very strong refutation from Oswald, but also a spiteful rider to the effect that the family misfortunes were nothing to do with her.

'You're not a Godslove,' he snapped, 'and never will be!'

The housekeeper's face flushed crimson with hurt and

embarrassment, and I tried to distract her attention by asking for the name and direction of the man who had been robbed of all his life's savings.

'Why would you want to know that?' she demanded ungraciously. 'In any case, it was some years ago. It has nothing to do with us.'

'If Master Chapman wants to know, tell him!' Oswald shouted. Then, moderating his tone and turning to me, he said, 'The man's name is Peter Coleman and he lives two doors away from the Bedlam. He's a woman's tailor, and to the best of my recollection, the robbery took place at the beginning of last year.'

'And when was the pyx stolen from the church?'

Oswald wrinkled his brow. 'Not long before, I think.' He raised his eyebrows at Arbella. 'Isn't that right?'

The housekeeper's only reply was to dump the plate of oatcakes on the table and withdraw without a word. A spot of colour burned in Oswald's cheeks, but he made no comment on her behaviour other than to pull down his mouth at the corners. He rose from the table, shrugging on his lawyer's striped robe which had been draped over the back of his chair.

'I must go. You are, of course, free to borrow Old Diggory whenever you wish. I shall see you this evening, probably sometime after supper as I shall be working late on a case with my clerk in chambers.' He held out his hand in a sudden gesture of friendship that he had not displayed hitherto. 'Find out what you can, Roger,' he added on a note of desperation at variance with his usual frigid manner.

'I'll do my best,' I promised, 'but I can't work miracles, Oswald, and sooner or later I, too, must go home. I have a living to earn.'

He waved a dismissive hand as though such a triviality were unimportant and hurried from the room. I went upstairs again to where my loved ones were still soundly asleep, thrust my knife into my belt and put on my cloak, for the early May morning had turned cold and showery. Today I had thankfully abandoned my smart new clothes for the old familiar hose and jerkin which fitted me in all the accustomed places and were as comfortable as a second skin.

Moreover I should be far less conspicuous, just one of the crowd.

A few people were coming out of St Botolph's as I neared the church, so I guessed that prime had just finished. I therefore went inside to speak to Father Berowne. He greeted me with delight.

'You're just too late for the service, Roger,' he said, his eyes twinkling with suppressed laughter. 'You must have overslept. What a shame! I know you must be sorry, but come and have some breakfast with me. I'm sure Ellen can find enough for two.'

I declined on the grounds that I had just eaten. 'I won't detain you for more than a moment, Father. I simply wanted to ask you about the pyx that was stolen from this church.'

He looked surprised. 'But that was over a year ago. Why do you want to know about that?'

'There has been another robbery. At the Arbour, yesterday. A ring belonging to my wife was taken. Clemency and Oswald mentioned the previous thefts.'

'Thefts?' he queried sharply.

'It seems that a man called Peter Coleman was also robbed, of his savings.'

'Peter? Ah, yes! I'd forgotten that. Well . . . there's nothing much to tell, I'm afraid. This is a poor church and the pyx was one of the few valuable things it possessed. It was silver-gilt and kept in that aumbry you see to the right of the altar.' The priest shrugged. 'The lock in those days was flimsy and easily broken, unlike the one you see on it now. By the greatest good fortune, the two candlesticks, also silver-gilt, had been removed by myself for cleaning on the very morning of the robbery.' He grimaced. 'And that's all I can tell you, Roger. Although, as I say, why you should want to know . . .' He broke off, smiling at someone who had just entered the church behind me. 'Mistress Rokeswood! You wish to speak to me?'

I turned. Arbella was standing in the doorway, and I had the fleeting impression that she was a little flustered. But if she were – and I could think of no good reason why she should be – she recovered herself immediately, walking forward and saying calmly, 'I've come to confession, Father. I haven't been since last Wednesday.'

Sir Berowne nodded, waving her towards the confessional and raising his eyebrows at me, an indication that it was surely time for me to leave.

I took the hint, wished them both good-day and left, walking the length of Bishop's Gate Without until I reached the Bedlam. Already the shrieks and cries from within were loud enough to chill the blood, but I had grown used to them by now. I counted back two houses and knocked on the door.

After a few moments' delay, it was answered by a small, wizened man whose most prominent feature was a large pair of ears, giving him the appearance of some woodland sprite. He was holding a needle and thread in one hand, and behind him, I could see a long trestle table covered with lengths of material. Several bolts of cloth stood against one wall and a pair of scissors dangled from the belt at his waist. He regarded me uncertainly.

'Yes? Who are you?' His voice was astonishingly deep for such a little man. 'If you're wanting a gown for your wife, I'm sorry but just at present—'

I interrupted his apology to explain my business, receiving in return the sort of blank look I had got from Father Berowne, and an almost identical response.

'But that was a year and more ago.'

Once he grasped the fact, however, that my interest was serious, he seemed anxious to talk about his loss, inviting me in, clearing a space on the table and producing two beakers and a jug of what he assured me was the best home-brewed ale in London. (And while accepting this with a pinch of salt, I have to admit that it was by no means the worst ale I have ever tasted.)

'What do you want to know?' he asked.

'Who, apart from yourself, knew where you kept your money?'

'No one,' he answered, his little face puckering with distress. 'I had dug the hole myself, most secretly, when I first came to live in this house. A woman's tailor, sir –' he indicated with a sweep of his hand the jumble of coloured silks and velvets that littered the trestle – 'does not make a great deal of money. Thrifty goodwives make their own gowns and only those with money to spare can afford my services. And I dare not overcharge or I lose such custom as I have. But I'm unmarried and live frugally – a habit I learned from my mother, herself a sewing-woman – so I was able to save steadily against the day when my eyesight begins to fail me and my fingers to thicken and become misshapen — '

'In other words,' I interrupted, smiling, 'you had a fair sum put by.'

He nodded ruefully. 'But,' he was quick to add, 'it represented many years hard work. So, as I said, when I first came here, I dug a good, deep hole beneath the floor, over against that wall there –' he nodded towards the back of the cottage – 'placed the money in its leather bag inside, stuffed the remaining space with scraps of old material and smoothed earth over the top. Then I stood that chest over the spot. The hole was not easy of access, I assure you, and I used to curse myself for having made it so difficult whenever I had money to put away.'

'People, though, must have suspected you of having a secret hoard,' I suggested. 'A single man, living alone, making a reasonable living but spending little, would be bound to give rise to that sort of speculation.'

He shrugged. 'I suppose so. But the strange thing was that when I returned home on the day of the robbery, nothing appeared to have been disturbed. The house had not been ransacked, neither upstairs nor down. Everything seemed to be in order until I went to put away the day's takings that same evening. It was only when I had moved the chest and scraped away the layer of earth that I realized the hole was empty. The bag full of money had gone.'

This put a different complexion on the matter. 'So someone knew exactly where it was hidden?'

'But how could they?' he protested excitedly. 'I never told anyone of my hiding-place.'

'It's no good saying that!' I retorted irritably. 'You must have mentioned it to someone, it stands to reason. It beggars belief that a chance thief, or even an acquaintance who suspected you of hoarding money could go directly to the right place without prior knowledge of its location.'

'I told no one,' the tailor reiterated, growing rather red in the face, his ears seeming to stick out even further from his head.

'Could anyone ever have looked through the window and seen you stowing your money under the floor?' I asked with sudden inspiration.

He shook his head decisively. 'I never did so until after dark, even in the summer months, when the shutters were fast closed and the door locked.'

'And there's no back entrance to this house? No one could have crept in and spied on you without your knowledge?'

'There is, but that, too, was always locked once dusk had fallen.'

'A mystery, then,' I said, finishing my ale. 'The church, too, was robbed, or so I've been told.'

Once again, Master Coleman nodded. 'That was not long before my money was stolen. Sacrilege! Father Berowne was distraught. He told the congregation after Mass the following day and begged the guilty party to come forward and confess. He promised that no further action would be taken if the pyx were restored. But of course it never was. I'm a good son of the Holy Church, sir, and one morning shortly afterwards, when he was here visiting me because I was sick, I offered to head a subscription to raise money to replace it.'

'And was your offer accepted?'

My host shook his head sadly. 'Sir Berowne thanked me, but doubted if other folk would be so generous. I suggested the people at the Arbour, but he was loath to ask them. He said they had troubles of their own. One of the ladies had been seriously ill and another sister had recently died from eating a poison mushroom.' He regarded me curiously. 'You're staying with Lawyer Godslove, aren't you? And now another of his sisters has gone missing, or so I've heard. Such ill-luck!' He shuddered. 'There's evil at work there, sir. And you say that the robberies have started again. A ring belonging to your wife? You need to be careful. Misfortune can be contagious.'

I rose to my feet. 'So my wife believes. She is anxious to go home to Bristol as soon as maybe.'

The tailor got up with me. 'She's wise,' he said and accompanied me to the door. 'I hope I've been of some use to you; that you've learned whatever it is you wanted to know.'

I thanked him without giving him an answer. The truth was that I wasn't at all sure what it was I had hoped to glean from him or what it was exactly that I had wanted to know. As I had said to Adela, I had been following one of those inexplicable hunches that possessed me every now and then. Or were they indeed directions straight from God? I was never quite certain: I only knew that they had to be obeyed.

Once outside the tailor's cottage, I debated whether or not to return to the Arbour and saddle Old Diggory for the ride into the city, but in the end, decided against it. For one thing, my old clothes would consort ill with a thoroughbred horse and draw people's attention to me. For another, the walk would do me good; I was growing lazy and putting on weight. I was used to going everywhere on my own two legs and had never been comfortable in the company of horses, a rather stupid animal in my estimation. I had my knife in my belt, and this, together with my height and girth, would afford me sufficient protection.

As I passed through the Bishop's Gate, I noticed that there was no sign of any workmen.

'The repairs are finished, then,' I remarked to the gate-keeper.

'God be praised,' he answered devoutly. 'All that noise! Banging and hammering and shouting and cursing! It was enough to drive a man out of his wits, so it was. Not,' he added petulantly, 'that it's much better now that the Duke of Gloucester's taken up residence at Crosby's Place. Such a to-do and people coming and going at all hours. Still, it's further down the road and not right in your earholes like the masons and the hod-carriers, which is summat, I suppose.'

'Is the king staying there, as well?' I asked.

The man gave a vigorous shake of his head. 'Lor' love you, no! He's lodging with the Bishop of London, or so I was told by one o' Gloucester's men. Temporary, like. Rumour is,' he added confidentially, warming to his theme and blatantly ignoring the impatient queue that was building up behind me, 'his uncles want him moved to the royal apartments in the Tower, but they want his brother, the little Duke

of York, to go with him for company. Trouble is, he's in
Westminster sanctuary with his mother and sisters, and Queen
Elizabeth, well, she don't want to let him out.' The gatekeeper blew his nose in his fingers. 'S'pose you can't blame
her, not after what happened to her brother and other son.'

I took no notice of the old lady who was prodding me in
the back with her stick. 'They were only arrested.'

'Ay!' The gatekeeper again nodded his head. 'And imprisoned up north, so Gloucester's man tells me.'

He was a fount of information and I would have liked to
stay and gossip with him longer, but the clamour of indignant
voices behind me was growing too great to be ignored.
Reluctantly, I took my departure and walked on down Bishop's
Gate Street Within. Long before I drew abreast of Crosby's
Place, I could hear the hum of activity and saw at least five
messengers wearing the Gloucester livery ride out, all in the
space of five minutes. And just as I reached the turning into
the Poultry and Eastcheap, I was forced to one side of the road
as the duke himself swept past. Thankfully, he was surrounded
by a vast number of attendants and men-at-arms, so failed to
notice me, although I was able to get a good look at him.

Never of a high colour and always with something of the
pallor of ill-health about him, he appeared even grimmer and
more drawn than usual, as though he had the weight of the
kingdom on his shoulders. Which, undoubtedly, he had.
Moreover, he was, and always had been, a man of the north,
of the moors and mountains and wide open spaces of his
beloved Yorkshire, and had never been happy in the south.
London, I knew, particularly irked him, making him feel
caged. But I reckoned that there was more to it than that. If
his version of what had happened at Northampton were true
– and I, for one, believed it – then his life had already been
endangered; Sir Edward Woodville was at sea with half the
royal treasure along with him; and somewhere at the back
of his mind – or perhaps in the forefront of his mind – was
the belief that he, and not his nephew, was the rightful king.
But he had no proof. And as long as his mother chose to
remain silent, there was nothing to say if the information I
had brought him from France the previous year meant
anything or no.

I waited for a minute or two until the ducal procession, obviously heading for Westminster, was out of sight before proceeding on my way, the length of East and Westcheap, in the direction of St Paul's and Old Dean's Lane.

There was all the customary early-morning bustle of good-wives sweeping yesterday's dirt and stale rushes out of doors, throwing slops and excrement into the central drain, shaking dusters out of windows, so I was able to station myself opposite Roderick Jeavons's house without being too noticeable and watch while Mistress Ireby, like her neighbours, busied herself making the place habitable again for the new day. She seemed, for the moment at least, to have no assistance, although I would have expected the good doctor to employ at least one maid. But it was possible that the girl (or girls) lived out and would eventually appear full of excuses as to why she had overslept and was late. For now, however, it was the doctor's sister who plied the broom and disposed of the rubbish, but with such an irritable expression on her face, and with such constant glancing up and down the road, as to suggest that my theory was probably correct.

I was just pondering how to insinuate myself into the house and persuade Mistress Ireby to show me the cellar which she had denied was there, when the wheel of fortune suddenly spun in my favour. A neighbour, a stout goodwife, from a house a few doors distant came squawking along the street, obviously in some distress and begging for Mistress Ireby's help. I was unable to hear the exchange of words between the two women for the crash and rumble of a passing cart, its iron wheels screeching over the cobbles in a more than usually ear-splitting fashion, but whatever the problem, it was of sufficient urgency to cause the doctor's sister to drop her broom and hurry away with her friend, leaving her door wide open.

I didn't hesitate, but was across the street and into the house in almost less time than it takes to tell. If Mistress Ireby returned quickly, then I should have to make up some story of having been unable to get an answer to my knock and, finding the door ajar, entering to see if she was inside. A feeble enough tale and I doubted if she would believe me, but I wasn't prepared to pass up this golden opportunity to lay Oswald's suspicions to rest once and for all. I felt certain I should find nothing, but convincing my host, once I had informed him of the cellar's existence, was another matter, and only my sworn assurance that I had investigated it for myself would suffice.

Locating the cellar door took me a little longer than I had anticipated as it was not where I had expected it to be, under the stairs leading to the second floor or somewhere in the entrance passage. I finally discovered it in the kitchen, at first mistaking it for a cupboard until, having looked everywhere else, I at last opened it in desperation. It was locked, but there was a key hanging on a nail beside it; and there, facing me, was not, as I had assumed, some precious family silver or other treasure, but a flight of steps leading down into the darkness.

A hurried search of the kitchen provided me with a candle in its candleholder, and having lit it at the fire and descended the steps, I found myself in what seemed to be a surprisingly capacious cellar for the size of the house above it. Needless to say, it was empty except for a few barrels of what was probably wine or ale, along with various pieces of broken furniture: two-legged stools, chairs with no seats and the like which householders invariably dispose of in such places. But of Celia in chains, or in any other form of restraint, there was no sign. Nor had I ever expected to find one. This, I thought grimly, would put an end to Oswald's nonsense and allow me to make enquiries elsewhere. (Although to be honest, where exactly I had at that moment no notion.)

I started to mount the steps again, hoping that I might be lucky enough to get out of the house before Mistress Ireby returned. But just as I was halfway up, I heard a girl's voice calling, 'Mistress! Mistress! Where are you? I'm sorry I couldn't get here earlier, but one o' the little 'uns was sick this morning.'

My guess about the maid who was late had proved to be unnervingly accurate and I hesitated, loath to make a sudden appearance which would most likely send the poor girl into a fit of hysterics. But that hesitation was my undoing. I heard the girl muttering angrily to herself, something about leaving the door open again, about it being dangerous and about someone falling down the stairs one day and breaking her neck. A second or two later, the cellar door slammed and I heard the key grate as it was turned in the lock.

I was a prisoner.

SIXTEEN

Of course, all I had to do was hammer on the door and shout for the woman to come and let me out. But would she? There was always the chance that having assumed she had captured a thief, she would rush out to get assistance and I would find myself facing an angry, probably armed, mob whose members would attack me first and ask questions afterwards. There was also a possibility that, on her return, a furious Mistress Ireby would refuse to recognize me and hand me over to the law. And the consequences of that could be disastrous, for there was no disputing the fact that I was trespassing; and although I had no doubt that Oswald Godslove would come to my aid, I wasn't sure that even so I would not be clapped up in prison.

I stared around me from my position halfway up the stairs and pondered what to do for the best. The ghostly light from the flickering candle-flame filled the cellar with shadows, making deep hollows of darkness that seemed to stretch into infinity beneath the vaulted arches. Once again it occurred to me that the cellar was far too large for the house, and in the same moment I remembered houses in Bristol which shared cellars with a neighbour, with no intervening wall below ground to mark the division between the two dwellings. I wondered if that could be the case here and what it could avail me if it were.

I recollected that while I was standing opposite Roderick Jeavon's house, watching, I had had a vague impression that the one next to it on the right-hand side was empty. I tried to recall what had given me that feeling, but was able to conjure up no good reason except that the shutters were firmly closed, just as they had been on my previous visit with Oswald. But even if the place were empty, it would be the greatest stroke of good luck if the cellar door should have been left unlocked. Could I really expect the wheel of fortune to spin in my favour twice in one day? Well, there was only one way to find out.

I descended the steps for a second time and made my way across the dusty floor space, walking, ridiculously, almost on tiptoe as though afraid to make the slightest sound. I didn't for a moment believe in my own reasoning, and it was with genuine astonishment that I found myself standing at the foot of a flight of steps identical to that on the other side of the cellar and leading upwards to a similar door at the top. I mounted swiftly, my heart pounding, and cautiously raised the latch, anticipating resistance, but, miraculously, the door gave under my hand.

It was unlocked. The wheel of fortune had favoured me again.

I must have stood there for several seconds trying to conquer my sense of disbelief before quietly pushing the door open and stepping, not this time into a kitchen, but into a narrow passageway that appeared to run the length of the house from front to back. The street door was only a yard or two from me and, even in the dimness of the shuttered gloom, I could see that it was not just unbolted but that the key hung on a nail beside it. I immediately froze where I stood. This was too much good fortune not to have some catch attached to it – and I was right. A man's voice spoke from a room on the other side of the passage, almost opposite the cellar door.

'You'll get word to everyone on that list by tomorrow afternoon, Will. Arrange a meeting here for the morning after if possible, or whenever it will be convenient for them all to come. You must be sure to tell them to enter by the back way from the lane that runs close to the city wall. On no account must they try to enter from the front. You understand that?'

'I do, my lord. And can I assure them that they are unlikely to be disturbed here?'

'Most certainly. This place belongs to a kinsman of mine who is at present residing in the country and isn't likely to return to London for some months. You have the list safe? Good. Now, off you go.'

I stepped back behind the cellar door, almost closing it, but not quite. There was something going on here that had the smell of treasonable activity about it, and I was curious to see who might be involved. But no one appeared immediately.

'I see you haven't mentioned Lord Howard,' the second voice said; the voice belonging to the man addressed as 'Will'.

There was a scornful laugh. 'There are times, my lad, when you're not very astute for a lawyer. For a start, John Howard was never a close friend of mine nor of King Edward's.' There was a sudden break in the voice as the speaker mentioned our late sovereign, but it was quickly mastered. The tone became harsh again. 'And Howard wants nothing more in this life than to regain the duchy of Norfolk for himself and his family. He won't risk anything. He'll be toadying to Gloucester, flattering him for all he's worth. And also –' and here the voice spoke with such quiet venom that it made me shiver, grown man as I was – 'he'll be licking the arse of that misbegotten son of a viper who's wormed his way into Gloucester's affections, Henry of Buckingham.'

'Not Lord Howard, then,' replied the voice of Will, a faint edge of sarcasm informing his words.

Evidently 'my lord' heard it, too, because he answered sharply, 'Be careful of that tongue of yours, Master Catesby. I can easily find another lawyer. Members of your profession are ten a penny.' I wondered fleetingly what Oswald would have said to this sentiment before concentrating once again on what was being discussed in the room opposite. The first man went on, 'You'd better buy some wine. Rotheram and Morton are both particularly fond of malmsey.' He gave a short laugh. 'There must be something about it that appeals especially to the clergy.'

There was an infinitesimal pause. Then, 'You want me to purchase and bring this wine along the day after tomorrow?' the lawyer enquired in a flat little voice that should have warned his companion that he was not best pleased. 'No doubt you would like me to serve it, as well?'

'Good idea,' 'my lord' agreed. 'It'll save having another servant present.'

I grimaced to my self. That 'another' was not going to sweeten Master Catesby's mood.

I was right. The lawyer's voice, when he spoke, was cold

enough to have frozen a monkey's balls in summer. 'How many of us?'

A brief silence ensued while the first man must have made a swift calculation. 'If everyone accepts my invitation there should be eight of us. Jane – Mistress Shore – will be present. She's agreed to be the messenger between us and Westminster Sanctuary.'

I caught my breath. This, then, that I was overhearing was a plot involving the Queen Dowager and her family. If I were to be seen now, I didn't doubt that my life would be worth less than a groat. I drew back further behind the cellar door, but still keeping it open a crack, enough for me to peer through and see without being seen.

The door opposite was flung open and to my astonishment Lord Hastings, the Lord Chamberlain and lifelong opponent of the Woodvilles, came out. And yet, at the same time, I was not astonished. Only the previous day I had noted his expression of angry discontent and affronted dignity as he was forced to ride behind the king and my lord Gloucester, while the position he had expected to occupy was usurped by the Duke of Buckingham. But what did genuinely astound me was the speed with which he had turned his coat.

He spoke over his shoulder to the lawyer Catesby, still within the room. 'Follow me out the back way and be sure you lock the door and take the key with you. Don't forget to send me word of what's happening and if the morning after next is convenient for all. If it is, you'll be here in advance of the appointed hour with everything ready for our arrival.' He added viciously, 'If you're not, I'll have your guts for garters. I mean that, Will. We dare not risk people like the Bishop of Ely and the Archbishop of York being caught skulking around a back alley.'

'I shall be here, my lord. You need not worry.'

'Damn well see to it that you are,' was the ungracious response.

And a moment later, Lord Hastings, one time boon companion of his sovereign in all the excesses of his hedonistic life and now fallen from grace, brushed past my hiding place on his way to the back door with never a glance in my direction. I stayed where I was, hardly daring to breathe, and after a short delay, the lawyer emerged into the gloom of the passage.

From the little I could see in that dim light, I judged him to be somewhere around forty, perhaps more, perhaps less. He stood, briefly, staring towards the back door of the house through which Hastings had vanished, with a total lack of expression on his small, tight face. Then he, too, let himself out of the house by the same way and I heard him lock the door behind him. Breathing a sigh of relief, I gave him a few minutes start before slipping out of the front door as unobtrusively as possible, pausing only to replace its key on the nail, and closing it, unlocked, behind me. Then I walked up the street and turned right into Paternoster Row.

I sat on the grass in St Paul's churchyard, resting my back against a tombstone, contemplating the conversation I had just overheard, what it meant and what, if anything, I should do about it.

The answer to the second question was simple. Nothing: I refused to get involved. I had no doubt at all that Timothy Plummer would greet me and my information with open arms, but before I knew it I should be up to my neck in the spy's schemes and everything else would be subordinated to them. My own affairs would have to wait and there would be an even longer delay in getting home to Bristol. Guilt consumed me but I hardened my heart. I had been embroiled enough, more than enough, in the fortunes of my lord of Gloucester.

For I felt sure that this plot – if that was what indeed it was – concerned him. Hastings, arrogant and full of self-importance, could not stomach being overlooked for a man such as Henry of Buckingham, member of the royal family though he might be. But what exactly was the Lord Chamberlain planning? Was it merely a coup to contain the Duke of Gloucester's powers and oust Buckingham from his suddenly exalted position as the favourite? Or was it more sinister than that? Was the duke's life in danger?

I caught my breath. If that were the case, then I had no choice but to go at once to Timothy and tell him all that I had overheard, whatever the consequences to myself. But

after a few moments quiet reflection – in which, I have to
admit, self-interest played no small part – I was persuaded
that whatever was being hatched by Hastings and his erstwhile enemies, no physical harm was meant to my lord of
Gloucester. They would not dare. As the victor of the Scottish
war, the reclaimer of Berwick for English soil, he was too
popular with the general mass of people, even here in the
south, to run the risk of murdering him. And yet . . .

And yet wasn't that what he claimed had happened at
Northampton? Or had the Woodvilles simply intended to take
him prisoner until they had established themselves in the
chief positions of dominance? I didn't know. My head reeled.
All I knew for certain was that I had no wish to become
entangled. Had I not, when I first heard of King Edward's
death, congratulated myself that I was far from London and
had no prospect of going there? But God had decreed otherwise; and now here I was, quite by chance (or was it God's
will?) pitched headlong into what seemed to be a treasonable
attempt to unseat Duke Richard and prevent him influencing
the young king.

I half-rose to my feet, then sank back again against the tombstone as the thought occurred to me that perhaps I had no need
to do anything. I remembered the tone of the lawyer Catesby's
voice and the stony expression I had glimpsed on his face as
he stood in the passageway, staring after Hastings. I was willing
to wager that the Lord Chamberlain, by his contemptuous treatment of his underling, had made an enemy, one who might '
yet turn on his master. Of course he might not, but I felt the
idea exonerated me from any immediate action. I would wait
to see what news the next few days brought forth, and meantime I would concentrate on my own business.

Quarter of an hour later I was at Blossom's Inn, making
enquiries as to any carters travelling to Bristol within the next
day or two and willing to take a woman, three children and
a dog as passengers; the children, of course, being little short
of angelic and the hound a model of obedience and good
behaviour.

'And if you believe that, you'll believe the moon's made
o' green cheese,' said a voice behind me.

I swung round and there was a grinning Jack Nym. I stared
at him in disbelief, unable to accept that the luck was still
running my way, and once more made uneasy by the reflection that it couldn't possibly last. The wheel was bound to
spin soon in the opposite direction.

'Jack!' I exclaimed, clapping him on the back, 'what are
you doing here again so soon? Twice to London in less than
a fortnight? No, no,' I corrected myself. 'That's not possible.'

'Never been home yet,' he grumbled. 'Got an offer from
a glass-maker out Clerkenwell way to carry a load to Clifton,
and I've been hanging about these past ten days waiting for
the bugger to close the deal and make me a fair offer. But
he won't pay my price so now I've had enough. I'm showin'
him the two fingers.' His eyes brightened. 'Did I hear aright?
You and Adela and the children are going home? What a
piece of good fortune. I can take you tomorrow. You won't
pay as well as the glass, but you're better company so I'm
not complaining.'

'Not me,' I explained. 'Just Adela and the children. Oh,
and the dog.' He snorted. 'I shall be making my own way
home sometime later.'

Jack groaned. 'What you got yourself mixed up in now,
Roger, eh? Dang me if I ever knew such a man for getting
tangled up in other people's doings. I wouldn't be married
to you for nothing. That wife o' yourn deserves better, I can
tell you!'

'I know it,' I admitted, 'but I've given my word to assist
some relations of hers who are in trouble. If I can that is. I
can't break my promise.'

He shook his dead despairingly. 'Don't bother explaining.
It ain't nothing to do with me, thank the Lord. Just be here
with Adela and the children and that wretched cur first light
tomorrow and I'll see 'em safe home. You needn't worry.'

I insisted on paying him for the family's transportation
there and then and promised to have everyone assembled,
without fail, in Blossom's Inn yard at an early hour the
following morning. Then, with a much lighter heart, I returned
to the Arbour.

The news that they were to start for Bristol the next day
was received by my family with mixed emotions. There was

a certain amount of sadness, although the overall feeling was one of relief. The air of depression that had hung like a pall over the house since Celia's disappearance had inevitably affected everyone's spirits, and judging from the whispered conversation I overheard between Nicholas and Elizabeth at dinner, they were already looking forward to seeing their own home once more. Even the week's journey on a jolting cart which lay ahead failed to dismay them, and the fact that I was not to be a member of the party in no way blunted their excitement. It was left to Adela and, surprisingly, Adam, to express dismay at my absence.

'You come, too,' my son said, regarding me severely.

'I'll follow you as soon as I can,' I assured him.

He looked as if he didn't believe me, not without good reason. I was always disappearing from my family's life and constantly breaking promises to return when I said I would. He had learned to distrust me. Adela felt the same way and urged me to go with them.

'I should never have involved you in my cousins' affairs,' she said regretfully as we took a walk together that afternoon, leaving the children in Arbella's care.

We followed the track northward, away from the city – where the filthy, clamorous streets ran higgledy-piggledy in all directions and the houses blotted out the light with their overhanging eaves – and into the open countryside; mile after mile of sun-kissed fields, with trees and hedgerows bursting into leaf in the warm spring weather and not a dwelling nor a person in sight as far as the eye could see.

'Sweetheart, I can't abandon them now,' I said, and repeated the old arguments. 'They've been good to us, to you and the boys especially, and they are in desperate trouble. I can't bring myself to be that uncaring.'

She sighed and rested her head against my shoulder as my arm encircled her waist. 'No. Oh, Roger, I'm sorry. It's all my fault. Why did I ever allow myself to listen to that evil woman?'

My conscience smote me and I paused to stop her mouth with a kiss.

'It's all right,' I murmured. 'It's all right. But you do

see that I must stay? For a little while, at least, until I'm
convinced that there is nothing more I can do?'

I didn't add that I might now have another reason for wishing
to remain in London that had nothing to do with the Godsloves.
Indeed, I wasn't even prepared to admit it to myself. How
could I? Hadn't I told myself that the Duke of Gloucester's
affairs were nothing to do with me?

'Yes, I know,' Adela said miserably, returning my kiss
with fervour. 'And you say that there's no trace of Celia in
Dr Jeavons's house, not even in the cellar which his sister
denied was there? Why do you think she did that?'

I shrugged. 'I think Ginèvre Napier was right; for no better
reason than that Mistress Ireby wanted to be rid of us. Nothing
more sinister than that.' I glanced around, noting that the shadows
were lengthening across the grass. 'We have to go back, sweetheart. It will soon be suppertime and Oswald will be home. I
must break the bad news.'

Adela nodded. 'And my poor legs are aching. We've walked
a couple of miles at least, I should think. But at least I've had
you all to myself. We haven't passed another soul. No one
seems to live this way.' She glanced up at me. 'Now, why are
you frowning?'

'I don't know,' I answered slowly. And it was true that I
didn't. But something was suddenly making me uneasy, prodding at my memory, and yet I couldn't think what. It was the
same feeling I got whenever I saw Julian Makepeace.

I said quietly to myself, 'You'll have to do better than this,
Lord, if you want me to solve this mystery for you. You know
very well that I'm just a mere mortal. I can't be expected to
do everything on my own.'

'What are you saying?' Adela asked curiously. 'You were
mumbling something.'

'I was just humming to myself.'

'Oh well, that explains it.' My wife laughed. 'You never
could master a tune.'

Oswald was quietly furious that I had kept Ginèvre Napier's
intelligence to myself, and was at first inclined to accuse me
of not having inspected the cellar properly.

'You should have told me and I would have come with you,'

he said with suppressed violence. 'I wouldn't have had any hole-and-corner nonsense! I would have forced Mistress Ireby to open up the cellar. I would have threatened her with the law and then I would have made a thorough search.'

'I did make a thorough search,' I answered wearily. 'You have to believe me, Oswald, there is nothing down there except a few barrels of wine or ale and some odd pieces of broken furniture. For heaven's sake, man, just accept the fact that Roderick Jeavons is not holding Celia a prisoner anywhere in that house. We must look elsewhere.'

'You have to believe him, my dear,' Clemency broke in. 'If Roderick is the culprit, then he is not hiding her there.'

'And maybe he is not hiding her at all,' I said. 'Maybe he has nothing to do with Celia's disappearance. By the way,' I went on before Oswald could say anything more, 'I have made arrangements for Adela and the children to go home tomorrow. Our old friend, Jack Nym, has been disappointed of a load of glass and is more than willing to convey them to Bristol instead.'

Clemency once again expressed suitable regrets while Sybilla and her brother made a half-hearted attempt to echo her sentiments, but without much success. Arbella didn't even bother, merely reiterating her earlier words that I ought to accompany them as there appeared to be nothing I could do if I stayed.

'You should go home,' she said.

'Hold your tongue!' Oswald told her roughly. 'This is nothing to do with you. Roger has promised to help us and he's a man of his word.' He took a great gulp of air like a drowning man. 'I have commitments that I can't ignore and he's my eyes and ears while I'm otherwise engaged. Celia *must* be found.' He didn't add 'alive or dead', but it was implicit in his tone. He was frightened.

To distract his unhappy thoughts I said, 'The word on the street is that the Archbishop of York has become disaffected from my lord of Gloucester. Do you know any reason why that should be?'

The lie was successful if only for a moment or two. Oswald even managed a superior smile. 'Thomas Rotheram's an ageing, timorous old fool,' he answered scornfully, 'who should never have been given the post of Lord Chancellor. Do you know what he did, when he heard about the arrests at Northampton? He rushed to Westminster Sanctuary and gave the Great Seal into the Queen Dowager's keeping. Dear God!' His good lawyer's soul was outraged. 'The Lord Chancellor should *never* relinquish the Seal into anybody's hands but the king's. Of course, he realized his mistake almost at once and got it back again, but the damage was done. Everybody knows about it. The Inns of Court were buzzing with the news. You can be sure that Gloucester won't forgive him for it. Rotheram will be removed from the chancellorship as soon as maybe. Of course he's a Woodville adherent to his fingertips. I've always fancied that the stupid old dotard is more than a little in love with the queen.'

So that explained why the Archbishop of York was involved in this plot of Hastings – if plot it was. But the conviction was growing in me that something was afoot. I took a deep breath and put it resolutely out of my mind.

Adela and I put the children to bed soon after supper in spite of their protests that it was far too early and that they would never go to sleep. (In fact they were all three asleep in a surprisingly short space of time.) Nicholas and Elizabeth were still excited and eager to be home. Adam again surprised me by putting both arms around my neck and kissing me.

'You promised to come home soon,' he reminded me.

'And so I will,' I assured him.

'What's happened to him?' I asked my wife as we went downstairs. 'He never used to be this fond of me.'

Adela gave me one of those pitying looks that women reserve for men when anything to do with children is mentioned.

'I told you, he's growing up. He's always been a sensitive child.'

I took her word for it, but it wasn't the boy that I remembered. Then again, perhaps I had never been at home long enough to get to know him.

We decided to go for one last stroll in the wild, overgrown garden and went out through the kitchen, where Arbella was overseeing the washing of the supper dishes.

'You'll need a cloak,' she said to Adela. 'There's a breeze

sprung up since this afternoon. Take that old blue one of Celia's that's hanging on a peg in the passageway.'

She was right. A chill wind was rustling the trees and grasses and making the little clouds scud across the evening sky, chased by darker ones marching up over the horizon. We went as far as the side gate and looked over it into the copse, but all was silent except for the singing of the birds. It was here that Adam had last heard Celia's voice, talking to someone. But who? After that she had just vanished.

Adela shivered in spite of the cloak which she had wrapped around her, or perhaps because she was suddenly conscious of the fact that it belonged to Celia.

'Let's go in,' she said.

That night, I was barely asleep – or so it seemed – before I started to dream. I was at once back in the house next door to Roderick Jeavons's, trying to get out of the cellar, but the door was locked fast. I kept hammering on the wood until I could see that my hands were bleeding. No one came although I could hear a voice speaking on the other side of it. I could feel the desperation rising inside of me because I knew that what this voice was saying was important. I knew it had a message for me if only I could make out the words . . .

Then, as happens in dreams, I was standing on the other side of the door in the long passage that ran from front to back of the house, and standing beside me were Hastings and the lawyer Catesby. They were both looking straight at me, but didn't seem to notice I was there.

Hastings was saying, 'I said eight of us, Will, eight! Eight children! Eight of them! You can imagine the noise! And what's more, I don't like that blue cloak you're wearing. The colour doesn't suit you and it belongs to somebody else. You'd better get wine for eight. The archbishop's going to bring the Great Seal.'

'You can't do that,' I said, stepping forward, and Catesby caught me by the shoulders, shaking me hard . . .

'Wake up, Roger! Wake up! You're having a bad dream!' It was Adela's voice and her face that was bending over me, a pale oval in the darkness. I was bathed in sweat.

It took me a moment or two to get my bearings, then I gave an uncertain laugh and stroked her cheek.

'It's all right, sweetheart. I was riding the night mare, that's all.'

'It felt like it,' she said. 'You were tossing and turning and moaning to yourself so much I thought you'd fall out of bed. Are you all right now?'

'Yes, of course. It's Arbella's cooking. It lies heavily on my stomach sometimes. Go back to sleep. You have a long day's journey ahead of you tomorrow.'

Satisfied, she snuggled into my side and was soon gently snoring. I, on the other hand, lay wide awake, staring into the darkness trying to interpret my dream.

SEVENTEEN

I t was still barely light the following morning when I said goodbye to Adela and the children (and of course Hercules) in the courtyard of Blossom's Inn. St Laurence the Deacon, in his flowery border, looked down benevolently upon us from his sign which swung gently to and fro in a faint, barely perceptible breeze. Jack, anxious to get started, contained his soul in patience while we took our fond farewells.

'I give you four weeks,' Adela said as she held me tightly and kissed my cheek. 'Do you hear me, Roger? If you are no nearer solving this mystery in a month's time, you are to make your excuses to Oswald and Clemency and Sybilla and start for home. Promise me. I won't leave unless you do.'

'Four weeks,' I agreed, returning her embrace. 'As near as possible,' I added as a sop to those uneasy reservations which always plagued me.

She flashed me a suspicious look as, with Jack's help, she stepped into the back of the empty cart. A basket of food and drink had been supplied by Arbella and I handed over a purseful of money to meet her immediate needs. (I had spent very little in the past three weeks since leaving Bristol thanks to the generosity of the Godsloves – yet another reason why I felt unable to abandon them.) Jack climbed on to the driver's seat and was about to give the command 'Gee up!' when Adam suddenly scrambled towards me, standing up in the tail of the cart.

'Remembered,' he announced cryptically, ignoring his mother's reprimand and leaning over to put his arms around my neck. 'Woman,' he said, adding impatiently as he encountered my uncomprehending stare, 'Woman talking to Celia in the garden. Remembered!'

I took a deep breath. 'You mean that the day you overheard Celia speaking to someone in the garden at the Arbour it was another woman's voice you heard? You're sure of that? Think carefully, Adam. It's important.'

He nodded. 'Sure,' he said.

'You haven't been up until now.'

He gave a weary sigh: adults were such a trial. 'Told you. Just remembered. Didn't remember before. Do now.'

I kissed him soundly. 'You're a very clever boy.' He shot me the same sort of leery look that his mother had given me (he was unnervingly like her on occasions). He knew when he was being patronized. 'I mean it,' I assured him and kissed him again.

Then they were off. I stood waving until they were out of sight, lost among all the early-morning traffic of the streets, before entering the ale-room of the inn and ordering myself a large pot of the very best brew. The place was fairly deserted at such an early hour of the morning and I was able to sit quietly at a corner table without being disturbed by garrulous neighbours, all longing to share their life histories with me.

I was thankful that I had things to think about or parting with my family would have been less bearable. We seemed to have grown exceptionally close during the twelve days I had spent at the Arbour in spite of the doom and gloom surrounding us, and for a brief while I worried that I was losing my taste for freedom. But by the time I was halfway through my second pot of ale, the feeling of being unencumbered, and therefore at liberty to please myself without any restraint being placed upon me, had returned in full force. I was my own man again.

I considered my dream of the previous night, and not only that. In the hour just before dawn, that hour when there is a sudden shift in the light, I had jerked wide awake with the words of Margaret Walker ringing loud and clear in my head: 'I recollect my poor father going to see them once, on his own. He came back absolutely appalled. I can remember him exclaiming, "Eight children! Eight of them! You can imagine the noise! All of them talking and shouting together!" I think it made him thankful that he only had the one.' William Woodward had been talking about the Godsloves.

The dream and subsequent memory had plainly been evoked by Lord Hastings's mention of eight conspirators (and yet again I added the qualification 'if that's what they are') but I was still unsure of the number's significance. I knew I was being obtuse and that God was prompting me towards a solution of this mystery concerning Oswald and his siblings, but for the moment all was still dark. And why had I dreamed about Celia's blue cloak? This explanation was also hovering just out of reach, like the butterflies I used to try to catch as a boy in the countryside around Wells, but which always eluded my destructive, grasping fingers. Furthermore, my walk with Adela the previous afternoon kept obtruding on my thoughts just as though it, too, ought to have some special importance for me.

I pushed away my by now empty pot and stretched my long legs out in front of me under the table, closing my eyes and trying hard to concentrate on all the facts I had gathered about the Godslove family, the chief of which was that they had some terrible secret hidden in their past – provided, that was, that my little kitchen maid had not misinterpreted what she had overheard. If this were indeed the case, then it was more than possible that they had an enemy out there somewhere; an implacable foe ready to do them harm and bent on vengeance. But vengeance for what? And how long had they – or he or she – been biding their time? I decided that the moment had come, Adela no longer being present to be embarrassed by my behaviour, to tackle the remaining three family members on the subject.

I suddenly realized that Oswald had never provided me with the names of any former clients who might possibly hold a grudge against him, in spite of his having promised to do so. Did this mean that he knew of somebody who hated him; somebody whom he had wronged or failed or allowed to be condemned when he knew the person to be innocent? Oddly enough, I didn't think so. I felt convinced that he was genuinely unaware of anyone connected with his calling as a lawyer who would go to such lengths as murder – or paying others to do murder for him – simply for the sake of revenge. And yet I felt certain that, deep down, Oswald was afraid of something to which he refused to admit. The terrible secret? Most probably. That is, if there really was one . . .

I stood up abruptly, knocking over my empty pot. This was getting me nowhere. I was going round in circles, the trouble being that I wasn't sure what to do next. I remembered Adam's parting words that it was a woman he had heard talking to Celia just before the latter disappeared, so if Roderick Jeavons was involved, could it have been his sister, Mistress Ireby, delivering a false message to lure Celia away? And then it occurred to me to wonder why Celia had not returned briefly to the kitchen, to inform Arbella or one of the maids that she was going out and where she was bound. She must have stepped indoors, into the passageway, for a second or two to fetch a cloak, because Father Berowne had seen her wearing one. And it would have been only the work of a moment to put her head around the door to speak to the housekeeper. But then again, had it really been Celia that the priest had seen or had he been mistaken . . . ?

Of course he had been mistaken! He had said the woman had been wearing a blue cloak, and Celia's blue cloak was still hanging in the kitchen passageway. Adela had put it on the previous evening when we had gone for our farewell stroll in the garden. That was what my dream had been trying to tell me. But even so, I still had no clue as to what had happened to Celia or where on earth she might be.

I sat down again and called for a third pot of ale while yet again I tried to figure out what to do next. It seemed to me that I was getting in a muddle. This was one problem which I seemed unable to solve and I hated to be defeated. It was an affront to my pride.

'Drowning your sorrows, Roger?' asked a familiar voice.

I turned my head and saw Timothy Plummer sitting alongside me. He gave a lugubrious smile and whistled for the pot boy.

'You don't look any too happy yourself,' I retorted, my conscience pricking me as I wondered if I should tell him what I knew – or thought I knew – about the Lord Chamberlain. But self-interest won and I kept silent. 'Is anything the matter?'

'*Anything the matter?*' he spluttered. 'With the duke's life in danger every hour of the day! And you ask if anything's the matter!'

'Is his life in danger?' I enquired uneasily. 'I thought the Woodville bid for power had been scotched. Someone told me that Earl Rivers and Sir Richard Grey and Sir Thomas

Vaughan have been imprisoned up north where they can't do any further harm.'

'And the Queen Dowager is still in Westminster Sanctuary,' he snapped back, 'at liberty to plot and scheme. Edward Woodville is at sea with half the royal treasure and her other brother, our precious Bishop of Salisbury, is spreading sedition and lies wherever he can.' He took a swig of the ale which the pot boy had just set before him. 'I tell you, Roger, the duke is a worried man. His whole way of life is like to come crashing down about his ears if the Woodvilles have any say in the matter. For years now he's been sovereign in all but name in the north. The late king let him have his way in everything, and rightly so. Duke Richard has been the most effective and just administrator that part of the country has ever known. Yorkshiremen adore him, and that's no exaggeration. Of course, it ain't endeared him to the Percy family who've grown used to having it all their own way for centuries past. They'll do him an ill turn if they can. And then there's the little king himself. A Woodville to his fingertips if all I hear is true, and none too happy with his Uncle Richard. Not, I suppose, that you can blame him, poor little bugger. But you can't help remembering the late King Henry and Humphrey of Gloucester. I overheard our own duke mention it to Buckingham only the other day, how Good Duke Humphrey died in very mysterious circumstances as soon as his nephew was old enough to rule for himself.'

'Worrying,' I agreed, but half-heartedly. I had worries of my own to concern me.

'How long are you staying in London?' Timothy asked, draining his cup. His tone of voice put me instinctively on my guard.

'Not long,' I answered quickly. 'In fact Adela and the children and Hercules have already left for Bristol. That's why I'm here. A friend of ours, a carter who's been disappointed of a load, is able to take them all the way home. I shall follow them as soon as I can.'

'Hercules?' Timothy queried with a puckered brow.

'My dog.'

'Dear sweet virgin! You mean that mangy cur you dignify with the name of dog?' He moved closer to me on the bench

and lowered his voice. 'Listen, Roger. Don't be in too much
of a hurry to leave the capital. The duke may need your
services before all's done. I don't know what's in the wind
– in fact I don't know for certain that anything is in the
wind – but I do know I'm feeling damned uneasy. A sixth
sense is telling me that all's not well. It's no good asking
me why, but I'll say this. Ever since you got back from
France last year, Duke Richard has been unsettled. Even up
north, where he's usually at his happiest and most carefree,
he's been preoccupied. And after news reached us of King
Edward's death, well . . . He was upset naturally. Grief-
stricken. He was devoted to his brother, as you know better
than most people. But there was more to it than that. Of
course he assembled all the magnates of the region, had a
solemn Mass sung for the repose of the late king's soul and
then, himself included, made everyone swear an oath of alle-
giance to the new young king. And yet . . .'

'And yet?' I prompted, my attention caught in spite of
myself.

The spymaster shrugged. 'There's something about him I
can't quite define. An edginess, a withdrawal into himself,
an unhappiness almost, as though he's constantly wrestling
with some knotty problem that the rest of us can't be allowed
to share.' He called for a second pot of ale before continuing.
'And the business at Northampton shook him to his very
foundations. I don't think he imagined that the queen and
her family would move against him so swiftly and with such
malice. If it hadn't been for Henry of Buckingham being
privy to the Woodvilles' intentions and then deciding to throw
in his lot with his cousin instead of his in-laws, it's more
than probable that by now Prince Richard would either be
a prisoner at Grafton Regis or – even more likely – he would
be dead. Murdered like the previous Duke of Gloucester, poor
old Humphrey.'

'And you think that Buckingham was telling the truth?
About the plot, I mean. Not just trying to curry favour with
the man who will undoubtedly be nominated as Protector by
the council?'

Timothy was indignant. 'Why would he need to curry
favour? As husband of the Queen Dowager's sister he'd have

done as well, if not better, to have stayed with the Woodvilles. It's a serious threat, Roger. As Spymaster General I know for a fact that men have already been despatched to man the fortifications on the Isle of Wight and at Portsmouth. Furthermore, Sir Thomas Fulford and Sir Edward Brampton have both been ordered to sea to intercept Edward Woodville and his merry band of pirates who are apparently trying to join up with some French privateers, at present threatening the southern coast.'

I grimaced. 'As bad as that, eh?'

'If not worse.' He shook my arm. 'So keep your ear to the ground, my friend, and if you see or hear anything – anything at all – let me know at once. And, as I say, don't be in too much of a hurry to leave London. You may be needed. It's a great piece of good fortune you being here just at this time.'

If he hadn't added those last two sentences, I would have told him what I knew there and then. Indeed, I had drawn a breath ready to speak. But at his words, I expelled it again and sat silent, staring into my empty beaker. I realized that if I was not to be inveigled into Duke Richard's affairs by Timothy Plummer I had best keep quiet about the house in Old Dean's Lane and what I had overheard. I also had to apply my mind to this business of the Godsloves and either come to a conclusion as quickly as was humanly possible, or express my regrets and shake the dust of the capital from my boots as rapidly as I could.

I rose to my feet. 'I'll-er-let you know if I hear anything, Timothy,' I said, lying through my teeth. 'I shall be resident in Bishop's Gate Street Without for a while yet, I daresay.' I crossed my fingers behind my back.

He nodded. 'See that you do. By the way, what do you know about the Bishop of Bath and Wells?'

'Robert Stillington? Nothing much, Why do you ask?'

Timothy swallowed his ale. 'No reason, except that he's from your part of the world. And he's turned up at Crosby's Place a couple of times lately and been closeted with the duke.'

'Has he now?' I sucked my teeth thoughtfully. 'In case you've forgotten,' I said, 'let me remind you that the bishop

was very close to the Duke of Clarence. In fact he was imprisoned for a while round about the time of Clarence's trial and
execution. It might have been a coincidence, of course. And
then again it might not.'

Timothy looked sick. 'You're right. It had slipped my mind.
I must be losing my grip on things.' He also stood up and
straightened his tunic. 'I'm unhappy about the way things
are going, Roger, and that's a fact.'

'And where are they going?' I asked.

The spymaster sighed. 'I don't honestly know, and that's
the problem.' He squared his shoulders and drew himself up
to his full height (which was a little below my own shoulders). 'But just remember what I've said to you. If you hear
or see anything, anything at all in the least suspicious or that
you think I ought to know about, get in touch with me at once.
If I'm not there, a message left at Crosby's Place will bring
me up to this house you're staying at as soon as possible.'

Once again, I nearly spoke, but once again self-interest
held me silent. We walked together down St Lawrence's Lane
into Cheapside, but there we parted, he striding off in the
direction of the Strand and Westminster and I loitering on
the corner. Various cries of 'Hot sheep's feet!', 'Pies!', 'Ribs
of beef!' reminded me that I had breakfasted very early with
Adela and the children, and that my belly was now rumbling
with hunger. I approached the beef vendor.

'How many ribs for a farthing?' I asked.

'Eight. Got yer bowl with you, sunshine?'

'No . . . No, I haven't,' I said slowly. There it was again.
What was it about the number eight that bothered me so
much? I became aware that the street-seller was speaking.
'I'm sorry, what did you say?'

He cast his eyes up to heaven (or what we could see of it
between the overhanging eaves of the houses). 'I said, dozy,
I'll lend you a bowl.' He took one from a pile on the edge of
the tray strapped around his neck. 'And that'll be another
farthing until I get it back.' He ladled eight ribs into the bowl,
adding, 'I'll be around here fer a bit yet awhile.'

I thanked him and retreated to lean against the nearest wall,
out of the path of the constant stream of traffic that screeched
and rumbled its way along this busiest of thoroughfares, while

I sucked the ribs clean of meat and upended the bowl to drink the gravy. I had just finished and was looking around for the vendor in order to return my empty basin, when I was pounced on by a vaguely familiar figure who shouted, 'It's you again, is it?'

Adrian Jollifant! By sheer ill-luck I had chosen to prop myself against the wall of the silversmith's shop. I gave an elaborate sigh. 'What do you want with me now, sir?'

He looked me up and down. 'Damn me if I can make out who or what you are,' he complained peevishly. 'One time you're dressed up as fine as five pence, mounted on a decent horse, another time you're playing the country bumpkin but buying a ring for your wife, and now you look like a servant, but talk like an educated man.' Without giving me a chance to reply, he continued, 'Where's that thieving rapscallion Oswald Godslove? Is the old sod going to sell my house back to me or is he not? I warn you, he'll be sorry if he doesn't.'

I turned to face him. 'And if he won't agree, which I can tell you here and now is the case, what will you do to him, Master Jollifant? What *can* you do?'

I must have looked and sounded fiercer than I intended because he backed away, stuttering, 'D-don't you dare hit me again or I'll have the law on you, whoever you are. And being a friend of that cursed robber won't help you!'

I calmed down a little. 'I have no desire to hit you,' I said, 'and only did so before because you attacked me first.' I put two or three paces between us to demonstrate that I meant him no harm, and as I did so, caught a flicker of movement at the second-floor window which bellied out over the street. 'Who's that upstairs?' I demanded sharply.

The silversmith stared at me for a moment or two as if I had taken leave of my senses before his anger got the better of him again. 'What in the devil's name has it got to do with you?' he asked furiously. 'It's my old father if you want to know.'

I could see that he had left the shop door open. To distract his attention, I stooped and put the beef-seller's bowl carefully on the ground; then, before he could divine my intention, I straightened up and made a dash for it, through the shop, vaguely aware of the gaping mouths of the apprentices, to the flight of stairs beyond. At the top of this was a narrow landing and, because of my familiarity, five years earlier, with the old Babcary shop, I knew exactly where to find the steps leading to the upper floor. Once there, I could see a door partially open and, without any hesitation, pushed it wide and went in.

The pathetic occupant, a white-haired, rheumy-eyed old man, sat trembling on his bed, the frayed end of the rope which normally tethered him to the bedpost held limply on one hand.

'I-it snapped,' he whimpered. 'It-it wasn't my fault, Adrian. I-it just snapped. I only had a peep out o' the window. No one s-saw me. I-I promise.' He was terrified, and, I guessed, with some reason. A stick stood in one corner of the room, a nasty thin cane which could wreak havoc with the flesh. And as my eyes grew accustomed to gloom, I noticed raised wheals on the backs of the old man's hands and on one of his cheeks.

As I moved into the light filtering through the grime of the windows, he stammered, 'Wh-who are you? Y-you're not my son.'

'No, I'm not,' I answered grimly and swung round furiously as Adrian Jollifant puffed and panted his way into the room.

'Get out of here!' he shrieked. 'Get out! You're trespassing!'

'And you're trying to murder your father!' I accused him. 'You're mistreating him, and starving him, too, by the look of it. Mistress Napier told me that there were rumours you'd done away with him, but she thought he was just ill and confined to bed. Well, he is confined to bed, isn't he? He's tied to it, and until the rope snapped he couldn't even reach the window. Just helping him on his way, are you? And no doubt you'll give him a splendid funeral once he is dead so that all the neighbours can come and pay their respects. And, of course, they will all accept that you really are the master of the shop at last.'

'It's none of your business,' Adrian Jollifant screamed. 'He's a meddling, stupid old fool who thinks he knows better than anyone else. I hate him! I've always hated him! Now get out!'

'Oh, I'll get out,' I said, advancing and towering over him.

'And the first thing I'm going to do is to inform all your neighbours what's going on here. I'd be prepared for some very angry visitors if I were you. Not to mention representatives of the law you're so fond of invoking.'

He blenched. 'You-you wouldn't do that,' he faltered.

'Just watch me,' I snarled, and seized hold of the cane. 'But before I do, I've a good mind to give you a thrashing.' He shrank back. 'Oh, don't worry,' I sneered, suddenly sickened by him, 'I won't touch you. But I shall carry out my promise to tell your neighbours about your father's plight unless I get your solemn word that your treatment of him will alter. I'll tell you something else,' I added. 'Again according to Mistress Napier, there's been talk that you might have murdered your first wife in order to marry your second. And if people realize that you and she have been trying to murder your father, there may be more than just talk. There may be accusations brought.'

The silversmith looked so terrified now that I felt almost certain that the rumours concerning him and the first Mistress Jollifant were true. I pressed home my advantage.

'And there's another condition for my silence.' I seized him by the shoulders, pinning him back against the bedchamber wall. 'You'll leave my friends, the Godsloves, alone. You'll give up this insane pretence that somehow the Arbour belongs to you. Now!' I let him go and wiped my hands down the side of my breeches. 'I'll be back in three days to see that you've amended your ways. If not, or if I'm denied entrance, I shall carry out my threat. But before I go, you are going to give me permission to search the whole of this house, attic to cellar, just to make sure that you're not holding Celia Godslove a prisoner.'

I could tell by the blank expression on his face that he neither remembered Oswald's accusation of Sunday nor understood what I was talking about. Nevertheless, he made no effort to stop me, even following me downstairs to detail one of the apprentices to show me round the cellar. If looks could have killed I would have been a dead man, and I experienced a few qualms about descending into the depths, but he made no attempt to follow me, a circumstance for which I was truly grateful.

By the time I had finished my search, I was convinced that, whatever else he was or was not guilty of, Adrian Jollifant was not Celia's abductor. I had looked under every bed, in every cupboard, in every place, however absurd, where there was even the remotest chance that she could be hidden. If nothing else had convinced me, the return to the shop of the second Mistress Jollifant would have made up my mind for me. She might have dimpled cheeks and a sweet little turned-up nose, but she had a gimlet eye and a mouth that shut like a trap when, as now, she was displeased. Her husband would have had no chance to conceal another woman in the house while she was around. I gave her a brief bow and left the silversmith to explain my presence as best he could. Had he been a different sort of man, I would have wished him luck. As it was, I hoped he would get all that was coming to him.

As I left the shop, I said, 'Remember! Three days.'

Then I was gone, walking eastwards along Cheapside.

So that was that. Adrian Jollifant was no longer a suspect as far as I was concerned. And I felt as reasonably certain as it was possible to be that Roderick Jeavons was not the culprit, either. So who was this implacable enemy of the Godsloves, determined to eliminate them all one by one? And what, if any, significance did the number eight have? God was doing his best to enlighten me, but I was proving to be singularly obtuse, probably because there was another, greater distraction nagging away at the back of my mind. Did I tell Timothy Plummer what I knew? Was the duke's life truly in danger? Were the Woodvilles really plotting his downfall? Did this strange uneasiness which seemed to have the city in its grip have any foundation in fact?

I didn't know. And I doubted, at that point, if anyone else did either.

EIGHTEEN

As I walked eastwards along Westcheap towards the Poultry and the Great Conduit, I realized that I had never reclaimed my farthing from the seller of hot beef ribs, and had carelessly left my bowl somewhere outside the silversmith's shop for any fool to stumble over. I also realized, with a certain amount of unease, that I was growing adept in the dubious art of housebreaking, even though I had committed no other crime. Indeed, one might argue that on both occasions I had been trying to uncover a crime, and in the case of Master Jollifant's father had actually prevented one. (It was my avowed intention either to return to the shop in a few days' time or to apprise Ginèvre Napier of my discovery and leave that redoubtable dame to deal with matters in her own fashion. Either way, I felt that the old man would now be safe.)

Having eliminated the silversmith and the doctor from my enquiries very nearly to my satisfaction – I reluctantly acknowledged that there might be some small salient fact that I had overlooked regarding one or both of them – I now had to look elsewhere for my murderer. And at the risk of repeating myself, let me again say that I was conscious of the fact that God was doing his best to point me in the right direction but that my mind was clouded with other concerns. Or, at least, with something that I was desperately trying not to make my concern.

My thoughts were therefore in a turmoil and I walked blindly, bumping into people, almost getting run down by several carts, trampling over a flower-seller's tray – which he had placed on the ground while he eased his shoulders – and ruining his blooms, knocking into a pieman's stall and generally getting cursed up hill and down dale for my pains. Finally, I fell over a legless beggar, sitting on his little wheeled trolley near the Great Conduit, as I tried to get myself a drink of water.

'Stupid oaf!' he shouted furiously as I assisted him to regain his balance. 'Why don't you look where you're bloody well going?'

'Sorry! Sorry!' I apologized. 'Are you hurt?'

He felt himself cautiously in various insalubrious places before resuming his former pitiable expression. 'I think I'm a' right,' he finally admitted grudgingly. 'All the same –' he rattled his begging bowl suggestively '– I might've bin laid up fer a week or more, and then what would've become o' my poor fambly? Eight childer me an' my goody've got between us, bless the little perishers.'

Once again, I expressed my regrets, dropped more money into his bowl than I would normally have parted with, drank some water from the conduit, then went slowly on my way, the beggar's last words ringing in my ears.

'Eight childer me and my goody've got between us . . .'

And those other words of William Woodward, Margaret Walker's father. 'Eight children! Eight of them!'

My legs dragged themselves to a stop as revelation dawned and I just stood there, buffeted by the passers-by whose imprecations were as nothing to those I was heaping on my own head. Of course, of course! Eight! My heart was hammering in my chest, and I had almost set out along the Poultry and the Stocks Market, heading for Bishop's Gate Street, when I changed my mind and veered right from the Great Conduit into Bucklersbury. It was as well, before I took action, to make certain that my facts were correct and that there was no room for doubt.

I entered Julian Makepeace's shop, still gloomy in spite of the warm May sunshine outside, and was met by Mistress Naomi, looking prettier and even more pleased with herself than when I had first seen her. The reason was not far to seek as she flashed her left hand with a ring prominently displayed on the third finger; not a wedding band, but plainly a pledge of some kind or another. I was obviously expected to comment, but my mind was too taken up by my recent discovery to waste time on polite conversation.

'Is Apothecary Makepeace in?' I demanded.

Naomi made a little moue of disappointment. 'I'll find out,' she said, and flounced off to the living quarters behind the shop.

A second or two later, Julian appeared, exuding his usual aura of good health and unabashed friendliness.

'Master Chapman, how nice to see you again. What can I do for you? Nothing amiss with your family, I hope?'

'No, no!' I answered hurriedly. 'They've gone home to Bristol. Master Makepeace, there is something I must make sure of. You told me that after your mother married Morgan Godslove, you and Reynold went to live with an aunt—'

'Grandmother,' he corrected me.

'Grandmother, then,' I continued impatiently, 'who lived in Candlewick Street. You told me that neither of you ever lived with her in Bristol.'

'That's quite correct,' he agreed, puzzled but smiling.

'Are you quite sure?' I persisted.

He gave a little laugh. 'Quite sure.'

'Then did you and Reynold perhaps pay a visit to the house at Keynsham after your mother's marriage to your stepfather?' I suggested.

'No, never. My brother and I didn't see our mother again after her wedding day. I daresay that may appear strange to you, but travel was arduous and expensive and our grandmother was a poor woman. And Morgan Godslove gave no indication of desiring our company. Moreover, within three years of the marriage, our mother had born her new husband two children of his own to add to the four he already had by his first wife. He had no need of Reynold and myself. On the contrary, I imagine he was pleased to be rid of us so easily as we should only have meant two more mouths to feed. As for Mother herself, she was not a maternal woman. Our grandmother had always been the constant, steadying influence in Reynold's and my life from our earliest days, so it was no penance for us to live with her permanently. Whether or not our mother would have shown more affection for Martin and Celia than she did for us we shall never know. Within six years of her second marriage she died of the plague, and our stepfather was a widower for the second time.' He frowned. 'You still look uncertain, Master Chapman. It would seem that there is something about my story you fail to understand.'

We were interrupted for a few minutes by customers; a woman who bought syrup of calamint for a child with a bad cough and another who wanted extract of feverfew to make into a poultice for a sprained wrist.

'Be very careful with it,' Julian advised the latter as he handed over the little box. 'Keep it well out of the reach of your children. Concentrated feverfew can be poisonous.'

The woman thanked him and departed.

'And now!' Julian turned his attention back to me. 'Master Chapman, what is bothering you?'

I took a deep breath. 'When I was first told the history of the Godslove family, the person who gave me the details said that her father – a distant kinsman of Morgan Godslove who had visited the family at Keynsham – was horrified by the fact that there were *eight* children in the house. But by my reckoning I can only make it six: Clemency, Sybilla, the sister who died after eating mushrooms—'

'Charity,' Julian supplied.

'Thank you. Yes, Charity and Oswald from the first marriage, and your half-siblings, Martin and Celia from the second. If, as you say, you and your brother were never present, not even for a visit, who were numbers seven and eight?'

My companion considered the question. 'Could this kinsman of the Godsloves have been mistaken?' he asked at last. 'Is it possible that he miscounted? Six children stampeding around could possibly appear more numerous than they actually were.'

That, I knew, was true. When Nicholas and Elizabeth were playing one of their games, upstairs at home in Small Street, it could often sound like an army on the march.

'I suppose it's possible,' I conceded reluctantly, but then shook my head. The number eight had recurred too frequently during the past few days for me to ignore it. God's finger was inexorably pointing me in a particular direction. 'Nevertheless, I don't think so,' I added. 'My informant was adamant that her father said eight.'

Julian Makepeace chewed a thumbnail, as intrigued by the problem as I was. Meantime, I cudgelled my brains trying to remember all that Margaret Walker had said. Suddenly, memory sharpened.

'Wait! Something's coming back to me. I can recollect Margaret – the woman who told me the story – saying that after the death of his second wife – that is after your mother's death – Morgan Godslove decided against marrying again. Instead he hired a housekeeper. And,' I went on triumphantly, 'I can even recall her name. Tabitha Maynard! That was it. But a few years later, she and Morgan were both drowned in a tragic accident. The two of them were aboard the Rownham ferry when it capsized in a terrible storm. Master Makepeace, is it possible, do you think, that this Tabitha Maynard had children of her own? Children who would have gone to live in the Godslove household when their mother became Morgan's housekeeper?'

The apothecary stared at me for a moment or two, then sadly shook his head. 'I'm afraid I wouldn't know. After my mother died, all communication with the Godsloves ceased. Not that there had ever been much: one short letter announcing her death was all we received, and I knew nothing more about the family until they moved to London when Oswald was about fourteen. Clemency brought Martin and Celia to visit us, but we never had a great deal to do with any of them, even then. As for this housekeeper, I've never heard any mention of her until now.' He smiled apologetically. 'I regret I can't be of more help on the subject. But of course the people to ask are Oswald and his sisters.' He rubbed the side of his nose reflectively. 'If there were children, I wonder what became of them?' Almost in the same breath, he answered his own question. 'I suppose they would have been reclaimed by their mother's kinfolk.'

'Yes, I suppose they would,' I agreed, and held out my hand. 'Thank you for being so patient with me, Master Makepeace. I just wanted to be sure that the extra two children could not possibly have been you and your brother. By the way, am I to congratulate you?'

He looked bewildered. 'Congratulate me?'

'I noticed Mistress Naomi was wearing a ring.'

His eyes twinkled. 'Oh that! She just chooses to wear it on her wedding finger and I don't dispute her right to do so.'

'But you bought it for her?'

'I bought it as a favour from an old friend of mine who was in urgent need of ready money, that's all. There's nothing more to it than that.'

'I see,' I said and once more held out my hand. To enquire further would be to intrude upon his privacy to an unwarrantable degree. And I liked him as much as I had liked his brother. I wished to stay friends.

I retraced my steps to the Great Conduit and from there walked slowly homeward through the Poultry and the Stock's Market, busy with my own thoughts and taking little heed of what was going on around me. I did notice, however, that several enterprising street-sellers had exchanged their usual goods for trays of 'coronation specials': cheap miniature replicas of bits of the regalia and little dolls in royal purple, distressingly bad wooden effigies of our young boy-king. I resisted the temptation to buy one, in spite of knowing how much Elizabeth would love it.

As I turned into Bishop's Gate Street Within, I was forced into the side of the roadway by a bevy of horsemen all wearing the Duke of Gloucester's blue and murrey livery, the animals' coats gleaming like satin in the pale spring sunlight. And there in the middle of them was the duke himself, his small, dark face tense between the swinging curtains of almost black hair. (I remembered people who had known the late Duke of York saying that Richard was the only son who truly resembled him).

I withdrew into the shelter of the houses on the left-hand side, hoping to remain unseen, but suddenly the cavalcade came to a halt. The horsemen nearest to me shifted their mounts to allow the duke a passage through their ranks, and I noted with amusement their utter astonishment that the mightiest subject in the kingdom should stop to speak to a ragamuffin such as I appeared to be.

'Roger!' He was riding a big, handsome black with white stockings and a pair of flashing, brilliant, imperious eyes. He himself was still dressed from head to foot in deepest mourning and I noticed a network of fine lines around his eyes which had not been there when I last saw him and told of strain. All the same, he spoke cheerfully enough. 'I was told that you were in London.'

I dutifully bent the knee and kissed the hand he extended towards me, but at the same time snarled, 'That idiot, Timothy Plummer, I suppose.'

There was a hum of outrage from the duke's escort that I should speak to him in such a fashion, but he only smiled and went on, 'You're lodging near here, I understand. Don't run away, will you? I may need to send for you. I'm living at Baynard's Castle with my mother for the time being.'

I muttered something unintelligible and he nodded before riding off, his retinue clattering after him, to vanish through the gates of Crosby's Place.

My determination to return to Bristol as soon as possible was now stronger than ever. I had to concentrate all my energies on solving this mystery of the Godslove family and discovering what had happened to Celia. Not that I entertained much hope of finding her alive. All my instincts now told me she was dead.

Supper that afternoon was a strange meal without Adela and the children to cheer our spirits. Even Hercules's absence was mourned: Clemency admitted that she missed his cold, wet nose nudging her for tit-bits.

To begin with, there were only the four of us, Clemency, Sybilla, Arbella and myself, but halfway through the meal Oswald arrived home and took his place at the head of the table. He seemed tired and out of sorts, a condition aggravated by none of us having any news to report of Celia.

He took a few spoonfuls of mutton stew, but refused the freshly baked oatcakes that Arbella offered him.

'There's a rumour going around the Inns of Court,' he said, 'that the executors of the late king's will are refusing to administer it so long as the Queen Dowager and her children remain in sanctuary. For the time being, the goods are to be put under ecclesiastical sequestration.'

None of us made a reply to this nor did Oswald seem to expect any. He lapsed once more into moody silence; a silence

I finally broke with my information about Adrian Jollifant and the discovery I had made concerning his father.

'He permitted me to search the entire house, including the cellars,' I said, stretching the truth only a very little for the sake of brevity. 'Celia is not being concealed by Master Jollifant, so we can forget him as we can Dr Jeavons.'

'Not necessarily,' Oswald retorted grimly. 'One or the other may already have murdered Celia and buried her body.'

The three women cried out at that and Sybilla, as usual, burst into noisy sobs. I waited for these to subside before pouring myself more wine and looking slowly around the table. Clemency shifted uncomfortably, as though she guessed that something portentous was coming.

'After your stepmother, the former Widow Makepeace, died,' I said quietly, 'I understand that your father engaged a housekeeper, a Mistress Maynard. Tabitha Maynard.' I hesitated a moment, debating whether to present my next statement as question or fact. I decided on the latter. 'She had two children. I don't know what sex they were; if they were two boys, two girls or one of each. But I know that she had them.'

'A boy and a girl,' Sybilla burst out. 'Henry and Luc . . .' Her voice tailed away as she realized that Oswald was glaring furiously at her and had even raised a hand as though to strike her. 'Oh . . . I-I'm sorry.' Her eyes filled with tears. 'Sh-shouldn't I have said anything?' She started to cry again.

'Why can you never keep your mouth shut?' Oswald thundered at her.

Clemency hushed him sternly and put an arm around her sister's shoulders. 'There, there, Syb,' she comforted the younger woman, frowning at her brother. 'There's no reason at all why Roger shouldn't be told.' She added significantly, 'There's no mystery about it.'

'No. No, of course not,' Oswald agreed hurriedly, realizing his mistake. 'I'm sorry, Sybilla my dear. I've had a very trying day and I'm worried out of my mind about Celia.' He turned to me. 'Yes, our housekeeper – Tabitha Maynard as you so rightly say – had two children. A boy, Henry and girl, Lucy.' He forced a smile. 'May I ask what your sudden interest in them is?'

'How old were they?' I asked ignoring his question.

'Oh . . .' He looked vaguely towards his elder sister. 'What would you say, Clem?'

Clemency was brisk. 'When our stepmother died and Mistress Maynard came to look after us, I should say that Henry was about six, a year younger than Oswald. Lucy was a little older, nine perhaps, or ten. Probably ten. She was fifteen when Father and her mother were drowned on the Rownham ferry.'

'And what happened to them after that? Did they continue to live with you?'

Sybilla nodded eagerly. 'Yes, they did.'

I moved so that I was looking directly at her on the opposite side of the table. 'But they didn't come to London with you, did they?' I asked gently. 'What happened to them?'

Sybilla immediately became confused. 'I . . . I . . .' she began, glancing wildly first in her brother's direction, then at her sister.

Once again, it was Clemency who stepped smoothly into the breach. 'Neither Henry nor Lucy wished to remove to London, so they decided to return to their mother's family – a sister or cousin or someone – who lived in the village of St Bede's Minster.'

'But—' Sybilla began, obviously bewildered.

Oswald hissed at her to be silent. 'Yes, of course. I recollect now that's what happened. I was only fourteen or so at the time,' he explained. 'Clem would have been nearly thirty. That's why her memory is so much better than mine. But you still haven't explained your reason for asking these questions, Roger.'

I glanced towards Arbella, sitting at one end of the table, her lips slightly parted, her eyes wide with curiosity, the raisin pasty on her plate quite forgotten in her interest in the story. Clemency, ever swift on the uptake, began stacking the dirty dishes.

'Time to wash up, Arbella,' she said firmly in a tone that brooked no argument. 'I'll call one of the girls to help you clear the table.'

The housekeeper flushed resentfully at what amounted to a summary dismissal, but had no option except to obey. She was not the mistress of the house yet, however much she would like to be, and probably knew deep down that she never would be. She moved as slowly as she dared, but in the end, with the maid's help, she was forced to retire to the kitchen.

Clemency sat down again at the table and regarded me straitly. 'What's this all about, Roger?' she asked. 'You obviously have something to say that you don't want Arbella to hear.'

'Arbella is perfectly trustworthy, you know,' Sybilla protested in her usual vague, woolly-minded fashion. 'She's been with us now for quite a few years.'

'I'm not questioning Mistress Rokeswood's character,' I said. 'I'm sure she is most reliable.'

'But for some reason you don't want her overhearing what you have to say to us, is that it?' Clemency half-looked towards her brother, then changed her mind. When I inclined my head, she went on, 'Does that mean that it – whatever "it" is – reflects badly upon us?'

'Not necessarily,' I replied quickly before Oswald could start to bluster. 'It depends what your answer is.'

Oswald was on his feet, every inch the lawyer. 'You have no right to catechize us about anything,' he pronounced in his best courtroom voice. 'Clemency! Sybilla! You are obliged to say nothing.'

Sybilla looked frightened, but Clemency said, in an elder sister tone that I had never heard her use before, 'Sit down, Oswald, and don't make a fool of yourself. You want Master Chapman to discover who's been terrorizing us, don't you? Who killed Martin and Charity. You want to find Celia or . . . or her . . . her body.' She took a deep, steadying breath and nodded at me as, most surprisingly, Oswald obeyed and resumed his seat. 'Well, Roger, what is it you want to ask us that you don't want Arbella to know about?'

'I want to know what really happened to Henry and Lucy Maynard.'

'We've told you what happened,' Oswald began, but once again, Clemency intervened.

'Be quiet, brother! It's time Roger knew everything. He's been handicapped by our reticence, our inability to tell the truth, from the start.'

'It has nothing to do with that,' Oswald said positively. 'I keep telling you.'

'It may have no bearing on the matter,' Clemency agreed. 'But we don't know for certain. And even if it doesn't, for my own part, I can't help feeling that heaven is punishing us for our sin.' Sybilla began to grizzle again, but her sister ignored her and turned to me. 'You want to know what happened to Henry and Lucy Maynard? We sold them to the Irish slavers working out of Bristol. You may think that the trade, which was outlawed by both Church and state, ended centuries ago, but—'

'I think nothing of the sort,' I interrupted. 'I know that it still exists.' I didn't enlarge on the subject, although I saw avid curiosity in all their eyes. 'Why did you sell your late housekeeper's children to the slavers?'

'We needed the money,' Clemency replied simply. 'Oswald wanted to study law and we knew – at least, Charity and Sybilla and I knew – that it would be as much as we could afford. We wanted the best for Oswald, so we had to move to London and quickly. He was already fourteen. Consequently, the house at Keynsham was sold for less than it might have been had we had more time at our disposal. Moreover, the Maynards, who were nothing to us . . .'

'We'd only let them stay on with us after Tabitha died out of the goodness of our hearts,' Sybilla chimed in indignantly. 'They weren't Godsloves, after all.'

'They intended to accompany you to London?' I queried.

Clemency bit her lip. 'It never occurred to them that we didn't want them. After seven years, I'm afraid they regarded themselves as a part of the family. It was partly our own fault. We should have asked them to leave when Father and their mother died. Unfortunately, we were quite fond of them and stupidly let them remain.'

'But now you didn't want them any more?'

Clemency sighed. 'It sounds so callous when put like that. But no, once the decision was taken concerning Oswald and the move to London, and once money became an object with us, they were just two more mouths to feed.'

'We did ask them to leave,' Sybilla pointed out self-righteously, wagging her head from side to side.

'They had nowhere to go. There was no kinswoman living in St Bede's Minster.' Clemency suddenly dropped her gaze, avoiding my eyes. 'I don't know whose idea it was to rid ourselves of them and make money at the same time. Maybe it was Charity's, maybe it was mine.'

'Well, it certainly wasn't mine,' Sybilla cut in virtuously. 'But it was the right decision, all the same.'

'Hush, Syb,' her sister commanded tartly. Clemency hadn't looked up, but she must have guessed at my expression.

'So you sold them to the Irish slavers.' This then was the 'terrible secret' my little kitchen maid had heard mentioned. 'You knew where to find them?'

Clemency nodded. 'I had been visiting Bristol all my life, and everyone in the city knows about "little Ireland".' Her voice became almost inaudible. 'It wasn't difficult to arrange for Henry and Lucy to be abducted.'

'I keep telling you, Clem,' Oswald broke in angrily, 'this . . . this persecution can have nothing to do with the Maynards. You've always been quite adamant that neither of them could have known that you and Charity and Sybilla were behind it.'

'I didn't think they did,' Clemency admitted desperately. 'We just took them into Bristol one morning and . . . and made some excuse to leave them in the vicinity of Marsh Street for a while. We'd previously arranged with one of the slavers where they would be found. I daresay, to be sure, he was watching when we left them. Certainly, they had vanished by the time we returned and we've never seen anything more of them from that day to this.'

'I hope you got a good price for them,' I said before I could stop myself.

Clemency flushed a dark red, but her only answer was, 'Good enough.' She added defensively, 'I've always heard that the Irish treat their slaves very well.'

I didn't remark that well-treated or not, slavery was never the same as freedom. There seemed to be no point: they knew that as surely as I did. Instead I asked, 'And it has never occurred to you that this Lucy and Henry Maynard might be behind all your troubles?'

'No, of course not,' Oswald said, bringing his hands down on the table and once more getting to his feet. 'If they'd known the truth, why would they have waited all these years to get their revenge?'

NINETEEN

I didn't believe him.

I realized with sudden clarity that the possibility, although not the probability, of it being the Maynards had been lurking somewhere in the back of his mind, firmly suppressed, from the very beginning of this unhappy saga. It accounted for his indifference to my suggestion that any of his past, or even present, clients might be responsible for the terrible vengeance being wreaked upon his family, and his persistent failure to supply me with a list of names. It also explained his determination that Roderick Jeavons should prove to be the culprit. The doctor not only had a strong motive, but Oswald hated him because the man had the temerity to be in love with Celia. My previous suspicion that the lawyer was himself in love with his half-sister had now become a certainty – and it was, moreover, absolutely necessary that there should be a suspect with a good enough reason for the vendetta to obviate those two ghosts from the past.

After his outburst, Oswald stumped from the room, leaving me alone with Clemency and Sybilla. I looked at the former and raised my eyebrows. 'What do you think, mistress?'

She appeared suddenly much older than her fifty-odd years and put up a frail hand to push back a tress of hair that had escaped from beneath her cap.

'I don't know,' she said. 'But from the beginning, ever since things started to go seriously wrong, I've been afraid that we were all being punished for our crime. Although,' she added desperately, 'as Oswald says, if Lucy and Henry knew all along that we were to blame for their capture, that it was not just chance, why would they have waited so long to take their revenge? And why would they have killed Reynold Makepeace? Our stepbrothers were unknown to them. And how would they have discovered where to find us?'

'I can't give you answers to all your questions,' I said. 'But as to the third, finding you would have presented little difficulty. They knew you and your siblings intended coming to London, and they knew the reason why. They would only have needed to ask around the inns of court to discover a lawyer named Godslove, and once he had been pointed out to them, following him home would have been a simple enough matter. As for why they waited so long, that would have depended on a number of factors; when they left Ireland for one. And having found you, they may have been in no hurry to execute vengeance. They could have relished seeing you suffer as they had suffered, and were in no mind to bring it to a swift conclusion. Slowly, one by one, they are eliminating the whole family. First attempts are not always successful, as witness you and Sybilla, but that probably doesn't worry them. In some ways it makes the chase more fun and prolongs your misery.'

'But where are they? *Who* are they?' Clemency asked in trembling tones, her face as white as the broad collar protecting the shoulders of her gown. Then suddenly, like Oswald, she heaved herself to her feet, slamming both hands down on the table top and making her sister jump. 'No! I don't believe this is the answer! I won't believe it! Lucy and Henry had no idea that we were behind their seizure by the Irish slavers. Charity and I had been most careful to go in disguise to that inn in Marsh Street when making the necessary arrangements, and we were careful to be nowhere near when they were taken.'

'You don't think the slavers themselves knew and revealed the truth?'

But even as I asked the question, I guessed it to be unlikely. The Irishmen who carried on their illegal trade with the help of Bristol's respectable citizens, were men who knew how to keep their mouths shut. Nor were they interested in the whys and wherefores of their nefarious transactions or in exchanging small talk with their victims. It was a business like any other, though perhaps more lucrative than some, and as such, respect for the client was paramount. So when Clemency answered firmly that she thought it impossible, I was forced to agree with her.

We joined Oswald in the parlour and, by tacit consent, the rest of the evening passed without further discussion of the subject, even though it was the one uppermost in all our minds. We speculated where Adela and the children might be spending their first night on the road, I expressed my total confidence in Jack Nym, and we speculated in a desultory kind of way about Oswald's news concerning the late king's will. But eventually, and much earlier than usual, we parted company and went to bed. As I mounted the stairs, I could hear Arbella still clattering angrily around in the kitchen.

I woke suddenly in the middle of the night, my heart pounding and my hands groping for the comfort of Adela's body, only to realize, of course, that I was alone. The door to the children's room stood open, emitting a deafening silence, and there was no Hercules, snuffling and whining pitifully to be allowed on to our bed.

I sat up, pushing the hair out of my eyes and passing a hand across my damp forehead, trying to pinpoint what exactly had woken me. I had been dreaming, I was sure of that, but, most unusually, was unable immediately to recall my dream. I had been in the apothecary's shop; I could still see the rows of bottles on the shelves, the bunches of dried herbs, the pestle and mortar on the counter, and I had been talking to someone. Julian Makepeace? No, he had not been present, I would swear to that. His housekeeper, young Naomi, then? Yes, that was it. I even recalled being able to smell the faint scent of rosemary that emanated from her gown. She had been saying something to me, but what? I shut my eyes against the shadows of the room, the empty beds, the feeling of loss, and concentrated hard . . .

Her face, as I had seen it in my dream, flashed suddenly and vividly before me. She was holding up her left hand, a small, triumphant smile curling the sensuous mouth. 'Do you like my ring?' she had asked. 'Do you like my ring?'

And it was at that moment that I had recognized it. It was Adela's ring, the one I had bought for her from Master Jollifant's silversmith's shop. The one that had been stolen from the Arbour. It was the shock of that recognition that had wakened me, bringing me out in a sweat.

I opened my eyes again, accustomed now to the darkness and able to make out the lineaments of the furniture and the faint grey light around the shutters. What was it that Julian Makepeace had said when I had quizzed him about its purchase? 'I bought it as a favour from an old friend of mine who was in need of ready money, that's all.' But who was the old friend? And what was he or she doing with a stolen ring? Was he or she the thief? Or had this person come by it in all innocence? Well, I had only to visit the apothecary's shop again to find out, and I would most certainly do that first thing in the morning, after breakfast.

I found I was shaking with excitement, and tried to calm myself by eating a little of the bread and drinking some of the water which Arbella, ever mindful of her domestic duties, had placed beside my bed for my 'all-night'. I had just reached for the water bottle a second time, when a slight noise made me push back the bed curtain and look towards the door. The latch was being very slowly and cautiously lifted, but it was stiff with age, like so many others in the house, and had to be dealt with firmly. It resisted all attempts to treat it gently.

I eased myself out of bed as silently as possible, intending to station myself behind the door when it opened and thus surprise the intruder. But as I returned the water bottle to the tray, my hand shook and I dropped it on the floor where it rolled a little way before fetching up against the clothes chest with an almighty thud. Cursing, I called out, 'Who's there? Who is it?' and in getting out of bed, slipped in one of the puddles of water left by the bottle's contents and sat down heavily, giving my spine a nasty jar in the process.

I forget which particular profanities issued from my lips; suffice it to say that they were not for repetition and would have provoked Adela's censure had she been there. I wrenched open the door with a fury that almost broke the latch and stepped out into the passage.

Needless to say, it was empty. I glanced to right and left, but no sign of life disturbed the shadows. The house was as quiet as the grave, not even a faint snore breaking the silence. I went back to bed and, hopefully, to sleep, persuading myself that I had been mistaken. But I dragged the chest across the doorway, all the same.

Bucklersbury was its usual busy early morning self as I picked my way through the overflow from the common drain and entered Julian Makepeace's shop for the second time in twenty-four hours. He was busy at the counter, selecting pills from a large tray in front of him, and counting them into little boxes. Absorbed in his task, he did not immediately look up as I entered.

'. . . six, seven, eight, nine, ten. And what can I do for you, s . . .?' His voice tailed away as he recognized me and he made a comical grimace. 'Master Chapman!' he exclaimed, but was too polite to utter the word 'again'. Nevertheless, I could hear it in the inflection of his voice. He smiled resignedly. 'Have you by any chance come to buy something this time?'

I regret that I didn't even bother to reply to this soulful query, so anxious was I to get an answer to my own question. 'Master Makepeace, who sold you that ring?' He looked so affronted, angry almost, that I was forced to explain the circumstances and the reason for my enquiry. 'So you see,' I finished lamely, 'why I need to know.'

'If you are correct, yes,' he said gravely, and going to the door at the back of the shop which opened into the living quarters, called, 'Naomi, my dear, please come here and bring the ring I gave you.' There was a moment's pause before she appeared. 'Show it to Master Chapman,' he instructed.

The pretty face assumed a mulish expression. 'Why should I?'

The apothecary sighed. 'Just do as I say.' And before the girl realized what he would be about, he had grabbed her left wrist and forced her hand towards me. 'Is that your wife's ring, Master Chapman?' Naomi gasped in protest and tried to pull free, but Julian Makepeace's grip remained firm. 'Is it?' he repeated.

I nodded, adding, 'I'm sure the silversmith, Adrian Jollifant, will, if necessary, confirm that it's the one he sold me.'

'No!' Naomi put her hands behind her back and turned to her lover (I felt certain Julian was that). 'It's mine. He shan't

have it. He's lying. You heard what she said. She said it had
been given to her when she was a young girl and she hated
having to part with it.'

'Who said?' I demanded urgently.

The apothecary pulled down the corners of his mouth.
'Where did you say your wife lost the ring, Master
Chapman?'

'She didn't lose it. It was stolen from the Arbour. Someone
must have got into the house.'

Julian Makepeace shook his head sadly. 'I doubt that, my
friend. You see it was Arbella Rokeswood who offered it to
me.'

'*Arbella?*' For a moment or two I stared at him incredulously, but then things began to fall into place. For a start,
who of the Arbour inmates would have been the most likely
to try to enter my bedchamber the previous night? Not Oswald
or his sisters: they would have no reason to do so. But if
Arbella . . . My heart was pounding again and I had to grip
the edge of the counter. If Arbella were really Lucy Maynard
and was beginning to fear that I suspected the truth, might
she not make an attempt to silence me? She would surely
not balk at another murder, having killed, or helped to kill,
a number of times already . . .

But *was* she Lucy Maynard? Perhaps her story that she
was in need of money had been the truth. Maybe she had
taken Adela's ring for just that reason. On the other hand, I
had little doubt that she was paid well enough by the
Godsloves; her food and shelter were supplied and, as far as
I could see, she had few wants of her own. And what of her
apparent passion for Oswald? Was that just simulated as an
additional part of her disguise, if she were indeed the long
lost Lucy? Or had she, at some point in her masquerade
genuinely fallen in love with him?

I suddenly became aware that Naomi was screaming the
most unladylike obscenities at Julian Makepeace, and that
he was offering me the ring which he seemed to have prised
from her finger by force.

'Take it, Master Chapman,' he was saying. 'I believe you.
It's yours. Why should you lie about it? It will teach me not
to do old friends a good turn in future.'

'Master Makepeace,' I said, leaning towards him and raising my voice, 'you say Mistress Rokeswood is an old friend. How old? What do you know about her?'

It was his turn to look startled. 'I-I've known Arbella for several years now. She's always come here to buy the family's medicines when they were needed. And other things like fleabane for keeping the fleas at bay, and alkanet for colouring cheeses and a mixture of my own – gall nuts and iron and alum – for dying hair. A pleasant woman, pleasantly spoken, politer by far than my stepsisters' previous housekeeper, who—'

I interrupted him unceremoniously. 'She's only kept house for the Godsloves for the past year or so, then?'

'Three years. Maybe four. I can't remember. Does it matter?'

'Perhaps.' I held out my hand. 'Master Makepeace, I can't tell you how grateful I am that you believe my story and for returning Adela's ring. I suppose . . . I suppose Mistress Rokeswood didn't mention why she needed money so urgently?'

He eyed me curiously. 'No, nor did I ask.' He glanced ruefully at the door at the back of the shop through which Naomi had just that moment flounced, oozing enough ill-will to make any man wince in anticipation of the tirade to come. 'What will you do? Will you confront Mistress Rokeswood with the theft? I shall certainly be wary of her in future.'

'I don't know,' I answered cautiously. 'I must think it over. It might be awkward to accuse her while I'm still a guest at the Arbour.' I saw that he was about to dispute this argument and went on hurriedly, 'I'll relieve you of my presence. Thank you again for being so understanding. If ever I can do anything for you . . .'

'As a matter of fact, there is,' he said, smiling faintly. He took a small box from the shelf behind him. 'This is Father Berowne's extract of feverfew. He likes to keep some handy for making poultices when he hurts himself working in that garden of his. If you're passing his door, will you give it to him?'

'Of course,' I answered, putting the little box into my pouch, glad that there was something I could do in exchange for his unconditional acceptance of my story. He came out from behind the counter and moved towards the shop door to open it for me, but I stayed him with a hand on his arm. 'I recall you saying that extract of feverfew is poisonous. Could it be administered in a drink?'

For a moment, he looked startled, then laughed. 'It would be difficult. In that form –' he nodded at my pouch – 'it's very bitter. An infusion of the flowers and leaves can be used to alleviate headaches and ease women's monthly pains, and mixed with wine and honey they are a good cure for melancholy and dizziness. But when the plant's juices are concentrated, the result, as I say, is bitter.'

'Is there any way in which the taste might be disguised?' It was my turn to laugh at his anxious expression. 'Don't worry. I'm not planning to do away with anyone.'

He looked shamefaced. 'No, I didn't really think you were.' He considered for a moment. 'I suppose if you smeared a little of the extract around the rim of a beaker, the drinker might not notice it. I daresay it wouldn't prove fatal, but it could make a person ill.'

'Thank you,' I said. 'You've been extremely patient and most understanding.' I glanced towards the opposite door. 'I hope you make your peace with Mistress Naomi and that she won't make you suffer too greatly.'

His eyes twinkled. 'Oh, I don't think she'll do that, but it will cost me another ring I don't doubt. Women!' he added. 'But we can't do without them, I suppose.'

I walked back along Bucklersbury deep in thought. The muckrakers were by now busy at work on the central drain and the night-soil removers, with their noisome little carts, were going from house to house emptying the privies, while several roisterers, already drunk even at this early hour of the morning, rolled out of the Voyager, something that would never have happened in Reynold Makepeace's day. But I hardly noticed any of these things – or if I did, paid them no heed – being deep in thought.

Why would Arbella Rokeswood be in need of money? And another thought intruded before I had formed the answer to my question. Adam had recollected that the person he had

overheard talking to Celia in the Arbour garden had been a
woman. Could it possibly have been Arbella? Almost at once,
I realized that if that were so, then it would explain why
Celia had failed to inform anyone else that she was going
out. She would naturally have assumed that the housekeeper
would tell them where she was. And she had most probably
gone at Arbella's instigation.

Having by this time reached the Great Conduit again, I
paused for a drink and to splash my face and hands with
water. Feeling somewhat refreshed, I returned to my first
question: why was Arbella suddenly in need of money? And
what for? The answer came with the memory of something
I had said to Oswald; that it must cost a great deal to hire
bravos willing to kill to order. And immediately I remembered those other two thefts: the pyx taken from St Botolph's
Church and the stealing of the tailor's savings from his
cottage near the Bedlam. Father Berowne had said that the
pyx was stolen over a year ago and Peter Coleman had said
much the same thing about his gold. And in the autumn of
the preceding year, Martin Godslove had been set upon,
apparently by street robbers, and murdered, while within the
past few months or so, Sybilla had been injured by falling
masonry from the Bishop's Gate wall.

I remembered something else as well; three things, in fact.
The first was how Arbella had kept urging me to return to
Bristol with Adela and the children; the second was her reluctance to tell me the tailor's name and address until bullied
into it by Oswald; and finally, I recalled Arbella's appearance at the church the day before yesterday while I was
talking to the priest. My initial impression had been that she
was flustered by the sight of me. But with her usual self-
possession, she had quickly recovered her countenance and
allayed any curiosity on my part by announcing she had
come to confession.

I realized that I was walking up Bishop's Gate Street
Within without any clear idea of how I got there. It was
quiet today, quieter than it had been at any time since my
arrival a fortnight previously; although I had to admit that
that St George's Day now seemed more like two months
than a mere two weeks ago. And for one of those two weeks

I had been ill, thanks to an excess of Father Berowne's elderflower wine . . .

Or had that really been the cause? I drew out the little box from my pouch and contemplated it, another suspicion taking shape in my mind. Yet more memories surfaced; one in particular: the tailor's story of how he had volunteered to head a subscription to replace the stolen pyx during one of Father Berowne's visits to him. The offer alone would have implied that he had money put by, and although he had not actually said as much, I suspected it to be more than possible that he had confided further in the priest, even going so far as to disclose his treasure's hiding place. It would have been the natural thing to do, and the tailor had been emphatic that nothing had been disturbed during the robbery. Whoever took the money seemed to have known exactly where to look for it . . .

I paused, leaning against the wall of Crosby's Place, biting my lower lip between my teeth and trying to discern where my galloping thoughts were leading me. Were they really saying what they appeared to be saying? That Father Berowne was a murderer and a thief? That he was in reality Henry Maynard? But even as I told myself that the idea was ridiculous, I could hear in my imagination the priest's Irish lilt and his hasty denial that he had ever seen that country. His explanation had been that he must have picked it up from his father, who came from around Waterford, and I had said . . . What had I said? I struggled to remember. I had said that the slavers used the coves and inlets around the port to land their illegal cargoes, and he had known instantly what I meant. There had been no need to explain to him the details of Bristol's infamous trade with their southern Irish neighbours.

Arbella Rokeswood and Father Berowne, could they truly be Lucy and Henry Maynard? Charity Godslove's death by mushroom poisoning could so easily have been arranged by the housekeeper, as could the mysterious illness that had so nearly disposed of Clemency. And my own indisposition after toping with the priest might well have been caused not by too much elderflower wine, as I and everyone else had assumed, but by something administered either in the drink itself or smeared on the cup.

The more I considered the idea the more plausible it seemed, and the less I was able to reject it. And if money was again becoming an object with the pair, it must surely mean that they had another plan afoot to dispose of one of the three remaining siblings; a plan which entailed the assistance of someone other than themselves, as in the deaths of Martin Godslove and Reynold Makepeace and the attempted murder of Sybilla. And what of Julian Makepeace? If it had been considered a part of the couple's revenge to dispose of not just the culprits, but anyone else remotely connected with them, then the apothecary's life might also be in danger. I have often heard people carelessly use the expression 'my blood ran cold', but now I knew what was meant in good earnest. I found I was shivering convulsively in spite of a bright sunny morning.

I heaved myself away from the garden wall of Crosby's Place just as the gates were opened and two young men in the Gloucester livery rode out, carrying on a loud-voiced conversation from which anyone within earshot might gather that they were bound for Baynard's Castle with an important message for the duke, and also, in the next day or two, that the young king was to be moved to the royal apartments in the Tower. At any other time, such a titbit of news might have caught my attention, but at that moment, I was interested in no one's affairs but my own. I walked on slowly, passing under the Bishop's Gate – merely giving an unresponsive grunt in reply to the gatekeeper's attempt at conversation – wondering what it was best for me to do. Obviously, I must impart my suspicions to Oswald and his sisters as soon as possible, but would they believe me? And if they didn't, would they be right to be sceptical? Would it not be better for me to try to discover more definite proof of my suspicions before speaking to them?

It was then I became conscious of the fact that I was still clutching the box of feverfew extract in one hand. I had promised Julian Makepeace to deliver it to Father Berowne on my way back to the Arbour, a good enough excuse, if one was needed, for calling on the priest. Of course, he could well be from home, visiting a member of his flock . . .

I experienced another jolt to the pit of my stomach as yet a further memory obtruded. On the day of Celia's disappearance, when I had questioned Father Berowne, he claimed to have heard the children playing in the garden that morning because he had been on his way to visit one of his parishioners who lived further up the track. I remembered his exact words: 'A poor, childless widow who has been unwell.' Yet when Adela and I had gone for our stroll two evenings since, we had come across no other dwelling anywhere near the Arbour in spite of having walked some considerable distance. So what had he been doing in the vicinity of the house? Had he, indeed, even been there? If not, why had he lied? No one had accused him of anything. It was simply one of those unnecessary embellishments of an untruth provoked by a guilty conscience.

This last recollection convinced me even more that my theory was correct: Father Berowne and Henry Maynard were one and the same person. And if only Oswald and his sisters had seen fit to confide in me from the very beginning, I might have reached this conclusion much sooner. I could see why they hadn't, of course. Selling two innocent children to the Irish slavers was not the sort of admission anyone wanted to make, not even to themselves, and most certainly not to a stranger. Only her secret fear had forced Clemency to speak out in the end.

As I approached St Botolph's everything lay quiet and still in the morning sun. There seemed to be no sign of life anywhere, although the church door stood open, inviting all those who wished to communicate with God to enter. I went in briefly to return thanks for the solution that I trusted was the answer to my prayers and to beg pardon for doubting that I should receive it. As I was leaving, I sent up a brief admonition to God not to desert me, just in case I should prove to be in any danger.

I knocked on the door of the priest's house, but there was no reply. I tried twice more, but each time was greeted with silence, so I strolled round to the side of the cottage and the small garden where Father Berowne – for until I was certain of his true identity, I could not think of him by any other name – dug so diligently to produce something green from the stony soil. At the back, out of sight of the road, two pigs grunted at me from their sty, big, ugly brutes that stank to

high heaven, while a goat, tethered to its post, regarded me
with a pair of evil yellow eyes. An attempt had been made
to grow a few herbs, and the vegetables I had noticed on my
first visit appeared, if anything, even sallower and more
drooping than before. But the thing which really drew my
eyes was a patch of freshly turned earth some six feet by
three. Just the right size for a grave . . .

A hand fell on my shoulder and I jumped. A soft laugh
sounded in my ear. 'Admiring my new seed bed, Master
Chapman?'

I spun round. The priest was standing there, smiling at
me. I hesitated for a long moment before deciding to take
the plunge.

'Am I addressing Henry Maynard?' I asked him.

TWENTY

'I told you I thought he was growing suspicious,' a second voice said, and there was Arbella standing behind the priest. She had come so quietly round the corner of the cottage that I had not even noticed her approach.

'Mistress Rokeswood.' I gave a slight bow in acknowledgement of her presence. 'Or should I say Mistress Maynard? Mistress Lucy Maynard?'

She returned my greeting with an inclination of her head. 'You may call me Mistress Rokeswood. It is indeed my name. My married name. And I was christened Lucy Arbella.'

This shook me a little. 'But you don't deny that you are Lucy Maynard, Tabitha Maynard's daughter?'

She smiled. 'No, I don't deny it. How long have you known?'

'Not *known*,' I corrected her, 'and not as long as you seem to think. I *guessed* after Julian Makepeace told me this morning that you were the person who had sold him the ring I bought for Adela; the ring that was supposed to have been stolen from the Arbour by a chance thief.'

At that, her brother jerked his head round to look at her. 'You fool!' he exclaimed bitterly. 'What possessed you to get rid of it to someone so well known to the family as the apothecary? Why? When there are so many fences in London who would have bought it from you?'

'For half its true value,' she flashed back, adding vindictively, 'And what mistakes have *you* made, Henry, that Master Chapman should suspect the truth about you?'

I was happy to enumerate them. I wasn't sure what the couple's next move would be and calculated that if I could get them quarrelling, I might be able to make my escape before they realized what I was about. Unfortunately, Father Berowne – or Henry Maynard as I must now think of him – was not so easily duped and, without waiting for me to finish speaking, moved suddenly and speedily to stand behind me, producing from the sleeve of his gown a long-bladed and very sharp knife. I could feel the point sticking into my back through the thickness of my shirt and tunic.

'Just walk slowly into the house, Master Chapman,' he said politely, but with such an undertone of menace that I shivered involuntarily. He chuckled softly. 'Oh yes, you're right to be afraid. I shan't hesitate to use this. I'm inured to killing by now. One more death amongst the rest won't worry me.'

I didn't doubt it. Any hopes I might have entertained of making a sudden run for it, were frustrated by Arbella walking immediately ahead of me, so that anyone observing us from the roadway might have been puzzled at seeing the three of us in single file. Except, of course, there wasn't anyone about. In my experience there never is when you want them.

We entered the cottage and the priest motioned me to sit down at the table on the side farthest from the door. He sat opposite, the knife laid ostentatiously between us and his right hand resting suggestively on the hilt. Arbella, having carefully shut the door behind her, sat where she could see us both.

'Where's Celia?' I demanded abruptly. 'What have you done with her?'

Henry smiled. 'What do you suppose? You've just been looking at her grave.'

I stared at him. Even now I knew the truth, he didn't look like a cold-blooded killer. With his short, slight build, his innocent blue eyes, his curly hair and, above all, the youthful air that clung about him, belying the fact that he must be approaching forty, it was almost impossible to believe him guilty of the various crimes I knew must lie at his door.

As though he could read my thoughts, he suddenly leant towards me, his usually benevolent expression contorted into a vicious mask. 'If you know as much as you seem to do,' he said, 'then you have to know what happened to my sister and myself as children. The Godsloves sold us into slavery in Ireland because we had become a burden to them. And also for money. *Money!*' he repeated. 'Money so that their precious brother could become a fine London lawyer. Do you wonder, when we finally discovered the truth, that we wanted our revenge?'

'Why did you wait so long?' I asked, intrigued in spite of myself and the disgust I felt for this murderous pair.

It was Arbella who answered. 'Because we didn't know for certain.' Her lip curled disdainfully. 'It might surprise you to hear that although, as we grew older, the suspicion of their complicity occasionally crossed our minds, we couldn't bring ourselves to believe it. You see, our mother was a distant cousin of the Godsloves, so we were in some, admittedly remote, degree kin to them. Of course, Clemency and Charity and Sybilla didn't deign to regard us as such. To those three, we were merely the housekeeper's children.'

'So how did you find out that your suspicions were correct?' I queried. 'Something must have brought you to England.'

'What brought us to England,' Henry said, 'was the death of my brother-in-law, Seamus Rokeswood, and a natural curiosity to discover what had become of the Godsloves in the intervening years. Seamus, you see, was the master who had bought us from the slavers and brought us up. He was a widower, years older than Lucy, but he took a fancy to her and when she was old enough, he married her. He had always treated us with great consideration – most Irish are good to their servants – but for the latter part of his life he was an invalid and she wouldn't leave him. But when he died, we were at last free to do as we pleased. Seamus had left Lucy a little money, enough for our immediate needs and we were able to take ship to Bristol, from where we made our way to London. Our enquiries around the Inns of Court soon located a Lawyer Godslove – Oswald Godslove – and after that, there was no difficulty in finding out where he lived.'

'And it so happened,' Arbella put in, 'that fortune favoured us. The Arbour had just lost its housekeeper, and Clemency was looking for another. I offered my services and was immediately accepted.' She gave a little crow of laughter. 'And as if that weren't sufficient good luck for two people, the parish priest of St Botolph's had recently disappeared. My brother simply took his place.'

'Are you really a priest?' I asked, looking across the table at Henry.

He grinned. 'Let's say I'm a sort of hedge-priest. I was known around Waterford for my hell-fire sermons.'

'But did no ecclesiastical authority ever question your right to be in charge at St Botolph's?'

That made him laugh out loud. '"Ecclesiastical authorities"!' he mocked. 'Don't you realize that parish priests are
the scum of the earth, the poorest of the poor? No one cares
if they live or die or just run away, as my predecessor did.
The stipend – if it ever gets paid, that is – is often less than
six pounds a year. Most of the poor devils can't write their
own names. As long as a parish has a priest, and the parishioners aren't complaining of the lack of one, the authorities
are more than happy to ask no questions. I doubt if anyone
outside the parish boundaries was even aware that a change
had taken place.'

There was silence for a moment or two while I digested
this information. Then I shrugged.

'Very well,' I said at last. 'So the wheel of fortune spun
your way. What next? Did none of the Godsloves recognize
you?'

Arbella sneered. 'Why should they? Nearly twenty-five
years had passed. We shouldn't have recognized them if
we hadn't known who they were. For quarter of a century,
they hadn't given us a thought. And Celia and Martin would
have been too young to remember us with any clarity.'

'And Reynold and Julian Makepeace wouldn't have known
you at all,' I said viciously. 'They'd never set eyes on you
or had anything to do with you.'

Both brother and sister looked genuinely bewildered.

'No, of course they hadn't,' Henry agreed.

'Then why did you have Reynold murdered?' I demanded
furiously.

Henry blinked, staring at me as though I had gone a little
mad. Then, slowly, a look of comprehension dawned and he
started to grin.

'You think we had Reynold Makepeace killed! Do the
Godsloves believe that, too? Dear oh dear! No, no!' He shook
his head. 'Reynold's death had nothing to do with us. It was
just what it seemed – a fatal stabbing during an ale-room
brawl.'

For a moment, I was unable to take it in. 'You're saying
you didn't pay to have Landlord Makepeace murdered?'

It was Arbella's turn to laugh, 'No, of course we didn't.
Why should we? He was nothing to us and no blood relation

to the others. Besides, at that time Henry and I were still unsure if Clemency and Charity and Sybilla really had been involved in our capture by the slavers.'

'But sure enough to try to poison Clemency,' I accused her.

Once again there was silence while the siblings looked at one another.

'Oh dear, oh dear!' Henry repeated, smiling broadly. 'What misapprehensions you've all been labouring under. We didn't try to poison Clemency. Her illness was a fever of the brain as everyone so rightly thought at the time. But –' and he leaned towards me, the smile replaced by a grim tightening of the lips – 'it was during that illness that she believed she was going to die and confessed her sins to me as her parish priest. *All* her sins.' He bared his teeth in a wolfish grin. 'Including, of course, the greatest of them – how she and her two sisters had rid themselves of the two children of their erstwhile housekeeper who had become an embarrassment to them, and made some much needed money out of the necessity, as well.'

My brain was reeling, not least because I realized that God had tricked me into this investigation by planting in my mind the belief that my old friend, the landlord of St Brendan the Voyager, had been one of the victims of this series of killings.

'You didn't arrange the stabbing of Reynold Makepeace?' I repeated stupidly, staring from one to the other of the two smiling faces.

'No,' Henry Maynard said.

'No,' echoed Arbella.

'And until Clemency fell ill and made her confession, you had no proof that your suspicions regarding her and her sisters were correct?'

They both shook their heads. 'But once we knew the truth,' Arbella went on, 'we set about getting our revenge. We didn't care how long it took. Indeed, it was all the sweeter for being protracted. At first, they naturally had no suspicion that they were all under sentence of death, not even when Charity died from mushroom poisoning. That was my idea and such a simple thing to arrange. But after Martin Godslove was set

upon and killed by street robbers, they began to be afraid
and suspect that someone was trying to get rid of them all.'

'I thought they seemed unusually quick on the uptake,'
Henry interrupted, 'but now I see why. Quite erroneously,
they had added their stepbrother's death and Clemency's
illness to the list of mishaps that had befallen them.'

He spoke pleasantly, conversationally, as though he were
discussing the weather. It brought me out in a sweat.

'You paid those men to rob and murder Martin Godslove,'
I accused him, 'with the money you'd stolen from the tailor,
Peter Coleman, and what you'd raised from selling the pyx
you, yourself, had taken from the church. Where did you
find these cutthroats?'

Henry looked astonished. 'In this city,' he said, 'you can find
anyone to do almost anything for money; in the taverns, the
brothels, the stews, along the waterfront, anywhere, in fact,
where poverty reigns. And poverty is king of the London streets,
believe you me! I've seen more real misery here than ever I
saw in Ireland.' He laughed. 'But it isn't just the poor who are
willing to take bribes. My sister will confirm that we had no
difficulty at all in finding one of the masons working on the
Bishop's Gate wall who was quite willing to push a block of
masonry down on Sybilla's head. Unfortunately it didn't quite
work out as we had hoped, but it gave her and the rest of them
a nasty fright. And next time, we shall use a surer method.'

I ignored this unnerving implication that there would be
a next time, and demanded, 'Why wreak your vengeance on
Martin and Celia? They could have had nothing to do with
their elder siblings' schemes. They were too young. So was
Oswald if it comes to that.'

'They were Godsloves,' Arbella said viciously. 'They bore
the name, and that was enough for us.'

'But,' I argued, grasping at straws, 'you told me yourselves that your experience in Ireland wasn't too bad. That
the Irish treat their servants well.'

'And you think that excuses what was done to us?' Henry's
voice, raised to a sudden shout, made me jump. 'We were
sold into slavery! Robbed of our freedom! Two children who
had done no harm to anyone! Sold by the people we trusted
most!'

There was no reply I could make. He was right, of course. But whether it justified the revenge they had taken was another matter and I wasn't sure of the answer.

'Is Celia really dead?' I asked. I suppose I was hoping against hope that they had been lying.

'Oh yes, she's dead,' Arbella said. 'It was easy enough to lure her down here. I just told her that Henry wanted to see her. She came straight away, glad, I think, to have something to take her mind off her quarrel with Roderick Jeavons.' She added with a smile, 'You mustn't think she suffered. Henry is very quick with his knife. He cut her throat before she had much time to realize what was happening. We fed most of her to the pigs but we gave what was left a decent burial. We told you, that was her grave you were looking at in the garden just now. Later, Henry or I will plant some flowers on it. It should look very pretty by next spring.'

I could feel my belly heaving and for the next few moments had to concentrate hard to prevent myself from being physically sick. I refused to give them the satisfaction of believing I was either disturbed or afraid.

But I was afraid. I was only one against two, and I was under no illusion that, having revealed their guilt, they were about to let me go. I should be quietly despatched with Henry's knife and then suffer poor Celia's disgusting fate. Who would suspect the parish priest, of all men, of doing away with me? His calling was his best protection, but in any case, Arbella would undoubtedly provide him with an alibi. I should simply disappear in mysterious circumstances. There might be a little flurry of interest for a while, but I should soon be forgotten, just one more of the many dozens of people who vanished from the London streets almost every day of the week and were never again accounted for. Adela, of course, would come up to London to search for me when I failed to return home, but I doubted that she would find me – or what remained of me after my body had been mauled by the pig . . .

I gave an involuntary shudder and looked across the table to see Henry Maynard grinning evilly at me, still fondling the handle of his knife. Arbella's gaze, too, was fixed on me, watching my every move. I was not only outnumbered, but was also heavier, and therefore somewhat slower, than my chief adversary.

God, I admonished Him silently, You got me into this situation. You tricked me into it! It's up to You now to get me out.

The words had barely formed in my mind, when I heard footsteps on the path outside. I slid my fingers under the edge of the table and waited, my heart in my mouth. The next moment, the latch of the cottage door lifted and the housekeeper, Ellen, stepped inside.

'Father,' she was beginning, 'I've brought your—' But she got no further.

There was another woman with her, but I didn't stop for introductions. As Henry half-turned on his stool and Arbella's eyes momentarily swivelled towards the newcomers, I leapt to my feet, pushing over the table in Henry's direction and, at the same time, making a grab for the knife. As the priest's stool toppled backwards and himself with it, I just managed to grasp its handle, even though my ·fingers were slippery with sweat. My recollection of the next few seconds is hazy, but I recall dropping to my knees beside him where he lay amid the rushes, jerking his head back against my chest and holding the blade of the knife to his throat. A woman was screaming and a basket had fallen from nerveless hands, a shattered clay bowl and a mess of stew spilling out across the floor.

'If you make a single move,' I warned Arbella, 'this knife goes straight into your brother's throat.'

She glared at me, but then looked, almost imploringly I thought, towards the second woman who had accompanied the housekeeper into the cottage. I didn't dare take my eyes off Arbella or slacken my hold on my prisoner. The slightest inattention on my part could be just the opportunity the evil pair were hoping for. So I was totally unprepared for the familiar voice which smote my ears.

'Don't kill him, Master Chapman. He hasn't harmed me.'

'*Celia?*' I demanded incredulously, removing my arm from about Henry Maynard's throat and turning to stare up at her. 'Celia! He-they t-told me you were dead.'

The priest, taking advantage of my state of shock, struggled to his feet. I also stood up slowly, feeling dazed, while Arbella did her best to soothe Ellen's hysterics and revive her with a cupful of elderflower cordial. Then, with her brother's help, she righted the table and stools, scuffing the broken bowl and its contents to one side along with some of yesterday's rushes.

When I would have spoken, Celia held up an imperative finger, commanding my silence, before turning to add her voice to that of Arbella in persuading Ellen to go home.

'It's just one of Father Berowne's drunken parishioners,' she explained, as Ellen seemed not to recognize me. 'He'll behave himself now that I'm here. You've had a nasty shock, my dear. Go home and lie down.'

The housekeeper, who was regarding me with round, scared eyes, much as she would have regarded one of Old Nick's henchmen from hell, eventually, after more persuasion, took her departure, leaving behind her a sudden silence which, for a minute or two, no one seemed able to break.

Finally, I asked, 'Where have you been these last six days, Celia? We've been looking for you everywhere. You must have known we thought you were dead.'

'I've been staying with Ellen.' she said. 'Oh, Henry and Lucy intended to kill me when they lured me down here, but when it came to the point, Henry couldn't bring himself to do it. They told me their story instead, and I was so incensed, so angry – so furiously angry – with what Clemency and Charity and Sybilla had done to them that I agreed to play their game, for a while at least, and vanish without letting the others know what had become of me.'

I stared at her in disbelief. 'This precious pair had your brother murdered,' I shouted. 'Your brother, Martin, as innocent of their fate as you are yourself. They killed Charity and tried to kill Sybilla. He –' I jabbed a finger in Henry's direction – 'even tried to poison me.' And I slapped down on the table the box of feverfew extract, pushing it towards the priest. 'Julian Makepeace asked me to give you this. A little smeared on the rim of a cup or beaker can be quite deadly, he tells me.'

'I had no intention of killing you,' Henry denied sullenly. 'I could recognize your sort at once. The sort that sticks his nose into everything as soon as he scents a mystery. I hoped if I made you ill that you'd go back where you came from and take your family with you.' He shrugged resignedly. 'I should have known better. I should have known that even if you sent your wife and children away, you'd remain behind, dogged to the last.' He regarded me, pale but defiant. 'So? What do you intend to do?'

'He will do nothing,' Celia, to my great astonishment, answered for me. 'At least, not immediately. He will accompany me home, and by the time that Clemency and Sybilla have been put in possession of the facts, and by the time that they have sent to Chancery Lane, or even, perhaps, to Westminster, and brought Oswald home to hear the story and raise the hue and cry, the two of you should be clear of the city and lost somewhere in the countryside. The choice of direction naturally is your own, but if I were you, I should make for the coast and take ship to France. Later you can make your way home to Ireland.'

Henry looked at his sister and smiled faintly at the mutinous expression on her face. 'I'm afraid, Lucy, my dear, that we have no choice. Not unless you fancy trying to overcome the pair of them, which would be foolishness. Not only is Master Chapman fully forewarned of any such move on our part, but he is also armed with my knife. And I don't doubt that Celia could prove a match for you. Moreover, the box of feverfew extract suggests that Julian Makepeace knew where Roger was bound when he left the apothecary's shop. The law would soon be hard on our heels.'

'Are the other Godsloves to go unpunished then?' Arbella demanded angrily.

'They won't go unpunished,' her brother answered quietly. 'The knowledge that it was their own wrongdoing that brought retribution upon them will stay with them for the rest of their lives. Furthermore, I suspect that Celia has no intention of returning to live at the Arbour.' He raised an eyebrow at her as he spoke.

She nodded. 'You're right. I shall marry Roderick Jeavons if he still wants me. I've always been fond of him and he'll make me a good husband, I'm sure of that.' She glanced at me. 'Let's be off, Roger.'

'No,' I said, backing against the door and pointing the knife blade at Henry Maynard. 'These people are thieves and murderers. They should not be allowed to escape the penalty for their crimes. I'll stay here and watch them while you go for assistance.'

Celia clicked her tongue impatiently. 'And what proof do we have of anything they've done? They've told you themselves that they are innocent of Reynold Makepeace's stabbing and Clemency's illness. Charity's death seems, on the face of it, a simple accident, as does Sybilla's mishap. And you'll never find anyone willing to admit to pushing a block of masonry over on her, any more than you'll be able to discover the footpads who were paid to murder my brother. Or,' she added after a second or two's thought, 'any more than you will persuade Clemency and Sybilla to own in public to the wrong they committed all those years ago.'

I considered her words. There was a great deal of truth in them. All the same . . .

'Checkmate,' Henry said softly.

'Not necessarily,' I snapped. 'If I were to go to the Duke of Gloucester and disclose to him the details of this affair, I'm sure he would believe me. He trusts me, you see. And he dislikes injustice as much as I do.'

Celia nodded. 'Adela told us something of the work you've done for the duke, Roger, so I, at least, know that that is not an idle boast. But there is injustice here, on both sides. I cannot excuse the misery that these two have caused, but neither am I able to overlook the fact that the initial wrongdoing was that of my half-sisters. And I have little doubt that Oswald, although only a boy of fourteen at the time, both knew of the plan and condoned it.' She shivered suddenly. 'I realize now that there has always been something about him that repelled me. I would just never let myself admit it before. So!' She smiled at me. 'We will do things my way, if you please. After all, I have been more injured than you. I lost my full-blood brother.'

In the end, I allowed myself to be talked into doing as she wanted; not, I regret to say, because her argument altogether convinced me – although, as I mentioned earlier, there was something in what she said – but because I knew that

to do things my way would mean the possibility of a long
delay before I could set out for home. With luck, I might
now find myself in Bristol within a week or two . . .

And so indeed it was that two days later, on Friday, the
ninth of May – the day that the young king rode in procession through the London streets to the royal apartments in
the Tower; the day that his coronation was set for Tuesday,
June the twenty-fourth; the day that my lord of Gloucester
despatched more men to reinforce those already manning the
fortifications of Portsmouth and the Isle of Wight – I set out
westwards on my journey home, if not with a spring in my
step and a song on my lips, then at least with less dissatisfaction than I had anticipated.

Celia had been quite correct in assuming that neither
Clemency nor Sybilla would be willing to admit to selling
the Maynards to the Irish slavers. Oswald had been a different
matter. He was all for revenge, for raising the hue and cry
to lay the fugitives by the heels, and was almost struck dumb
with rage at their escape. I thought at one moment that I
should have to defend both Celia and myself from physical
violence. But his sisters restrained him, pointing out with
some asperity that, being only a boy at the time, he could
easily be exonerated from the charge of slave-dealing; a
charge which, even if it could not be satisfactorily proved,
would be mud which stuck.

They were all three in a state of shock after learning the
true identity of Arbella and 'Father Berowne', but to Oswald
it was as nothing to the shock of Celia's scorn and her
decision to marry Roderick Jeavons. Indeed, had I not person-
ally escorted her and her baggage to Old Dean's Lane that
very afternoon, where she awaited the doctor's return, I truly
believe that Oswald would have found some way to keep
her prisoner at the Arbour. As for me, he could not bear to
have me in his sight, and it was only Clemency's insistence
that I be allowed to rest for a day before setting out on my
homeward journey, that enabled me to remain for that night
and the next.

I took the opportunity of the day's grace thus granted me
to write a letter to Timothy Plummer concerning what I
had seen and heard at the house next to Roderick Jeavons's.

This I entrusted to Clemency, extracting her promise that its delivery to Crosby's Place would be delayed until the following Monday, by which time, God willing, I should be well on my way home, using those hidden paths and byways known only to foot-travellers, out of the reach of mounted men – if, that was, Timothy should decide to send after me.

And so, in the pale sunshine of a warm spring morning, a bundle of those clothes which Adela had not taken home with her slung across one shoulder, my cudgel in my hand and sufficient money for my needs in the pouch at my waist, I strode, whistling tunelessly, along the track towards Reading. The little king was safely on his throne, the Woodville plot against the duke had been foiled, the plotters in prison, I had solved the Godsloves' mystery for them, however unsatisfactory the outcome, God was in His heaven and all was right with my world . . .

But Fortune, that fickle jade, was about to spin her wheel in a totally unforeseen direction, affecting king and commoner alike. Nothing would ever be the same again.